B~FOUR

B~FOUR

a novel by
Sam Hodges

ST. MARTIN'S PRESS
NEW YORK

Production Editor: David Stanford Burr

Design by Judith Christensen

Library of Congress Cataloging-in-Publication Data

Hodges, Sam.
   B-Four / Sam Hodges.
     p. cm.
   ISBN 0-312-07647-9
   I. Title.
  PS3558.O34343B4 1992
  813'.54—dc20   92-4033
                       CIP

10 9 8 7 6 5 4 3 2

Dedication

For Kit Lively, who took in the green or champagne-colored stray kitten and (later, also a little green) me; for my mother, Marion Lowe Hodges, who has saved every one of my newspaper articles, even those run on B-Four and beyond; and in memory of my father, Jake Hodges, who was my first and best reader, and who was always telling good stories when he wasn't busy being one.

Acknowledgments

Mike Mayhan, a true Southern gentleman and first-rate reporter, began to call himself "B-Four" while in a brief slump covering medical news for the Birmingham *Post-Herald*. I worked there, too, and went to lunch with him, and laughed at him, and in the halls conspicuously joined other reporter scruffs in calling him "B-Four." His discovery of B-Four as a proper noun and state of mind suggested this book to me. Bill Dawson, also of the South, affirmed and extended the sense of humor I began to notice in Birmingham.

Other people, programs, and institutions have sustained me as a writer over the years. They include Cleo Hudson, the late Dorothy Gipson, Nancy Elcock, Anne Edelstein, C. J. Hribal, Tommy Hays, Jay Hamburg, Bailey Thomson, Bill Banks, the University of Michigan Fellowship for Journalists program, the Warren Wilson College MFA in Creative Writing program, the Florida Division of Cultural Affairs, and the Orlando *Sentinel*. Jeff Lowe and Jeff Grzelak read behind me for accuracy on the Civil War and on Civil War reenacting. To them, to everyone: thanks, Roll Tide, strike the tent.

B~FOUR

Chapter One

Rosy dawn had not yet broken over Birmingham, Alabama, when Beauregard Forrest and his father, both dressed in Confederate uniforms, turned into the parking lot of their nearby International House of Pancakes. Their black Cadillac Seville pulled a narrow silver horse trailer occupied by a single, well-fed gray gelding.

They had gone by the newspaper first. Beauregard, these past three months, had been a cub reporter for the *Birmingham Standard-Dispatch*. He had just come under its benefits policy, a lean one that included flu shots, glaucoma screenings, and free newspapers. Though Mr. Forrest subscribed, his *Standard-Dispatch* had not come this morning—at least not yet—so they'd stopped by the newspaper for freebies. Each carried one as they climbed out of the sedan and walked across the spongy asphalt parking lot to the restaurant with its familiar high-pitched, blue-shingled roof. They ducked around the PLEASE WAIT TO BE SEATED sign and took a sticky booth in the back.

But for the laminated IHOP menu in his hands, Beauregard looked like a Mathew Brady photograph from one of the Forrest family's many books about the War Between the States. His dusty gray infantryman's uniform hung loosely on his thin frame. The bill of his forage cap cast a crescent shadow on his pale, unlined forehead. There was, in the daguerreotype gravity of his bearing, a

1

suggestion of innocence irretrievably lost. But in fact he was just deciding between blueberry and Silver Dollar pancakes.

Mr. Forrest, hidden already behind the business section, looked more than a little like Robert E. Lee. He had the uniform, the beard, the longish gray hair combed the other way, Lee's way. As president and major stockholder of City of Birmingham Bank, Mr. Forrest could easily afford to underwrite key engagements on the flourishing War Between the States battle reenactment circuit. This he did. None of the other soldiers, obligated as they were to him for powder and rations, openly questioned his right to portray Robert E. Lee.

"Coffee?" Beauregard asked, tilting their table's copper-insulated pitcher at an inquisitive angle. The business section did not rattle or come down. Nor did Mr. Forrest grunt affirmatively or negatively from behind it.

Beauregard shrugged, then filled his own mug. He added no milk or sugar. Reporters, he had learned at the *Standard-Dispatch,* drink coffee black.

The early morning IHOP staff did not seem even idly curious about the two Confederate soldiers in nonsmoking. Beauregard knew from talking to them that they had high standards for the unusual. As employees for an all-night restaurant with a liberal coffee refill policy, they routinely served professional wrestlers, female impersonators, contestants on break from the tractor pull. Confederate soldiers floated well within this odd mainstream. What's more, the IHOP staff knew the Forrests; Beauregard and his father ate here before most reenactments. And each Tuesday evening from eight to nine-thirty, the staff roped off two long tables for the Birmingham chapter of the War Between the States Roundtable, over which Mr. Forrest presided.

Mr. Forrest enjoyed needling the restaurant workers about whether the International House of Pancakes would ever give official recognition to the Confederate States of America. He lowered his newspaper and started right in when Rico, the swarthy, Brooklyn-born assistant manager, drifted over with a replacement pot of fresh coffee.

"All I want is for the Confederate flag to fly with all your other flags," Mr. Forrest said. "With Portugal and Sweden."

"And where—where would you have me fly this flag?"

Rico always took Mr. Forrest seriously.

"On a pole outside."

"Impossible," Rico said. "We've been over this."

"By the table syrups, then. *Little* flags."

Mr. Forrest was so much an IHOP regular that a waiter automatically brought over his prereenactment order of grits, scrambled eggs, link sausage, and wheat toast soaked in butter. Beauregard got Silver Dollar pancakes. He submerged them in a multicolored pond of available syrups. First, though, he had to use a spoon to pry the syrup pitchers out of the sticky wooden syrup-pitcher tray. As he ate, he read the B section of the *Standard-Dispatch*.

Beauregard's colleagues at the *Standard-Dispatch* did not call him "Beauregard" or "Beau" or "Forrest" or even "Kid." They called him "B-Four," short for section B, page four of the newspaper. That was as close to the front page as his articles ever got.

He had been hired as a cub reporter only because Mr. Forrest's bank had money in the newspaper. Mr. Forrest thought a few months as a reporter would improve Beauregard's verbal SAT score, which was necessary if he was going to get into the school Mr. Forrest wanted him to attend, Washington and Lee University. Actually, Mr. Forrest had conceived various strategies for how Beauregard could improve his verbal SAT score. "Think in complete sentences," he had commanded late one night, peeking into Beauregard's room after Beauregard had already turned off the light. "I do. Lee did. They don't have to be long sentences." He had also bought for Beauregard *Thirty Days to a More Powerful Vocabulary* and other books of its kind. The newspaper idea, though, he liked best. So the day after Beauregard graduated from Birmingham Military Academy, Mr. Forrest made a couple of phone calls, then sent him down to the newspaper.

He was not well received. City editor Bubba Shealy told everyone, including Beauregard, that he would not have minded having Beauregard as a copy clerk, someone to fetch coffee and take dictation; but Mr. Forrest had insisted, for vocabulary reasons, that Beauregard be a full-fledged reporter. Shealy outspokenly considered himself overworked, underpaid, and understaffed. It rankled him to think that Beauregard, not even a fast typist, was holding a spot that might otherwise be occupied by some bright and hungry Midwestern journalism school graduate.

So, enjoying it, he seized on the nickname "B-Four" and stuck Beauregard with Metro Briefs, obituaries, Pet of the Week, and stories of small consequence—Kiwanis fish fries and house fires without injuries. He gave him a quota of Metro Briefs, six to eight

3

a day, a sort of B-section woodpile that kept Beauregard chopping and stacking press releases throughout the day. Shealy checked the computer often to see if the Metro Brief queue was full, and if it wasn't, he sent Beauregard terse reminders through the computer message system. For today's edition, the scrambling Beauregard had improvised a Metro Brief about the reenactment practice to which he and his father were headed. He made it the last Metro Brief, because Shealy, who might well have rejected it as insufficiently interesting to the general public, usually sent the package straight to the copy desk after reading the first brief or two.

"Ready?" Mr. Forrest said when he had cleaned his plate.

"Not quite, sir."

Beauregard, finishing the last of his pancakes, could see Mr. Forrest searching for something to say. Mr. Forrest didn't like a lot of talk before a reenactment practice. A little, though, was only civil. "That Rico," he said finally, a conspiratorial smile lifting his gray mustache.

"Sir?"

"All that gold jewelry he wears. Those sideburns. What could he be thinking of?"

Beauregard wiped his lips with a creased paper napkin, then crumpled it decisively. "I like Rico," he challenged. He dropped the napkin and took a last swallow of coffee. "Ready."

They paid the bill, then headed north with the horse trailer through lightly zoned Birmingham suburbs and on into the rolling, intermittently populated countryside. Beauregard drove. Mr. Forrest sat on his right, his sheathed saber carefully wedged into the space between the seat and the door.

Day had broken. Golden light, having made its way over and around the many thousands of longleaf, slash, and loblolly pines, dappled them inside the Cadillac. It had a lovely and warming effect.

"Air conditioner," Mr. Forrest commanded.

"Yes, sir."

As soon as Beauregard nudged the switch to COOL, the air conditioner clicked on and went about its work silently. In fact, the whole car was quiet, the top-of-the-line Cadillac sealing off all but a minimum rumble of road noise, even from this low-grade, pebbly, county-maintained highway.

Just then, though, Mr. Forrest pushed in a cassette tape of War Between the States songs. It was a rerelease of a 1960 Folkways recording by Stockton Pye. "Goober Peas" was first up. The "peas! peas! peas! peas!" chorus boomed around the leather interior.

"Do we have to listen to that now?" Beauregard said finally, raising his voice to be heard. "All those peas, so soon after breakfast?"

"Gets me in the mood."

"Couldn't we just hear the news?"

"No," Mr. Forrest said. "This."

"Dad."

"No! And from here on out, call me 'sir.' We're getting close to the battlefield."

Beauregard brooded for half a mile, then steered the car close to the road's shoulder, knowing his father preferred the center line. He looked peripherally, expecting satisfaction at the sight of his father, tense. Beauregard had keen peripheral vision, the result of years of cutting his eyes warily to see what his father or older brother Jackson might be up to. This time Mr. Forrest had his eyes closed. He was humming along to "Goober Peas." Beauregard, conceding this skirmish, angled the large car back toward the center line.

They'd fought for years, not opponents but comrades, in these War Between the States reenactments. For Mr. Forrest, reenacting had proved the perfect hobby, combining his love of the outdoors with his armchair scholar's interest in the War Between the States. Reenacting also provided him a good physical workout. He kept his locker in the executive room at the downtown Y but rarely went there.

"I'm a little cool now," Mr. Forrest said, eyes still closed.

"Right, sir," Beauregard said, then flicked the A/C switch.

As a boy, Beauregard, too, had loved reenacting. Any boy would have. Camping out, wearing a uniform, toting a rifle, simulating the running through of some adult male's abdomen with a blunted bayonet—these experiences he'd felt lucky to have. When Mr. Forrest took up reenacting, Jackson was in his late teens, a standout high school football player, too old to want to don a Confederate uniform. Beauregard was just the right age. He had a precocious love of golf, too, and he'd managed to do both in those early years. But as time passed, Mr. Forrest plunged deeper and deeper into his hobby, insisting Beauregard go with him every weekend. Golf got pushed aside. That was all right, too, but as Beauregard reached his

5

middle teens, reenacting began to seem strange, even geeky—a kind of chess club in the field. There were no girls in reenacting. So while he still reenacted with his father, he was more conscript than volunteer. He intended to confront his father about this and about something else. He'd do it today, only later, after they'd fought.

"Goober Peas" faded into "Tenting Tonight," which faded into "Lorena." Beauregard had always liked this sad tune, especially Stockton Pye's rendition, with its acoustic guitar solo. After "Lorena" came "Just Before the Battle, Mother," a tune Beauregard did not like. He'd not minded it so much until Jackson had begun to parody it, putting an obscene, biker twist on "mother." Now whenever the real version played, he couldn't get Jackson's version out of his mind.

Within an hour they arrived, Beauregard parking in a clearing with all the other vehicles. The tall grass was mashed flat by an assembly of Jeeps, Broncos, and Ford trucks, as well as a few sedans and hatchbacks. They got out, Mr. Forrest toting his sheathed saber, Beauregard a .557-caliber long Enfield rifle musket. He reached back in for his haversack and cartridge box and canteen.

Once he had his gear well situated, Beauregard opened the trailer gate and coaxed out the gray gelding. It took some doing. He was a handsome but disappointingly unspirited steed. Though only seven years old, he spent an uncommon amount of time folded up on the ground, a habit which in the early years had prompted Mr. Forrest to make frequent and expensive false-alarm calls to the veterinarian. For a long time the Forrests had abided by the name the original owners had given him, "Snuffy." But Mr. Forrest had lately begun to call him "Traveller," after Robert E. Lee's horse.

"Mawn, Snuffy," Beauregard said, tugging the bridle.

"Traveller," Mr. Forrest corrected from the far end of the Cadillac.

"Right," Beauregard said. " 'Traveller.' Mawn, Traveller."

It was a cloudless day, warm and humid. They walked a narrow, straw-laden path into middlingly dense woods of pine, oak, and sycamore, passing two dozen modern campsites. Farther on they found a similar number of sites in which campers lived without conveniences—lived, as much as possible, as troops in the War Between the States had.

This was standard procedure at major reenactment events and

even at some practices. Modern campers slept in trailers with bathrooms, gas stoves, and battery-powered TV sets. Authentic campers slept on the ground and dug latrines. They shaved, if at all, with straight razors. They drank chicory coffee and ate hardtack: small saltless biscuits. When he and Beauregard camped, Mr. Forrest insisted they camp authentically. Beauregard would wait until his father was asleep, then slip over to the other camp, where the modern Confederates were popping popcorn, throwing crushed Budweiser cans at one another, and watching the late movie on portable TVs.

At the path's end they came to a much broader clearing, the site of this day's reenactment practice. Perry Winter, a claims adjuster who served as Mr. Forrest's second-in-command, spotted them and yelled, "He's here! Fall in! Inspection!" The seventy-five or so soldiers who had been chatting in little circles formed a shuffling gray line. Beauregard tied the horse's reins around a tree trunk and joined the far end.

They were a first-rate unit, known throughout the reenacting community and even in the movie industry, having been used as extras in two feature films and a miniseries set during the War Between the States. Each reenactor had well over a thousand dollars invested in guns and uniforms. Each had passed Mr. Forrest's basic "war knowledge" test, a multiple-choice examination that Beauregard sometimes helped to grade. Many of the men portrayed particular soldiers. "Living history," it was called, and they did extensive research on their soldiers. Mr. Forrest said a first-rate living history reenactor tried, as he himself did with Lee, to create the interior as well as the exterior life of his soldier. It was not unlike what Beauregard understood to be method acting— something he'd read about in a Style section story.

As usual, Mr. Forrest inspected his troops closely. His standard, as with camping, was the appearence of authenticity. He looked hard for high school rings, wrist watches, MIA bracelets—any telltale signs of now. Once, Beauregard remembered, he had ripped stripes off a sergeant caught with a transistor radio and ear plugs on the morning of the Alabama-Auburn football game. This time he found the men clean.

Mr. Forrest congratulated them, then barked out the day's agenda. First, drill. Then they'd split up into Confederates and Yankees. They'd have a good old-fashioned powder-burning exercise. Most of the time they tried to reenact some specific battle or maneuver within a battle, but today's action would be unscripted. Nothing fancy, either, just soldiers at opposite ends of the field converging and shooting powder at one another.

Beauregard would be a Yankee. Many Southern men refused to be Yankees—just couldn't do it, even for the greater good of authenticity—but Mr. Forrest had taught Beauregard that it was a sign of reenactment maturity to go both ways. So after drill he slipped on one of the blue mesh tank tops that designated "Yankee" and trotted down the field to his position. Men were making a last check of their gun barrels and wishing each other well with conspicuous, hand-on-shoulder solemnity. The skirmish began when Mr. Forrest, up on Snuffy/Traveller, cut the air with a baroque swoop of his saber. Rifle shots and powder filled the air.

Beauregard felt obligated to stay alive for the first few minutes, but he died as soon as he reasonably could. It was his custom these days. He was happy to be cannon fodder, any fodder. He saw an opening, squeezed through the blue mesh line, and ran forward to receive the precisely aimed but bulletless rifle shots of a Rebel soldier seventy-five yards down the field. "Taking a hit," reenactors called it. He crumpled without melodrama into the dewy grass.

As always, Beauregard found it pleasant to be there, dead, the battle raging above and around him. He knew he was a good dead man. Others—including his father—had told him. For one thing, he didn't overdo the death itself, as did so many. Moreover, he could convincingly relax his fingers and legs, his breathing was imperceptible, and he could go long stretches without opening his eyes or blinking, depending on whether it was a closed- or open-eyes death. He had great tolerance, too, for field discomforts. Neither anthills nor chiggers fazed him.

He began this particular death, as he had so many recently, by thinking about his newspaper career. He liked the work but hadn't quite got the hang of it. He didn't yet have the skepticism, nerve, and thinking skills that seemed as natural as breath to the best reporters, such as his deskmate, the legendary Price. Nor had he mastered the lean, muscular writing style *Standard-Dispatch* editors favored. He struggled with what people in the newsroom called a "nut graph"—a short paragraph, high up, that focused the story. Price wrote beautiful nut graphs: perfect little pecans, compact and meaty. They came so easily that sometimes, for sport, he would throw in a second one near the end of the story, to see if Bubba

Shealy would notice. Price's stories routinely made front page. He hadn't written a Metro Brief or obit in years.

As he lay there, a motionless **S** in the tall grass, Beauregard began to wonder how the *Standard-Dispatch* would cover his own death, should he expire sometime soon in an accident or from illness. Maybe Price would volunteer to write the obit. If so, it would probably be on page one, above the fold, with a beautiful little nut graph. Beauregard could see the funeral, too, everyone crying, especially the Midwestern women reporters at the *Standard-Dispatch* who had been so patronizing to him. His premature death would shock them into a recognition of their own mortality. One of them, Rochelle perhaps, would cry so hard that the assembled mourners would conclude that she and Beauregard had had a meaningful fling, and that that was why she was crying, because sex would never again be so good.

Beauregard, still an **S**, enjoyed this sad reverie as the guns blasted overhead.

Just then, though, a Rebel cried out in imagined pain and died a B-grade movie death near him. The soldier's leg actually came to rest against Beauregard's exposed right calf. There was an unwritten spacing agreement among the fallen at reenactments, and this rube, whoever he was, had violated it. Beauregard raised one eye. It was Barry Pollard, teenage son of Ralph Pollard, a Tarrant City septic tank contractor who camped authentically. Barry, a rotund, rosy-cheeked private, always seemed to be dying on top of others. The rumor around the modern camp was that he enjoyed dying on top of other men; that was why he reenacted. Beauregard hadn't thought much about it, but now Pollard had a leg on him. His hardtack-and-chicory breath, authentically rancid, drifted into Beauregard's face.

"Back off, Pollard," Beauregard commanded, corporal to private.

Pollard did not back off. In fact, he began to move his leg against Beauregard's, as if Beauregard had asked him to scratch an itch.

"Back *off*," Beauregard repeated. "That's an order."

"I can't hear you," Pollard said, an irritating melody in his voice. "I'm dead."

"Turkey."

Beauregard did something he almost never did as a fallen soldier: turned his head. Then he began a slow, invertebratelike movement away from the other soldier. It was risky, because his father or some

9

other officer might notice and reprimand him. Despite his growing disaffection from reenacting, he took pride in his deaths and did not want to be caught moving. He wormed away as subtly as he could. He had gone about a foot when, abruptly, all shooting stopped. Afraid he was caught, he peeked again.

From his horizontal perspective, he saw nothing but weeds and dead soldiers sprawled like loosened hay bales across the broad field. He sat up for a better look. His father was gesturing wildly at a small group of men and women, neither Confederate nor Yankee. They faced him, arms folded. They were dressed as knights, squires, friars, and wenches.

"Who's that?" Pollard asked. He too had sat up, as had all the dead.

"I don't know," Beauregard said. "I *think* it's the Birmingham Society for Creative Anachronism."

"What?"

"A medieval reenactment group. We marched with them in a parade one time. They must want the field."

"Oh, shit."

"Yeah," Beauregard said. "I better get down there."

He collected his rifle and jogged toward the confrontation, arriving in time to hear his father challenging the knight, poking his breastplate and saying, "You *got* a gauntlet, man, throw it down!"

"Easy, Dad," cautioned Beauregard, a little winded now.

Mr. Forrest wheeled and pointed. "Son, you stay out of this."

But the knight clanked past Mr. Forrest and over to Beauregard. He gave him a square, official-looking slip of thin pink paper.

"Old man Calhoun rented us this field," the knight said, his voice resonating oddly from within his helmet. "We've got it all day. That receipt's signed and notarized."

"We're not moving," Mr. Forrest said.

Beauregard, studying the paper, said, "Maybe we should go. This paper looks legal, Dad."

"Damn it, we've always used this field," Mr. Forrest said. "My bank holds the mortgage on it. Go ask Calhoun."

Beauregard had no answer to that. It seemed to him that Calhoun would retain the right to rent the field, even if it was mortgaged; but he wasn't sure. Mr. Forrest snatched the official-looking paper, wadded it, and threw it at random. A gust carried it to the feet of the squires, who stepped back a bit. Raising his voice so everyone could hear, Mr. Forrest said, "If they want the field so bad, let 'em take it from us!"

A conspiratorial cheer arose from the gray- and blue-mesh troops. Mr. Forrest swung up on Snuffy/Traveller and reined around toward them. "Men," he said, his tenor voice quavering a bit at the prospect of genuine field leadership, "we're all one army now. Assume your positions at the far end of the field."

They did, enthusiastically, many of them whooping. Mr. Forrest reined back toward the knight. "In the spirit of chivalry, I give you ten minutes, sir," he said. He made a show of checking his antique pocket watch. "I suggest you prepare." With that, he galloped off to his troops.

The knight let the hoofbeats fade, then turned to Beauregard, who had waited around in hopes of a quick compromise. "The old man—he's kidding, right?" the knight said.

"I don't think so," Beauregard said.

"Will those rednecks do what he says?"

"Those rednecks," Beauregard replied slowly, with edge, "are surprisingly well disciplined."

"Jesus Christ."

The knight gathered the other medievalists around him. Beauregard, lingering a respectable distance outside their circle, could hear the debate when it grew loud, which was often. The friars and one or two of the wenches wanted to fight, but the knight and squires favored appeasement. A vote was held. Soon they were all walking morosely off the field.

When it became clear that they had won by default, Mr. Forrest's troops yelled their best Rebel yells. The small trees that dotted the field seemed to sway from this bloodcurdling wind. But as the men grew hoarse, then silent, disappointment set in. They had wanted a real fight—a chance to see, for example, how much damage their blunted bayonets really could do to a knight's armor. Their regret hardened into ennui when Mr. Forrest insisted that they resume practice. The men went reluctantly back to their positions. Beauregard died again, far afield from Barry Pollard.

The practice was nearly over when Beauregard, eyes closed, heard a siren in the distance. It was unnerving to hear an urban sound so far back in the woods. The awful whine grew louder. Soon it was on them, and the shooting stopped again. Beauregard looked up.

The medievalists had returned with a sheriff's deputy. His two-

11

toned Plymouth squad car bounced slowly across the field toward Mr. Forrest and Snuffy/Traveller. The medievalists strode behind, except for the knight, who rode unhelmeted and smug in the front seat with the deputy.

The deputy parked next to the horse, then he and the knight got out. Mr. Forrest dismounted, facing the deputy as everyone else circled around. Mr. Forrest, his gray hair and beard matted a bit from perspiration, his face flush, looked more than ever like Robert E. Lee. The deputy by contrast was a young, egg white man, short with narrow, sloping shoulders. His brown uniform was a size too big, as was his broad-rimmed hat. Whatever his police academy background, the buckle in his voice suggested he'd never been instructed in how to handle anything like this.

"Mr. Forrest?" he managed to ask.

"Yes, I am!" Mr. Forrest answered at once. "And who, pray tell, are you? The sheriff of Nottingham?"

"You w-watch your tongue."

"Listen, son," Mr. Forrest said, squaring in front of him. "Your ancestors, which side did they fight on?"

"In what?"

Mr. Forrest flushed but kept his composure. "The War Between the States," he said.

"Oh." The deputy sniffed, thinking. "Rebel, I reckon," he decided. "We ain't really looked back. Now listen here . . ."

"Of course they were Confederates," Mr. Forrest said, "like my ancestors and the ancestors of all my men here. Tell me, honest. Would you give the boot to us, the few men willing to spend a hot September Saturday to keep the Confederate heritage, your family's heritage, alive?"

"W-well . . ."

"You don't have to answer," Mr. Forrest told him. "I know the answer. Let's resume, men."

Just then the knight stepped from behind and draped a heavy arm around the deputy's shoulder. The metallic sensation surprised and unnerved the deputy, who jumped forward and spun back around, hand on his service revolver.

"Hey, I'm sorry," the knight said. "But you are going to arrest them, aren't you?"

The deputy straightened up, coughed a little. "I don't know," he said. "I don't think so. I can't think of a law."

"Jesus Christ."

12

"You watch your tongue."

The deputy, scowling purposefully now, went back to the patrol car, opened the passenger door, and grabbed the gray, palm-sized speaker of his police radio. "I'm gonna call this in," he threatened to no one in particular. He cleared his throat again and brought the speaker up close. He opened his mouth, even began to gesture with his free hand, but said nothing. After a few seconds he put the speaker back into the plastic holder next to his radio.

"I can't think of the police signal for what this is," he conceded quietly. "It ain't a real fight. It ain't a domestic disturbance. What *is* this damn thing?" When no one answered, he shook his head, then leaned defeatedly against the squad car. "Can't think of the signal, can't think of the law," he said. "Maybe I shouldn't even be a sheriff's deputy."

Beauregard stepped forward. "Buck up," he said.

A friar in back called out, "Doing fine, young man. Doing fine."

The deputy swallowed, then nodded gratefully—he would go on. He reached again for the police radio and asked to speak to the sheriff. When the sheriff came on, the deputy sat in the car and shut the door. Beauregard could see him explaining, then listening, then finally laughing in relief. Once out of the car, he announced the sheriff's decision that both sides would leave the field.

The medievalists protested mildly, but the decision suited the War Between the States reenactors. It was getting on; they were dog tired. Even Mr. Forrest seemed ready to head over to the modern camp for the traditional postreenactment spread of deli sandwiches and cold Budweiser.

Before anyone left, the deputy insisted on a written report. Beauregard helped with the spelling and used one of Mr. Forrest's antique-looking maps for the accompanying diagram. As he some-times did with reporting, Beauregard got carried away, his sheet becoming an inky blur of topographical notations, position coordi-nates, and curved arrows illustrating troop movements.

Driving home, all was quiet in the Cadillac. Not even Mr. Forrest wanted to hear "Goober Peas." When they pulled in to the garage at New Arlington, their ten-acre estate named for Lee's, Beauregard cut the motor and turned to his father.

"Dad, I've got something to say."

Mr. Forrest was looking down at his gray lap, idly flicking away brambles that had attached themselves during the long afternoon.

13

"Don't, Beauregard," he said quietly. "I know. I acted badly out there."

"Oh, not so bad," Beauregard said, thrown a bit by this rare admission. "It was a totally unexpected situation. You were under a lot of stress."

"Lee never complained about stress."

"He might have. We don't know everything he said. . . . But listen, Dad. I want to tell you something. I'm leaving New Arlington. I've got an apartment."

"What?" Mr. Forrest was staring at Beauregard now.

"Sir, I'm the only young person at the paper who still lives at home. Even the copy clerks have apartments. I want to give it a try—just until it's time to go to Washington and Lee."

"No."

"Sir, please."

"Quit saying 'sir' so much. It's rank salesmanship, the way you say it." He looked away again. "I won't pay for you to have an apartment."

"You won't have to," Beauregard said. "I can make it on my salary. It'll be tight, but I can do it."

Mr. Forrest shook his head. "Rent, utilities, furniture. Son, you have no idea."

"Jackson loaned me some furniture," Beauregard said, "and a buddy of his owns the apartment building. He's not charging me any deposit."

"Jackson?" Mr. Forrest laughed bitterly. "That's just great."

"He's your son and my brother. He wouldn't steer either one of us wrong."

"I don't like the way your brother lives," Mr. Forrest said. "Too much sex."

"Dad, it'll be all right."

"No. I don't think so."

Beauregard, having anticipated this early resistance, tried another tack. "Look, Dad," he said. "I'll do better at Washington and Lee if I have some experience living on my own. This way, I'll get over being homesick before I ever get to college. I'll know how to do laundry, pay bills, organize my time. Dad, you know as well as I do that I'll need every advantage at a tough school like Washington and Lee. I need to go in with confidence, and living on my own for a while will give me some of that."

Mr. Forrest didn't answer immediately: a good sign. Beauregard knew he'd been right to frame his argument in terms of surviving at Washington and Lee.

"Not that I'm agreeing, but who would load Snuffy for me on Saturday mornings?" Mr. Forrest asked finally.

"You mean Traveller?" Beauregard said.

"Traveller! Traveller!" He was hitting his forehead.

"I'd come around for that."

"And Sunday lunch at the country club?"

"Of course."

"When would this great migration occur?"

"Today, Dad. I've already got the key."

"I see."

A brief lull followed, but Beauregard could feel what was coming. His father liked to end conversations by quoting Lee. As boys, Beauregard and Jackson had been able to earn spending money by memorizing Lee's farewell to the troops after Appomattox, and other of their father's favorites. Beauregard could almost hear his father considering and rejecting various Lee remarks. "It is good that war is terrible, else we might grow too fond of it"—no, that wouldn't be the one. After a few tense seconds, Mr. Forrest leaned toward Beauregard and said, "If you're absolutely sure this is what you want to do, I've got just one thing to say."

"Yes?"

Mr. Forrest opened the car door and stepped out, catching his saber in the shoulder harness briefly. He freed himself, then leaned back in.

"Strike the tent!"

The remark hung in the air like skywriting. Before it could dissipate, Mr. Forrest slammed the car door and went into the house.

Beauregard knew quite well that "strike the tent" was supposed to have been the last thing Robert E. Lee ever said; but he also knew that there was no finality when his father said it—for he said it fairly often. Sometimes he said it in irritation, but usually he said it as a general statement of affirmation, like the Frenchman's *"d'ac-cord"* or the University of Alabama fan's "Roll Tide." Saying it now meant he wasn't really all that upset.

Beauregard pulled the trailer around to the stables, then fed and watered Snuffy/Traveller. He unhitched the trailer, parked the Cadillac, and went into the house. He got his things—clothes,

15

books, golf clubs—and loaded up the van Jackson let him drive around town.

As he drove down the long red-brick driveway, past the cannon pointed north, just in case, Beauregard wondered why deep down he had wanted his father to have a real tantrum over his leaving. Certainly he wished his father had been too hurt to wrap things up with a cool recitation of Lee's best-known quotation. Oh, well. At least now he was loose from all that. He could come in from the gray, join the real world. He pressed down on the accelerator and hurried on to his new place.

The newspaper wasn't too far out of the way, so he decided to stop by there, check his phone calls, his mail. He'd grab a plastic foam cup of black coffee and look available. At the very least, he would impress Bubba Shealy by showing up on Saturday. Shealy might even have an assignment for him—a hastily called press conference, perhaps, or a political banquet in the black community. Some of the Midwestern reporters, liberals all, felt uneasy about going into Birmingham's black neighborhoods, especially after dark. Not Beauregard. "Black neighborhood?" he could hear himself telling Shealy. "Be glad to. Just let me grab a notebook."

But as he prepared to pull into the newspaper's parking lot, Beauregard remembered he was still wearing his Confederate uniform. Quickly, before any of his colleagues could see him, he switched off his turn signal and drove on to his new home.

Chapter Two

Southside, where Beauregard took an apartment, helped refute the old Atlanta argument that Birmingham was a minor league city, raw, sooty, and regressive, without great indigenous business institutions like Coca-Cola and Delta Airlines and CNN, without great academic institutions like Georgia Tech and Emory, without major league sports or even much civic leadership, and in fact still under the grinding boot of Yankee steel barons who practiced philanthropy only above the Mason-Dixon Line. Southside was lovely.

It was especially lovely in spring, when the dogwood and azalea bloomed so bright, lavishly pinkening and whitening the rolling landscape; bloomless, though, it still made a compelling argument for midsized Southern city living. Southside's main street, Highland Avenue, wound around three well-tended, well-used city parks. Standing on the other side of Highland, and along its oak-canopied side streets, were old, porch-dominated homes that managed not to look like one another. Southside had many apartment buildings, too, and though a few looked like Days Inns, most were sturdy red- or brown-brick buildings of three to five stories and indisputable character. All kinds of people lived in these buildings: old and middle-aged, who enjoyed freedom from the tending of one-acre suburban lawns; young, mostly students and beginning professionals, who enjoyed the modest rents and near-urban bustle; gays, generally unharassed; and blacks, a few anyway, also generally unharassed. Price and other reporters from the paper had talked up Southside, so Beauregard found a place there, in a building owned by a friend of his brother's. The building looked like a Days Inn. His one-bedroom apartment, upstairs, with splintery doors, smudged Sheetrock, aquamarine shag carpeting, and a good view of the Dumpster, was what he could afford on a cub reporter's salary.

Beauregard spent the late afternoon and early evening after the reenactment unpacking his clothes and rearranging the few pieces of spare furniture Jackson had sent over. Beauregard's room at New Arlington looked like a little museum, covered as it was with Confederate flags and portraits of Confederate generals. He'd brought none of that with him. He'd also left behind his three shelves of War Between the States books, his half dozen albums of War Between the States songs, and even his War Between the States chess set, with Grant as one king and Lee as the other. His could have been an Ithaca, New York, apartment, so bereft was it of Confederate matter. Just being in the place gave him a new, civilian feeling. He bit off four scraps of masking tape and put up a Jimi Hendrix black light poster Jackson had left in a closet at New Arlington. He stepped back and looked at this, his apartment's sole decoration. Good but not good enough. He went to a grocery store and bought a two-dollar cactus, then came home and flooded it.

Just before midnight, he climbed into bed with *All the President's Men* and *Thirty Days to a More Powerful Vocabulary,* two of the books he'd brought along. His father had given him the latter book a couple of months ago, but Beauregard had progressed no further than "Day Four: Words for Mature Minds." Now, in the interest of a higher verbal SAT score and admission to Washington and Lee, he would get down to it. He would study thirty minutes every night. He turned to his bookmark and found the next word, *vicarious.* He looked at how long it was, looked at all the vowels. He shut the book and opened *All the President's Men*. Any words he learned this evening he'd probably forget, tired as he was. He'd start again tomorrow, fresh, with a cup of instant coffee. For now he'd just read a few pages of this other book, which was, after all, career-related. Price, the best reporter at the *Standard-Dispatch,* had recommended it. It was a gripping, informative, and (to Beauregard) very attractive book. The reporters came off quite well. He'd seen the movie *All the President's Men,* too, and he especially liked

18

it when Dustin Hoffman, playing the scruffy Carl Bernstein, leaned with dangling cigarette over the typewriter and pounded out a story, all the while grilling a source on the telephone. Beauregard had started smoking a little because of that scene—and because Price smoked. He stayed up later than he meant to reading *All the President's Men.* It took his mind off the strangeness of being alone in an apartment so sparsely furnished that a spoken word echoed. About 1:00 A.M., he tossed both books onto the other side of the bed, cut the reading lamp, and lay back.

Security lighting from the outside walkway leaked through the sheer drapes and illuminated the Sheetrock wall ahead of him. Beauregard could hear laughter downstairs in the parking lot—a couple, man and woman, laughing. It sounded like precoital laughter, or postcoital, or maybe they were just doing it in the parking lot. Could people do it laughing? He considered the Sheetrock. Illuminated this way, it looked like a blank front page of the *Standard-Dispatch.* He sat up and filled the "page" by imagining a story under his byline. Something about a county commissioner, missing funds, a mistress. "Exclusive to the *Standard-Dispatch.*" He rolled over and faced a darker wall. The notion of a commissioner's mistress, of anyone's mistress, led him to imagine a woman in bed with him for a meaningful fling. The odds were long against it, but what the hell. She would be skinny like him, short, too, a woman he could envelop as he was enveloping the spare pillow just now. She'd be the kind of woman who, after the mutually satisfying sex, would curl up and put her head on his chest. She wouldn't withdraw or complain that his chest was too bony, because in point of fact her own chest was rather bony, and so she was tolerant, sensitive even, and knew what most people don't, that the skinny too have their story. Beauregard had one. At sixteen, he'd sent off for Joe Weider weight-gain powder. He'd endured it and even gained a few pounds until Althea, the New Arlington housekeeper, mistook it for rat poison and spread it behind the kitchen stove and cabinets. Beauregard sometimes thought Mr. Forrest had *told* her it was rat poison. He didn't like the idea of Beauregard gaining weight. He wanted his reenactors thin and even hungry-looking, like the real Confederate troops. During weekend trips he put heavier soldiers on half rations.

In the morning, Beauregard got up early and walked down to a convenience store to buy a Sunday *Standard-Dispatch.* He brought it back and read carefully as he drank a first, then a second, cup of instant black coffee. He'd had his usual quota of bad dreams, but it felt good to wake up in his own place. His friends from Birmingham Military were in their freshman dorm rooms, no doubt. Meanwhile, he had his own apartment. Anything might happen here. Poker parties; Southside women dropping by. After reading the newspaper, he putted a few golf balls across the shag carpeting. He even stepped back and tried to "read" the carpeting, the way professional golfers read greens. Beauregard had been a good golfer, six handicap and dropping, until his father had insisted that he reserve weekends for reenacting. He'd never putted on a green as bad as this carpeting, though. It was like U.S. Open rough. He set the putter aside and went back in the bedroom to get his copy of *Thirty Days to a More Powerful Vocabulary*.

Before he got there, the phone rang.

"Beauregard Forrest," he answered on the second ring.

"Roll Tide."

"Jackson!"

"Furniture arrive?"

"Yeah," Beauregard said, looking around. "It's not bad."

"Hungry?"

"Yeah."

"Mawn over. I'll throw a couple of steaks in the skillet."

Within a minute, Beauregard had hung up the phone, locked up his apartment, and begun the short drive over the mountain to Jackson's place.

Beauregard got along well with Jackson, but he was aware, because everyone told him, how different they were. They looked different. Beauregard was thin—so much so that he wore T-shirts for bulk as much as warmth or sweat protection. He had a too-ripe Adam's apple and a barber-college haircut. One of the barber college instructors was Little Willie Arnold, son of Big Willie, the New Arlington caretaker. Beauregard went to the barber college every third Wednesday as a gesture of loyalty to the Big and Little Willies. Little Willie was loyal in his own way, trying to steer Beauregard to one of the more promising undergraduates; but, inevitably, Beauregard emerged nicked and tapered, little bits of toilet paper stuck to his face and the dark brown hair on his neck trailing unevenly into his dress shirt and blazer.

Jackson, by contrast, retained the sinewy physique he'd had as a walk-on free safety for the University of Alabama football team. He lifted weights and modeled part-time for a local department store that supplied him the latest sports coats and casual wear. William cut his hair. William—who had had his middle and last names legally deleted—owned a salon in the exclusive Mountain Brook suburb of Birmingham. He cut only the hair of truly attractive customers. When the PGA Tournament came to Birmingham, he had rejected the great Jack Nicklaus. Something about the Golden Bear's blond locks and broad forehead offended William's sense of proportion—made him nauseated, really, he told people. But he took Jackson right away.

Beauregard, after the short drive, pulled up to the guard shack of Devonshire Oaks, where Jackson owned a condo. A guard in a white helmet and khaki shirt waved him through. He drove past the tennis courts, then the swimming pool, where two young women in string bikinis received the sun with a languor and openness that made Beauregard grip the steering wheel. It was as if they expected the sun to be worshipping *them,* the way they had dressed and positioned themselves. Beauregard drove on, parked in a visitors spot, then walked across the lot to Jackson's and let himself in.

"Roll Tide," greeted Jackson, who wore a red Alabama jersey over white tennis shorts. He was arranging ketchup and steak sauce bottles on the kitchen table but stopped long enough to thrust out a hand.

Beauregard took it and shook with the force he and Jackson always shook with: hard, but not competitively so. "Roll Tide," he said.

He knew to prepare the iced tea and shred the lettuce and microwave the Tater Tots. Jackson, spatula in hand, tended the steaks to the brothers' agreed-upon medium-well texture.

Soon enough they were eating their meal and talking about family and work.

"So," Jackson said, cutting into his steak, "what did Marse Bob say about you moving out?"

"Don't call Dad 'Marse Bob,' Jackson," said Beauregard, working the ketchup bottle.

"I'll call him whatever I want to call him, Roll Tide," said Jackson, who didn't need much if any context to say Roll Tide. "What'd he say?"

Beauregard, watching the ketchup dribble out, said, "First it was no, then I talked him into it, then he said, 'Strike the tent.' "

"That was it?"

tooth hat. It was dark in the room, drapes drawn against the late morning sun. Jackson leaned forward and pushed a cassette into the VCR below his large-screen color Sony.

"What's this?" Beauregard asked.

"A tape from 'PM Magazine,' " Jackson said. "They're doing a thing on me tomorrow night."

"Have you seen it?"

"No. Haven't had a chance."

The tape began not with Jackson but with a light feature on the Bill Johnson Club, convening in Fort Worth, Texas. Only Bill Johnsons could belong and there were hundreds in the Southwest alone. Now, for the "PM Magazine" audience's amusement, the members held a quick mock election. Bill Johnson won. Next a security guard shouted across the convention floor, "Phone call for Bill Johnson!" Everybody stood. In a more serious vein, the "PM Magazine" correspondent interviewed members as to the advantages and disadvantages of having so common a name. They proved uniformly, Bill Johnsonesquely, inarticulate. Then he interviewed Billie Johnson: she of the women's auxiliary.

"Enough of this Bill Johnson shit," Jackson said, fast-forwarding. "Let's have some Jackson Forrest."

"Yeah," Beauregard said.

Jackson found his segment and turned up the volume. The local "PM Magazine" celebrities, Frank and Wendy, said that tonight's Birmingham feature concerned another familiar name, Jackson Forrest, formerly of the University of Alabama football team.

"Roll Tide," Jackson said.

"Jackson was short but slow!" Frank joked.

"Shit," Jackson protested.

"That's right, Frank!" Wendy said. "But Jackson's not *slow* when it comes to business! And he's not *short* on cash!"

Beauregard watched the rest of the tape, although he knew the story of Jackson's business, Get Down! Inc., quite well. For a handsome fee, Jackson created bachelor parties and other events that he guaranteed would be unforgettable and successful, or your money back. In ten years, he had never given money back. He supplied music, scenery, hostesses, hosts, food, drink, party favors, blue films—whatever was necessary to the party in question. Jackson had learned the basics of party-giving as a Kappa Alpha at the University of Alabama, but he had gone way beyond that, even to the extent of formulating "principles of party science," which he

24

hoped someday to market. He *prepared* for a party, interviewing the client at length to determine who would be attending and how they might best be entertained. If the client had ideas for the party, Jackson fulfilled them; but if the client left it up to Jackson, anything might happen, and it would usually be amazing. He had a number of notorious "theme parties" that people asked for, including "Declining Rome," "The Old South," and "Batista's Cuba." Of course, these cost extra money. Jackson charged top dollar, but people seemed quite willing to pay. His business had set record profits in each of the last twelve quarters, with healthy surges at Christmas and during the May and June bachelor-party season.

The "PM Magazine" report as filed by Wendy and Frank did not mention theme parties or hostesses or blue films. There was a hokey shot of Jackson putting a keg into place at a party, another of Jackson in his office going over party options with a potential client. His brow was deeply, responsibly furrowed. He might have been explaining life insurance. Wendy and Frank described Jackson as a creative, enterprising young man who had taken an amateur institution and made it both professional and highly profitable. Wendy called Jackson a "pioneer of the party industry," crudely emphasizing the alliteration. She nodded hard when Frank added that Coach Bear Bryant would have been proud of Jackson.

Jackson turned to Beauregard. "Did you know Coach Bryant had just one testicle?"

"The Bear?" Beauregard said. "Just one?"

Jackson sniffed. "I can't say for sure," he qualified. "But an assistant coach told me that."

"In what context, Jackson?"

"I'd been hit hard in the groin during practice. I was rolling around, moaning. Coach Hooper came over and said not to worry. Winked at me. Said Coach Bryant was riding fine on one wheel."

"Roll Tide," Beauregard said.

"Roll Tide," Jackson said.

"Hey," Beauregard said, teasing Jackson. "Maybe I could do a story on that. A feature story. 'Men with One Wheel.' "

"No way, bud."

"I could build it around Coach Bryant. He could be my nut graph."

"No way!" Jackson cut him off. "Everything I ever say about Coach is off the record. *Everything.* I'm serious, Beauregard. He made us team captains take an oath."

Jackson leaned forward and ejected the tape, then put it in its plastic box. He got up and went back into the kitchen. Beauregard followed, and they began to clean off the table. It was clear that Jackson wasn't going to be giving Beauregard any career advice. His mind was on the "PM Magazine" spot. He started thinking out loud. First, he told Beauregard, he'd make a list of ways to take advantage of the publicity. Maybe after a while he'd go down to the office and line up some of his hostesses to field phone calls. He'd get his girlfriend, the Morsel, to help out. She had the kind of low, husky voice young men liked to hear over the phone. When she said, "Get Down!" they very much wanted to.

Beauregard finished cleaning the kitchen while Jackson made notes in his study. As he scrubbed the greasy skillet, he thought about his brother, all the women he knew, all the money he made. Then he thought about Price, and how little money *he* made. Beauregard had once visited the senior reporter's tiny white frame house on the eastern fringe of Southside. Price had boiled hot dogs for the two of them, then used the remaining hot dog water to make instant coffee, black.

Beauregard had never seen such a thing. The coffee wasn't half bad, though. Thinking about it made him want a cup right now. He put some water on, then lit a cigarette. He stood there smoking and pantomiming Dustin Hoffman as Carl Bernstein, typing like a son of a bitch.

Chapter Three

Reporters on the *Standard-Dispatch* were supposed to arrive for work at nine A.M., but they drifted in at various times, a few earlier than the appointed hour, most later. Beauregard usually got to work early, and the Monday morning after he moved into his new apartment proved no exception. He was at the newspaper just before eight. He wore a blue blazer, a white dress shirt, a gray-and-crimson-striped tie and scruffy wing tips. He carried a leather briefcase full of out-of-town newspapers and reporter's notebooks.

On the way to the coffee station he passed colleagues from advertising, promotions, circulation, and accounting.

"Mornin', B-Four," many of them said, enjoying his nickname, rolling it around in their mouths like a hard candy.

"Mornin'," he said, not letting on that the nickname bothered him. "How's it goin'?"

Everyone had coffee. They carried the white plastic foam cups ahead of them like small lanterns. Beauregard had decided that coffee was as much an illumination at the *Standard-Dispatch* as the long fluorescent cylinders buzzing overhead. It wasn't just the reporters, like Price. Everyone drank coffee. Coffee in the morning, coffee at lunch, coffee in the afternoon, coffee, coffee, coffee, as if the employees had enlisted in a public relations campaign to persuade the larger world that Birmingham was not a sleepy town.

To Beauregard, a plastic foam cup of black coffee was an essential prop in the romance of journalism; by day's end, his desk was a snowy forest of them. He liked the feel of warm plastic foam, the sight of rising steam. He thought a desk littered with empty plastic foam cups suggested a reporter who cared more for the First Amendment than for calm nerves or fresh breath. He linked coffee not with cancer but with breaking news, late hours, and gruffly affectionate city editors who, in the gut wrench of a major story, advised trusted reporters, "Gonna be a long one. Anyone wants a second cup, I'm buying."

This hadn't happened to Beauregard. When a major story broke, Bubba Shealy busied him with more Metro Briefs and obits. But as he carried his plastic foam cup to the newsroom he cheered himself with the prospect, however distant, of coffee-induced camaraderie.

He set cup and briefcase on his gray metal desk. His desk, professionally cluttered with files and press releases, faced Price's. Price was there already, working the phone. He cupped the speaker long enough to acknowledge Beauregard and begin an exchange of "mornin's."

"Ready to kick journalistic ass this mornin'?" Price asked.

"Ready."

When Price went back to the phone, Beauregard looked across the newsroom. No other reporters had made it in yet.

Like some fisherman with a favored stream or pond, Beauregard preferred the newsroom early in the morning. The stillness promised big, page-one catches, if only he'd keep throwing his line out and be patient. Beauregard liked the newsroom anytime, but this was the best—before it filled with reporters and editors, before deadline tension thickened the air, before he had to start calling near-in and outlying funeral homes.

The *Standard-Dispatch* newsroom was about the size and shape of a junior high basketball court. Decades of rising smoke from cigarettes, cigars, and (over in the editorial writer's cubicle) meerschaum pipes, had yellowed the ceiling tiles. A fresh coat of guacamole green paint covered the concrete block walls. Drippings of that same paint drew attention to the linoleum floor, which was liver-colored and buckled badly over by the copy desk. Reporters stepped over those buckles, as well as exposed wires and abandoned electrical outlets, on their way to do stories about other companies' safety violations. Upstairs in the executive suite, tasteful prints and lithographs graced the paneled walls. On the newsroom's concrete block walls hung enlarged black-and-white photographs of sink-holes, plane crashes, and Bear Bryant.

Beauregard draped his blazer over the back of his swivel chair, then sat and shuffled some press releases as he listened to Price work the phone. Price was following up a front-page story from the day before. A gun-wielding Birmingham man had entered a discount clothing outlet and forced several terrified people to try on various outfits. No one had been hurt—physically, anyway. At city editor Bubba Shealy's request, Price had set aside an investigative project to do a quick psychological profile of the perpetrator, now safely in custody.

"But Doc," Price was saying, "you're a psychiatrist. This guy's crazy, right?" A pause, Price listening, then: "That doesn't mean he's not crazy, Doc."

Price was only in his midthirties, but with his Camels and Vitalis-moistened hair, his loosened ties and eyeglasses bandaged at the temples, he looked more like an authentic reporter, more like *The Front Page,* than anyone else at the *Standard-Dispatch.* He complained to Beauregard that the business wasn't as interesting as when he'd started as a copyboy, fresh out of high school. Computers had removed from the newsroom its best sounds—the clatter of manual typewriters under deadline, the hum of the wire service Teletypes, the bells of those Teletypes during major breaking stories: assassinations, coups, and hurricanes. Price lamented the moving of the printing plant to a separate building. He'd liked the newsroom better when it smelled like ink. Management, though, he noted, was as scummy as ever.

"Readers don't understand those big psychological terms, Doc," he was saying now. "They understand words like 'crazy.' Let's tell 'em he's crazy."

He was well read, Price, and witty in a hard-edged, cynical way. Price-isms were repeated, even memorized, in the newsroom. It was Price who observed that the *Standard-Dispatch* was on the buttering, rather than the cutting, edge of journalism; Price who predicted that Alabama legislators would one day reveal themselves to be a troupe of European surrealist performance artists; Price who suggested "Better than Tulsa" as the slogan for Birmingham's latest promotional campaign. Price was writing a hard-boiled detective novel in the newspaper's computer system. He called it *That's Close Enough,* after the young Midwestern reporters at the *Standard-Dispatch* who so often said "that's close enough" during phone interviews in which sources tried to explain the intricacies of municipal bonds or water management policy.

He bore in on the psychiatrist.

"One of the cops tells me there was a color scheme at work. The suspect gave them only yellow and green clothes to wear. Some Dacron in everything. What might that mean?" Furious, two-fingered typing. "Uh-huh, uh-huh."

Beauregard much preferred Price to the Midwesterners. They were nice enough, most of them, but they regarded the *Standard-Dispatch* as the first stop on a road that would lead next to the *Atlanta Constitution* or the *Charlotte Observer,* and later on, quite possibly, to the *Philadelphia Inquirer* or the *Washington Post.* Weekends found them either at a Southside bar or the downtown Insta-Copy, running off résumés, cover letters, and clips. They made fun of Birmingham. Price did, too, but he'd grown up here, he was a homeboy, and so had the right. The Midwesterners, with their out-of-tune-guitar-string voices, couldn't quit talking about how popular the tractor pull was in Birmingham. As if it weren't popular anywhere else, as if the Midwest, the so-called breadbasket, had no tractors. They made fun of Beauregard, too—not to his face, but he'd overheard them. Once, in the outgoing mail basket, he'd read a postcard sent by Rochelle, who covered city hall. "We've got this kid reporter," she'd looped meanly across the narrow white space. "Everybody calls him 'B-Four' because that's where his stories land. No experience, no journalism school, but his old man runs a local bank, so 'sonny' gets to be a reporter. Incredible. And the pizza tastes like shit here. . . ."

She wasn't bad-looking, though, Rochelle. A big woman, handsome, with nice skin and lovely, layered black hair. Should things turn around, should he make front page, say, and establish his nickname as ironic, thereby earning more serious attention from the eligible females on staff, Beauregard felt he could over-look her open-mouthed chewing of gum and Yankee use of "Jesus Fucking Christ" as a mild newsroom oath.

Price was still typing. Beauregard rolled back from the desk, then stood and reached for his coffee. Each morning, soon after getting in, he made a brief, coffee-sipping circuit around the newsroom to check his mail and the bulletin board. It was time for that easy, pleasant ritual. He walked past the library, which he and Price, traditionalists, called the morgue; past Style, with its stack of *GQ* and *Vogue* magazines; past Sports, with its narrow AstroTurf strip for in-house putting tournaments between editions; past Business. Business, Price liked to say, was slow. Beauregard walked on, peeking into the cubicle where the editorial writers viewed with alarm declining SAT scores, mounting third world debt, and just about everything else.

Every reporter had a mail slot at the newsroom's far end. Price, having worked at the paper so many years, always had a box full. Beauregard often went two and three days without mail. Approaching, though, he could see an envelope wedged into his box. A few steps closer he recognized the Humane Society stationery.

Beauregard knew without opening it that the envelope contained a press release and a black-and-white glossy of the Pet of the Week. He grimaced. He liked the people down at the Humane Society, and he certainly didn't have anything against dogs, but there was no future in Pet of the Week. He'd never make front page with Pet of the Week. Still, it was mail.

He stuffed the envelope into his shirt pocket and moved on to the bulletin board. A quick inspection revealed nothing new. Last year's notice about free flu shots was still up, as was this year's Media League softball schedule. Bubba Shealy had yet to remove his long, angry memo insisting that reporters be more courteous. Reporters had crowded the margins with obscene words and drawings.

The final stop on Beauregard's tour was the city desk. The monotone drawl of a female dispatcher interrupted the police scanner's static. She gave some numerical signal—Beauregard didn't know what. Price knew the signals. He complained about the scanner and all the other new and corrupting technologies in newspaper work, but he kept up. He even had his own beeper, not a mediocre staff beeper, but state of the art. As yet, Beauregard had no beeper. Shealy hadn't offered to let him use a staff one ("We need you, we'll find you") and it seemed presumptuous to invest in one. It was a small thing, much smaller than a front-page story, but Beauregard wanted to earn staff beeper privileges. He wanted to be in his father's office, or Jackson's, and have the thing go off. He could see their large nostrils flaring with new respect.

Back at their desks, Beauregard listened as Price made the inevitable conquest.

"Doc, I understand about compulsions, and tendencies, and the Oedipal thing, and green being the color of life. But it sounds to me like he's a little crazy. Hey, if you're uncomfortable with speaking plainly like that, you could refer me to some other psychiatrist in town. You probably don't need the publicity anyway. The *free* publicity." A tense pause, then more typing. "That's good, Doc, very good." Price cupped the receiver again and, with triumphantly arched eyebrows, informed Beauregard, "Doc says this guy 'shows signs of mental imbalance.' "

"Roll Tide."

"Roll Tide."

They did high fives over their desks, Price retreating just long enough to thank the psychiatrist, confirm the spelling of his name, and get him off the phone.

"Cigarette?" Price said.

"Yeah."

They happily enshrouded themselves with Camel smoke.

"Good work, Price."

"Shit."

"No. That's front page."

"Shit."

Price took a vacuumlike drag on his Camel, then exhaled at a thirty-degree incline. "You're the one making progress," he said.

"No, uh-uh, I don't think so," Beauregard said. He waved away enough smoke to see Price clearly. "You think so?"

"Remember your first week?"

"What about it?"

"You thought the medical examiner was a newspaper for doctors."

Beauregard grinned lopsidedly, ruefully, again waving away smoke. "A tough week," he conceded.

"Shealy sent you to that little trial, the one for receiving stolen property. You sat in the jury box."

"Hey, nobody told me it was a jury trial," Beauregard protested. "I just wanted to be close."

"That was a weak excuse then, B-Four," Price insisted, "and it's still weak. But my point is that you wouldn't make those mistakes now. You know things like that now."

"I know a few things. I know I never make the front page."

"You get bylines."

"Everybody gets bylines. I want front page."

Price fogged and wiped clean his bandaged eyeglasses. They were bandaged, he'd told Beauregard, in protest of management's refusal to include any money for eye care in the latest of a series of lean benefits packages. "Don't get your heart set on making front page anytime soon, B-Four," he said. "It's a mistake to set your heart on something you can't control."

"A page-one story's a page-one story."

"No. Somebody has to decide it is."

Beauregard wanted to follow up with a question—"Bubba Shealy's not that crazy about me, is he?"—but suddenly he heard Shealy's distinctive approach.

He was a large, lumbering man who wore the long-sleeved power dress shirts of middle management but undercut the effect with inattentive shaving and pimento-cheese-stained ties. The impressive bulge in his double-knit pants was from an aspirin bottle, which shook like a maraca as he walked. The shaking aspirins, along with Shealy's labored breathing, let reporters know he was coming. He came over a lot, in part because he had a problem delegating authority—so much so that he'd let the assistant city editor's job go unfilled for more than a year. Shealy was an Auburn graduate and defensive about it, as were many of the other Auburn grads Beauregard knew in Birmingham, a University of Alabama stronghold. They constituted a kind of put-upon ethnic minority, flinching a little under the daily barrage of "Roll Tides."

Shealy rarely bothered with "mornin's." Nor did he, at day's end, sign off with the Birminghamian, "Have a good 'un."

"Shrink say he's crazy?" he asked Price.

"In so many words."

"Did you find out whether there'd been any complaints about him in his neighborhood?"

"I did. Lots."

"Think anybody else has got all this? The TV stations?"

"No way."

Shealy pumped a fist, did a brief elephant jig in his tasseled loafers, then got behind Price and began to massage his shoulders, as a trainer would a boxer.

"How crazy is he?" he asked, kneading hard.

"Crazy as a bedbug," Price said.

"Shit! That's great!" Shealy shifted into rapid, short-range karate chops across the middle back.

Price pulled away. "The shrink didn't really say that, Bubba," he said. "Shrinks don't talk like that. He *did* say the guy shows signs of mental imbalance."

"Did he say *how* imbalanced the guy is? On a scale of one to ten?"

"I didn't ask him that."

"Call him back."

"No way!" Price swiveled even farther away from Shealy, then drew in and blew out an extralong drag of Camel smoke, to show exasperation. He looked at Beauregard. "Editors," he observed bitterly, shaking his head. "Management scum."

Shealy cheerfully capitulated. "Hey, Price, we don't really need that one-to-ten business. 'Imbalance' is fine. Let's go for coffee."

Beauregard knew he was not invited. This was strictly a city editor–senior reporter thing. Cubs need not apply. He shuffled some more press releases as he watched the two men walk away. He could hear Price recounting the phone call. He was drawing it out, round by round, himself and the psychiatrist, two verbal heavyweights. When he reached the part where the psychiatrist gave in, Shealy got behind Price and began to massage his shoulders again.

Beauregard put out his cigarette and logged on his computer. He checked the schedule Shealy had made for him.

Reporter: B-Four. Day(s): Monday thru Friday. Stories working: Pet of the Week, Metro Briefs, obituaries.

The schedule was essentially the same as last week's. The three items were exactly the same, though Shealy had rearranged them, putting Pet of the Week first. Beauregard assumed this meant he was to make Pet of the Week top priority. Pet of the Week, he thought to himself without irony, has become my albatross.

Before Beauregard, every *Standard-Dispatch* reporter assigned to Pet of the Week had regarded it as a dog story, literally and figuratively. They gave Pet of the Week hit-and-run treatment: Read the press release, look at the glossy photo, write the story. In and out. Twenty minutes, max. Use words like *frisky*.

"Ranger" is the Humane Society Pet of the Week. A frisky, six-month-old mixed breed, he's available at a nominal cost to anyone with a loving home.

Beauregard, unburdened as other reporters were with lots of other stories, went deeper. He actually got into the van and went down to the Humane Society. He had them get the dog out and pose it in various positions. Sometimes he asked to be alone with the dog. He took page after page of notes. Back at the paper, he spent not twenty minutes but most of the afternoon writing. He searched for fresh approaches to structure and for ways to use new words from *Thirty Days to a More Powerful Vocabulary*. He searched for metaphors. Although the copy desk laid on the same old headlines ("Good with Children"; "Had His Shots"), Beauregard's Pet of the Week copy was, according to Price, unlike any the *Standard-Dispatch,* or any other newspaper, had ever published.

The rich, earthy smell of the metal cages, the early morning light spilling down the concrete corridor in bright, geometric shapes, sunny rhombuses and parallelograms, the brassy concerto of barking—all combine to send a signal of life, life abundant, to a visitor to the Humane Society.

But for "Chigger," whose heritage combines the best of three or four of the canine world's noblest breeds, the cages in question are an antechamber to almost certain death. . . .

The clock is ticking for him. Tick, tick, tick . . .

Chigger does not know his fate, could not, being a dog. His cage opens. Here he comes. Note the moist purple of his lapping tongue, the lovely rhythm of his toenails on concrete, the large walnut eyes: intelligent, loyal. To call him "frisky" is to extract one small nugget from the vast gold mine that is the English language. "Irresistible," "incomparable," "indefatigable"—all these adjectives apply, and more.

Tick, tick, tick . . .

And on the story would go.

Though the extra effort had yielded no compliments from Shealy, the Humane Society management appreciated Beauregard's work. A Beauregard dog had never failed to get adopted. Often, on the mornings after his column ran, a line of hopefuls curled around the kennel like Russian shoppers. Once there had even been an incident, pushing, and Beauregard had gotten a Metro Brief out of it. The only other problem was that sometimes "Jigs" or "Spunky" or "Tidbit" didn't quite live up to Beauregard's description.

A guy had called last week.

35

"Nice dog, understand, and we'll keep her," he'd said. "But she won't eat nothing but sausage."

"Is that right?" Beauregard had said, trying to sound sympathetic.

"*Pure pork* sausage."

"Man."

"Likes it microwaved."

The memory of such calls and the earthy smell of the cages firmly in mind, Beauregard began reluctantly to collect the notebook and pen he would need for another trip to the Humane Society. Camel smoke stopped him.

It was Price, looming.

"Where you heading, B-Four?"

"Humane Society."

"No. Uh-uh."

"Afraid so, Price. It's Pet of the Week time again." Beauregard held up the press release and glossy photograph. It would take every adjective he had to sell this aging Chihuahua.

"*No,*" Price repeated. "I talked Shealy into giving you an out-of-town assignment."

"Price—you're kidding."

Price shook his head. "It's just a speech, but at least it's out of town. I was supposed to go, but I can't, because of this other thing I'm working on. This craziness."

Beauregard looked at Price long enough to see that he meant it. Then, grateful, he thrust out his hand. He was from a hand-shaking family. During the early years at New Arlington, he and his father and Jackson would all shake hands before retiring to their respective bedrooms. Even now Beauregard's impulse was to initiate a handshake at any meaningful occasion involving two or more males.

Price made the handshake brief. "It's not a front-page story," he said. "Section front, maybe. Maybe not even that."

"Section front," Beauregard repeated, a little hypnotized. He snapped out of it. "Should I take a beeper?"

"Not to Tennessee. Won't reach that far."

"Tennessee?"

"Mawn," Price said, winking behind his bandaged glasses. "I'll walk you out."

Chapter Four

Beauregard had long wanted to visit the University of the South at Sewanee, Tennessee. It occupied, with Washington and Lee, The Citadel, and the Virginia Military Institute, a place on the short list of colleges his father considered fit for him. Each was thoroughly Southern. Each had played a role in the War Between the States. W&L, where Lee served as president after the war, was especially hallowed ground, the runaway favorite. But Sewanee, as the school was known, had made the short list, so Beauregard wanted to see it.

He was elated when Price informed him that the Tennessee assignment was to go to Sewanee to cover the speech—sermon, really—of an English archbishop. The publisher of the *Standard-Dispatch* was Episcopalian. Not particularly devout, Price said, but his wife was; so local and even regional stories of interest to Episcopalians got good coverage in the *Standard-Dispatch*.

Beauregard and Price stood in the Get Down! Inc. party van shade, Beauregard carrying extra notebooks and pens, Price yet another plastic foam cup of coffee.

"Bring back a receipt on everything, B-Four," Price said. "They have to reimburse you."

"How'd you talk Shealy into letting me go?"

"Easy. I just said, 'It's a speech, Bubba. Anybody can cover a speech.' "

"Well, thanks again."

"Don't mention it." Price looked at his watch. "You better get going. Remember what I told you. One with the road."

" 'One with the road.' Got it."

It was warm and clear, the downtown trapping of early morning haze having disappeared to wherever it went to—surely a very hazy place. Beauregard pulled out of the parking lot, waving at Price in the rearview. The morning rush hour over, he eased down surface streets to a connector highway. Soon he was on the interstate, angling northeast toward Chattanooga.

Besides wanting to see Sewanee, he felt glad and even lucky to be on the road. Price got most of the few trips allotted to *Standard-Dispatch* reporters. They were day trips mostly, though occasionally the *Standard-Dispatch* advanced him enough money to stay over at some bed o' nails motel. Walking Beauregard out of the building, he had talked almost mystically about becoming "one with the road." Price's method was to get a plastic foam cup of black coffee, light a Camel, nudge in a good cassette tape, preferably some New Orleans rhythm-and-blues band that few people in Birmingham had heard of, and find a cruising speed that seemed compatible.

One with the road.

Beauregard aspired to this but knew it wouldn't be easy in the party van. Few trips in the party van went entirely without incident. Jackson's company was well known in the state, and the sight of his Get Down! Inc. logo, with its rainbow background and inverted champagne bottle exclamation mark, often prompted other drivers to honk at Beauregard. Sometimes at red lights they'd roll down their windows and ask how much a bachelor party cost or how many bananas to put in a banana daiquiri. One time a cop had stopped him. Blue lights flashing, he'd wanted to know if Jackson needed part-time security help. Such interruptions, just the threat of them, usually put oneness with the road well out of Beauregard's reach.

What's more, he felt he had to hurry to Sewanee. This might not be front page, but it was his chance for section front, and he didn't want to miss one word of the sermon. So he postponed oneness, concentrating instead on passing every vehicle the sluggish party van was capable of passing. His only stop was at a Stuckey's to buy gas and take the dribbly, old man's piss that came after just one cup of coffee. Two cups of coffee, drunk in quick succession, yielded a fine, virile, high-arc piss, but Beauregard had hustled out of the newspaper building before his second cup. He endured the inferior piss, bought two more cups of coffee, carefully tore little drinking triangles in their cloudy plastic lids, bought a couple of out-of-town newspapers to read later, then climbed back into the van and headed north again.

Beauregard encountered a clot of traffic soon after the exit, but he got through it and for a long time drove unbothered. He sipped coffee and thought about Sewanee. Odd that he'd never been there. It was close to Chattanooga, a city he and his father knew well. They'd reenacted there and toured the major battle sites, Lookout Mountain and Chickamauga, where the Twenty-second Alabama Regiment lost more than half its men. No side trips to Sewanee, though. Beauregard had an idea of what it looked like from the college catalog. A leafy place, on a plateau in the hills, with stony Gothic-style buildings.

There was farmland along the interstate now, and some grazing cattle. Kudzu overtook various abandoned barns. Beauregard, speeding north, enjoyed the sights peripherally. He liked the way farmland rolled up here. Liked the colors. Soon, though, he was in the midst of more pine trees—a green-and-black wall of them on either side. He searched the glove compartment for a cassette tape, but failed to find one, instead pulling out a stapled booklet he hadn't known was in there. He propped it on the steering wheel and took the first of a series of stolen glances.

The blurry typing across the top of the white construction paper cover described the booklet as "a loose adaptation of the *Kamasutra,* ancient Indian guide to 'love science.' " Below the typing, in bigger, crudely stenciled lettering, was the title *I Can Suit Ya!* Below that came more typing, with the author's name, "Jackson Forrest," and his dedication, "To the KA pledge class in my charge. Long may you suit the women in your life. Roll Tide."

As traffic permitted, Beauregard flipped through the pages, amazed. Jackson, he'd thought, had told him everything; but he'd never mentioned this sex manual. Someone else had done the drawings, but Jackson had renamed the positions and explained them in his own words. "Shady Grove" was one position. "Way Down South" was another. The most advanced position, the one that most intrigued Beauregard, was a low, nasty, contortionistic thing called "the Catfish." Beauregard had perused Jackson's collection of *Penthouse* magazines and even previewed blue movies with him in preparation for the bachelor party season, but he'd never seen anything like the Catfish. He doubted whether the *Kama-sutra* author had either.

Despite heavier traffic in the stretch before Chattanooga, Beauregard kept finding more and more occasions to look down at *I Can Suit Ya!* After a while, he was not only not one with the road, he was almost off the shoulder. He looked up to see the van angling past a speed limit sign toward a concrete embankment. Shaken, he whipped the van back into the right lane and shut the booklet back into the glove compartment. The Catfish stayed with him.

In Chattanooga he changed interstates, taking the one that headed north toward Nashville through hill country. He got off a half hour later at the exit he'd circled on his atlas, then headed west toward Sewanee on the federal highway.

Beauregard had done his best, but he knew he was running a little late as he drove on to the campus. He parked on Georgia Avenue, then jogged across lawns and sidewalks to All Saints' Chapel. It was cooler up here, but he arrived sweaty and in a huff, his striped tie blown back over his blazered right shoulder. He would tour the campus after he'd finished his story. He was eager to see if any large monument existed to the memory of Edmund Kirby Smith, an underrated Confederate general who taught math at Sewanee for many years after the war. There might be something as well for Leonidas Polk, an Episcopalian bishop who had helped found the school and gone on, despite his vestments, to serve as a brave but only middlingly competent general in the Confederacy, dying finally in the Atlanta campaign. Beauregard wanted to see the campus newspaper office, too, and the student center, and the nearest golf course. Maybe he'd start playing golf again, once he got to college. In any event, the thing to do now was to concentrate on reporting and writing the archbishop's story.

Beauregard entered the chapel and saw that it was full of young men in coats and ties and young women in dresses. He also spotted students and professors in unzipped academic gowns. At Sewanee, Beauregard knew from the catalog, upperclass students with good grades got to wear academic gowns. Got to or had to? He couldn't remember. All but a few of the students sat on the hard, sinners' chairs that faced the altar. He leaned against the back wall with a half dozen stragglers. No one glanced his way.

How long had the service been going? Beauregard couldn't tell, but he was glad he'd hustled from the van, because the organ music was ending now and the boldly robed archbishop was climbing the stairs of the wooden pulpit. The archbishop began reading his sermon, gesturing occasionally and forcefully with his right hand. Beauregard removed his notebook. Quickly, reportorially, counting rows and seats per row and stragglers, he estimated the crowd at a thousand—a full house. He noted the beauty and dignity of the chapel, especially its stained glass, but also the flags of the Confederate states hanging from poles connected to the stone walls. He turned his attention to the students, expecting general raptness, but instead he found many instances of glazed incomprehension, even among the gowned. Puzzled, he leaned back and prepared to collect a few quotes from the archbishop.

More trouble. He could hear the archbishop well enough, but the words made no sense. The archbishop uttered them with a strange, off-putting cadence, as if someone were goosing him from behind at irregular intervals. Beauregard lowered his notebook and looked around for help.

"Latin," whispered the young man on his right.

"What?"

"*Latin.* The sermon's in Latin."

"Oh . . . Well, thanks."

"Forrest?"

"Sheffield? Lance Sheffield?"

The young man's moist, chipped-toothy grin confirmed Beauregard's identification. He and Beauregard had attended Birmingham Military Academy together. Sheffield, still wearing thick glasses and a military school haircut, still sporting little scars over his pale hands and fingers, was two years older than Beauregard. Beauregard remembered his reputation: a thoroughly decent fellow, but preoccupied with collecting knives and sabers. They walked out to the vestibule.

"I'd forgotten you went to school here," Beauregard said.

"Yeah," Sheffield said. "I'm a junior now. Still playing golf, Forrest?"

"Not so much."

"Still fighting the Civil War?" He was grinning again, but not mockingly. He'd been over to see Mr. Forrest's reenactment sabers. In fact, he was a good candidate to join the unit, once he got out of college.

"That's on hold, too. Still doing knife tricks, Sheffield?"

"Yeah."

41

"I'll never forget that talent show," Beauregard said. "You threw those Barlow knives way up in the air and caught them coming down. Caught them *by the blades*. The cadets went nuts. Honestly, I never heard them stomp the floor so hard."

Sheffield shrugged modestly. "They were Randall knives, Forrest, but I'm doing much harder tricks now," he said. "Unfortunately, there's no knife club here, like at BMA. Hey, Forrest, how *are* things at the Bowel Movement? I haven't been back in a while."

Even fairly reverent Birmingham Military Academy cadets, such as Beauregard and Sheffield, had called it "Bowel Movement Academy." Beauregard and Lance had attended during the so-called soft BM years, when uniforms and drill were required only on Fridays. Jackson belonged to the hard, daily era.

"All right, as far as I know," Beauregard said. "They're talking about letting girls in."

"Now that we're gone, right?" said Sheffield, rueful.

"Right."

"Mother told me you're working for the newspaper. She sees your byline."

"Yeah," Beauregard said. "That's why I'm here. They sent me to cover this thing." Beauregard, frowning, thumped his reporter's notebook. "Latin, huh?"

Sheffield nodded. "Quite a few things are in Latin around here. The diplomas, for example, which is a hell of a note. We've got graduates who can't read their own diplomas. . . . Hey, I hope to be one."

"You will be."

"I imagine so," Sheffield said. "It's hard, but not that much harder than the Bowel Movement."

"Are all the sermons in Latin?"

"No, Forrest. This is the first one in years. The archbishop—or maybe it was the dean—got a bug up his ass. There's this feeling we should all know Latin."

"Any idea where I could get a copy of the sermon in English?"

"I see a stack of papers over there."

Sheffield waved a nicked hand and went back inside. Beauregard walked over to the stack. The archbishop's text was all there, on multiple sheets, typed and stapled; but these, too, were in Latin. Beauregard slipped a rolled-up copy into his blazer pocket and went back inside.

The archbishop cadenced on. Beauregard, text in hand, tried to keep up, but his attention wandered to images from *I Can Suit Ya!* Frowning, he doodled musketry on his copy of the sermon.

Finally the archbishop sat. There followed more music, some pageantry, communion, more music and pageantry, a benediction, a headlong rush for the doors. Beauregard tried to make his way down front for an interview. Fleeing undergraduates blocked his way.

By the time Beauregard reached the far end of the chapel, the archbishop and his entourage had left through the back. Beauregard caught up as they slammed the doors of their black stretch limousine.

He tapped the driver's tinted window. It rolled down, revealing an older black man in a brown, broad-brimmed chauffeur's hat.

"No, sir, no autographs," the driver said, pointing a bony finger at Beauregard's notebook. "This is a man of God we're carrying in here, not Willie Mays."

"I'm a reporter," Beauregard explained, reaching for his press card. "I need a word with the archbishop."

Leaning over from the other side of the front seat was a heavy, gray-haired woman in a blue dress and pearls. Her scent and rouged makeup reminded Beauregard of boyhood hours spent on the laps of the United Daughters of the Confederacy. "The archbishop had a press conference earlier," she informed gently.

"That's the first I heard about it," Beauregard said.

"Everyone else was there."

"Yes, ma'am. But I didn't know."

The woman sighed deeply, then turned and looked into the back of the limo. After receiving some sort of signal, she turned back around. "All right, what questions do you have? I'll try to answer."

Beauregard coughed a little, for time, then said, "I'd really rather talk to the archbishop directly. No offense, ma'am."

"He's tired."

"Won't take but a minute."

"*No.* Ask me or ask nobody. That's the decision here, young man."

Beauregard could tell she was serious and that she had the backing of the archbishop, who was literally behind her. Maybe he would join in if she got something wrong or if he found one of the questions particularly interesting. "All right," Beauregard said. "First the basics. How old is he?"

"Sixty-six," she said.

"When did he get here?"

"Flew in to Atlanta yesterday, from London."

"Family?"

"Wife and three grown children."

"Has he been to the United States before?"

"Many times," she said. "What else?"

"Sewanee?"

"What?"

Beauregard looked up. "Has he been to Sewanee before?"

"I don't think so." She turned around, then back. "No. One more question."

"What was that sermon about?"

The woman shook her head. "No, now," she said. "No, no, no. We've got things to do. Eddie, drive on."

"Please," Beauregard said, keeping his head in the window space. "I know the archbishop is in there. Let me talk to him for a minute. I really need this story."

From the hidden recesses of the limousine an upper-class British voice—the archbishop's?—projected charitably, "Which newspaper do you represent, young man?"

"*Birmingham Standard-Dispatch,* sir."

There was a droll pause, then the voice cracked a joke Beauregard could not quite make out. The driver and woman in the front seat were still laughing when the window rolled up and the limo began to pull out.

Beauregard stood in the cloud of exhaust, notebook at his side. It was pep talk time. He knew he shouldn't take the rejection personally. Price, over hot dogs and instant coffee, had once outlined for Beauregard a hierarchy of reportorial entrée. At the top of the paper napkin he'd put the *New York Times* and television networks. Next came other major newspapers, the *Washington Post* and the *Los Angeles Times,* then the wire services. At the bottom Price had put the *Birmingham Standard-Dispatch.* As a joke, he'd penciled in *The Watchtower,* the Jehovah's Witnesses' newspaper, in the margin next to the *Standard-Dispatch;* but he'd been quite serious when he'd told Beauregard not to take rejection personally. It was the lot of the reporter, he'd said, especially one working for the *Standard-Dispatch.*

As he continued to stand there, the limousine having escaped into traffic and disappeared from view, the problem of quotations began to weigh on Beauregard. The question was not whether to use quotations—Shealy demanded them—but whether they should be in English or Latin. This had never before come up. Accuracy seemed to demand that the quotations be reported as spoken. On the other hand, the story might get better play if written entirely in English. Then again, none of his English stories had cleared Section B.

He found a pay phone and tried to call Price. Busy. He knew better than to call Bubba Shealy with such a question. Shealy would spread it around that he'd had to ask, just as he'd told everyone about Beauregard sitting in the jury box. Beauregard tried Price again: still busy. He shoved the quarter back through and made a collect call to Jackson's private line.

Two rings, then, "This is Jackson Forrest."

"Collect call from Beauregard," an operator said. "Will you accept?"

"Beau who? Beau what?"

"Please, Jackson," Beauregard said.

"All right, operator."

Beauregard explained.

"Latin," Jackson advised flatly.

"You sure?"

"Beauregard, look," Jackson said. "At this point you don't even have any English quotes. And, anyway, you have to take risks sometimes. Remember when Coach Bryant went with the wishbone offense? Here he was, a man who'd coached some of the greatest drop-back quarterbacks of all time, coached Kenny Stabler, coached *Joe Namath,* yet he made the switch to an option attack. Lots of people around Birmingham thought he'd lost his mind. *I* thought he had. The wishbone worked, though. We started boning teams big time. It was like the old days, tremendous lopsided victories, and all because Coach took a risk. Of course, to be fair, integration had something to do with it. Nothing quite like adding another race to the talent pool."

"Take a risk, huh?"

"Take a risk. Absolutely. Roll Tide."

Beauregard found an empty classroom and sat down with his notebook to write. His impulse, as with Pet of the Week, was to go on the literary offensive. Don't hold back. Use as many words as possible from the early chapters of *Thirty Days to a More Powerful Vocabulary*. Use metaphors. He knew he should reconcile this urge with Shealy's preference for a lean, muscular style, the Associated Press style—but Shealy might not be editing this story. Without an assistant city editor to share his editing load, he sometimes ended up sending Beauregard's copy right on to the desk.

After a few scratched-out tries, Beauregard arrived at a first paragraph, a "lede" paragraph, as it was called and spelled in newspapering.

SEWANEE, TENN.—The Archbishop of Canterbury, resplendent in garb, reserved, if not icy, in demeanor, gazed out at a sea of young faces at the University of the South yesterday and uttered an address that, at its all-too-soon conclusion, yielded from the hands below those young faces a wave of applause sufficient to propel him across the Atlantic and back to England, from whence he, 66, had come via airplane just two days before.

Beauregard read the lede aloud, for rhythm. Then again for content. He was satisfied. He knew a little bit about metaphors from military school English courses, and he felt proud of himself for the consistency of this watery one—proud of "icy" and "sea" and "wave." If only the archbishop had come by boat . . .

Time for a quote. Beauregard pulled the Latin text from his pocket and began to scan it. He guessed that the words *christus* and *deus,* liberally used in the text, meant "Christ" and "God." Surely any quotes with forms of those words would be safe, coming from an archbishop. He found one of about the right length, inserted it, then went on with the rest of the story, sprinkling in more "christus" and "deus" type quotes along the way.

When he finished, he went back to the pay phone and called the newsroom. Shealy answered. Beauregard was unnerved to hear him say he would edit the story and even take the dictation. They got started, Beauregard reading the lede aloud, slowly. He could tell by the way Shealy typed—starting, then stopping, then starting again in a cluttered rush—that he was editing ruthlessly.

"Give me a quote, B-Four," Shealy said. "It's time for a quote."

Beauregard tried to approximate the archbishop's cadence.

"Whoa, B-Four," Shealy said. "The phone line did something strange. Give me that last part again."

Beauregard did, letting up on the cadence.

"Again."

"Bubba," Beauregard said, voice flat now, "the sermon was in Latin."

There was a silence in English. Then came Shealy's breathing noises, little fruit-fly wheezes that damned to hell Beauregard's decision to use Latin quotes. Beauregard could see the story moving off the section front and backward through the paper, past even the county extension agent's pesticides columns, past Metro Briefs.

"You know, B-Four," Shealy said at last, almost eerily calm, "the crazy thing is I don't have to do this for a living. Just the other day my brother called. He wanted me to join him in his taxidermy business. I'd do fish, he'd do game. Birds we'd do together. 'No, Donnie,' I told him. 'I'm a newspaperman. I've got ink in my veins.' Do you know what he said?"

"No, sir."

"He said, 'Little brother, you're an idiot.' He also said I was a big disappointment to the family, college graduate and all, still not making jackshit for money. Then he started in on what a bad job the paper does covering hunting and fishing. B-Four, he knows I'm in charge of news, not sports. They don't *pay* me enough to be over news and sports. If they did, I'd make changes."

"Bubba, listen . . ."

"No, B-Four, *you* listen. Do you have any idea what the archbishop's talk was about?"

"Something about Jesus. I assume it was favorable."

"A reporter never assumes, B-Four. I've told you that a hundred times. Now go find somebody who can translate the sermon. It's an accredited school. There ought to be a classics professor, a good student, somebody. But call me back in a half hour, regardless. We're getting close to first-edition deadline."

Beauregard got directions to the classics department, but this late in the afternoon he found no professors or students. He thought about going to a dormitory and stopping people at random, or maybe buying construction paper at the campus store and making up a READ LATIN? sign to walk through the library. Then he had a better idea.

He jogged back to the party van and drove to the Kappa Alpha house, which he'd passed driving in. He crossed the lawn to the one-story stone structure. He knocked on the door.

No one answered. Through a side window, Beauregard could see a line of young men in a narrow hall beyond the front room with its framed oil portrait of Robert E. Lee. They'd loosened their ties and removed their shoes. They were taking turns jumping. The jumper would take two steps, then leap at an angle toward the ceiling. It was a game, obviously, the object to graze the ceiling with the top of one's head.

Beauregard thought, This is college? But he had an urge to get in line. He wasn't a bad jumper. Even failing to graze the ceiling in front of all these strangers seemed preferable to dealing with Shealy again. But he was on deadline; the paper was counting on him. *Price* was counting on him, not to mention the publisher's wife. He knocked again.

The game proceeded, but another KA, carrying a paddle and sandpaper, answered the door. He was a tall young man, gaunt in the face. He wore an Atlanta Braves baseball cap and a blue-and-white T-shirt that said I'D RATHER BE IN CHAPEL HILL.

"Yes?" he asked. "What is it?"

Beauregard explained that he was a reporter from Birmingham and that his brother, Jackson Forrest, had been a KA while at the University of Alabama, and as a favor to him, and in the spirit of Robert E. Lee, father figure to KAs everywhere, he, Beauregard, would appreciate a little help translating the archbishop's sermon. He held up his copy.

The KA waved Beauregard inside with the paddle.

"Let me see that goddamn sermon," he said with determination.

As Beauregard handed him the copy, a cheer went up in the back, a little guy having dislodged a ceiling tile. The KA by Beauregard ignored the celebration and concentrated on the sermon. He brought it close to his face, then turned away and held it up to a shaded lamp mounted on the wall. He left it there a long time, but Beauregard was not encouraged. He could tell that the KA's squint was not a squint of translation.

"I just don't know, man," he said as he handed the sermon back to Beauregard. "All of us take Spanish. You *might* try the Dekes."

But by then the half hour had elapsed. Beauregard excused himself, fought off a knot of arriving KAs intrigued by the Get Down! Inc. party van, and drove back to the pay phone. He almost wished he didn't have the coins to start the collect call to Shealy. As usual, though, he had a conservative pocketful, all denominations.

After Beauregard explained that he hadn't been able to find a translator, Shealy told him to finish dictating the story without quotations. A little later he told him to look for it in tomorrow's D section, unless there was an E section. Then he hung up.

Beauregard had time now to tour the leafy old campus, but he didn't feel like it. He was upset, dispirited. He blamed himself and Jackson, but he also held it against Sewanee that it was the site of his latest failure as a reporter. That was unfair, he knew, but he didn't feel like being fair. He climbed back into the party van.

It would have been a long drive in any event, because of the distance and the sluggish van. Now it seemed especially long. When he got to the interstate, Beauregard retreated south in a right lane, fifty-five-mile-per-hour funk. He didn't stop at Stuckey's for black coffee. Nor did he admire the gently rolling fields or robin's egg blue of the sky, on its way to puce now as late afternoon dissolved to early evening. He stared straight ahead. Normally, his keen peripheral vision would have picked up the sight of the archbishop's limousine by the side of the road, hood up, doors open, driver, aides, and most honored passenger all poking helplessly at the large, overheated engine. But this was not a normal drive.

Chapter Five

Beauregard got back to his apartment in time to watch the last half of "PM Magazine." He unlaced his wing tips, settled into the shag carpeting, and switched on his little black-and-white TV with the bent aerial. The spot about the Bill Johnson Club ended. Suddenly, once again, Jackson filled the screen.

Here he was putting a keg into place, going over party options with potential clients, explaining with furrowed brow his principles of party science. The editors had added a scene in which Jackson told of taking his KA pledges to Pamplona, Spain, for the running of the bulls. It was a stretcher—Jackson had gone there for a summer foreign study program, and there was only one other KA in the group, and he was a junior Spanish major from Argentina—but Jackson's modest, understated telling made the story credible.

As the segment proceeded, Beauregard paid close attention to Jackson's nostrils. They were huge dark affairs, black lagoons, the pink ridges above them levees holding back a flood tide of skin. Mr. Forrest had flared nostrils, too. Once, rocking on the front porch at New Arlington, he had put forth his theory that many great men had flared nostrils. General Lee had them, of course. So did Stonewall Jackson and P. G. T. Beauregard. Even two of the more interesting minor Confederate generals, Sterling Price and Simon Bolivar Buckner, were well endowed that way. Beauregard was a small boy when he heard his father's theory. The degree of flare in his nostrils, his potential, remained in doubt. He went through adolescence preoccupied not just with when he would have facial hair, if he would have chest hair, and whether the morning shadow cast by his penis against the plastic shower curtain was of a manly length. He also worried about his nostrils. They never did flare. Oh, he could flare them, but they always returned to their pinched, nothing-special width. He'd learned to live with it. Mr. Forrest and Jackson were the Forrests with great nostrils.

There was one last shot of Jackson shutting and locking the glass door of Get Down! Inc. He looked wholesomely tired, like some worker ant heading home to the hill after a long hard day. The lens zoomed in as he turned the key, and there he was, bigger than life, nostrils flared, left hand running backward through the sparkling trajectory of his William-cut hair.

"Latin, huh?" Beauregard said aloud as he leaned forward and switched off the little TV. "Take a risk, huh? Thanks, Mr. Catfish. Thanks a whole hell of a lot."

Beauregard dropped like dead weight back down into the shag. He meant to stretch out and look at the stained ceiling and loosen his tense muscles and think about nothing for a while, but his hand brushed against a paperback. He dug it out of the carpeting. It was *Thirty Days to a More Powerful Vocabulary*.

He got up and sat in the wicker chair Jackson had sent over, then turned on the reading lamp he himself had taken from his room at New Arlington. He looked at the book. It should have been, but clearly wasn't, dog-eared. He'd vowed to study a chapter a night so he could be through in time for the SAT, but he hadn't kept that vow. Learning words in isolation was slow-going, dull, a mental trench-digging. Also this reading lamp was hot. After one page, let alone a chapter, his face felt flushed and he began to perspire inside his T-shirt. The back cover of *Thirty Days* said "MAKE WORDS YOUR SLAVES!," but that was hard to do when you were sitting under a hot lamp sweating like a sharecropper.

He turned again to "Day Four: Words for Mature Minds." *Vicarious* was still the next word. He reviewed the definition, considered the sample sentences, then noticed the word was from Latin. He scanned the rest of the chapter. They were all from Latin, these mature words. He tossed the book aside.

Beauregard suddenly felt dizzy. He realized he hadn't had a full meal since breakfast. He didn't have much to eat here, so he changed into jeans, a jersey, and tennis shoes, then got back into the van and drove across town to Taco Bob's.

Unless he went to Jackson's for a T-bone steak and shredded lettuce, Beauregard usually dined at Taco Bob's for the barbecue or at a fast-food salad bar for the roughage. If he felt at all regular, he went to Taco Bob's. He liked the food there, and he knew Taco Bob.

Taco Bob was Vietnamese. A slight man with thick black hair and skin the color of powdered coffee creamer, his real name was Thanh Ho, and back home he'd been both a restaurateur and a soldier for the South Vietnamese. After the Communist takeover, he'd bought his way out of Saigon, escaping with his large family on a rickety boat that dodged Thai pirates all the way to Malaysia. Eventually they'd received sponsorship to the United States, specifically Birmingham, where Taco Bob, known then as Ho, went to work as custodian for one of the local Baptist churches. The Women's Missionary Union outfitted him and his family with secondhand clothes, rented them a small house in a transitional neighborhood, and invited them to Sunday morning and evening worship services.

All went well enough until another Baptist church tried to hire Ho away. He played one personnel committee against the other, irritating both, causing both to withdraw their offers. Not that Ho cared. As he told Beauregard later, all those verses of the hymn "Just as I Am" had begun to test his patience. They changed a person, he complained, and not necessarily for the better.

He opened a Vietnamese restaurant, which struggled, despite the good soups and vermicelli and spring rolls and fish sauce. Jackson was one of his few regular customers. He'd even used Ho to cater an occasional Asian-themed party. Jackson confided that Birminghamians felt vaguely unpatriotic about eating at a Vietnamese restaurant, given how the war had turned out. Ho would do better with a less emotionally charged cuisine.

So, with money borrowed from Mr. Forrest's bank, he bought a foundering Mexican restaurant called Taco Bob's. He assumed everything—the mortgage, the name, the sombrero.

He did well enough at Mexican but eventually deduced that Birminghamians preferred barbecue above all other foods—preferred it to sex, really. He began in spare hours to study the art of barbecuing. He read books, attended seminars. He visited black neighborhoods where women in curlers and men in shower caps cooked pork outside in huge rusting grills, using the corner tele-phone booth to take orders. He learned to choose only the best hickory wood, to cook the meat slowly over low heat, to let the sauce serve as sweetener rather than moisturizer, to drip the fin-ished product over white bread and sell it in plate-shaped plastic foam containers with runny dollops of cole slaw and baked beans, the way Birminghamians liked. When he was satisfied with his expertise, he made Taco Bob's a barbecue joint. As final touches, he replaced the glass door with a screen door, installed an Elvis-only jukebox, and tacked Bear Bryant posters up all over.

Mr. Forrest—breaking bank rules of confidentiality—had con-firmed for Jackson and Beauregard that Taco Bob grossed more than $450,000 in that first year of barbecue. Customers by the hundreds defected to him from other joints. Things got even better the next year, when he expanded the dining room, added a drive-through window, and introduced counter and mail-order sauce sales. He was able to move out of his transitional neighborhood, buy private music lessons for his children, insist that people call him "Bob" or "T. B."

Beauregard, because he was a Forrest, got treated as family at Taco Bob's. He was there more than Jackson. Jackson breezed in and out, nodding with satisfaction at the crowded dining room, but Beauregard stuck around to talk. Beauregard quietly considered himself Taco Bob's link to the mind of Birmingham. Beauregard had encouraged him to say, "Have a good 'un," at the end of conversations and, "Roll Tide," during pauses and lulls. Although Taco Bob struggled with the *l* sound in *Roll,* and seemed never to have quite grasped the expression's meaning, customers ap-preciated his efforts at school spirit and assimilation.

When Beauregard arrived at Taco Bob's, he found a long line at the counter. As usual, he got in the back. And, as usual, as soon as Taco Bob saw him, he came from behind the counter and took him by the hand and brought him back into the kitchen through the swinging white doors. Taco Bob's family and other help were there, all wearing sombreros as they prepared the barbecue and side orders. Beauregard barely had time to wave at them as Taco Bob pulled him into a small paneled office decorated with family photo-graphs and supply company calendars.

Taco Bob left briefly, returning with a pork plate and two mason jars of iced jasmine tea.

"Here go," he said, distributing everything on the gray metal office desk.

"Thanks, Bob."

"Check sauce."

"Don't have to," Beauregard said. "I know it's fine. It's always fine."

Taco Bob removed his sombrero and hung it by the string on a nail in the paneling. He sat, then took a red plastic comb from his apron pocket and ran it back through his full, neatly parted black hair.

"Cheer me up, Bob," Beauregard said, cutting across a tender flap of barbecue with a plastic fork and knife.

"No have good 'un?" Taco Bob asked, angling his head in concern. "Have bad 'un?"

"Very bad 'un, Bob. One of the worst."

The lines in Taco Bob's amber forehead crinkled black and deepened. He looked as if he understood about bad 'uns, as if he might have had a few himself. Beauregard knew he had and felt a little ashamed of his own small problems. Suddenly, though, Taco Bob put his mason jar on a coaster on his desk and started walking toward the far end of the office.

"Come here, Beaugard," he said on the way. "I cheer you up. I show you something."

Beauregard put down his utensils and followed him to the back. Taco Bob stood in front of an easel which held an enlarged architectural floor plan. Beauregard, looking over his shoulder, tried to make sense of it. It was a house, that was pretty clear; but it seemed to have an oversized kitchen and dining room, and far too many bedrooms even for Taco Bob's large immigrant family, extended now by cousins he'd managed to buy out of Vietnam. Writing occupied the drawing's bottom right-hand corner.

"Bed and barbecue," Beauregard read aloud.

"What you think?" Taco Bob asked.

Beauregard shrugged. "We don't get that many tourists in Birmingham."

"Picking up."

"I never heard of a bed and barbecue."

"My idea. New."

"Have you done any marketing research?"

Taco Bob nodded. "Very promising. And my gut say, 'Go for it. Ro' Tide.' What your gut say?"

Beauregard put a hand on Taco Bob's right shoulder. "You better ask Jackson or my father," he deferred. "They're the businessmen in our family."

While Beauregard finished the pork plate, Taco Bob fetched him a fried apple pie with two scoops of vanilla ice cream. Beauregard ate that, too, alone, because Taco Bob had to get back to the kitchen. As he ate, Beauregard thought about the bed and barbecue. The crazy idea amused, then depressed him. Taco Bob would make it work. Everybody but Beauregard made things work. Jackson started a party company, earned big bucks, got on TV. Their father ran one of the city's largest banks, not to mention a first-rate reenactment unit sought after by film producers. Price routinely made front page.

And Taco Bob, Lord. He'd achieved wealth and local fame against astounding odds. He probably made more in a day through mail-order sauce sales than Beauregard had made all summer. As for his children, well, they overachieved, too. His eldest daughter, Toni, just a year older than Beauregard, had finished first in her class at West Side High and now attended Georgia Tech on full scholarship. Beauregard didn't want to know what she'd made on the SAT. It'd be more depressing than this new bed and barbecue.

When he finished the fried pie, he found a trash can for the plastic foam plate and plastic utensils, waved again at Taco Bob and the kitchen crew, then pushed open the swinging doors and walked back through the lobby. Taco Bob's food, so good going down, always landed heavily. Beauregard took a breath and pushed open the screen door, then lumbered across the gravel parking lot to the party van.

He hoped his Sewanee story didn't get buried in the E section, as Shealy had threatened. He'd never been so far back in the paper. Even if he escaped E section, his Sewanee debacle would become a B-Four story, an internal one, one they'd tell in the newsroom. He could hear them embellishing the story on the copy desk. He could see the abbreviated version in derisive postcards sent home by staff Midwesterners.

He got into the van and headed downtown, intending to go by the newspaper to see just where in the first edition his story had been played. After that, he figured he'd do some Metro Briefs, to catch up. Maybe Shealy wouldn't be so hard on him if he knew he'd worked late to keep the Metro Brief queue full.

Traffic was heavy on Eighth Avenue. He'd forgotten it was

Monday night—professional wrestling night at the auditorium. He might have escaped through back streets, but now he was trapped in traffic and fumes. Creeping along, he noticed two successive cars with Confederate-flag plates. A few civilian cars passed, then came a third Confederate vehicle, a truck on big muddy tires. The flag plate itself was shiny clean.

As a boy, Beauregard had loved the Confederate flag. He'd kept a large framed one in his bedroom. Mr. Forrest and Beauregard would sometimes discuss the history of the flag—flags, really, because there had been several, including the distinctive battle flag designed by P. G. T. Beauregard after all the confusion at Manassas. That was the kind of thing Beauregard and Mr. Forrest knew.

But in recent years, Beauregard had begun to feel a little uneasy about the Confederate flag. He'd even had a bad dream about it. It was like that other nightmare—Lee at Calvary, Jesus up on Traveller. In this dream, the flag became an angry man. The red background was his skin and the inverted V at the bottom was his furious mouth. Stars of the upper V constituted his hard, accusing eyes. He had lots of eyes, and no ears, which made him more menacing. Flag Man spoke in a gruff voice, and he wanted to know if Beauregard was going to reenlist or sneak back home to work the farm, as so many other Confederate soldiers were doing. Beauregard started to say, "Reenlisting, of course. No problem, Flag Man." But before he could speak, Flag Man fluttered once, angrily, and Beauregard woke up.

Beauregard had seen Confederate flags at Sewanee. They'd be flying high at Washington and Lee, no doubt. Idling here in the wrestling traffic, he suddenly wished he'd be starting college outside the South. He could transfer back, of course, but he'd like for a while to be somewhere where no controversy simmered about waving the flag, integrating the fraternities, or singing "Dixie." He'd like a semester at least at some big anonymous university without regional identification or even much tradition—some university with pass-fail courses, coed dorms, a bowling alley.

Traffic thinned past the auditorium. He drove on to the newspaper. Price, in his battered yellow subcompact, was pulling out of the parking lot as Beauregard pulled in. He noticed Beauregard, waved, then reversed to a clear spot under a mercury lamp. Beauregard pulled up beside him, driver's window to driver's window.

"Let's talk, B-Four."

"Okay, Price."

Beauregard, still feeling the pork plate and fried pie, hoped Price wouldn't suggest going to IHOP or Waffle House or Dunkin' Donuts or one of the other all-night places where the senior reporter met his many sources. Beauregard wouldn't be obligated to eat anything, of course, but the last thing his queasy stomach needed was to be near all that IHOP or Waffle House syrup. The doughnut place, with its new tuna fish croissant, wouldn't be much better. He was relieved when Price got out of the subcompact and lit a cigarette.

He climbed out of the van and stood by him. The lamp illuminated them harshly. A breeze blew through the parking lot, but it was gentle, not enough to extinguish a cigarette lighter or lift the ropelike strands of Price's Vitalis-moistened hair. Price offered, and Beauregard accepted, a Camel. They leaned against their respective vehicles and smoked without speaking.

After a minute, Price's beeper sounded: first the beep, then a voice fighting through the crackle. It was Shealy, wanting to know what stories Price had going for the rest of the week. Price swatted at the beeper's OFF button as Shealy was still speaking.

"You're not going to answer it?" Beauregard asked.

"Not tonight," Price said. "I'm tired tonight, B-Four. Sometimes this job gives me a headache."

"Take some time off, Price. You've got plenty of comp time."

"Yeah, but time off gives me a headache, too. If I'm going to have headaches, I'd rather have them trying to make something happen."

"Headaches with a future."

"Exactly, B-Four. But I do get tired. And I don't make enough money."

Beauregard, cigarette dangling from his lips, nodded. He felt a little guilty whenever he heard Price complain about money. He made less than Price, of course, but as a bank president's son, he could afford a miserable salary. Price couldn't. He was in his thirties now, wanting to buy the little house he rented, wanting to get married eventually. Beauregard changed the subject.

"How'd it go with your story today?"

"Okay, I guess," Price said. "The psychiatrist called back to find out exactly how I was going to quote him. I told him I was too busy to talk. Told him I was on deadline, which I was. He may be pissed tomorrow."

"Yeah."

"Well, screw him," Price said, flicking ash. "He's an idiot. They all are. Hey, I heard you had some trouble up at Sewanee."

"Great. Everybody knows."

"Not everybody, B-Four."

"I figured Shealy'd get a kick out of telling everybody, once he cooled off."

"He didn't tell everybody," Price insisted. "He told me and one or two others. Well, maybe several others." Price paused, then added lightly, encouragingly, "Some people are off on Mondays."

Beauregard took a last drag of his cigarette and then, exhaling, said, "I tried to call you, Price, to find out what I should do about quoting the archbishop. Your line was busy, so I called my brother. I don't know why I thought he'd know. It seems pretty stupid now."

"Don't be too hard on yourself."

"I should have known better than to use Latin quotes."

"We all make mistakes, B-Four." He dropped and ground out a cigarette, then fired up another. After the first puff, he said, "Overall you're not doing too bad. Sure, your writing's a little florid, a little overdone. *Baroque* wouldn't be too strong a word. But you know grammar and you spell pretty well and you're not afraid to ask questions. Of course, we need to work on your questions. You don't ask the right questions, or maybe it's that you don't ask them the right way. I don't know. Anyway, that'll come with time and practice. My point is that you work hard, which should be enough to get you on the front page of a rag like the *Standard-Dispatch*. At least eventually."

"It's not happening, Price," Beauregard said.

"I know it isn't."

"Shealy doesn't like me, does he?"

"Actually," Price said, stretching his arms in a kind of postdeadline calisthenic, "it isn't so much that he doesn't like you. It's the circumstances. Shealy likes to hire his own people, and you were forced on him. Plus, he's not too crazy about your father and your brother. Plus, he's management scum."

"What's he got against my father?"

Price paused, obviously reluctant, then sighed out more Camel smoke. "A few years ago Shealy went to your father's bank for a boat loan," he said. "They turned him down."

"But Dad's the bank president," Beauregard said. "He wouldn't have had anything to do with Shealy's loan. Not personally."

"With an insecure guy like Bubba, everything's personal," Price said. "Especially a boat loan."

Beauregard saw a large circulation truck pulling away from the *Standard-Dispatch* building. It was filled no doubt with D or E sections containing his story. They'd be landing all over the metro area soon, in coin boxes, on dewy lawns, through office door slots. People would be wondering why his story—a story about a sermon—didn't have even one lousy quote.

He looked back at Price. "What's Shealy's problem with Jackson?"

Price shrugged, then said, "As you know, B-Four, Bubba went to Auburn. Your brother played football for Alabama. So there's that. And once, when Shealy was a sportswriter for the Auburn paper, your brother gave him a controversial interview. He told Shealy the Auburn quarterback had an arm like a Quaker gun. Shealy figured that was a compliment and put it in his story. I don't know what a Quaker gun is, but it's definitely not a compliment. The Auburn quarterback cornered Shealy and shoved him up against a locker—to prove he had an arm, I guess."

Beauregard paused, imagining the scene, then explained quietly, "A Quaker gun was a log Confederate troops painted black, to make it look like a cannon. It didn't have any firepower, of course. It just sat there looking like a cannon. The Yankees would see all the Quaker guns, assume they were cannons, and pull back to keep from getting annihilated. The Confederates had to play tricks like that because the Yankees had so many more soldiers and weapons. John Magruder used to march his troops back and forth, all day long, a kind of human Quaker gun. The Yankees thought he must have a huge army, but really he only had a few thousand troops. This was in April of 1862, Price, on the peninsula east of Richmond, the Siege of Yorktown."

"Well, Shealy hates your brother."

"I see."

"It's like this, B-Four. Shealy figures you'll be off to college before long. Until you leave, he's going to get a measure of revenge by sticking you with Pet of the Week and Kiwanis fish fries and obituaries of people who really didn't do that much. You're probably good enough to make front page, but you're not going to, at least not unless you come up with something awfully good. Shealy's just not very interested in seeing you succeed."

"Damn," Beauregard felt obligated to say, but really he felt better. At least he knew what he was up against. And Price had said it—he was probably good enough to make front page.

"What should I do, Price?"

"Call your old man. Tell him to complain to the publisher. With any pressure, Shealy'll give in and you'll start getting front-page stories right and left. You'll be sick of them, like I am."

"I can't do that."

"Why not?"

He knew why but couldn't say. The reason was Robert E. Lee, and Price wouldn't understand. Mr. Forrest had long ago taught Beauregard and Jackson to ask themselves in times of moral quandary, what would Robert E. Lee have done? The question was to be their touchstone, their Golden Rule. He'd even had the bank's printing department make up laminated, wallet-size cards of the question for them to carry around and consult as necessary. Jackson joked to Beauregard that moral quandaries were rare in party science, once you were in it. But Beauregard, eager as he was to break free from his Confederate upbringing, still found the Lee question helpful. Just recently he'd used it to decide whether to return a grocery cart from the far reaches of the parking lot (yes) and whether to take home extra sugar packets from a fast food restaurant (no). Here it was helpful, too. Lee wouldn't have pulled strings to make front page. He would have handled the matter himself, with dignity and flair.

"I'm going to leave Dad out of this," Beauregard said finally. "If I get a good enough story and do it right, nobody, not even Shealy, can keep me off the front."

They remained by their vehicles, neither speaking. Beauregard had never before rejected a Price suggestion. This wasn't the sort of rejection that would end their friendship, or even change it much, but a decent interval had to pass before they went on as if nothing had happened.

At last Price said, "Well, hell. I'll search my 'tips' file to see if there's anything strong for you to look into."

"Thanks, Price."

"Screw the city editor from Auburn. Roll Tide."

"Roll Tide."

They did an awkward high five in the semidarkness, then Price got into his battered subcompact and drove off. Beauregard jogged to the press room and picked up a wet, inky first edition from the reject barrel. He took it to a corner and looked for an E section.

Yes, damn it; there was one. He started at the back page and went forward, investigating with dread, as if searching closets for a burglar. No Sewanee in E. He repeated with the D section, then the C section. Nothing. Finally, on the B-section front, below the fold but above a Midwesterner's interview with the outgoing grand jury foreman, he found his story on the archbishop.

Section front!

He'd never had such good play. Maybe it was a slow news day, or maybe his story just fit the hole the desk had, or maybe—in fact, probably—the good play was a function of the publisher's wife's interest in Episcopalian affairs. But what of that? The story didn't look out of place on the section front. It read reasonably well. Shealy had edited aggressively, but it was still Beauregard's work. With quotes and fresh art, it might have gone above the fold or even made the inside of Section A.

Beauregard went back and got another twenty copies.

His mood brightened as he walked to the parking lot. The barbecue and fried pie had begun to digest. He'd made section front. Making front page was a taller order, and the intelligence from Price about Shealy's boat-loan-and-Quaker-gun grudge was hardly encouraging; but at least Beauregard felt now that he was capable. *Price* felt he was capable. That was something.

Driving home to Southside, windows lowered, crisp air coursing through the party van, B sections a pleasant weight on his lap, he felt better than he had all day. He wouldn't worry about catching up on Metro Briefs. He'd catch up tomorrow, early, then do his quota of obits, then do Pet of the Week, then with Price's help start thinking of some way to make front page.

Chapter Six

By noon the *Standard-Dispatch* had lost its freshness, but at breakfast it was still new, still the thing to talk about and read over grits, eggs, bacon, sausage, and buttered biscuits. Price and the Midwesterners worried openly about the future of newspapers, given the decline in circulation and death of so many afternoon dailies; but at breakfast, everybody grabbing for it, the newspaper seemed as essential as forks and knives.

Since becoming a reporter, Beauregard had haunted various breakfast spots, always sitting in a booth and watching people reading the *Standard-Dispatch*. He felt a little like a movie actor slipping into a matinee of his own show. Still a bit player, he knew better than to be disappointed that the papers were more often folded at the front page or sports than at his B section. He took general pleasure—vicarious pleasure—in the sight of people reading, say, a Price story. His day would come.

The cafeteria in the basement of Jackson's building was a first-rate spot to eat breakfast and watch people reading the *Standard-Dispatch*. The fluorescent lighting was bright, the coffee refill policy generous. Many of the accountants, lawyers, and insurance brokers who breakfasted there seemed in no hurry to set the newspaper aside and go upstairs to work.

Beauregard drove to Jackson's building early on the morning after Sewanee, meaning to tweak him about the Latin advice, to run by him the decision not to ask their father's help in making the front page, and to see if he'd join him downstairs for breakfast.

But as soon as he got to Jackson's office, Jackson put him to work. All Jackson's staffers had stayed late the night before to answer calls prompted by the "PM Magazine" spot. Jackson alone had made it back, and he needed help answering the phones, ringing off the hooks already.

He positioned Beauregard at the receptionist's desk and told him to catch lines two and three.

"Uh, Get Down," Beauregard said to the first caller.

"Let me speak to Jackson Forrest," responded an older male voice, frayed but confident.

"Mr. Forrest's on another line. May I take a message?"

"Son, let me just ask you, then. I was watching TV last night. Did he really take his KA pledges to Portugal for the running of those bulls?"

"Spain, sir."

"But did he?"

"I don't know anything about it."

"Nobody got gored, I hope. Nobody from Alabama."

"I really don't know."

"Maybe I'll call Jackson later."

"Do. He'd like to hear from you."

As the calls came in, Beauregard grew more and more confident saying, "Get Down," eventually adding the exclamation mark. He provided basic information and took messages on a pink pad with lines and boxes. Once, though, he put a call through.

Jackson came out a few minutes later.

"Good move, letting me talk to that guy," he said.

Beauregard nodded. "He said it was about a business deal. I thought it might be important."

"Could be. He's with a blender company in Boston, Roll Tide. He saw 'PM Magazine' and got the idea that I could endorse their ten-speed. He's talking print ads, some TV, maybe even my picture on the box. Who knows what will happen, but their advertising guy's supposed to call me this afternoon."

"Have you ever used one of their blenders?"

"I don't think so."

"Get one and try it," Beauregard suggested. "Get one at lunch, before the advertising guy calls."

Jackson nodded. "That's a good idea. I'll have Debbie run out to the mall, as soon as she gets in and we have breakfast. By the way, I'm buying your breakfast."

"Thanks, Jackson."

"Least I can do. . . . There's your phone."

Half an hour later, when Debbie the receptionist arrived, Beauregard drifted into Jackson's office. Jackson, wearing a white dress shirt but as yet no tie, was on one line with another holding. Beauregard walked around, noticing things.

It was a long, narrow room with a good view of Vulcan, the fifty-five-foot cast-iron "god of fire" statue that stood atop Red Mountain, the city's southern border. Jackson's carpeting was silver, his wallpaper fleur-de-lis. On one side of his teakwood desk, near the window, flourished ferns and flowering plants tended by a service whose employees wore green jerseys and water tanks and beepers that Beauregard frankly envied. On the other side of the desk, set into the wall, was a chalkboard on which Jackson kept a color-coded schedule of upcoming parties. Beauregard sat on the chintz sofa and looked at one of the pamphlets—"slicks," Jackson called them—that explained the company history and party options. Above him an antique ceiling fan stirred the air conditioning. Finally Jackson got off the phone.

"Beauregard, this could be big," the older brother said, standing up and beginning to tie a red tie he'd picked up from his desk. "I've always thought I could go national, if I got the right break. This 'PM Magazine' may be just the thing. Now it's up to me to take advantage."

He sat back down in his executive's chair and motioned for Beauregard to come around. Beauregard did. Leaning over Jackson's broad right shoulder, he could see a yellow legal pad full of jottings in Jackson's large, angular script.

NEW GOALS FOR GET DOWN! INC.

1) FRANCHISES. Steep fee in exchange for name and advertising. Quality control crucial. Unannounced on-site inspections (by me) a must.

2) BOOK. Mass-market paperback elaborating my principles of party science.

3) VIDEO. My principles again, with party footage and music.

4) SEMINARS. Major cities and college towns.

5) TV SHOW. How-to series, like those on gardening,

home repair, bass fishing. Great for cable or PBS. I could
host.

Jackson looked back for Beauregard's assessment. "Very ambi-
tious," Beauregard said.
"I know. It won't be easy."
"You see the paper yet? I made B section front with that Se-
wanee story."
"The one I helped you with?"
"Well, yeah."
"That's good, Beauregard. Really. I'm proud of you."
"About those Latin quotes, though . . ."
"Save it," Jackson said. "We'll talk over breakfast. I want to hear
all about your trip."
When Jackson finished knotting his tie, they took an elevator to
the basement, then walked down a short corridor to the cafeteria.
On the way they passed acquaintances and friends of Jackson's from
the building.
"Seen you on TV last night, Jackson." . . . "Looked good last
night, Jackson." . . . "Jaybird, son, how much do you *pay* for
advertising like that?"
Jackson managed without breaking stride to acknowledge every
remark. A wink here, a smile there, a passing high five—they knew
he'd heard them. Beauregard walked beside him, literally in his
shadow, feeling like a caddy or aide-de-camp.
At the cafeteria the brothers eased through the hot-table line,
choosing this and that, collecting silverware and coffee mugs, then
sat down with their modestly crowded trays. It was a good day for
watching people read the newspaper. All over the cafeteria people
had sections of the *Standard-Dispatch* up in front of them or folded
by their breakfast trays. After walking to the cafeteria in Jackson's
shadow, Beauregard savored the sight like a round of applause. He
sipped coffee in anticipation of remarking on the sight to his
brother, and of telling him the Sewanee story, every twist and turn
of it, especially the Latin dead end; but then Jackson whispered,
"Oh, God. Here comes Billy."
"Who?"
"Billy McArthur. Of the Birmingham Boosters."
Beauregard turned to see McArthur walking forward with a tray
covered by dishes, glasses, cups, and saucers. He didn't look as good
as his mug shot, which appeared fairly often with *Standard-Dispatch*

business stories in which he was quoted as Boosters spokesman. In person he was short, heavy, and pale, and he rather obviously wore a wig. The wig was black, his real hair dark red. The place where they met looked to Beauregard like school colors. McArthur had on a white dress shirt, and he wore the seersucker suit so popular with Birmingham businessmen and lawyers. Mr. Forrest owned a closet full of them.

"Mornin', men!" McArthur said generally, taking a seat and distributing the items from his tray.

"Mornin'," Beauregard said. Jackson just continued eating.

"You were wonderful on 'PM Magazine' last night, Jackson," McArthur said.

"Thanks," Jackson mumbled.

"Don't thank me," McArthur said, jostling the table as he took his seat. "I'm thanking you. A national spot like that is terrific publicity for the city of Birmingham."

Beauregard had never met McArthur but knew of him from Jackson and Price. McArthur was executive director of the Boosters, a more intense splinter group of the chamber of commerce. He was legendary for his zeal in promoting Birmingham and his hatred of Atlanta. Lots of Birminghamians hated Atlanta. After World War II the two cities had been roughly equal in size and importance, but since then Atlanta had grown rapidly, received much favorable attention by the national media, and attracted major league baseball, football, and basketball franchises. Meanwhile, Birmingham had seen its steel industry decline, endured one racial crisis after another, got called "Bombingham" and "the Johannesburg of the South" by the national media, and even lost its minor league baseball team. Things were much better now. The baseball team was back. The city had a black mayor. Some of the best cardiologists in the country—in the world—practiced in Birmingham. National publications had written about "surprising Birmingham," with its favorable business climate and low cost of living. But McArthur and many Birminghamians still hated Atlanta.

McArthur's particular hatred, Price had told Beauregard, was inflamed by an incident at a National Boosters Convention a few years back in New Orleans. Atlanta Boosters had gotten him drunk and talked him into getting a tattoo. It was, according to Price's sources, just a small, blue forearm job that said ECONOMIC DEVELOPMENT, but now McArthur had to wear long-sleeved shirts all the time.

66

"I've been talking to my friend at Delta," McArthur said, cutting into quadrants a tall, glistening stack of pancakes.

"And?" Jackson said.

"He likes our idea. Says a discount for people flying to your bachelor parties could be 'mutually beneficial.' Those were his exact words."

Jackson looked up from his breakfast. "How soon can we move on this?"

"Here's the thing," McArthur qualified. "He's not quite as high up at Delta as I remembered."

"What are you saying?"

"He promised to write a memo."

Beauregard, cutting his eyes, could see Jackson staring at McArthur. Jackson's saber-sharp stare—almost as sharp as their father's—was something else that hadn't made the final editing of the "PM Magazine" spot.

"He really does like the idea," McArthur scrambled. "In fact, he wants me to take him to one of your parties."

"To help him write a better memo?" Jackson asked.

"Exactly."

"Screw it. I'll call United."

McArthur, wounded, glanced over at Beauregard.

"Who's this here?" he asked almost accusingly.

"My little brother," Jackson said. "Beauregard Forrest."

"Ah!"

They shook hands over the salt and pepper shakers. McArthur had a moist, warm, spongelike grip, surely a liability in his line of work. Beauregard felt a little sorry for him.

"You must have a hard job, Mr. McArthur," he said, buttering the conversation as he buttered a last crust of toast.

" 'Billy,' please."

"Okay, Billy."

"I do have a hard job," McArthur said, setting his utensils down and looking straight at Beauregard. "Very hard. People have no idea. They think it's just conducting tours, sending out brochures, giving a little slide show at Rotary. That's the easy part. What's hard, Beauregard, is changing attitudes, here and everywhere else. People in Birmingham have what I call a 'civic inferiority complex.' You try to get them to do something new, something exciting, and they say, 'Well, hell, Billy, it's just Birmingham, won't work here, not here, not first, let's let somebody else try it,

Billy, make sure it's a good idea, then maybe bring it here, once everybody knows about it.' I hear that all the time. That's why Jackson's business is so important. It's new. It's cutting edge. It's important in and of itself, but also as a symbol. People are going to begin to think of Birmingham as a great party town, and that can't help but improve our image. Better that than idle steel mills and firemen hosing down little black kids, right?"

"Right," Beauregard said.

"Pass the salt, Beauregard," Jackson said. "The grits are way too flat this morning."

Beauregard passed the salt. McArthur waited until Jackson was through, then took the shaker and dusted his own grits. People were leaving the cafeteria now, their sections of the *Standard-Dispatch* left behind with their trays and cutlery and wadded paper napkins.

"It's always going to be real tough, though," McArthur continued without prompting. "Take this theme park thing. Atlanta's had one for years, Six Flags over Georgia. We've never had one. I almost had that crowd from Dallas talked into putting one in here. I had a good site for them. I had some financing. When they got hung up on the theme, I told them, 'Look. It doesn't have to be about Coach Bryant. That was just our opening position. We're flexible. Make it about dolphins if you want to, or cowboys and Indians.' But of course they backed out. They decided Birmingham couldn't support something like that. So there goes a year of my work right down the toilet. Hell, it took me five years to get a French restaurant here."

Beauregard looked up. "You mean Ooh La La?"

"Well, yes," McArthur conceded. "And I'd hoped for a classier name."

Jackson dropped his fork onto his plastic tray. "Got to go."

"Wait a minute, Jackson," McArthur said. "I want to show you something."

He pulled a greeting card from an inside seersucker pocket and set it by Jackson's tray. Beauregard, from the other side, could see that the cover was a pen-and-ink drawing of the immaculate little ballpark where the minor league team, the Birmingham Barons, played home games. The drawing included the tier of stands, the pennants fluttering in the breeze, the Coke and popcorn salesmen, the players in and around the dugouts; but the emphasis was on small—small stands, small crowd, small press box. Everything small.

Jackson opened and read the card, then turned it so Beauregard could read. The caption, written in block letters, said, WELCOME TO BIRMINGHAM, A REAL MINOR LEAGUE TOWN!

Beauregard and Jackson exchanged wondering glances, then Jackson said to McArthur, "So?"

"What do you mean 'so'?" McArthur said.

"So? So what? It's fairly clever. What do you want me to say?"

"It's not *clever,* Jackson," McArthur said. "It's poisonous. It just reinforces this whole civic inferiority complex business. The thing is, though, it's selling. The merchants say young adults are buying these cards and sending them to their college friends in bigger cities."

"It's just a novelty item, Billy," Jackson said. "I wouldn't worry about it."

"It's my business to worry about it. The merchants are talking T-shirt."

Beauregard set his tray to one side but held on to his coffee mug. "Who's behind the card?" he asked.

"Good question," McArthur said. "The Atlanta Boosters are behind it. They're the ones putting this card out."

"Billy," Jackson said. "They've got better things to do."

McArthur shook his head. "I've known these people for ten years, Jackson. This is exactly how they work. Remember that joke that goes, 'What's the best thing ever to come out of Birmingham?' "

"Sure I remember," Jackson said. " 'Interstate 20.' I ought to remember, as many times as I've heard it."

"That's my point!" McArthur said, rising from his chair. "We all have! All of us who travel! And, damn it, the Atlanta Boosters are responsible. They hired a gagman to write several jokes about Birmingham. They picked the best one, then gave it to all the morning disc jockeys in Atlanta. From there it spread. Now I hear it everywhere I go. I heard it in Denver two years ago, in Knoxville last year. Knoxville! Can you imagine!"

"What are you going to do about it?"

It was more a taunt than a question, the way Jackson said it, but McArthur was ready. "I might have some plans," he said.

"What?" Jackson demanded.

"Let me just say this. Very soon some Birmingham men will be making a little trip to Atlanta. When they get there, they'll follow my instructions."

"And do what?"

"That's really all I can say."

Jackson shrugged. He looked at his watch, then stood with his tray. "Got to go. I'm not learning anything here."

"Wait," McArthur said softly, almost desperately, catching Jackson by the wrist and guiding him back down. "I'll tell you a little more. The Atlanta traffic, which is plenty bad already, will get much worse when my men arrive."

"Why?"

"That I cannot tell you."

Jackson stood again. McArthur pulled him back down. Beauregard, admiring Jackson's technique, wondering if it might be applicable to reporting, poured himself more coffee from their table's copper-insulated refill pot.

"Okay, here's the scoop," McArthur said. "These guys go in separate cars. They arrive in the afternoon, a weekday. They split for different traffic arteries, all of them crucial. They go to Five Points, Little Five Points, Brookwood Station, Piedmont, and Peachtree. A few even go out on the interstate. At about four P.M., they pretend their cars are stalled. They raise their hoods, scratch their heads. Meanwhile, traffic backs up and all the Atlanta radio stations, the same ones that spread the Interstate 20 joke, will be playing my ad about how much simpler life is in Birmingham, how much less traffic there is."

"Who pays for these ads?" Jackson asked.

"I've got some Boosters money. A discretionary fund."

"Slush fund?" Jackson asked.

"Well, yeah."

"What day's it going to be?" Jackson said. "I'm over there a lot. I don't want to get delayed, if I can help it."

"I'm not sure yet, Jackson. I'll give you a call."

"Be sure you do. Now, no kidding, I've got to get back upstairs. I've got a million things to do today."

Beauregard, figuring they'd talk about Sewanee during their escape to Jackson's office, rose too. But Jackson said, "You stay with Billy until he finishes his breakfast. You've got time, right?"

"I guess so."

"I'll try that Delta guy again, Jackson," McArthur said. "I'll really lean on him."

Jackson gave the tiniest, most grudging of nods, then walked off to the cashier's counter. McArthur said to Beauregard, "Remarkable young man, your brother. If we had more like him, in various industries around town, we wouldn't have to worry about Atlanta. As it is, though . . ."

And off he went on another long harangue about his job. Nobody appreciated him, not even his board of directors. Some of them flatly distrusted him. He was an outsider, from Kentucky, a border state, and he'd been educated back east at the University of Georgia. He'd gone to extraordinary lengths to prove his loyalty, even having the profile of Coach Bryant burned into the McArthur family rocking chair that he kept in his Birmingham Boosters office. Still, they regarded him warily.

Beauregard only half listened. He was irritated with Jackson for bolting before they could discuss Sewanee and for abandoning him to McArthur. They sat alone now in this section of the cafeteria. Across the way, a busboy tossed newspapers onto a cart with dirty dishes and trays. On McArthur droned. Whatever boosting Birmingham needed this day could wait until he'd told his life story to the no-longer-nodding Beauregard.

Suddenly, though, a reportorial synthesis began to take place in Beauregard's brain. Birmingham men paid to tie up Atlanta's traffic? . . . Raised hoods, scratched heads? . . . A *slush* fund? . . .

This sounded like a story, maybe even front page.

Chapter Seven

Leaking was a fairly new word for Beauregard, to go with *obsequious, importune, asceticism, mulct,* and others he'd learned from the early chapters of *Thirty Days to a More Powerful Vocabulary*. Price had explained that leaking in journalism was when sources gave a reporter information for a reason. They might leak for the public good, but more often for economic advantage, or political leverage, or to settle a score. Leaking was common in Washington, D.C., Price explained. Not in Birmingham. In Birmingham it was still catching on, like frozen yogurt. Even someone as good as Price took only one or two reportorial leaks a month.

As he made the short drive from Jackson's office to the newspaper, Beauregard wondered if Billy McArthur had been leaking the details of the Atlanta traffic campaign. It hadn't come up, but surely he knew Beauregard was a reporter. Anyone in McArthur's position read both papers, front to back, and paid attention to bylines. Or should. But why leak such a story? To have a witness? Possibly. McArthur's *hubris,* another vocabulary word, might have gotten to him, causing him to want a reporter to document his triumph over the Atlanta Boosters. Maybe not, though. McArthur had only yielded details of the operation because Jackson kept threatening to leave the table. If the operation didn't go as planned, McArthur would look bad. He'd misfired before, most notoriously when he invited representatives from Tunisia to attend the Birmingham

International Friendship Fair. Having encouraged them to make their own travel arrangements, for which he promised full reimbursement, they flew by mistake to Birmingham, Michigan. A flurry of phone calls tracked them down, but they steadfastly refused to come south and set up their booths of indigenous foods and leather goods. They liked Michigan. The weather was cool, the people friendly. They had box seats for a Detroit Tigers game. Price wrote the story for the *Standard-Dispatch* and it was, he said, embarrassing for McArthur. Who could say whether he leaked or merely blabbed the Atlanta operation? All Beauregard knew to do was go with it. Any reporter would.

He parked the party van in the newspaper lot and hustled inside. He wanted to see Price, but he decided to make a quick stop by the downstairs coffee station, which occupied the dead end of a carpeted L-shaped corridor. When he got there the coffee had just stopped dripping. Excellent. He'd get the first, best cup and wouldn't have to make the replacement pot. What a grim chore that was, emptying the grounds, putting out fresh coffee, pouring the water. People would drift in and watch expectantly. It was close quarters in the station and no consensus existed about how much coffee and water to use. Sometimes, with his keen peripheral vision, he could see people shaking their heads at his admittedly strong proportions.

As he poured himself the first cup, he tried to anticipate Price's strategy for the Atlanta story. Surely he'd suggest finding a source among McArthur's men: somebody on the inside. He might even want Beauregard to go to Atlanta with the men. If so, it would be another long day, like Sewanee, only worse with all the traffic; but it would be worth it. No way could Shealy keep this story off the front page.

Plastic foam cup in hand, he started back. He had barely cleared the door when he heard a familiar drawl coming from around the corner and far down the hall. It was heading his way, the tone one of mirthful complaint. He stopped to listen.

"Can't even send him to a speech! Not even a speech! He leaves with English, phones back Latin!"

"Hee-hee."

Shealy. And he had someone with him—someone chuckling. It sounded like that lanky, glad-handing advertising man he talked fishing with most mornings. What was his name? B. J.? Whatever, there was no way to avoid them, given the design of the corridor.

All he could do was hasten the encounter or stand there. He stood there.

"So that's why we call him 'B-Four'," Shealy said. "Only now we may have to call him 'Quid Pro Quo.' "

"Or 'C'est La Vie.' "

"That's French, B. J."

"Is that right? I guess you're right."

Beauregard stood rigidly, judgmentally, cup in hand. When they rounded the corner, the sight startled them.

"Oh," Shealy said, jaw and voice unhinged. "It's you."

"Yeah, me," Beauregard said cooly. "Beauregard."

"Well, uh, mornin'."

Beauregard withheld his "mornin' " but gave the men a grudging nod. Then he ducked around them and strode toward the elevator, spilling coffee all the way. As he pushed the UP button and waited, he could hear the faint far-reachings of deep, spasmic laughter from the coffee station.

Alone now, Beauregard wanted to kick or throw something, but he couldn't, not on an elevator, not with half a cup of coffee. What assholes they were! If ever there was an occasion for revenge, for tit for tat, for quid pro quo ("Yes, Bubba," he imagined himself saying, "I know what it means"), this was it. A work slowdown on Metro Briefs and obits would be one way. Better would be to do a story Shealy would have to put on the front page. He'd run this by Price right away.

But when Beauregard got to their desks, Price was on the phone. He was slumped down, his spine a hypotenuse to the straight back and base of his swivel chair. He used both hands for typing and pinned the phone between his left ear and collarbone. Price always emerged from long phone interviews with a red, wrinkled ear, "phone ear" he called it, and he talked of the condition with pride, as if it were proof that he did his job better than other reporters.

Beauregard draped his blazer over his swivel chair, then sat and tried again to think through the Atlanta trip. If McArthur had some men in mind to tie up Atlanta's traffic, he might have worked with them before. The newspaper's morgue would have a "Birmingham Boosters" file, so a good next step would be to search that file for stories involving large groups of men. If there was one, with names, he'd have potential sources to contact. A long shot, but worth a trip to the morgue.

Just as Beauregard rose to go there, his phone rang. He sat back down.

"*Standard-Dispatch,* Forrest."

"B-Four?"

"Yes?"

"This is Haney in the lobby."

"Yes, Mr. Haney."

"Somebody here to see you."

"Be right down."

He put on his blazer and took the stairs, to avoid Shealy. This lobby person would have a press release no doubt: Metro Brief fodder. People stopped by all hours of the day with press releases, and many if not most of the releases were handwritten, with leaning, verbless headlines across the top. Part of Beauregard's job was to fetch these releases and turn them into publishable Metro Briefs. He had gotten to know Haney, the lobby guard, quite well.

But when Beauregard arrived at the lobby, no one stood with Haney at the guard's table. Haney, a sliver of a man with stiff gray hair, wore the white shirt and blue stretch pants that all *Standard-Dispatch* guards wore. A ring of keys bounced importantly on his right hip. He was vigilant about his lobby. Now, seeing Beauregard, he pointed to a far corner of it, over by Classifieds. Beauregard looked that way and noticed a young woman holding a small dog.

A complicated shiver went through him, part panic, part delight. He recognized the dog as "Booger," one of his first Pets of the Week. Beauregard remembered his description: "a happy mingling of the smaller breeds, more Boston terrier than anything else, with a compact and powerful black-and-white body, a cheerful disposition, and for those interested in security, a bark that would reverse an attacking street gang." Light praise by Beauregard's standards. In truth, Booger had struck him as one of the worst of the Pets of the Week. Ugly, mean, bad to slobber—this was Booger. His name, a Humane Society throwaway, had struck Beauregard as hauntingly appropriate.

But the young woman! She was, from this distance, an unconventional beauty, the kind most young men in Birmingham were too foolish to appreciate, which meant Beauregard might have a chance. She was at least as thin as he was. She was about his age. She had a rosy complexion, a thin nose, and long reddish blond hair that puffed out as if she'd washed it a dozen times in a row.

It was a hoopskirt of hair: something to hope to get up under. She wore faded jeans, sandals without socks, a billowy white blouse, and a black vest. The blouse, unbuttoned at the top, was an encouraging contrast to the cameo-brooched fortress dresses of the arranged dates Beauregard had taken to Birmingham Military dances.

He ambled over, establishing eye contact about halfway. She stood with the dog on her shoulder but didn't return Beauregard's smile. She looked angry. A clumsy moment of introduction ensued before she took hold of the conversation.

"This is not the dog you described," she said.

"Excuse me?"

"You didn't say in your article that he barks all night."

"I didn't know he did."

"I can't sleep. I can't study. I *have* to study. When you work all day and go to school at night, you make every moment count."

"I can appreciate that," Beauregard said, sweating inside his blazer. "Uh, where do you go to school?"

"Don't throw me off track. I came for a reason, not to chat. . . . Why didn't you write about the hot dogs?"

"What hot dogs?"

"That's all he'll eat," she said. "And I don't eat meat."

Beauregard nodded casually, although he'd never met a vegetarian. "All right, try this," he said. "Let him go hungry a day or two. He'll start eating dog food."

"Don't tell me what to do."

"Hey, it was just a suggestion."

"I didn't come here for suggestions. Don't you understand by now? I don't have to keep this dog. I'm *not* keeping this dog. This is not the dog you described."

And then, without waiting for any further defense or protest, she stuffed some papers in his blazer pocket, thrust the dog at him, and began to walk out. She turned just before the revolving door. She stood there a second, looking at Beauregard and the dog, her lower lip trembling, then turned again and hurried out.

As soon as she was gone the dog began to make noise. Two sharp barks came first, then a growl which rose to a high-pitched whimper.

"Booger, hush," Beauregard said.

Despite the extreme circumstances, which included the attention of everyone in Classifieds, Beauregard had managed to pay attention to the sway of the young woman's hips as she left. It wasn't the Robert E. Lee-like thing to notice, but he couldn't help himself. Unfortunately, he'd blown to hell whatever chance he had with her. She was furious. The proof was in her words and tone, but also in her extreme act: returning a dog after more than a month. Not that she'd neglected him. Pets of the Week ran together after a while, but this one seemed to have gained a few pounds. He was squirming now, again making that awful growl-to-whimper.

Haney, keys bouncing, walked over.

"You can't keep that dog here, B-Four. This is the lobby."

"I know that, Mr. Haney."

"Well, move it."

"Just give me a minute."

Beauregard looked at the papers. Yes, Booger's. And her name was Lorena Miles, which he liked. Not that it mattered: She was so angry at him. She'd included in the papers a photocopy of the Pet of the Week article, with large question marks and "yeah, right" inked into the margins. He put the papers back into his pocket, then shouldered the dog outside. They arrived in time to see her orange Vega lay rubber as she escaped from the visitors parking lot.

He looked at his watch: almost nine-thirty. One or two of the Midwesterners would be drifting in to work late any moment. If they caught him with a returned Pet of the Week, they'd be all over the story, telling it, beeping it if necessary, to Midwestern reporter friends at the school board or courthouse.

He hustled Booger out to the parking lot and put him into the back of the party van. He cracked a couple of windows, then jogged to the building for anything that might work as a water dish. Soon he was sloshing back with a plastic cereal dish full of water and a vending-machine hot dog. While Booger ate the wiener, Beauregard lined the van with old sections of the *Standard-Dispatch*.

Pep talk time again. Stay calm, he told himself as he locked the vehicle and again walked toward the building. Work your shift. Find the dog another home. Don't let this become a major obstacle to the Atlanta story or anything else.

But it was no use. Troubled by the lobby encounter, he found that even Metro Briefs taxed his concentration. He kept seeing the young woman thrusting Booger at him and walking away in her faded jeans. He also began to worry about how the dog would fare in the van on such a warm, humid day. Cracked windows and a cereal dish of water might not be enough.

Finally Price got off the phone.

"Mornin', B-Four."

"Mornin', Price."

"Ready to kick ass journalistically this mornin'?"

"Ready."

Beauregard began to tell him about the early morning encounter with Billy McArthur. Price fogged and wiped off his bandaged glasses as he listened but looked up often enough to seem genuinely interested. Beauregard had reached the part about the slush fund when Price's phone rang again.

"Just a minute, B-Four," he said, picking up. "*Standard-Dispatch,* Price. . . . Oh, hey there, Bonnie. Thanks for calling me back. You okay? . . . And Eddie, Jr.? . . . That's interesting. If he hangs with it, he'll be terrific. Daily practice is the key to learning any musical instrument. Tough on *you* though, him choosing drums. . . . I know, I know. . . . Listen, Bonnie, do you have access to those welfare-fraud files? . . . Could you pull a few for me? I've got names. . . . Hey, you're a sweetheart."

Soon Price was slumped back into his chair, hammering welfare-fraud information into the computer, lost in reporting another page-one story.

Beauregard wandered over to a dingy window that overlooked the employee parking lot. He could see the van but not Booger. The mutt was sleeping, probably, but what if he'd died of heat stroke? He'd be a long time explaining that to his sources at the Humane Society. He supposed he could just take Booger back there, but that would be embarrassing. Better to find a new home for the dog. He'd do it now, then get back to work.

He went back to his desk and dialed Jackson's office, but Jackson was on the phone. He called Taco Bob, but Taco Bob was meeting with a building contractor. Finally he called Big Willie, caretaker at New Arlington. Big Willie agreed to look after the dog, but only at New Arlington, and only if Mr. Forrest approved.

Beauregard hung up the phone. He would go to his father's bank, make his case in person. He needed to cash a check anyway.

Walking back out to the van, he could hear barking even before he reached the asphalt lot. The dog was fine, obviously: No sick dog could project like that. But Beauregard decided to go see his

78

father anyway. He couldn't concentrate on Atlanta or anything else until he found a new home for Booger.

The City of Birmingham Bank Tower had its own underground parking lot. Beauregard parked there, leaving Booger and taking an elevator to the spacious lobby. Chandelier light pooled on the polished granite floor. Customers leaned over glass-topped mahogany tables, filling out deposit slips and endorsing checks. Beauregard got into a teller's line but was discovered by a senior vice president who greeted him avuncularly and insisted on cashing the check himself. Soon Beauregard had his fifty dollars and was on the elevator, riding up to the executive suite. The doors opened and he faced Miss Bobbie, his father's secretary for as long as Beauregard could remember. A heavy, deep-voiced woman with a leaning silo of chemically black hair, she, too, greeted Beauregard avuncularly and told him to have a seat. Mr. Forrest was busy; she would work him in.

Beauregard sank into the tapered sofa, his attention falling on the large oil portrait hanging behind Miss Bobbie. It depicted the bank's board of directors and his father, before the beard.

The beard, Beauregard knew, was a signal event in his father's life. Mr. Forrest really was too conservative, too much the charcoal gray or seersucker suit, to grow a beard; but in those first reenactments he began to hear of his resemblance to Robert E. Lee. He'd long ago made the association himself but had confined comment about it to the dinner table and porch at New Arlington. The recognition by others coincided with the "living history" movement within reenacting. Mr. Forrest knew he'd need a real beard to get by as Lee. He decided to try growing one but waited until a vacation he and Beauregard had planned for touring battlefields in the Eastern Theater, principally Maryland and Virginia. They spent a scruffy two weeks on the road, Mr. Forrest itching and complaining but gaining confidence with each Holiday Inn. By the third week he was truly bearded, undeniably Lee-like. Even haughty Virginians were commenting. Back home bank employees reacted positively; after all, he was the boss. Reenactors cheered the growth sincerely.

"Your father can see you now."

"Thanks, Miss Bobbie."

Mr. Forrest was on the phone, sunk into the back rest of his executive's chair, but he acknowledged Beauregard with a brief smile and wave. He had his hair parted his own way, and he had on bifocals. He wore a white, button-down shirt and a striped red-and-silver tie. Behind him, on a wooden rack, hung the coat of one of his charcoal gray suits. In this setting—a paneled office, large and posh, with vases and framed prints and a map of greater Birmingham with red pushpins showing all the bank branch locations—he didn't look quite so much like Lee.

Beauregard took a seat opposite him.

"I don't mind loaning them that much money, Frank," Mr. Forrest was saying, "it's just that I'm not convinced the traffic is there for a strip shopping center. Site inspection is everything, and they haven't done it. . . . Well, I'm not so sure. . . . Listen, Frank, I'll call you back. Beauregard's here. . . . He's fine. He's working at the paper, getting ready to go to Washington and Lee. . . . All right, we'll talk tomorrow. Tell them to get hard numbers, the harder the better. . . . All right, fine. 'Bye."

He put the phone down, then looked at Beauregard. "Hey, hey!" he said, his tone and smile confirming pleasure at the surprise visit. "Strike the tent."

"Hello, Dad."

"How's life in your depressingly small apartment?"

"Very good, sir."

"I trust that thin walls, low ceilings, and an abundance of dust motes are all helping you realize your new goals of independence and precollege maturity."

"They are. Listen, Dad, I've got a favor to ask."

With some confidence, Beauregard made his pitch about Booger. He knew his father to be a reasonable man mostly, and sometimes even progressive. Well, maybe *progressive* was too strong, but he'd been the first Southern unit commander to take a stand against reenactors bringing along body servants. Nor did he allow epithets in camp or on the battlefield. He went out of his way to be friendly to the occasional black reenactor, always a Yankee.

"Where did this dog come from?" Mr. Forrest asked.

Beauregard shrugged. "Someone I know dumped him on me."

"Well," Mr. Forrest said, rocking back indulgently, "I don't see why we can't keep him for a few days."

"Big Willie promised to feed him during the week," Beauregard said. "I'll feed him Saturday, when I come by to load Traveller."

"A yard dog, right? I won't have one in the house."

"He can be a yard dog."

"Bring him by tomorrow."

"Not today?"

"No," Mr Forrest said. "Give Big Willie a chance to fix a place in the garage or barn."

"All right. Tomorrow, then. First thing."

"Come here, Beauregard. I want to show you something."

Beauregard went around to Mr. Forrest's side of the desk. Mr. Forrest had pulled from a drawer a thick black photo album. He began slowly to flip the pages, wetting his finger to help them along.

The photographs were of their reenactment unit—action shots, mainly, though a few captured life in the authentic camp. Beauregard recognized himself dead in a number of the photographs.

"Chambers took these, right?" he asked.

Mr. Forrest nodded. "Does good work, doesn't he?"

"He sure does."

"Look here. Look at the way Pomeroy's head emerges from the powder. It's like he's an extension of the howitzer or something."

"Very artistic. But he shouldn't be standing so close."

"I know. I've told him."

Mr. Forrest closed the book and put it back into the drawer. He stood, then walked over to a window, wrapping a finger in the cord as he peeked through the blinds.

"What are you up to, Saturday?" he asked.

"I plan to be working, Dad. I'm on to a pretty good story."

Mr. Forrest turned Beauregard's way, eyebrows raised. "We've got a good little skirmish set," he enticed. "The Tennessee boys are coming down. We'll have artillery."

"Can't make it, Dad. I'll load Traveller for you, but after that I've got to work."

There followed a brief, uneasy silence, Mr. Forrest staring at Beauregard from over the bifocals. He sighed finally, then turned again and looked back through the blinds. "And you're sure Big Willie agreed to take care of this dog?"

"I just spoke to him."

"He's so surly these days, Big Willie. So difficult. I still don't understand why he won't work Saturdays anymore."

"Sir, he's seventy."

"I've always paid him well."

They talked a while longer, Mr. Forrest wanting to know how Beauregard's vocabulary studies were going ("Fine, Dad") and informing him that the governor would be joining them for lunch

Sunday at the country club. This did not surprise Beauregard. The governor and his father were old friends. They lunched together whenever the governor was in Birmingham, which was at least once a month, more often during election years.

Beauregard went from the bank to his Southside apartment, with a stop at the grocery store for wieners and other emergency provisions. His lease prohibited pets, but this was just for one day and one night. He'd stress that if anyone objected. He left the barking dog, returned to work, got through his quota of Metro Briefs and obits, and went home early. He could hear Booger as soon as he opened the van door in the parking lot. He found that the little dog hadn't messed up the apartment in the slightest. Too busy barking, no doubt.

It was late afternoon now, tenants beginning to return home from work. Beauregard put on his Confederate uniform, the outfit he least minded soiling, and took Booger for a walk around the park. The dog did his business quickly, authoritatively, well off the sidewalk. Whatever trouble he didn't cause in the way of wastes, though, he more than made up for in noise. He barked at everything; everything alarmed him. The walk became a tug of war, Beauregard pulling on the terry cloth leash he'd fashioned from his bathrobe belt.

Back in the apartment, Booger observed early evening with another round of barking. The barking was intermittent now, not constant as before, but if anything louder. Neighbors turned up stereos. Neighbors beat the Sheetrock. Beauregard, pacing, couldn't help but think about the easier yard dogs of New Arlington. Finally, inevitably, someone knocked on the door.

Beauregard, Booger barking behind him, answered. Under the yellow, buggy patio light stood a middle-aged man, bald, in tennis shorts and a blue sports shirt. He wore flip-flops and held a can of Budweiser low in one hand.

"Yes?" Beauregard asked.

"You're not supposed to have a dog here."

"It's not mine. I'm just keeping him for a little while."

" 'No pets,' the lease says."

"It's just for tonight. It's kind of an emergency."

The man took a sharp, fed-up breath, then exhaled obviously and at length. The anger seemed to go out of him with the air. He looked down, toed the patio with a flip-flop, smiled just a little, then looked up and asked, "Got a cigarette?"

"Sure," Beauregard said, surprised. "Step inside."

While Beauregard searched the bedroom for Camels, then the kitchen for matches, the man waited in the front room. Booger shuttled back and forth, barking at each stop.

"Here go," Beauregard said, tossing the man the pack and matches.

"Thanks."

He lit a cigarette and took a long drag. "The wife made me come over here," he said, smoke filtering out of his nostrils. "My idea was to get out of the apartment for a while. Go to a movie or something. Go bowling." He looked down at Booger. "No offense, but that's the barkingest little dog I ever heard."

"He barks at everything," Beauregard conceded sadly. "Barks at nothing. At air."

"Worms?"

"He would if he saw one."

"I meant does he have worms."

"Oh," Beauregard said. "I don't think so. He's had his shots."

"What's his name?"

Beauregard, not wanting to get into it, shrugged. "I'm just keeping him for somebody."

The man knelt down, groaning over the sound of his knees popping. "Come here, little buddy." Booger did, cautiously, reducing the intermittent barks to a low, continuous growl. The man looked him over good, stroked him along the back and neck. "Sometimes a sock helps," he said.

"A sock?" Beauregard asked.

"I could show you."

"What kind of sock?"

"A white one. Long."

After Beauregard fetched an athletic sock from the dirty-clothes hamper, the man stroked Booger some more, then quickly tied the sock loosely around his jaws. After knotting the ends, he stood up like a rodeo cowboy who'd roped a calf in record time. "That should do it," he said.

"You're kidding."

"I don't hear a bark? Do you hear a bark?"

It was true. Booger sat quietly at their feet. He seemed to like the loose, smelly cotton muzzle.

"Who taught you that?"

"I'm an exterminator. We're always up against dogs. After twenty years, you learn things."

"Let me shake your hand." The man did, and they shook with feeling, as if they'd completed some long, arduous journey.

"Hey, I'm Beauregard."

"Felix."

"Good to meet you, Felix."

"Good to meet *you*, Beauregard."

"How long should that sock stay on?"

"Try it a couple of weeks. It's a hassle, taking it off for meals and water. But it beats hell out of all that barking."

They talked a while longer, or rather Felix talked, using the apparently rare occasion of a sympathetic listener to put forth his theories on insect behavior. Beauregard nodded faithfully for a while, then scaled back to mere eye contact, then failed to stifle a yawn.

"Hey, I better go," Felix said. "I've talked your ear off."

"Thanks for the help with the dog, Felix. By the way, his name's Booger."

" 'Booger,' " Felix repeated approvingly. "Listen, Beauregard, you should stop by our place sometime. We're just down the patio."

"I'll do it, Felix."

"I could show you my Ant Farms."

"One day real soon."

It was eerily quiet in the apartment with Felix gone and Booger not barking. Beauregard knew he should study vocabulary words or take more notes on how to do the Atlanta story, but he was tired and hungry. He made himself a peanut butter and jelly sandwich and turned on the TV. He watched the late news from his wicker chair, his interest quickening at the Channel 5 report on welfare indictments. That was a story Price was working. Beauregard could even see Price in the footage of the district attorney's press conference. He stood to one side, taking notes and touching his bandaged glasses. Beauregard guessed he was thinking of a penetrating question to ask. Knowing Price, though, he'd save it until after the TV crew had packed up and gone back to the station. He didn't give anything away.

Another knock on the door. Booger yipped but didn't bark. Beauregard struggled out of the wicker chair. It was probably Felix again, with an Ant Farm. Or maybe Jackson had come by to provide a post–"PM Magazine" update on Get Down! Inc. If so, Beauregard knew he might as well heat water for instant coffee. Jackson would talk half the night.

But when Beauregard opened the door, he didn't see Jackson or Felix standing under the harsh patio light. He saw the young woman from the *Standard-Dispatch* lobby. She had some kind of shift on now, and her hair was tied behind her. She just stood there, arms folded defensively, large brown eyes welling with tears. Beauregard decided distress became her, made her that much more of an unconventional beauty, even with bugs from the patio light swooping down like fighter planes across her face.

"I don't know what to say," she said finally.

"I do. Come in."

When she hesitated, he extended and rotated his left hand. After a second she brushed by him and knelt down for a reunion with tail-wagging Booger. Beauregard felt a surge of hope. She was here for the dog, of course, but he liked his chances.

Chapter Eight

Within minutes they were in the van, Booger too, on the way to a party she knew about. Beauregard had wanted to change out of his Confederate uniform, but she'd said no, uh-uh, it was perfect, everybody would be impressed, they were the avant-garde of Birmingham, they loved outlandish clothes, there might even be somebody in drag. She herself wore a stunning pink shift over a green jersey. The shift was bell-shaped, and extended to her ankles. It was solid pink to the knees, where a series of aqua and white stripes began. Below the stripes, just above the ankles, surprising quiltlike patches took over and further enlivened the outfit. Beauregard was admiring it peripherally as he drove them to the party.

"Tell me again you don't think I'm horrible," she said. She was stroking Booger, now affectionately grinding his socked terrier head into her bosom.

"I don't think you're horrible at all," Beauregard said.

"I missed him within minutes. I don't think I knew how much I cared for him until he was gone."

"It's hard to know what you feel with all that barking going on."

"You're not kidding."

"I know I'm not. Which way here?"

They'd come to a stop sign. She looked up from Booger, studied the intersection, then boldly pointed right. Beauregard eased down on the gas and made the turn. Traffic was light, almost nonexistent, this late at night on Southside. They drove on toward the neighborhood's east side, near the University of Alabama at Birmingham, a flourishing commuter school that Jackson and other hard-core Tuscaloosa graduates preferred to ignore.

"How'd you find me?" Beauregard asked.

"I called your office late this afternoon. They switched me to your desk. Some guy answered."

"Price?"

"That sounds right. I talked him into telling me where you live. He said you'd just moved, and he didn't have the new address. He said it'd take him a few minutes to get it, unless he just called you at home. I didn't want him to. I wasn't sure I'd have the nerve to come over. So I told him I'd wait while he tried to find it. He put me on hold, but pretty soon he came back on with the address. I asked him where he found it. He said, 'No comment' and, 'You didn't get this from me, sister.' He's funny. I'll bet he's a good reporter."

"Price is the best reporter at the *Standard-Dispatch*," Beauregard said flatly. "But, hey, you could be a reporter, getting my address like that."

"I probably could be," she said brightly. "I can talk people into things."

"Now which way?"

"Straight ahead."

She spoke in the soprano range of the basic Birmingham accent, which meant she neglected consonants, indulged vowels, paced everything for music and nuance. Beauregard liked that about her. He'd learned to appreciate hometown voices, working among the newsroom Midwesterners.

As they drove on, she slid over a bit, to look in the rearview. She used her free hand, the one not stroking restless Booger, to untie her hair. After a brief fluffing, it was a hoopskirt again, only inches from Beauregard. He fought to maintain his poise. As good as her voice was, her hair was better. He'd never been this close to such good hair.

She slid back.

"You're sure you don't mind that I put the sock on Booger?" he asked.

"Mind?" she said. "It's ingenious. I'll sleep now, and keep my job, and stay in school."

"To be honest, the sock wasn't my idea."

"No?"

"This guy in my building knew about it. An exterminator."

"Yes, but you saw the wisdom in the sock. Anyway, soon, maybe tomorrow, I'm off to Kmart for a half dozen extra pairs."

They pulled up to a stoplight and smiled at one another in the semidarkness. Beauregard recognized that some principle of acceleration was at work. Maybe it was the shared custody of a difficult Pet of the Week; maybe it was the late hour. Something was accelerating intimacy. Moments before he had been about to nod off in the wicker chair; now he was intensely awake, more awake than after two cups of black coffee, three cups, and beside him was someone new and attractive and sympathetic, someone who smelled good, her herbal perfume or shampoo a slight but consistent waft, overriding earthy Booger; yet nothing in this newness seemed strange, which was the strange thing. A naturalness marked these first few moments together, an agility, almost a grace.

Just then, as if in punishment for reaching such an optimistic conclusion, he noticed *I Can Suit Ya!,* Jackson's sex manual, on the dash in front of her. He had a sickening feeling that he'd marked the Catfish section. He didn't want her to see that—not yet, anyway—so he pointed to something in the distance, one of the lovelier homes of Southside, its porch and azalea bed visible by floodlight. As she turned to notice, he deftly snatched the book and slipped it under the seat.

"Pretty," she said, tossing her hair back again.

"Isn't it."

"All those rocking chairs."

"I know."

"The light's green now."

"Right." Beauregard pressed down on the gas. "And your name's Lorena, right?" he asked. "Like the old song?"

"What old song?"

"You don't know the old song?"

"Left at the next street. . . . No, Beauregard, left."

He made a hard, corrective turn, causing tires to squeal and old party equipment to slide from right to left in the back. Lorena and Booger caromed off the passenger door, bouncing back into Beauregard.

"Sorry," he said, savoring the contact.

"It's okay." She was righting herself and the dog. "What song?"

So, briefly, he told her about "Lorena," the ballad favored by so many Confederate troops, how all through childhood it had been his favorite song, especially the 1960 Stockton Pye version, though the Tennessee Ernie Ford version, cut a year or two later, with drums and a swelling male chorus, had much to recommend it.

A sad song, Beauregard added.

"Sing me just a little."

"Lord, no."

"Do," she pleaded. "Just the first verse."

"I couldn't. I like you."

"Please. I should know this song. After all, it's my name."

She was right, of course. He'd have to sing and singing wasn't one of his strengths, as other reenactors had been quick to point out around the authentic campfires. Bravely, then, from a sense of duty, knowing it wouldn't help and could possibly keep him from achieving his new goal of having a meaningful fling with her, he cleared his throat and warbled toward a key.

> The years creep slowly by, Lorena
> The snow is on the grass again
> The sun's low down the sky, Lorena
> The frost gleams where the flowers have been

"You get the idea," he broke off.

"God, it is sad."

"I told you."

"You have a nice voice, though."

"Lorena." He laughed a little. "I do not."

"Yes! Yes, you do!" She seemed to be convincing herself. "Now, slow down, Beauregard. That's the house right there."

They parked on a narrow street behind a half dozen other cars and vans, then walked to a two-story frame house with a weedy front yard and an outside, wrought-iron stairway. Lorena carried Booger, his oddly swaddled head bouncing over her right shoulder. As they climbed the staircase, she explained that the party was for Mike Band, an alternative rock group that had just released its first tape, *Open Mike*. The tape was done in Birmingham, she conceded, but was in no way amateurish. They'd packaged the tape well. The sound mix was good. The band, particularly the lead guitarist, had raw talent. Who could say how far they might go?

Beauregard, intimidated by the prospect of meeting Mike Band, not to mention the rest of Birmingham's avant-garde, was glad when no one answered Lorena's knock on the door. Now maybe they could go to IHOP, his turf, where the waiters knew him and his Confederate uniform. But before he could suggest this, Lorena opened the door and advanced inside with Booger. The music, smoke, and conversational buzz confirmed a party. He had no choice but to follow.

They passed through a dingy kitchen into a large main room with an unpolished wood floor and peeling white paint on the walls. The room was crowded with what Beauregard took to be an avant-garde density of paperbacks, magazines, art posters, and Salvation Army furniture. Maybe twenty-five people milled about, sipping beers, munching chips, talking. Another few occupied the patio beyond the glass sliding door. Music unfamiliar and not even immediately musical to Beauregard throbbed from stereo speakers nailed to the far wall.

As they made their way into the crowd, Lorena got European greeting kisses from a number of people. After each one she introduced Beauregard, noting, with some pride he thought, his status as reporter. She'd been right about his uniform. It elicited several admiring remarks. A lanky, red-haired woman in dark glasses and a camouflage jumpsuit ran a long, black-tipped fingernail up one gray sleeve while saying, "Wonderful irony. Real good fabric, too. Where'd you get it?" Before Beauregard could explain about the family-run business in Mississippi that supplied the vast majority of reenactor uniforms, grossing, by Mr. Forrest's estimation, at least a million a year, Lorena had pulled him away to meet someone else. In some respects it was like any other party—young women liking each other's hair; young men standing behind, mute and grinning—but in others it was different. No one shook his hand. Beauregard tried with the first couple of men, but they took his effort as more irony and just grinned back knowingly.

Booger was a smash. A girlfriend of Lorena's took him over, showing him to everyone, untying and tying back his sock, usually after one bark. Lorena and Beauregard trailed along, then Lorena got caught up in a debate about some movie he hadn't seen. He walked to the kitchen, popped a beer, drifted to a corner, and more objectively evaluated the party.

He decided at once that it violated most of Jackson's principles of party science. The beer, for example, was lukewarm. Gnats had pocked the dip. The music had to be talked over and the chair-to-body ratio was far too low. Most important, no host or hostess had emerged to give the party direction and involve the uninvolved: the people in corners.

Beauregard noticed a Mike Band album poster on a table and walked over to inspect it. On the poster the four band members wore black leather jackets, white T-shirts, and faded jeans. They stood against a brown brick wall of Sloss Furnace, the old downtown steel mill that survived as an industrial museum. The band members all had long, stringy hair and sneering, pout-lipped expressions. They all wore high-topped pointy black leather shoes. Beauregard could tell that they considered themselves badasses for wearing such shoes. They should try wearing reenactment shoes, he thought. Reenactment shoes, replicas of what the Confederate troops wore—when they were lucky enough to have shoes—were little more than leather boxes. Spend five minutes in them and your feet felt like brushfires. Spend a weekend, marching, and you could forget about going back to work or school in wing tips. It'd be Hush Puppies, if not bedroom slippers. These Mike Band wimps knew nothing about hard shoes.

The fine print at the bottom of the poster confirmed that everyone in the band was named Mike. What's more, all the songs on the tape the poster publicized had *Mike* in the title. The list included "Iron Mike," "Just Call Me Mike," "Mike the Girl," "Open Mike," "Mike, Mike, Mike," "Born to Be Mike," and "Hey, Mike!"

Beauregard was studying the fine print to see where exactly in Birmingham the tape had been recorded when he noticed someone approaching from the side. He looked up to see a short, squat, wavy-haired young man moving into position in front of him. Although smiling, he was squared off, as if to block any right or left movement by Beauregard. He wore a white blazer, pink shirt, and loose black pants with silver stars all over them. His white lapel sported an I LIKE MIKE BAND button. He carried a long-stemmed wineglass. He seemed at once part of, and not part of, the avant-garde crowd. He'd definitely been into the chips. He had a rolled-up bag of them under his arm.

The young man tapped the poster. "I do their bookings and p.r."

"That so?" Beauregard responded politely.

"Yes. And other bands. Ever heard of Jesus Shriner?"

"I don't know. Maybe."

91

"Local Anesthetic? Redneck Anglophiles?"

"Pretty sure."

"All my bands."

He pulled a brochure from his coat pocket and handed it to Beauregard. It was a slick, like Jackson's, though not as professionally done. Beauregard opened the slick. It had booking information and grainy black-and-white photographs of the bands.

"Interesting concept, don't you think, Mike Band?"

"I guess so," Beauregard said. He was folding the slick and sticking it into a blazer pocket. "I don't really get it."

"They're making a statement," the promoter said impatiently. "See, when you're a Mike, not many people call you that, because it's so common a name. You're just Jenkins or Purcell, Turnipseed or Coleman. In my case Coleman."

Beauregard now knew better than to thrust out a hand to a member of the avant-garde, but he risked saying, "Good to meet you, Mike."

"No, I'm Steve. But that's a very common first name, too. Growing up, all the boys in my neighborhood called me Coleman. Girls did, too. Their mothers did. There was a harshness there, a kind of dehumanization. Potato chip?"

"No, thanks."

He withdrew the bag he'd briefly held out and shaken. "You may have faced the same treatment yourself," he said. "Lots of people have common first names. What's yours?"

"Beauregard."

"Beauregard?"

"Yes."

The promoter frowned again, then took another drink. "Anyway," he went on, "Mike Band is in reaction to all of that. They're quite serious about their statement. They won't let anybody in the band who isn't named Mike. They say they were Mikes first, then musicians. They're not real happy about *my* first name. To be honest, it's hell working with them, but I'll bite my tongue for talent. This is their tape on the stereo now."

Beauregard listened politely to what seemed to him a wrecking ball sound. Besides War Between the States songs, he liked singer-songwriter stuff, Gordon Lightfoot and James Taylor, and after a beer or two he enjoyed the soul music Jackson used to ignite parties; but he had never acquired a taste for alternative rock. It wasn't that he was a snob. He didn't much like classical music either. His father had been on and off the symphony board, and a few Saturday nights they'd actually had to go to the symphony, Mr. Forrest having forgotten to fob off the tickets on one of the bank vice presidents. They'd sit there, exhausted from reenacting all day, trying hard not to nod off, always failing, always awakening with a start at the battlefield boom of the timpani. This Mike Band stuff was worse than classical, though. Yet here was Coleman enjoying it. He had his eyes closed. He was nodding his head to the music.

"Good, huh?"

"Hmm," Beauregard straddled. "How long have they been musicians?"

"About a year and a half."

"Making money yet?"

"Starting to, with my help. . . . Say, Beauregard, are you in a band? I'm always looking for new acts."

"No."

"I noticed your uniform."

"Nope. No band."

The young promoter, pondering, bit his lower lip. "Maybe we could start a band for you," he brainstormed. "You could front it. I've got to tell you, Beauregard, I'm in love with that uniform."

"Thanks, but I better just stick with the newspaper."

"Newspaper?"

"I'm a reporter for the *Standard-Dispatch.*"

"Well, well, well."

They talked awhile longer, the young promoter pitching various Mike Band–related story ideas, Beauregard batting back that he was in news, not features, but agreeing under duress to pass along a business card.

He was relieved when Lorena tugged him away.

"Sorry about that," she said when they got to a corner. "Coleman's a bit hyper."

"He's all right."

"Where's Booger?"

"Still with your friend. They're over there."

"Oh, yeah. . . . Beauregard, you see that girl?"

"Uh-huh."

"She was in my psychology class last term."

"I meant to ask—you go to UAB, right?"

"Right. . . . She did her paper on how men cut lawns."

"What?"

"The patterns men make when they cut lawns. What those patterns might mean. The professor—a man, by the way—*loved* that paper. I got an *A,* but he gave her an *A plus,* the only one in the class." Smiling, she tapped her beer bottle to his beer can. "How do you cut lawns, Beauregard?"

The question unnerved him, but he managed to smile back. "I'll have to think about that one."

In fact, Big Willie had always cut the lawn at New Arlington— cut it with a big riding lawn mower that had a canvas bag to catch the clippings. If Beauregard had cut it, he'd have cut it Big Willie's way, straight up and back.

"Lorena!" A group across the way was calling for her.

"Come with me," she told Beauregard.

"I'll catch up in a little while. I need another beer."

In the kitchen Beauregard encountered a subsection of the avant-garde reviewing all the reasons except talent for their failed efforts to live as artists in New York City. Then they began to rip Birmingham. They swapped stories about the lack of local support for the fine arts, the scarcity of good bookstores, the absence of Thai restaurants. Somebody called Birmingham's northern suburbs "a landfill of poor white trash." Somebody else said Martin Luther King, Jr., could have written his "Letter from Birmingham Jail" from anywhere within the city limits. Beauregard grew more and more irritated with their commentary. It was darker than anything he'd heard from the newsroom Midwesterners. No sentence seemed complete without a nasal inflected "crap" or "Jesus Christ." They tried to disguise their Southern accents, but the more they drank the more the truth came through. Sometimes they'd start a sentence in New York and end in Birmingham. Other times they'd get the accents all jumbled. The result, to Beauregard's ears, was affected and mongrel. They talked like people from Florida.

Beauregard, walking back into the main room, noticed a thick tabloid stuck into a magazine rack. As he suspected, it was the *Village Voice,* which he'd heard about but never read. He was surprised as he thumbed through it to find that few of the articles answered the basic reportorial questions, who? what? when? where? how? or why?, or even gave the hometowns and ages of the people quoted. None of the opening sentences seemed written to hook the reader. He couldn't find a single nut graph. Disappointed, he wedged the fat newspaper back into the rack.

94

"Nice uniform."

"Thanks."

He caught the scent of marijuana drifting in from the balcony. Though he'd never smoked marijuana, Beauregard knew the aroma and effects of the weed all too well. Cadets from Birmingham Military would sneak off before Friday drill and smoke until their eyes were bloodshot. Beauregard, a squad leader his senior year, would catch hell for their wavy lines and dropped rifles. He had no use for marijuana.

He saw Lorena across the room, still talking to the group that had summoned her, still looking lovely in her hoopskirt hair and pink shift; but where the hell was Booger? He heard an isolated yip from the balcony. Braving the marijuana smell, he stepped to the opening of the sliding glass door. Streetlight roughly parallel to the second-floor patio illuminated the area just well enough for Beauregard to make out clothes and faces. He identified the Mikes, dressed and shod as on the poster. Young women in halter tops sat on the arms of the lounge chairs the Mikes occupied. Everyone was laughing corrosively. Looking closer, Beauregard saw that a Mike with particularly stringy hair and a safety-pin earring was holding Booger in his lap. He'd draped sunglasses on the dog's head and wedged a marijuana cigarette in the dog's mouth, hard by the white sock. The sock was tied tighter than before—much tighter. The young woman on the arm of the Mike's lounge chair had a Polaroid camera. Suddenly a bulb flashed in Booger's face. Clacking and a whir followed, then a snapshot spit halfway out and began to develop. Booger's blind twisting prompted more laughter and scattered applause from the patio crowd.

"Hey!" Beauregard yelled, his simmering indignation boiling over. "What do you think you're doing! Give me that dog!"

The crowd fell silent and watched as Beauregard, in a series of swift, authoritative movements, stepped forward, brushed off the sunglasses, tossed away the marijuana cigarette, loosened Booger's sock and grabbed the dog from the unprotesting Mike. Beauregard pivoted and pulled the snapshot from the camera, then began his retreat.

"Hey, who the hell are you?" a female voice asked nervously just before he reached the door.

"Yeah! Wait a minute, *asshole!*" yelled a Mike. But no one followed him. All was quiet in the apartment when he stepped in with bleary, red-eyed Booger. The rest of the avant-garde stared as Lorena hurried over.

"What happened?" she asked.

"Just look at this." Righteously, like an assistant district attorney showing a jury a damaging piece of evidence, he handed her the photograph. It was still developing. *Damn.* "Give it a minute," he said. "I'll be out in the van."

When he got there, he set Booger down on the floorboard, slammed the door, and collapsed against the seat. Sweat trickled inside his uniform.

Lorena had probably only brought him to the party out of guilt for having given up on Booger. Now he'd humiliated her in front of the entire avant-garde. He had half a mind to end the whole thing, just drive off and let her catch a ride home; but that would mean keeping Booger. He wasn't up to it. Though quiet now, the little dog reeked of marijuana. Beauregard could see himself getting stopped for some minor traffic offense and having to argue to the police, then later to Jackson or their father, that it was the dog that had been smoking.

When the passenger's door squeaked open, Beauregard jumped. Lorena climbed in without speaking. Before she shut the door and the overhead light went out, he could see her looking at him. She picked up Booger first, then reached over and squeezed Beauregard's right forearm.

"I spoke to them," she said quietly. "They're sorry. So am I."

"They put the flash right in his face."

"I know, Beauregard. It was cruel."

He was still collapsed against the seat, but he angled his head toward hers. "You want me to go back up there with you?"

"No. I've had enough of those jerks for one night."

"So have I."

"Can we go somewhere for coffee? Or is it too late?"

This was a surprise, but Beauregard decided that she wasn't being polite, that she must really want to go. It was too late and too much had happened already for her to pretend to want to go somewhere for coffee with him. "Of course we can go," he said, trying to modulate his enthusiasm. "I know a good place."

So, finally, he drove them to IHOP, where they left Booger locked and sleeping in the van. Inside they took a sticky back booth and ordered a pot of decaffeinated coffee. Beauregard was glad

Price wasn't there. Price laughed at decaf, just as he laughed at the herbal teas and Diet Cokes of the Style section writers.

Beauregard told Lorena.

"Price is the guy I spoke to, right?" she said, hands curled around her steaming mug.

"That's right."

"He called you 'B-Four.' So did the lobby guard."

"It's a nickname," Beauregard scrambled. "A newspaper nickname. Inside stuff."

"Like 'Scoop'?"

"Something like that."

Beauregard studied where his reflection would be, if the plastic-coated table had yielded a reflection. He needed a new topic. Quickly, as transition, he began to tell her what he was working on, playing down Metro Briefs and obituaries, playing up the possible trip to Atlanta with Billy McArthur's men. He laid it on thick, as he did in the paper with Pet of the Week.

"Interesting," she said. "Now sing a little more of 'Lorena.' "

"No, please. They know me here."

"Oh, all right. But why did you listen to Civil War songs when you were growing up?"

"It's a long story."

She held up the half-full pot, to show how much time they had.

So, shrugging, he began to tell her. She listened carefully, nodding like an apprentice therapist as he told how his mother had died after he was born, how his father had relied on friends and family and women from the United Daughters of the Confederacy to help rear him, how the UDC women had taken him to their quarterly meetings, holding him in their elaborately folded laps and fanning him with oriental hand fans during the old and new business. Rather than nursery rhymes or stories, his father had nightly read to him from War Between the States books, the good stuff only—Freeman, Wiley, Foote.

Her attention nourished him. If anything, she nodded too often, affirming statements he was still formulating. He hurried on through his early years at Birmingham Military, his entry into the world of reenacting, and his relationship with Jackson. Then he talked some more about their father, the good and bad, including his preoccupation with complete sentences and other disciplines.

"He didn't beat you or anything, did he?" she asked.

97

"Uh-uh, no, never," Beauregard said. He took a sip of coffee, then added, "He did have his saber around the house."

She didn't nod, just widened her brown eyes and leaned forward on her elbows. "What did he do with it?"

"Rattled it," Beauregard explained calmly. "As Jackson likes to say, at our house 'saber rattling' was no mere figure of speech."

"God, Beauregard. I'm sorry."

He shook his head. "That's just Jackson talking. It wasn't really so bad. Boys like a saber." He smiled, then poured more coffee for both of them. "Let's talk about you."

She took her turn, gesturing extensively, as before. Commentary tumbled out with the facts. Oldest daughter of a truck driver and an elementary-school teacher. Lifelong Birminghamian. Public schools, Baptist church—way too much Baptist church. She'd made good grades but bombed the SAT. She *hated* the SAT: the taking of it, just the idea.

"Who are they to measure my intelligence?"

"I know," Beauregard said.

"Or yours, for that matter."

More coffee. She went on. She was involved in all kinds of environmental groups, something that didn't particularly please her parents, who were quite conservative. She admitted that she had, in her early teens, engaged in screaming fights with her mother. Now they were friends. "Distance helps," she said. She'd recently moved into a small apartment on Southside, not far from where Beauregard lived. She worked days as a file clerk at the school board. Nights she attended UAB. An urban affairs major, and her best course this term was on the history of Birmingham. Still, poetry was her first love. She tried to write a few lines every day.

"See that?" She pointed to blue lights flashing on the street beyond the IHOP parking lot. Beauregard saw a police officer trying to question an enormous woman who leaned against an ancient battered Pontiac, her curler-filled head in her hands. "I see a poem in that."

It looked like a Metro Brief, if that, to Beauregard, but he said, "I know exactly what you mean."

They got back to his apartment building just after 3 A.M. She put Booger in her car, then lingered outside with Beauregard in the half-lit parking lot. It was cooler now. A quarter moon shone beyond the Dumpster. She put her hands in the pink shift's pockets and looked at him.

"You could have taken Booger to the dog pound," she said. "You didn't. I admire you for that. You're trustworthy."

Beauregard nodded. He hadn't thought about the pound.

"I do want him," she went on. "It was just the all-night barking. Now, with the sock, we'll be fine."

"Could I call to check on you? On him, I mean?"

"I'd like that."

"Good. I'll call you at the school board."

"Or call me at home. My number's in information. L. O. Miles, not Lorena."

Without removing her hands from her pockets, she reached forward and kissed him lingeringly on the cheek. Then she turned and got back into the Vega. She cranked the engine, then drove off, waving once in the rearview.

Beauregard waved, too. He was still waving when the car was out of sight. He knew she'd kissed and been kissed often at the party, but that was the avant-garde, that was Europe. His kiss was better. There was romance in it; he was pretty sure. He stood savoring the kiss, savoring almost everything about the evening, even Mike Band, even the Vega's fumes. When the fumes cleared he walked slowly back to his apartment, hands in his pocket, singing cheerfully and in uncharacteristically good voice the lugubrious old ballad "Lorena."

Chapter Nine

They became phone buddies. Beauregard enjoyed writing Lorena's numbers, home and work, on a three-by-five-inch card he placed in the *L* section of a small, dented metal box on his desk. The box was where he kept numbers for the police department, the fire department, the jail, the courthouse, the National Weather Service, the Humane Society, the Red Cross Blood Bank, Taco Bob's—all the important numbers. The Midwesterners had spiffy Rolodexes, but Price and Beauregard, traditionalists, held fast with three-by-five-inch cards and dented metal boxes. Beauregard didn't really need to put Lorena's numbers on a card. He'd memorized them right away. But reporters often searched each other's Rolodexes or dented metal boxes for numbers, and Beauregard liked the thought of the Midwesterners flipping through his *L* section and finding "Lorena." It would tantalize them to see that he had the card of a woman who wasn't a spokesperson or dispatcher, that he had her home as well as office number, and that he had her card filed intimately, under her first name.

He called three times in the two days after the avant-garde party. At first he opened with the too stiff "Beauregard Forrest, here," then loosened to "This is Beauregard," and finally, on the third call, he risked testing whether she knew his voice. "Beauregard!" she said in a stunning payoff. "I was hoping that would be you!"

Their conversations had a number of themes, including Booger, how well he was doing, when he might come off the sock. They talked about her environmental interests, her poetry reading, and her school work, particularly the course on the history of Birmingham. Her class had just taken a field trip to Tuxedo Junction in the city's Ensley section. She hadn't known that it was the inspiration for the big band standard "Tuxedo Junction" or that the tune was written by a black Birminghamian, Erskine Hawkins. Beauregard hadn't known that either, though he'd ridden by Tuxedo Junction with Big Willie many times.

"How's your Atlanta story going?"

"Fairly slow, really."

"I can't wait to see it. I know it'll be great."

Beauregard wanted very much to ask her out, and he sensed she wanted him to, but he felt that he had to finish the Atlanta story first. After all his bluster, he needed a front-page byline. He needed B-Four-ism solidly behind him.

Encouragingly, Price too had high hopes for the Atlanta story. He confirmed that it was page one material and predicted that it could be done fairly quickly. He even agreed to help Beauregard. They worked together on it all week, Price in moments stolen from major stories, Beauregard stealing his moments from Metro Briefs and obits. He felt bad about hurrying through obits. Having died himself so many times on reenactment battlefields, and having so often imagined his own obituary (written by Price) and funeral (packed house; young women crying) he felt kinship with the recent dead. He worked hard to swell their obits with club affiliations and hobbies and other facts gleaned from calls to the survivors. Unfortunately, he was pressed for time now. He and Price were working a big story. Everyone would just have to understand.

They went painstakingly through the McArthur and Birmingham Boosters files, but no reference to a group of Bear-Bryant-like men emerged. There were references to others, though, mainly people who had worked for the Boosters or served on its board of directors. Price secluded himself in the morgue for twenty minutes and emerged with a confusing (to Beauregard) list of potential sources. Price had cross-referenced everything, putting the names and numbers in what he called "priority boxes." He'd drawn lines between the boxes, but hadn't made clear what the lines meant or why certain names had priority and others didn't. Some names appeared in more than one box. Some were shaded and had little stars by them, also unexplained.

Beauregard and Price took turns making calls from the list. For three days they had no luck. Even Price seemed discouraged. No one knew anything. Finally, though, on Friday morning, Beauregard returned from the coffee station to find Price pumping a fist.

"A break at last, B-Four," he said. "Turns out somebody hired a bunch of old men to dress up like Bear Bryant for the pregame show at an Alabama game. This was years ago, before Bear died. They all wore houndstooth hats and ugly blazers. They all leaned against the goal posts. They were Bear to a T. The crowd loved it, but Bear was pissed. It gave him nightmares or something. Anyway, this sounds like something McArthur might have done."

"Your source doesn't know?" Beauregard asked.

"No. Not for sure."

Beauregard sipped coffee thoughtfully. "We can't just call the Boosters office and ask," he said. "That would tip them off."

"Attaboy, B-Four. Now you're thinking."

"Thanks, Price."

"Tell you what. You go through the Bear Bryant file. If we had a story or picture, it might be in there, rather than in the McArthur or Boosters file. As I get time, I'll make more calls from the list."

Beauregard felt good about getting away from the list, but the Bear Bryant file filled six cabinets. No Birmingham mayor, not even "crime," had so thick a *Standard-Dispatch* file. It was as if the paper had been the coach's diarist. Even now, Bryant dead, the file grew. There was the Bryant museum to write about, and periodic feature stories about the steady stream of visitors to his grave. Bryant anniversaries had to be observed: birth, death, key bowl victories. Visiting reporters had often used the Bryant file and, as a consequence, it was no longer in anything like chronological order. It was a haystack, only in beat-up metal drawers which slipped off their tracks. Beauregard would have to go through the whole damn thing.

Turning the yellow clippings over, one by one, was like reliving the nights upstairs with Jackson at New Arlington. Jackson was obsessed with Bryant and Alabama football. Obsession with Alabama football was considered normal in Birmingham, so Beauregard, interested but not obsessed, was the odd one. Beauregard knew the starting players, the key substitutes, the strength of the freshman class—enough to get by in conversations at the coffee station and the urinal. Jackson knew everything. All Beauregard could do was nod or say, "That's for sure," as Jackson droned on about an inside linebacker's bench press ability or Lee Roy Jordan's thirty-one tackles in the 1963 Orange Bowl. Jackson's specialty was Bear Bryant. He'd worshiped him at Alabama. Now, years later, he affected irreverence to the old man's memory; but Beauregard wasn't fooled. He knew Jackson had needed prescription drugs to get through the funeral—knew because he himself had picked up the prescription at that all-night drugstore near Taco Bob's. Beauregard had skipped school along with the other cadets to join the tens of thousands who lined Birmingham's streets for a look at Bear's hearse and the trailing limousines full of former Alabama football players, including Joe Namath in aviator sunglasses and a sharp black suit. But Beauregard had not been especially moved. He knew Bear was a great man. Bear had the won-loss record, the nostrils. But he'd never touched Beauregard's life the way Robert E. Lee had. Bear hadn't been confused with Jesus in his dreams.

"What are you doing, B-Four?"

It was Bubba Shealy, looming and casting a shadow over him. Shealy did that sometimes—stole up on reporters, in spite of his breathing noises and shaking aspirin bottle.

"I'm looking up something for Price," Beauregard said. He didn't want Shealy to know about this story yet. "Price is pretty busy out there."

"You caught up on Metro Briefs?"

"I think so."

"Good." Shealy dropped a hand on Beauregard's shoulder. "Listen, B-Four," he said, voice a bit softer. "I'm sorry about what happened the other day in the coffee station. That was uncalled for."

"Oh, it's all right, Bubba."

"Your story from Sewanee wasn't really that bad, apart from those Latin quotes."

"Thanks."

"Your writing needs work, of course. You need to weed out some of those big words and phrases. *Mulch* your writing a bit, B-Four. That's what you need to do. But you know that, don't you? You're working on it."

"I'm trying, Bubba."

Shealy looked around, making sure they were still alone in the morgue. "Listen, B-Four," he said. "You're not going to tell your

Dad what I said in the coffee station, are you? I know he's tight with the publisher."

"No, Bubba. I wouldn't do that. I'm not that kind of guy."

"Good man," Shealy said, sniffing and standing up straight. "You say you're caught up on Metro Briefs?"

"Yes, sir. You can check the queue."

"I don't have to, B-Four. I know I can trust a guy like you."

It was a relief to have made up with Shealy, but it was also intriguing to know how much Shealy worried about Mr. Forrest's friendship with the publisher. Beauregard had promised himself he would never exploit that friendship, but it didn't hurt to have Shealy thinking about the possibility. Price had probably mentioned it to him. That would be like Price, to suggest on Beauregard's behalf the possibility of a power play that Beauregard couldn't, in good conscience, make. Price encouraged him, looked after him, told him little things like hail is always "golf-ball-sized" in newspaper writing.

Beauregard, as he had time, continued the marathon exercise of going through the Bear Bryant files. By late Friday afternoon, he was still in the fourth cabinet. Price stopped by.

"Any luck?" he asked, swinging a leg over a folding chair across the table from Beauregard.

"Not for us, Price," Beauregard said. He held up a front-page clip. "But Bear just won another SEC championship."

"Roll Tide."

"Roll Tide."

Price stretched his arms back behind his head, exposing his late-in-the-day, continent-shaped underarm sweat stains. "Lord, I'm tired," he said. "Broke, too. You'd think they'd pay me well for all the work I do."

"I could loan you ten bucks."

"That's all right, B-Four. I'm not that broke. But thanks."

"Good story today? I saw you working the phones."

"Oh, pretty good," Price estimated. "I found this local guy who's all pissed off because his daughter's reading *The Canterbury Tales* in school. It was the "Miller's Tale" that got to him. He thinks it's corrupting. I asked if he'd ever read it, and he said, 'Yeah, in high school.' So I said, 'Well, it didn't do you any harm, did it?' He said, 'It was different then.' I said, 'Different, sir? Sir, how was it different?' He said back then it was in old-timey English. Said they used *arse* instead of *ass*."

With the word *arse,* the memory of Lorena walking ahead of him in faded jeans flashed into Beauregard's mind. *Ass* was heard many times each day in the newsroom and had no resonance, but the variant *arse* provoked associations. Beauregard's was with Lorena. It was a sexist first thing to remember about a young woman, especially someone like Lorena, good-hearted, a dog lover, a poet. He felt disloyal. He also felt warm in the face. He was *still* thinking about her arse. He tried to think of some blasé comment with which to cover himself.

"Ass, arse," he told Price. "What's the difference?"

"I know," Price said. "He's an idiot. They all are."

"But can you get *ass* or *arse* in the paper?"

Price shrugged. "I think so. Bubba's nervous, but he promised to try. Anyway, I'm not waiting around. I'm one whupped puppy. I'll jump back on that McArthur thing Monday, but for now I'm heading to the house. Don't *you* stay too late, B-Four."

"I won't, Price. Have a good 'un."

But Beauregard did stay late. He liked staying on duty when all other dayside reporters, even the indefatigable Price, had punched the clock. He sat at the morgue table sipping black coffee and turning yellow clips. The sun went down in the dirty plate-glass window over by Style. The police scanner crackled by the city desk. He kept on working. He was a workingman. The guys in his military-school class would be off at some rush party, freezing daiquiris and trying to impress the brothers. Meanwhile, he pulled a second shift. He took a dinner break about eight-thirty, driving to a nearby fast-food restaurant for a go at the roughage bar, then resumed file duty. By eleven, he was into the last cabinet. Turning fast now, fatigue eroding his patience and concentration, he looked only at headlines: BEAR WORRIED ABOUT MEMPHIS STATE; COMMODORES CONCERN BEAR; LSU UNDERRATED, BEAR SAYS; BEAR ON REST OF SEASON: "WOE IS ME."

And then, suddenly, he spotted the needle: a two-column photograph of twelve old men dressed like Bear Bryant. They had the checkered blazers. Their houndstooth hats rode forward on their heads. They formed a kind of chorus line in front of a goal post, arms linked, one leg up. The cutline gave the names of all twelve.

Beauregard stared at the clip, afraid that if he looked away it might disappear back into the file cabinet. He jogged to the Xerox machine to make insurance copies. When the last one spit out, the stack looked puny, so he made a dozen more. The bigger stack felt warm and substantial and smelled impressively inky as he carried it across the newsroom.

He put half the copies on Price's desk, half on his own. He folded the original and stuck it in his briefcase, in case the building burned. Then with rising excitement he dialed Price's home number.

Ten rings: no answer. Beauregard set the phone down. Price, he remembered, had a date most Friday nights. Beauregard wished he too had a date, or at least someone to share this discovery with. The few people left in the newsroom were busy getting out the last edition. He couldn't call Lorena this late on Friday night. Well, he could, but it would be bad form, and if she wasn't home, he'd be depressed. Better just to keep working toward the front-page story that would advance everything. He picked up one of the photocopies.

How would Price proceed? He'd do some more of that damn cross-referencing, probably. While he had the chance, Beauregard chose a simpler method, copying the twelve names in alphabetical order on a legal pad. He searched the phone book for numbers. He found a "Cecil E. Tipton," but not a "Cecil W." None of the other men was even that close to a listed number. He called information twelve times and found that two of the men had numbers, both unlisted. He remembered that Price and other reporters sometimes used the city directory, a supplementary reference book which carried the numbers, addresses, and even occupations of many city residents. He found that book in the morgue. Of the twelve, he got data on just one: Dewey Simpkins. The directory had no phone number for him, just a trailer park address and occupation: "Guard, Downtown Museum of Art."

Beauregard called the museum and got a recording that gave its hours. He decided to go by there the next day, after loading Snuffy/Traveller for Mr. Forrest. It would be Saturday, his day off, so he wouldn't get paid. That was all right. Making page one and impressing Lorena would be payment enough. He would drop by the museum, see if anyone knew this Dewey Simpkins.

Leaning back in his swivel chair, Beauregard could feel the elevation of his shoulder muscles, a sure sign that he'd put in a long, tense day. He stretched a bit, then slipped on his blazer, grabbed his briefcase, and walked out to the van. Light, slanting rain glistened the downtown streets. It was quiet out, except for the circulation workers bundling second editions over by the loading dock.

Beauregard pulled the van out of the lot and began the short drive to Southside. He figured he'd make a snack, study vocabulary words for thirty minutes, then go to bed. He'd have to be up early to load the horse for his father.

When he turned into the driveway of his apartment building, he noticed cars in all the parking spaces. He could hear rock music, too. Someone's party. He parked on wet grass by the Dumpster, then climbed the stairs and walked down the patio. Inside he could hear bass notes from the stereo of the party apartment—just bass notes, conducting themselves through the Sheetrock with depressing fidelity. Beauregard knew he couldn't sleep or study vocabulary words to such a pulse. He left his apartment and drove in harder rain to Devonshire Oaks, Jackson's place. The white-helmeted, khaki-shirted guard recognized the party van and waved him through. A light burned in Jackson's kitchen. Beauregard parked in a visitors spot, and hurried through the drizzle to Jackson's door. He shook himself dry, then tested the knob: unlocked. He pushed the heavy door open slowly.

"Jackson?"

"In here."

Beauregard walked through the kitchen into the den. Jackson, wearing only red gym shorts, lay stretched out on the tapered, earth-tone sofa. He was on his left side, facing the nearby color Sony and holding the remote control with his right hand, which dangled like a dead man's to the buffed parquet floor. A crumpled bag of chips and a Budweiser can were on the glass table between him and the TV, which was tuned to "The Tonight Show." Just now a starlet in a low-cut, high-slit dress was speaking single innuendos and double entendres to Johnny in a husky, mock-innocent alto. When she bent over to make a point about "yoga," the camera zoomed in on her cleavage.

"Is it dangerous to lick a television screen?" Jackson asked.

"I don't know," Beauregard said, clearing newspapers from the easy chair. "Maybe not, if you're on cable."

"That wouldn't make any difference."

Beauregard removed and draped his blazer, then went back to the kitchen for a Budweiser and an ice cream sandwich. He returned to the den and sat in the easy chair. Except for a single, shaded lamp across the room, the TV was the sole source of light. Blinking color images washed up like waves on Jackson's muscular body. As Beauregard unwrapped the ice cream sandwich, he considered this effect, as well as his brother's state of near undress.

"Anyone else here?" he asked.

Jackson gestured with a bare foot toward the master bedroom. "The Morsel's in there sleeping," he said. "She's worn out, Roll Tide." He flashed a wrinkled smile.

"Maybe I should go," Beauregard said.

"Stay. She'll sleep for hours."

Beauregard chased a bite of ice cream sandwich with a swallow of beer, then said, "You should call her by her real name, Jackson."

"Sometimes I do. Anyway, stop preaching."

"You serious about her?"

Jackson made a wavy, noncommittal gesture with his dangling hand. "I don't even know if she's serious about me," he said. "One day she talks about marriage and kids. The next day she wants to go into business for herself. Right now she wants to open a tanning salon. 'Donna's Bakery,' she wants to call it. Hell, it might work."

"Might," Beauregard agreed amiably. "Hey, I met a girl."

Jackson sat up. For all his macho bluster, he was keenly interested in others' romantic prospects, especially Beauregard's. "Tell me," he demanded.

So Beauregard told him about Lorena, beginning with the lobby confrontation, flashing back to Booger as Pet of the Week, fast-forwarding to the avant-garde party, then wrapping up with their status as phone buddies and the possibility, indeed likelihood, of a date.

Jackson listened carefully. When Beauregard finished, Jackson said firmly, as if delivering the final words on some hotly debated topic, "Godiva chocolates."

"What?" Beauregard asked.

"Get her a box of Godiva chocolates."

"Why?"

"Women love them."

"More than other chocolates? I don't understand."

As Beauregard finished the ice cream sandwich, Jackson explained that Godiva chocolates had something close to an aphrodisiacal effect on many, if not most, women. He wasn't sure if it was the sexy name or the milk-to-sugar ratio, but every accomplished bachelor he knew, every real swordsman, had a refrigerator full of Godivas. He'd seen Godivas on bachelor friends' bedposts, in their carpeting. He kept a box or two himself.

"Lorena's never even mentioned chocolate," Beauregard said, "much less Godivas."

"Trust me," Jackson said. "What does she look like?"

Beauregard gave a thorough, though hardly unbiased, report, beginning with the basics, then lingering a little too poetically on her hoopskirt of reddish blond hair and her naturally rouged face and forehead.

"She's not an albino, is she?" Jackson asked.

"Shut up, Jackson."

"If that's what you want in life, Beauregard, a love affair with an albino, then I'll support you one hundred percent."

"Just shut up."

Carson's next guest was the wholesome-looking woman who often appeared on the program with exotic animals from the California zoo where she worked. This time she had a gibbon. It was all over Johnny, running its tiny hands through his perfect silver hair. Jackson punched down the sound with the remote control.

"Let's talk business," he said.

"Yours?" Beauregard asked with edge. He was still smarting from the albino crack.

"Mine, then yours," Jackson said.

Jackson briefed Beauregard on all that had happened since the "PM Magazine" spot. The blender endorsement was still under negotiation, but he'd begun developing the curriculum for his two-day party science workshops. If those went well, he'd video-tape and market the highlights. He hadn't had time to explore the franchise thing, but there was no good reason to believe it would not happen.

Beauregard listened impatiently, awaiting his turn. When it came, he talked about the Atlanta story, reminding Jackson of the breakfast with McArthur, explaining how that had been the seed. He had begun to describe how different investigative reporting was from routine reporting, how it required persistence, wiles, and cross-referencing skills, when Jackson held up a hand.

"Hear that?" he asked ominously.

"No."

"I thought I heard the Morsel snoring."

"I don't hear anything."

"She must have rolled over." Jackson sighed big, then shook his head. "It's not just the snoring."

"What do you mean?" Beauregard asked.

"She takes up too much of the bed."

"Jackson," Beauregard said skeptically. "She's small, a morsel."

"I know! I know!" Jackson said. "It makes no sense, but it's true. I've got proof." Suddenly he was up off the couch and rummaging through a drawer below the mahogany chest that held athletic trophies and letters he'd won at Birmingham Military and the University of Alabama. He turned and tossed a handful of color photographs at Beauregard. "Just look at these."

They were of the Morsel, under the covers. She did indeed take up well over half of Jackson's antique four-poster bed. Her head was pillowed at the northwestern corner, but her body cut diagonally across the mattress, toward the southeast.

"You shouldn't have done this, Jackson," Beauregard said, studying the photographs, reacting impurely to the sight of the Morsel's bare, tan shoulder as framed by the white sheets.

"I had to," Jackson said. "She didn't believe me."

"Which camera did you use?"

"The Minolta. It was tricky, with that canopy. I wasn't quite sure how to do the flash."

"You did fine."

"Just wait till I get a tape recorder," Jackson said, gathering the photographs from Beauregard. "I'll nail her on the snoring. There won't be a thing she can say."

They watched the rest of "The Tonight Show," Beauregard sipping the last third of his beer. A new commercial for City of Birmingham Bank came on. It was a straightforward spot, satisfied customers giving minitestimonials on the bank's friendliness and reliability. Jackson and Beauregard agreed that the commercial was boring, especially compared with the old campaign, conceived by their father, that featured a cartoon Vulcan flying over the city and speaking with a pronounced Southern accent. Then the brothers began to argue about their father, Beauregard taking the old man's side, Jackson prosecuting and calling him "Marse Bob." It was a familiar argument, a dirt road the turns and gullies of which they knew quite well. Jackson considered their father a minor embarrassment these days, because of the reenacting obsession, and he claimed Mr. Forrest was jealous of him for making so much money in partying. Beauregard acknowledged that reenacting wasn't the usual hobby, wasn't golf or rose gardening, but he listed its merits, namely the acquisition of real understanding and respect for what the troops went through. He insisted that Mr. Forrest was secretly proud of Jackson, but deeply, perhaps permanently, miffed that the Get Down! Inc. account was at a competing bank.

"Better rates," Jackson said. "Free checking."

Beauregard shook his head reproachfully.

"Back off," Jackson said. "You're preaching again. Anyway, you know as well as I do that my personal account's at Dad's bank. Always has been, always will be. I just think it's better to keep the business funds separate."

Beauregard paused, then asked, "You going to be at the country club for Sunday lunch?"

"Yeah, but only because the governor's coming."

"I still go every week."

"I know, Beauregard," Jackson said. "That's because you're Dad's whipped dog."

"I am not."

"His Booger."

Beauregard stood. "That's it," he said, reaching for his blazer. "I'm out of here."

Jackson again held up a hand. "Hey, I'm sorry."

"Tough."

"Come on, Beauregard." He was frowning now. His nostrils were drawn up, and his voice had lost its team captain quality. "Stay for a while."

"No."

"Stay, Beauregard. I—I'm lonely."

Beauregard hesitated, then flopped back down. Jackson's rare display of vulnerability, real or not, couldn't be walked out on. Besides, "The Rifleman" followed "The Tonight Show." Beauregard had always liked "The Rifleman." Jackson suggested they play the "Rifleman Game," which they had invented as boys and still played occasionally. On slips of paper they guessed how many people the Rifleman, with his modified Winchester that could fire off a first round in .3 seconds, would kill this episode, and how many of those deaths his young son Mark would witness. Beauregard guessed three and one, Jackson five and two.

"I win," Jackson said as the credits rolled. "Roll Tide."

"You must have seen this episode recently," Beauregard protested. "You had both numbers exactly."

"So? I win, you lose." He was team captain again. "That means you have to go in there and sleep with the Morsel."

"Very funny, Jackson."

"I hope you brought your ear plugs. If you didn't, it could be a long night."

Chapter Ten

Beauregard drove to New Arlington before dawn to load Snuffy/Traveller into the horse trailer. It was a cool, damp morning, and the horse, no more a fan of these early disturbances than Beauregard, proved stubborn. "Mawn, Traveller" was not enough to lure him from his warm, hay-laden stall. Beauregard had to jerk the halter all the way to the Cadillac.

Afterward he sat in the kitchen with his father, who was already in uniform, hair combed back the other way. He had a new old pistol to show Beauregard.

"A Le Mat?" Beauregard asked, observing the French pronunciation and looking with squinted eye down the short barrel.

"Of course."

"Where was it made?"

Mr. Forrest smiled. "New Orleans," he said, thumping every syllable.

Beauregard whistled appreciatively. Made in New Orleans, the pistol was worth a lot more than if it had been made in France or England. The Confederates hadn't made many in New Orleans before the Yankees under General Ben "Beast" Butler occupied the city and shut down weapons production.

"Come with me today," Mr. Forrest insisted suddenly. "We'll get some breakfast at IHOP. And when we get to the field I'll let you carry the Le Mat. Not in the reenactment, of course, but later, around the authentic camp."

Beauregard shook his head. "I've got to work today, Dad. I thought I told you that."

"On Saturday?"

"I'm trying to find a guy. If I can, I might have a very good story."

Mr. Forrest fixed a stare on Beauregard. Tiny lines of tension, the lines of a general enduring insubordination from his own son, formed around his face. Finally he picked up the thin Saturday *Standard-Dispatch* and rattled it to where it fenced off the deserter.

Beauregard, frankly relieved at the break in eye contact, set the pistol down and walked back through the kitchen in search of coffee. He found the percolator unplugged. He glanced back at the table and noticed the open jar of instant coffee crystals.

His father, he remembered now, had an aversion to almost anything mechanical. He couldn't operate the microwave, couldn't program the VCR. He claimed the cruise control function on the Cadillac was lulling, therefore dangerous, but in truth he didn't know how to set it. He even had trouble operating the automatic tellers he'd pushed for so aggressively at the bank. Beauregard had always made the coffee, even before he was allowed to drink it, and the sight of his father reduced now to instant made him feel a little guilty for having moved out. His father could be a horse's ass—often was—but he didn't deserve instant. Beauregard made a mental note to call Althea. He'd get a timer for her and have her set the pot each night before going home. It wouldn't be fresh, with the coffee grounds sitting out all night; but it would sure taste better than instant.

Mr. Forrest only grunted from behind the newspaper when Beauregard announced that he had to be going. Beauregard paused at the door, awaiting some belated civility—"Good luck on your story," or something like that—but it didn't come. He let the screen door shut harder than usual and walked out to the party van.

The sun was coming up. The air was warmer, drier. If it didn't rain, as the paper had predicted, it would be a good day for a reenactment. The thought of having to track down this operative of Billy McArthur's, who might prove reluctant to talk or even hostile, who might even turn around and call McArthur, thus jeopardizing the whole story, now seemed quite a bit less appealing than dying on the reenactment battlefield or walking around the authentic camp with the Le Mat. It had to be done, though. Any advance at the paper and with Lorena depended on this story.

He drove to his apartment and closed the drapes against sunlight. Meaning to take a brief nap, he slept until noon. He awoke groggy and unable to remember anything about his dreams except that they were bad. He felt better after a sandwich and coffee. He would go to the museum and seek out this Bear Bryant look-a-like, this Dewey Simpkins. First, though, he returned to his bedroom and called Lorena. He cleared his throat as the dial tone sounded.

"Hello," she answered sleepily.

"Whatcha doing?" He instantly regretted both the obvious question and the falsely flip way he'd phrased it.

"Beauregard?"

"I'm sorry. I'll let you go back to sleep."

"I was just taking a little nap. What time is it?"

He looked at his clock radio's blue digital glow. "Half past noon. Sleep now. I'll call later."

"Oh, that's all right," she said, reviving a bit. "If it's that late, I really need to get up. . . . Hey, Beauregard, I tried to call you last night."

"You did?"

"I was going to suggest we do something. A movie or something. I wanted to see you. We've talked a lot, but I've about forgotten what you look like."

Beauregard sat up in bed. "I'll come over right now."

"No, Beauregard, that's okay. I've got things to do this afternoon."

"Tonight, then. That movie . . ."

"I can't tonight. I've got to get going on this paper for my history of Birmingham class." She yawned big into the phone. "Sorry. God, I *am* tired. I had to get up very early this morning."

"How come?"

"I had to proctor the ACT. Another office at the school board does the SAT, but we do the ACT, and it was my turn to help proctor. If my boss knew how much I hate standardized tests, I don't think she would have let me in the building. I'm subversive about it. I coughed all morning."

Beauregard hadn't yet told her he was supposed to take the SAT again in a few weeks. Nor had he told her about Washington and Lee. He started to tell her now, but on instinct held back. He trusted his sense of when not to talk. He'd developed tact, along with keen peripheral vision, during the many years with his father and Jackson.

115

"When did you have to be there for the test?" he asked.

"Seven-thirty," she said. "Which meant I had to get up at six-thirty. And I ended up staying out late last night. I ran into some people on Southside."

"No wonder you're tired."

Away from the receiver, where she couldn't hear, he hit the bed with a balled fist. He should have asked her out right away. Now she figured him—perhaps rightly—for a George B. McClellan. McClellan was the Yankee general who prepared thoroughly, sometimes brilliantly, but never seemed to attack, despite having an overwhelming advantage in troop strength. Beauregard couldn't bear to think of himself as a McClellan. It was late, but he would go on the offensive.

"How's Booger?" he asked transitionally.

"Fine. I'm looking at him right now."

"Lorena, we really should get together."

"We should," she said, but less emphatically. "I'll bet you're busy with that Atlanta story, though."

"That's true. I've got to try to interview a guy today."

"When's it going to be in the paper?"

"Soon, I hope. The big stories take longer. It's frustrating."

He waited, but she didn't affirm his frustration. Maybe she was nodding, but he couldn't see her. After an awkward silence she said, "Listen, Beauregard. I really better go. Call me when you have time."

"Okay, I will."

"Do."

"I just said I would."

Incredibly, he had snapped at her.

"All right, then," she said. "God."

Beauregard hit the bed again, then steadied himself. "I'm sorry, Lorena," he said. "I'm edgy. I was up late, too."

"Doing what?" she asked immediately.

He paused, encouraged that she cared. On the other hand, it was a little deflating to realize how easy it was for her to ask a tough question. He, the reporter, had to work up to such questions.

"I was at the paper most of the night," he said. "After that, I was over at my brother's."

"Oh," she said, prolonging the response as if she didn't quite approve, as if she knew, somehow, that hanging out at Jackson's

116

wasn't the highest, best use of Beauregard's time. "Well, get some rest, then," she said. "I'll talk to you later."

He hung up the phone and rolled back on the bed. This had not been a good conversation. Because he was on the phone so much these days, because success or failure as a reporter depended to so large a degree on reaching people and getting them to talk, he had begun to evaluate his phone conversations. This one was dog shit. Worse, the evidence was in that Lorena expected to see some important story by him in the paper. Someone as smart as she was would eventually figure out the nickname "B-Four." Even if she didn't, she was bound to run into some of the Midwesterners at a party or a club on Southside, and they would be happy to explain the nickname to her, at length and in much greater detail than they provided in their reports from city hall or the school board. He needed to work fast to lose the nickname or make it ironic. Pressure. He could feel the tiny hydraulic cranes along his shoulders begin to construct from the nearby muscles a model city skyline of tension.

Chapter Eleven

Light rain began to fall as Beauregard drove the party van to the Downtown Museum of Art. He flipped on the wipers. They squeaked badly but did the job. Only middling traffic this time of day in downtown Birmingham. Beauregard drove on, thinking about the task that faced him, about establishing a source.

Until he took the job at the newspaper, Beauregard had associated the word *source* with rivers and streams. Now he knew that a source was someone who gave a reporter valuable, hard-to-get information. The reporter knew the source's identity, but often no one else did, not even the city editor. The more sources a reporter had, the better. It was like SAT points, although a case could be made for having a few select sources—quality sources. Price had quality sources all over Birmingham. He had "courthouse sources," "police sources," "inside sources," "highly placed sources." Once, covering a dispute between two local grocers, he'd been delighted to quote "wholesale meat sources." Beauregard had no sources other than the Humane Society staff, and they'd talk to anybody. He wanted good sources just as he wanted front page and a beeper, but with Bubba Shealy sticking him with Pet of the Week, Metro Briefs, and obits, there had been no real need. He needed a good source now, though, to break the Atlanta story. Identifying this museum guard was the day's objective.

He parked on a side street, then hustled through rain toward the one-story, redbrick museum with the box holly shrubs and algae-covered fountain. He stepped inside and dropped a dollar in the padlocked donations box. On his left, in the glass-enclosed gift shop, he saw a handful of people fingering art posters and postcards. If he had time, he'd stop by there later. His apartment needed more decoration. He didn't know what Lorena liked in the way of posters. Something environmental or poetic, probably. He'd get a poster along those lines, maybe a couple of them, in case she ever came over again.

Only a few patrons joined him in the galleries. Two little tow-headed boys who looked like brothers giggled in front of an oil nude. Their mother, arriving late from the ladies room, shoved them toward the porcelain exhibit. It was quiet mostly, the only consistent sound the hush of the central air.

Beauregard wore a sports shirt, blue jeans, and white leather running shoes. His wallet rode one hip, a reporter's notebook the other. He followed his plan, pretending interest in the art of each room, pausing before one or two of its pieces, stepping back, then forward, then back again, squinting purposefully. He got into a rhythm—examine a painting or two, then smile at the room's guard, a friendly gesture that enabled him to see if the guard resembled Dewey Simpkins of McArthur's Bear Bryant campaign.

Strange about art, Beauregard thought, as he feigned thoughtful study of a murky landscape in the Early American room. At the newspaper *art,* like *source,* had its own definition. Art illustrated a story. "Got that wreck art?" Shealy would yell at a returning photographer. Art could be bar graphs of gasoline prices, mug shots of indicted politicians. On slow days photographers went looking for "feature art," wistful twilight shots of mothers swinging children in a park or old men playing checkers outside a barber shop. Editors cropped feature art as they did all other art. At the *Standard-Dispatch,* art had to fit.

Beauregard had gone through three rooms and three guards when he entered the Contemporary American room. He repeated his practice, this time examining a huge canvas, floor to ceiling, painted in a bathroom tile pattern of black and gold. Beauregard turned to find a guard to smile at. This one, he was startled to see, wore a houndstooth hat.

The guard dozed against a paneled wall in the narrow space between two abstract canvases. He wore a blue blazer over a white open-collared shirt and gray pants. His walkie-talkie was holstered.

He was a short, thin man with loose mottled skin and ears that jugged out from his houndstooth. He was a downsized Bear Bryant—the Bear at age sixty-two or win two hundred seventy-five, however one chose to measure. He was Dewey Simpkins. Beauregard could see the resemblance, the nameplate. The older man shook himself awake and met Beauregard's gaze. Beauregard smiled. The guard narrowed his eyes, suspicious.

Things were happening more quickly than Beauregard had planned. He'd really only meant to find his source today, not interview him. He'd planned to get Price in on that. Price would know just what to ask and how to ask it. Price began interviews softly, the subject's best friend, then gradually hardened them into inquisitions. Beauregard hadn't mastered the hardening part yet. Here came Simpkins, though. Rather than flee, Beauregard decided to wing it.

"Help you with anything?" the guard asked, more curious now than hostile. Even his voice was like Bryant's in the later years, a channel dredge that had forced the TV people to speed the tape on his telephone company commercials, because even Alabamians weren't understanding him.

"Well, uh, yes, that painting there," Beauregard said, spinning and pointing at a pink-and-blue abstraction. "Could you tell me a little more about it?"

"Like what?"

"Oh, I don't know. . . . How much is it worth?"

The guard glanced at it, his forehead lining deeply and skeptically below the rim of the houndstooth. "Hoss, if you're asking me personally, I wouldn't give you two dollars for it. Hell, I wouldn't clean fish on it. But other people, you know . . ." He looked right and left, making sure they were alone, then stepped toward Beauregard. "Tell you a little secret about that masterpiece, hoss. It hung upside down for two weeks."

"No," Beauregard said. "Really?"

"Hoss, I helped flip it!" He rotated his shoulders once to punctuate that revelation, then continued. "We had to flip it at night, after hours, the museum director and me. Somebody had sent him a letter that said, 'You got your painting upside down, hoss,' and in the envelope was a Xerox copy of it right side up, from some book or catalog or something."

The guard looked around the room, then stepped even closer. "Be honest," he went on, "I don't care for anything in here. Now

Room Ten's a good room. It's got our Remington, that bronze cowboy on a horse. *Nice* piece of work. Years ago, when I was at U.S. Steel and had tools to work with, I might have tried to make something like that. But this stuff in here is pitiful. Why guard it? Nobody comes in here. And check out those little plates by the paintings. Every last one says 'Anonymous Donor.' Hell, hoss, I don't blame 'em."

"Room Ten is good, though?"

"Room Ten." He had Beauregard by the arm now. Beauregard could smell alcohol on his breath, hear his dentures struggling to adhere. "I used to guard that room full time. That was my room. Then we got this new head of security, a colored guy, infirmative action. He makes us rotate."

"Could be worse," Beauregard said. "You could be in this room all the time."

The guard shook his head, impatient, as if Beauregard failed to understand. "See, hoss, I had a good thing going in Room Ten. I used to do wood carvings in that room. School groups would come in, I'd talk to 'em, explain things, show 'em my knife, let 'em take home some shavings. Believe me, they liked that better than anything else in this museum. But old Mr. Infirmative Action put a stop to all that. Said it wasn't professional. I told him I didn't think affirmative action was professional. I didn't say 'infirmative action.' I ain't *that* crazy. Anyway, next day we began to rotate. I'm in this prison cell three hours a day."

Beauregard didn't know how much sympathy to accord the guard's anecdote. He didn't have anything against affirmative action. On the other hand, he didn't want to end his chance for an important interview by being contrary. Price wouldn't. He'd heard Price express sympathy for all kinds of positions in the interest of securing an interview. He was for or against school prayer, gun control, a state lottery—all depending on whom he was talking to. Beauregard wasn't yet that limber, but he could at least maintain a studied neutrality. "Wood-carver, huh?" he said.

"Yeah." Simpkins reached into a blazer pocket and brought out a four-inch lacquered wood carving of Bear Bryant, complete with red jacket and houndstooth hat. He proudly handed it to Beauregard, who put it up to the light and admired it at different angles.

"Fifteen dollars," Simpkins said. "Plus tax, of course."

"Oh, no," Beauregard said, not bartering so much as reacting cautiously to the unexpected turn of events. "I couldn't. Really."

"Ten dollars, then. Screw the tax. Just screw it."

"Let me think about it."

No way did he want a Bear Bryant wood carving, but suggesting that he might buy one gave him leverage. "Hey," Beauregard said, as if the thought had just occurred to him. "Aren't you Dewey Simpkins, one of those Bear Bryants who did the pregame show a few years back?"

Recognition pleased the crusty guard. He took back the carving, said shyly, "I might be. Who wants to know?"

"I do," Beauregard said, pushing ahead. "I'm Beauregard Forrest. I work for the *Standard-Dispatch*."

The guard raised a mottled hand. "Whoa, hoss. This ain't no exposé of Bear, I hope."

"No, sir. Not of Coach Bryant. Certainly not."

" 'Cause he was a good man. I mean, he had his faults, of course, like the rest of us. He sure had a temper. And his language wasn't the prettiest I ever heard. And, as we all know, he dearly loved to pop a cork. But a good man. Say your little girl had a broken leg. You could run her down to Tuscaloosa and he'd sign the cast. He was never too busy for that, even before the Auburn game. I took Sonya a couple of times."

"He *was* a good man," Beauregard agreed, quietly reaching for his notebook.

"Raised money for all the big diseases," the guard said.

"I know."

" 'Course, now, he had those potato chip and telephone commercials, so I guess he could afford charity work. What I mean, it didn't put no big damn dent in his pocket, as it would have you and me. But he was a good man."

Beauregard tested his ballpoint on the first page of the notebook, then looked up and said as nonchalantly as he could, "Hey, how did Billy McArthur ever round up so many guys that look like Bear Bryant?"

The guard thought about it for a few seconds. Finally he said, "Hoss, I really don't know. I just wish he'd of checked with Bear first. Bear was *pissed*, let me tell you. I never seen one man so mad. He didn't hold it against us, though. What I mean, he signed our hats and everything."

The guard took off his houndstooth so Beauregard could see Bryant's bold scrawl on the leather band.

"Nice," Beauregard said. "Hey, you in on Billy's new deal? The Atlanta thing?"

The guard, looking into the bowl of his hat, chuckled low. "That damn Atlanta thing," he said. "Yeah, hell, I'm in it. I'm just crazy enough to be in it."

"When do you go over there?"

"Lord, I don't know. One day next week. I got the letter at the house." He put his hat back on, then looked at his watch. " 'Bout my break time, hoss. I got a ham sandwich waiting."

He tipped his houndstooth and started off toward the main corridor. Beauregard, on his heels, said, "Mind if I drop by your house tomorrow? We could talk some more. . . ."

The guard didn't look back, just rotated his shoulders again, which Beauregard took as a yes.

"Where is it?" he asked.

"Compton Road Trailer Park. Number sixteen. Name's on the mailbox."

Beauregard stopped and wrote that down. Then he called after the guard, shuffling down the hall, "Any particular time?"

"I'll be there!" The guard stopped and turned around. "No, wait. Come at two, hoss. I might ask you to give me a ride somewhere."

Beauregard spent the rest of the moist gray afternoon cleaning his apartment and putting up his new poster. He'd settled on a van Gogh, a flower thing, poetic *and* environmental. That evening he washed clothes. It was Saturday night, a grim hour for such a chore, but Beauregard went about it with curiosity, anticipation even. He'd never been to a Laundromat.

At New Arlington, all he'd had to do was put his clothes in the wicker hamper. He really hadn't had to do that—Jackson never had, instead just dropping things on the floor or, best case, draping them on a bed post or easy chair. But Beauregard felt that putting his clothes in the hamper was the least he could do for Althea. After all, she'd been good to him these many years, cooking macaroni and cheese the cheesy way he liked, pouring cherry sauce over his ham, stocking the refrigerator with Cokes, Dr. Pepper, Nutty Buddies, and ice cream sandwiches, applying first aid and sympathy as necessary. When he'd called her this afternoon, she'd done a mock boo-hoo about how old he was getting, then given him precise, bachelor-level instructions for how to wash, dry, and fold.

He chose the nearest of Southside's three public Laundromats. It was what Beauregard understood to be a basic Laundromat, quaking washers, incinerating dryers, hard plastic seats on which to sit and read religious tracts and orphaned sections of the *Standard-Dispatch*. Only a dozen or so people, women mostly, toiled under the harsh fluorescent lights. Beauregard found two washers together, separated his clothes into whites and colors, measured out and dumped in detergent, put quarters in the slot, and retreated with his red plastic basket.

He took a seat and thumbed through a *Standard-Dispatch* travel section. He read the Going, Going, Gone! column, this time about Nova Scotia, then got up and examined the Laundromat's bulletin board. On three-by-five-inch cards, people had printed advertisements for home improvements, Bible cassettes, tropical fish. A college student begged for a ride to New Orleans "any weekend."

Beauregard walked to the open door and watched the cars moving slowly down Highland Avenue in the light rain. Lorena would probably be in her apartment now, working on her history of Birmingham paper. He wanted to call her again, or maybe stop by with fresh coffee from the Southside Deli; but he wouldn't. It was too soon after the lousy phone conversation. He needed not to seem too desperate for her company. She might size him up as a B-Four in romance as well as journalism.

The transfer from washers to dryer went without incident. Beauregard sat down again and pulled a notebook from his hip pocket. He reviewed what he'd written in the party van after leaving the museum that afternoon.

> Dewey Simpkins—looks like Bear, but smaller . . . likes to talk . . . wood-carver . . . formerly with U.S. Steel . . . daughter—Saundra? Sonya? . . . meet at Compton Road Trailer Park, Sunday, 2 p.m.

Not a bad day's work. Tomorrow, if all went well, he'd gain Simpkins's confidence and establish him even more solidly as the inside source on the Atlanta campaign. Price would be amazed.

Beauregard's clothes still felt damp after the first cycle. He fed in another quarter and climbed on top of an idle washing machine. The clothes tumbled silently, clockwise, behind the dingy plastic window. Every so often an arm of his Confederate uniform would go by.

It was odd, ghostly even, to see the disembodied gray cloth rising and falling. He remembered the many B-grade deaths he'd seen on reenactment battlefields. His own were better, less conspicuous. His father had had him do a workshop on reenactment dying, and it had been well attended, some men taking notes, one guy video-taping. That was just last year, but it seemed far away now, looking as Beauregard was from the civilian perch of a Laundromat washing machine.

He hopped down and pulled open the dryer door. The clothes felt pleasantly warm and dry as he raked them into the plastic hamper. When he reached his Confederate uniform, though, it looked short. Wool. Hadn't Althea said something about wool? If she hadn't, she should have, because this uniform had shrunk by inches. Beauregard tossed it into the basket. There would be no reenacting for him anytime soon. If he ever did fight again, his father would be pleased by the shrunken uniform. Mr. Forrest preferred ill-fitting uniforms, big or small. He thought they more accurately reflected the make-do tenor of the times.

Chapter Twelve

Flickerwood was not Birmingham's oldest country club, but it was the oldest with a championship golf course and a progressive membership policy. Quite a few Jews and a handful of blacks belonged. Beauregard was proud that Mr. Forrest had been a force for change at Flickerwood. He'd even sponsored Taco Bob. According to Jackson, who had called last night with the report, Taco Bob would be at this Sunday lunch. Apparently Mr. Forrest saw in him a potential financial supporter for the governor's reelection campaign.

Beauregard, dressed in a fresh blazer, was the first of the Forrest party to arrive. He had some time, so he did something he hadn't done in ages. He walked all around, paying brief visits to the clubhouse, the pro shop, the garage, the grill. He saw old friends at every stop.

"That you, Beauregard?" "It's me, Tillman." . . . "Beauregard! Long time no see!" "Too long, Mr. Ben." . . . "Lookin' good, Beauregard." "Thanks, Dudley. It's the blazer." . . . "Give me a hug, Beauregard." "You know I will, Margaret. I've been missing your hugs."

Beauregard had spent a large part of his youth at Flickerwood. Summers, his father would drop him off in the early mornings, the dew still silvering the broad, oak-lined fairways. He'd play a quick eighteen holes, sometimes with a partner but usually alone, the

126

other privileged youth having slept much later. They'd wave at him from the first hole as he made his approach on eighteen. After his round, he'd swim for a while, then retire to the grill for a grilled cheese or club sandwich. Afternoons were for the driving range, the practice putting green, another round of golf. Along about dark his father would pull up in the Cadillac to fetch him home.

Some of this time was idyllic, some wasn't. He recalled with pleasure the whir of an electric golf cart under him, the metallic sound of a ball rimming then dropping into the cup, the wholesome soreness of his hands as he finished driving a third bucket of range balls. He could see the tumbler of Coke waiting for him at the grill, with crushed ice and two cherries, just the way Margaret knew he liked it.

On the other hand, none of the women at the club had seduced him. He kept waiting for it to happen. Jackson, who claimed to have been seduced four times, once by a college girl, three times by older women, insisted it was just a matter of time. All Beauregard had to do was be available, patient, and reasonably well groomed. So Beauregard would linger at the pool, toweling off longer than necessary, knotting and reknotting his trunk strings. Dressing for the grill, he'd try various colognes and levels of sideburns. Nothing worked. The women sat by themselves at the grill, loudly skewering absent friends and husbands. At the pool, they never flirted with Beauregard, never even lowered their bathing suit straps. When they spoke to him at all, it was to ask about Jackson or to see if Big Willie could come do some yard work.

Taco Bob arrived second for lunch, looking sharp in his charcoal gray suit and shiny wing tips. He wanted to know what to talk about with the governor, so Beauregard suggested a few safe topics, including Elvis Presley, who had been the governor's good friend. They chatted amiably by the gazebo until Mr. Forrest and Jackson arrived in separate cars. Then, just behind them, the governor's limousine and an accompanying state trooper's car rumbled down the brick driveway.

The governor hopped out of the limousine's backseat, then reached in for the coat to his pin-striped suit. He was a tall, broad man with a shock of black hair that cut boyishly across his pink forehead. He was smiling when he turned around. He always seemed genial and at ease with his old friends, the Forrests. The governor shook everyone's hand and slapped everyone's back, even Taco Bob's, though he'd just met him. They walked on into the club.

Their usual table was ready, but the governor wanted to shake more hands. He worked the room quickly, ducking under chandeliers, bending around lace-covered tables, shaking the hands of those men he didn't know well, massaging the necks of those he did, bussing old lady's cheeks, tousling young people's hair, telling everyone to come see him in Montgomery.

Finally they sat. Mr. Forrest had arranged for a quick serving, and now the white-jacketed waiters came with individual plates of roast beef, green beans, white rice, and corn pudding. They brought bread baskets, too, and two cut-glass pitchers of iced tea, sweetened and unsweetened.

The governor sat at the head of the table, Mr. Forrest and Jackson on either side, then farther down, not banished exactly, but at a slightly lower table leaf, Beauregard and Taco Bob. As always, the talk was apolitical—nothing Beauregard could write about or share with Price. It started with Alabama football, then went to Auburn football, then to the approaching deer hunting season, then to the crazy music the governor's children listened to, then to his father, eighty-three now and ornery as ever. Pleasant conversation. Mr. Forrest and Jackson submerged their animosity in the interest of a friendly lunch with the governor.

"Pass the salt when you get a chance, Jackson," Mr. Forrest said.

"Certainly, Dad. Be glad to."

"Thanks, Jackson."

"You're welcome, Dad. Anytime."

Eventually an attempt was made to include Taco Bob. The governor, between bites of roast beef, initiated it.

"Great country, America, isn't it, Bob?"

Taco Bob hurried to swallow a forkful of green beans. "Yes, governor," he said eagerly. "Great country. Very great. Yes, yes."

"Whereabouts you from in Vietnam?"

"Saigon, governor."

"That so." The governor wiped gristle from his mouth with a cloth napkin. "I was there once, years ago," he said. "Me and ten other young congressmen. A fact-finding trip. We went out in the field some, but mostly we stayed in Saigon." He grinned at Jackson. "You talk about a party town."

"Roll Tide," Jackson said.

Taco Bob cleared his throat, then raised a fork to get the floor.

He looked at the governor. "I have King jukebox," he announced importantly.

Beauregard, recognizing the governor's confusion, said, "He means an Elvis Presley jukebox. Every song on it is by Elvis, governor."

"I see."

"You knew Elvis?" Taco Bob encouraged.

"Knew him?" the governor said, wounded that anyone, even someone from Vietnam, would have to ask. "Bob, Elvis was a dear friend of mine. See, when I got out of law school I clerked for Judge Hoskins in Memphis. The judge lived up the road from Graceland, and he introduced me to Elvis. We shot pool together many times. I eventually left Memphis, of course, came back to Alabama, but we stayed in touch through the years. In fact, Elvis called me six months before he died. Wanted to give me a Cadillac. I said, 'Elvis, buddy, I got two already.' He just laughed."

"Great man, King," Taco Bob said.

"A musical genius." The governor had been buttering a bread stick but stopped now and pointed the slick blade at Taco Bob. "I wish to God Elvis had been born in Alabama instead of Mississippi. I swear I'd build him a monument as tall as Washington's. Hell, I'd raise taxes for it."

"Hank Williams was born in Alabama," Jackson said, refilling his iced-tea glass. "At least we can claim credit for him."

The governor, frowning, went back to buttering his corn bread stick. "I guess so," he said without enthusiasm. "I never much liked that real twangy shit."

"The iced-tea pitcher, Jackson? When you're through . . ."

"Here go, Dad."

"Thanks, Jackson."

"My pleasure."

Lunch broke up after strawberry shortcake. Mr. Forrest announced that he and the governor would be adjourning to New Arlington to drink coffee and talk more. Beauregard knew they would be talking politics. Mr. Forrest advised the governor informally, particularly on financial affairs, but also on other issues. He'd helped him on an educational matter soon after the governor took office. The governor, nothing if not bold, had wanted to offer Harvard land and tax breaks in exchange for building an adjunct campus somewhere, anywhere, in the state. If Harvard wouldn't come, he'd go to Yale, then to Princeton, and on down the Ivy

League. Mr. Forrest and other cool heads had talked him out of it. Good thing, too, Beauregard thought. Something like that would make the wires—would become a front-page "brite" in newspapers all over the country.

The governor wanted to see what the pro shop had in the way of graphite drivers, so Jackson and Taco Bob walked him there. Beauregard and Mr. Forrest strolled through the flower gardens, lingering finally by the gazebo. It was muggy out. They removed their coats, then leaned back against the shaded wood structure.

"I wrote Washington and Lee last night," Mr. Forrest said.

"Yes?"

"I want them to take you winter term, providing you do well enough on the SAT."

Beauregard turned toward his father, to make sure he was serious. Then he grabbed his arm. "Dad," he said, "I'm not sure I want to go that soon."

"Why not?"

"I've got a lot going on here."

"You don't mean that little job at the paper."

"That's exactly what I mean."

Mr. Forrest stared at Beauregard, then pulled his hand away. "Since I'll be paying your tuition, room and board, *and* spending money," he said with measured condescension, "I think it's only fair that I should have some little bit of say in when you go."

"Dad, listen . . ."

Mr. Forrest raised a hand. "Not now, Beauregard. Here comes the governor."

The governor, Taco Bob, and Jackson were indeed out of the pro shop and walking briskly toward them. The governor and Taco Bob walked ahead, Jackson just behind. Later Jackson would report that two things had been settled as the governor wiggled drivers in the pro shop. Taco Bob would contribute to the governor's reelection campaign, and the governor would cut the ribbon at the grand opening of the bed and barbecue. He'd even spend grand opening night there, in the Alabama Room, his campaign schedule and the first lady permitting.

Compton Road Trailer Park was in an old commercial district of east Birmingham. Discount water bed outlets and auto body repair shops hugged the weedy corners, their yellow trailer signs blinking and blocking the vision of motorists pulling out from side streets.

Beauregard, arriving from Flickerwood Country Club, was right on time for his appointment with Dewey Simpkins. He pulled into the trailer park, continuing down the narrow gravel strip until he saw the guard's trailer: a big sugar cube up on cement blocks. Beauregard got out of the van and walked to the door. He knocked.

"Who is it?" the museum guard yelled from within.

"Beauregard Forrest, *Standard-Dispatch*."

"Door's open."

Beauregard stepped inside, then looked left into the tiny kitchen. A stack of dirty dishes tottered in the sink. Cans of baked beans lined the unpapered shelf above. There was an odor from an overflowing trash can. It wasn't too bad, wasn't reeking, but it nonetheless hastened Beauregard's turn back to the living room on his right.

There, on the Naugahyde sofa, on the folding chairs, in the windowsills, on the linoleum floor, everywhere, stood four-inch lacquered wood carvings of Bear Bryant. The sight of the silent, unblinking houndstooth nation unnerved Beauregard. He felt as if he'd stepped into one of his bad dreams.

"Got a few left over," the guard said, bustling out from the back room.

"You sure do, Mr. Simpkins," Beauregard said.

" 'Dewey,' please."

"All right. 'Dewey.' And I'm 'Beauregard.' "

"Let's go, Beauregard."

"Where?"

"Perkins Field."

"You'll have to show me."

"I will. You bet I will. Mawn."

Simpkins wore plain black shoes, gray stretch pants, a blue short-sleeved dress shirt and a red Alabama baseball cap. His front pocket bulged with a pouch of chewing tobacco. His left hand held a tall beer can covered partially by a paper sack. As they drove, he sat on the edge of the party van's front seat, eyes focused forward, head jerking as necessary to give directions. At stoplights he'd swing open his door and drill the pavement with a brown rope of tobacco juice, an act he performed in one continuous motion, door swinging out, juice bisecting the open space, door swinging back. Beauregard admired the feat and told him, but Dewey wasn't

131

receiving compliments. His mind was on wherever they were going.

"All right, that's the ballpark up there," he said. "Get in the right-hand lane."

Perkins Field was a city ballpark, old but tidy. When they'd parked, Beauregard followed Simpkins to a spot along the waist-high, chain-link fence that bordered right field. Simpkins spit out the plug of tobacco juice and opened the tall beer. He took a sip, then leaned over the fence. Beauregard leaned with him.

A young women's softball game was under way. Slow pitch, but Beauregard could tell by the way they snapped the ball around that they knew their sport well. They had uniforms—one team green and white, the other red. Maybe a dozen fans occupied the bleachers behind home.

"Who's playing?" Beauregard asked.

"My daughter's team. Sonya's team. That's Sonya at third."

She was a tall, heavy girl with a long braid of orange hair that swung coast to coast along her broad back as she shifted weight and popped her glove with her right fist. Beauregard figured she was about his age, maybe a year older. She was all hunched over in her green-and-white uniform, awaiting a hot one.

"We could get closer than this," Beauregard said.

Dewey shook his head. "I ain't really supposed to be here," he said. "I ain't supposed to have nothing to do with Sonya. Her mama and me been fighting a long time."

"Oh."

"So we'll just stay right here."

Dewey watched Sonya as carefully as a professional scout would a major league prospect, his concentration breaking only for quick sips from his beer sack. Between innings, Beauregard tried to ask about Billy McArthur's Atlanta campaign, but Dewey was absorbed even by the warm-up tosses and would not respond.

It was broilingly hot along the metal fence. Right field wasn't shaded at all. Nor was the electric scoreboard lit, so Beauregard couldn't tell how far along the game was. It could be the ninth inning, it could be the third or fourth. It could be game one of a doubleheader. Beauregard had filled in once for the *Standard-Dispatch* team in a Media League doubleheader. The struggling little AM radio station they'd been scheduled to play was short on players and so had to forfeit the games officially. But they insisted on playing anyway, for the fun of it. Shorthanded, they'd tagged the *Standard-Dispatch* for eleven runs in the top of the first. Trotting in from center field, Price had told Beauregard and the rest of the dispirited *Standard-Dispatch* squad, "Let's get those meaningless runs back!" It had been hot that day, too, but at least right field, where the Midwestern manager had stuck Beauregard, had been mostly shaded. No such luck today.

Beauregard loosened his tie, rolled up his sleeves. This was the unglamorous part of investigative reporting, the part described much better in the book *All the President's Men* than in the Redford and Hoffman movie. Beauregard knew he should try to focus on the game. That way he'd have something to talk to Dewey about later. Price-like, he could ease the conversation from Sonya's performance to the McArthur operation. But Beauregard couldn't concentrate. Even over the rhythmic infield chatter *("You can't hit it! You never could hit it!")* he kept hearing his father's bombshell about early admission to Washington and Lee.

What would Lorena think? He hadn't mentioned W&L to her. He hadn't even mentioned that he was about to take the SAT, she was so touchy about it. Earlier, when the subject of college came up, he'd boasted that newspaper work was an education in itself but conceded that he might take classes at UAB eventually. She'd made the case for UAB's night school—the students were older, more motivated, full of practical advice and unusual perspectives. This history of Birmingham class, for example—some of the students had actually been in the 1963 children's demonstrations called for by Martin Luther King, Jr. They talked with authority about all that had gone on. Beauregard told her a class like that sounded good, and it did, and if this early admission situation hadn't come up, his father might even have let him take a course or two at UAB, as practice for W&L. Now, though, W&L was not only inevitable but imminent.

Simpkins elbowed him gently and pointed a mottled finger out toward the field. "Think they're lesbians?"

Beauregard, ambushed by the word and the fact that the museum guard, of all people, was using it, said, "Lord, Dewey. You can't tell somebody's sexual preference just by looking at them." He looked at the women, including Sonya, now taking her cuts in the batter's box. "Certainly not from way out here," he added.

"I don't think Sonya likes men," Dewey said with surprising detachment. "I know she's not real crazy about me. We were close when she was young, but later on, after her mama and me broke

133

up, it wasn't so good anymore. She fell in with this crowd here. Even though the judge told me not to, I try to go see her, try to call, but she don't want any part of it."

"She's just busy, Dewey."

"No, hoss. It's much, much more than that." He took a long drink from the sack, then wiped his mouth with his sleeve. "I honestly don't know what to do about it. I do know this, though. She's one hell of a softball player. You ask anybody in Birmingham softball about Sonya Faye Simpkins."

Just then, as if to prove the point, Sonya drove a low, outside pitch high over the left field fence. To cheers from her dugout and the stands, she tossed her bat and began loping toward first base, right fist thrust in the air.

"Hey, hey," Beauregard said, a little caught up. "She knocked the cover off that one, Dewey. Roll Tide!"

Beauregard expected an echoing "Roll Tide!" but instead saw Dewey beginning to climb the fence. The guard tumbled over, managing somehow to keep the beer sack erect.

"Dewey?" Beauregard said. "Dewey, what are you doing?"

But the guard had gotten to his feet and begun to run out toward the diamond his daughter rounded in triumph. He caught up with her, beer spilling now, as she reached second base. She hadn't noticed him until he fell in step.

Beauregard thought it was odd enough, the sight of someone jogging onto the field to circle the bases with a home run hitter in a softball game. It was even odder to see Sonya stop, pull away from her father, and scream right into his face *"No!"* with a visceral force that rivaled rebel yells Beauregard had heard on reenactment battlefields. Dewey staggered back as if shot by pistol at close range. Sonya glared at him, then trotted on toward third and home. Her teammates, quiet during the actual confrontation, erupted in applause. Beauregard decided they were cheering her rebuttal of the old man as much as her swat of the ball over left field.

Dewey, head down, turned now and walked slowly back toward the right field fence. It seemed to take forever for him to get there. Whatever adrenalin had propelled him the first time was all gone. Once Beauregard had helped him over the fence, the guard kept walking toward the party van.

"Ready to go, Dewey?" Beauregard called after him.

The guard just kept walking.

They didn't talk on the way back, nor did Dewey chew tobacco.

Every so often he would clinch his beer sack, as if a chill or mild electric shock had passed through him. Beauregard, seeing this peripherally, felt bad, too. It was as if Sonya's *"No!"* continued to resonate for both of them. Maybe the rejection was justified, maybe Dewey was reaping the bitter harvest of a neglectful or just plain screwy fatherhood; but Beauregard was sticking with him. He didn't seem like such a bad guy now. Besides, Beauregard needed a source.

When they got back to the trailer, he cut the engine and turned toward the museum guard, staring now at the floorboard.

"Dewey," he said. "I want to do a story on this Atlanta business with McArthur. I need your help. In fact, I want to come with you to Atlanta. That's the only way I can do this story right."

It took a few seconds for the request to sink in. Then Dewey looked over, face wrinkled in disbelief. "You want to come with me?"

"Yeah," Beauregard said. "Sure I do."

The guard shook his head. "Find somebody else, hoss. Somebody better."

"I want you, Dewey. Really. It's important."

More seconds passed. Then, rallying a little, the guard lifted his head and sniffed. "Well, if it's important," he said conditionally. "I *did* check that letter from McArthur. We leave tomorrow morning."

"Tomorrow?"

"Yep." He grinned, more himself. "You got a hat?"

"No, Dewey."

"That's all right. I got an extra houndstooth you can wear. Not the signed one, though. Nobody wears my signed one."

"I understand," Beauregard said.

"Mawn in the house," Simpkins said, squeezing the door handle. He was all the way back now. "Let's just make sure the spare fits."

Beauregard was in no hurry to smell Dewey's kitchen or see all those wooden Bear Bryants, but he would do what was necessary to get this story. He climbed out of the van and followed his newly established, highly placed source into the little white trailer.

135

Chapter Thirteen

Bubba Shealy's small, green, windowless office was cluttered with AP Stylebooks, which he handed out with rite-of-passage solemnity to interns and new hires. Tacked to the wall was an Auburn football calendar containing not only a schedule and numerical roster but also personal information about key players, their majors and favorite foods, mostly business and ham.

Beauregard and Price sat in the hard plastic chairs facing Shealy's desk.

"I don't know, guys," the city editor said. He was leaned forward, his elbows on a stack of yellow forms reporters filled out to get reimbursed for gas mileage. He wore a long-sleeved white dress shirt, monogrammed at the cuffs; but pimento cheese stained his necktie and brass cuff links. "This whole damn thing just sounds so farfetched. Even for Billy McArthur."

"No, Bubba," Price said, leaning forward himself. "This is just like McArthur. He's always this extreme. Remember the Michener thing?"

"Oh, God," Shealy said, squeaking back in his swivel chair, putting his hands behind his broad head, chuckling low. "The Michener thing."

"What Michener thing?" Beauregard asked.

"This was years ago, B-Four," Price said, turning toward him. "And we never could get it on the record. But apparently McAr-

136

thur tried to talk James Michener into doing a novel on Birmingham. McArthur thought that would be the perfect way to promote the city. It'd be a fat novel, millions of copies, in grocery stores and airports everywhere, and it'd be called *Birmingham!*, with an exclamation mark. He was going to set Michener up with research assistants, give him office space, a townhouse on Southside, a nice car. All Michener had to do was write fifteen hundred pages about Birmingham and put that exclamation mark in the title. Of course, like most of McArthur's ideas, it didn't work out. Michener sent a letter back saying he didn't do cities, only states and countries."

"I remember when *Alaska* came out," Beauregard said.

"Yeah," Price said. "And *Texas*. And *Poland*."

"I wouldn't have read *Birmingham!*" Shealy said, grinning again. "I'd have just read the Cliffs Notes."

Price laughed, then said, "I'd have *skimmed* the Cliffs Notes."

"Me, too," Beauregard said, grinning and keeping up.

"I always skimmed 'em at Auburn," Shealy said. "Old Cliff goes on way too long."

They all laughed now, Shealy so hard his aspirin bottle shook. Beauregard felt a sudden, cheering solidarity with Shealy and Price, an esprit de corps. It was good to be crowded with them and the AP Stylebooks in Shealy's little office. Beauregard shared their hard-bitten newspaperman's impatience with the pretentious and long-winded in life, with any story that couldn't be banged out under deadline with a hook opening and a tight nut graph and a snap-shut quote at the end. Nothing any of them wrote would ever have to be Cliffs noted.

The laughter died down.

"I just don't know," Shealy was saying again. "It still seems pretty damn farfetched. Birmingham men holding up traffic in Atlanta?"

"Give B-Four one day to check it out," Price said.

"What am I going to do for Metro Briefs?"

"I'll handle Metro Briefs."

Shealy shook his head, not in opposition to the plan—which was destined, because of Price's insistence and clout as senior reporter, to go forward—but in weary recognition of the manpower consequences. He looked at Price first, then at Beauregard. "One day," he said grimly, extending a thick index finger for emphasis. He rose from the squeaky chair and went back out to the newsroom.

Price and Beauregard did a high five behind his back, then

137

followed him, the other reporters watching and no doubt wondering what was up. Beauregard had gone by Price's rental house the night before to tell him about establishing Dewey Simpkins as a source. They'd drunk a toast with instant coffee, then Price, pacing the small, book-lined living room, had decided they should let Shealy know they had a good tip on McArthur. They wouldn't let on about Beauregard going to Atlanta, though, because Shealy would want Price to go. No, the thing to do was to make Shealy think Beauregard would spend the day knocking around Birmingham, asking questions, trying to get someone to talk. Meanwhile, he'd really be on his way with the Bear Bryants. If all went well, he'd file a story from Atlanta. Shealy would grumble, but he wouldn't have any choice but to run such a strong story on the front page, under Beauregard's byline. Price had an AP photographer friend in Atlanta who owed him a favor. He'd lean on him to shoot pictures of the Bear Bryants holding up traffic.

Once again, as he'd done before Sewanee, Price walked Beauregard to the parking lot. The climbing sun barely shone through the cover of gray clouds, but it was still hot and humid out, still a day to doff blazers. Beauregard tossed his over the passenger's seat of the party van, then climbed back out for final instructions.

"Get all the details you can," Price said.

"I will."

"And when you're in Atlanta, try to get a handle on whether you're really making the traffic situation worse. See what kind of a backup there is. Count cars, if you have to."

"Will do."

"Call me if some problem comes up. Call tonight, regardless."

"I will, Price. I just hope everything goes okay."

"You'll do fine. This is front page, B-Four. I can feel it."

They shook hands now, a firm, lingering handshake with some emotion in it, not unlike those Beauregard remembered from just before Malvern Hill and Pickett's Charge and other scripted re-enactments in which his side was about to be decimated. Price, no doubt, meant the handshake to be encouraging. It was clear that he cared intensely about this assignment. He'd been fairly lethargic in recent weeks, grumbling about money and his inability to buy the house he was renting. Just this past week, when he and Beauregard had done the Thursday shuffle to the bank to cash their paychecks, Price had held his up and asked aloud, "Why can't it be more?" It was like a philosophy question, the way he'd said it. Everyone in the teller's line had stared at him. But this Atlanta story, with its elements of intrigue, had him fired up again. He'd vowed last night to get started soon on his long-delayed series, "People Who Have Jobs at the Courthouse but Don't Really Do Anything."

Beauregard, excited, too, but also feeling pressure to produce, guided the party van out of the parking lot and onto the street that would carry him to west Birmingham and the Birmingham Boosters office. He glanced at his watch and saw that he was early. The Bear Bryants wouldn't be gathering for another twenty minutes. He was undercover, sort of, and didn't want to be the first to arrive; so on the way he killed time by pulling over at a strip shopping center with a convenience store and florist's shop. In a corner phone booth, he dialed Lorena's work number. He would tell her he was on his way to Atlanta.

But the receptionist said Lorena wasn't at her desk; she was in the basement, filing. She'd be down there all morning and most of the afternoon. No, Beauregard couldn't talk to her, because the basement had no phone extension. He could leave a message and hope Lorena saw it and called him on break. Beauregard declined the offer, feeling bad as he hung up. Here he was, about to embark on a reportorial adventure, to Atlanta, no less, and Lorena was in the basement filing. It was probably a dank, dimly lit basement with exposed pipes, abandoned office equipment, rat droppings in the corners. She was probably bent over a file cabinet, the bulging manila folders making vicious paper cuts in her fingers and hands. He knew about paper cuts. The morgue files were knives. Walking back to the van, he again noticed the florist's shop. He looked at his watch: There was time. He stepped inside and ordered a dozen roses sent to Lorena at her office. She'd have a bouquet on her file cabinet by early afternoon—Roll Tide!—and a "Fondly, Beauregard" note as well.

The Birmingham Boosters headquarters was in a squat, featureless, cream-colored building with a cartoonish plywood sign of a thermometer on the front lawn. Every so often a handyman with a paintbrush would raise the mercury level, to show progress in the Booster's year-round membership drive. Beauregard parked behind the building in a sloping asphalt lot with speed bumps and faded yellow lines. He had to park way down the hill, because all the near-in spots were filled by a fleet of amber, late-model Buick Electras.

Standing around the building's back door, looking like early birds for a soup kitchen, were a dozen or so men dressed in faded blazers and houndstooth hats: the Bear Bryants. They were of different heights, different ruined postures; but the striking thing was the concentration of identical hats. Beauregard had seen lone men around town in houndstooths, stumbling out of bars and leaning against lampposts, no doubt coaching with the help of cheap whiskey their own imaginary Alabama teams to Sugar Bowl victories and national championships; but he'd never seen a whole bunch of them. The sight was unnervingly like Dewey Simpkins's mobile home gallery of wood carvings. Beauregard, advancing up the lot toward the building, put on his own houndstooth and blazer. He'd waited until now to put on the hat, because he didn't want to risk a Midwesterner, any newspaper employee, really, seeing him topped this way. Now, though, his hat and a pair of wire-rimmed sunglasses in place, he was able to stand with the much older men and not feel too conspicuous. Dewey Simpkins picked him out, but the others went on talking, smoking, and sipping coffee on the lawn beside the back door.

"Mornin', hoss," Dewey said.

"Mornin', Dewey."

"Ready to roll?"

"I think so. How do I look?"

Dewey studied him for a second, then stepped forward and adjusted the angle of Beauregard's houndstooth way down, almost to his eyebrows, Bryant style. "Better." He turned and pointed to one of the Buicks. "We'll be in that jewel there, you and me," he said.

"Nice," Beauregard said.

"You better believe it's nice." Dewey spoke proudly, as if he'd purchased or even had a hand in designing the sleek vehicle. "It's got a big damn engine," he said. "Leather seats, whitewall tires. Hoss, it's got cruise control. We'll ride like kings!"

Just then Billy McArthur, dressed in a white button-down shirt, a narrow silver tie, and a brilliant green blazer, emerged from the back door with a clipboard. Someone had flipped a wooden crate over for him, and he stepped onto it, for height and authority. Although nattily attired, McArthur looked flush this morning, haggard. He studied his clipboard briefly, then squinted out at the assembly in front of him, as if they were a morning sun waking him to hangover.

McArthur was shaking his head now, the spittled corners of his mouth turned down judgmentally.

"Why are you wearing your houndstooth hats?" he called out. "This isn't the Bear Bryant operation. That was years ago. I told you in the letter that the Atlanta operation is one hundred percent different from the Bear Bryant operation. If anything, it messes us up for you men to be wearing those hats. Lord God a'mighty. Can't you men follow even the simplest instructions?"

The men, embarrassed, shuffled. Then, in a subtle but perceptible shift, the shuffling turned angry. One of the Bryants turned to another and said aloud, "Why can't we wear our hats?" Another one, to Beauregard's left, yelled, "What difference does it make, *McArthur?*"

The misterless use of McArthur's last name worked like lighter fluid on the Bryants' smoldering resistance, prompting applause, hoots, and derisive whistling. Dewey had told Beauregard that they were all former U.S. Steel employees, card-carrying union men. They had performed McArthur's last assignment only out of respect for Coach Bryant. They didn't much care for McArthur, hatchet man of the antilabor Boosters.

"All right, all right," McArthur said, hands way up as if he'd been arrested. "Wear the damn hats. I just hope nobody in Atlanta notices that today's traffic jams are all being caused by men in houndstooths. All right. The Electras are in the lot, where I said they'd be. The keys are in them. They all have central air and FM radio, as you requested."

"Are they demos?" one man asked.

"Well, yeah," McArthur said.

"I *figured* they'd be demos." The man folded his arms and looked around, apparently expecting the demo revelation to incite the men further, but it didn't.

"All right," McArthur went on, "remember my instructions. Drive to your appointed intersections, pop your hoods, lean over your engines, and look perplexed. If a cop shows up, tell him a wrecker's on the way. When rush hour is over you can come back to Birmingham. I'll be at Tidwell's Buick all evening to collect the keys and pay you. There's an envelope in each glove compartment with twenty dollars for spending money and twenty-five dollars for gas. You lose an hour when you cross the state border, but you should have plenty of time for lunch and maybe even a little sight-seeing before rush hour. But don't be late."

141

"When do we get paid?" one of the men asked.

"When you get back. I just said that."

"He don't hear too good," someone explained.

McArthur, studying his clipboard again, muttered, "That's his problem. . . . I guess that's everything. All right, I want to close with a few words of inspiration. Men, we're in an uphill battle against Atlanta on this economic thing. So many people from Birmingham go to Atlanta for sports events, concerts, shopping. You probably hadn't thought about this, but a lot of Birmingham couples take their honeymoons and second honeymoons in Atlanta. How many Atlantans do you think honeymoon in Birmingham? Hell, my own wife takes our little boy Billy over there to buy clothes and ride the Pink Pig around the toy department at Rich's department store. I can't blame her. For years, I've tried to interest the department stores here in a mechanical animal, a pig or a big squirrel, for the children to ride around the toy departments. They won't do it. Or they say they'll get back to me, only they never do. Meanwhile, our wives and children go off to Atlanta and come back with little 'I Rode the Pink Pig' stickers. So you can see that the work you're doing today is very important. Anything we can do to point out Atlanta's weaknesses—and traffic is the big one— works to Birmingham's advantage. It won't be easy standing in the middle of those intersections. It's a hot day, and there'll be fumes. But the Pig, men. Remember the Pig."

McArthur was sweating like one now, a pig, a stuck one. He dug into his pants pocket for a white handkerchief, which he used to mop his neck and forehead. Beauregard stood waiting with the older men. He'd ridden that Pink Pig a couple of times, visiting his Atlanta cousins, but hadn't thought about it in years until just last night. Price had mentioned McArthur's obsession with the Pig. He'd said that if McArthur ever did get Birmingham a pig, somebody here would probably steal it and barbecue it. Then, more seriously, he'd said that that was the trouble with McArthur, he wouldn't take advantage of barbecue and the city's other inherent strengths, instead trying to import toy department rides, theme parks, and French restaurants like Ooh La La. Price thought Taco Bob would be a better Birmingham Booster.

"All right, men," McArthur said, softening as he put away the handkerchief. "I know I gave you a hard time about those hats. Cut me some slack on that. I certainly didn't mean anything disrespectful to the memory of Coach Bryant. In fact, I'll send you off with a quotation from Coach. Coach often said, 'If you won't be beat, you can't be beat.' Think about that as you're driving to Atlanta. I'll see you when you get back."

After an awkward Nixonian salute-wave, he stepped off the crate and went back into the building. The men stood around for a second, then began to move toward the Buicks. The pace of the walking picked up the closer they got. There was a "Gentlemen: Start your engines!" feel in the air that had the old men and Beauregard hopping.

Dewey, striding ahead of Beauregard, called back, "What the hell did McArthur mean, hoss? 'If you can't be beat, you won't be beat.' "

"It's the other way around," Beauregard said.

"Still."

"I think it just means try hard."

Dewey, reaching the passenger's side of their Buick, shook his head. "I don't believe Bear Bryant ever said that. One of his assistant coaches *might* have. Not Bear. Bear Bryant always made good sense."

They got into the car and pulled into the line of vehicles moving herky-jerky from the parking lot. Drivers tested wipers, headlights, brakes. "I'm happy to take the first leg," Beauregard said, adjusting the seat and rearview mirror. "We can switch off at Anniston. That's about halfway."

"No, hoss. You got to drive all legs," Dewey said, buckling his shoulder strap. "See, I lost my license a while back. A cop pulls me over now and I'm in big trouble. To be honest, I don't know what I'd have done if you hadn't shown up. I guess I'd have risked it. But I'm real happy for you to do the honors."

"McArthur didn't check your license?"

"He didn't check nothing. Hey, you don't mind driving, do you? I mean, I'm giving you this story and everything."

"No, Dewey. It's fine. Really. I like driving."

Beauregard followed the long line of amber Electras down a surface street that would lead them to the interstate that ran east to Atlanta. The thing was, he did mind about driving, at least a little. It was true that he liked driving, and that the distance to Atlanta, three hours, was nothing compared with distances he'd driven himself and his father to reenactments; but he'd hoped to have some time to take notes on the trip. There might be a detail or two in the scenery or the weather or Dewey's thoughts that would make all the difference in his story. Color, editors called it. "Where's the color?" Shealy would yell at the Midwesterners, who were notoriously short on it. Beauregard prided himself on his ability to find color in even a Pet of the Week; but he was at a disadvantage now, because he was driving and couldn't take notes. Billy McArthur, with typical care, had hired a driver who didn't have a license.

The Electras began to separate once they got out on the interstate. Beauregard ignored the cruise control but kept a fairly steady speed. Dewey got out his chewing tobacco, only this time he spit into a paper cup, not out the door as he'd done during their brief trip to the softball field.

He talked between expectorations about how lucky he'd once been. Fifteen years ago he'd had a new house, a new car, an old truck, the good job at U.S. Steel. Once in late June he'd worked an overnight shift, then driven the truck to Daytona Beach to meet Jeanette and little Sonya, who'd been at the Smiling Dolphin Motel all week. They had a fine day at the beach, a fine night at a seafood restaurant, and the next morning they headed back to the beach, all three of them slick with Coppertone. As Dewey helped Sonya build a sand castle, Jeanette waded out in the surf only to have a big wave wash her glasses right off her. Badly nearsighted, she'd stumbled back, crying to Dewey that she wouldn't be able to drive her car to Birmingham. It was Sunday, she'd wailed, no optometrist would be open, she was supposed to be back at work first thing Monday, she might get fired. Dewey waded out to where he thought the wave had ambushed her. For an hour, to the sound of the surf and of Jeanette yelling that it was no use, that people on the beach were laughing at him, he dived down looking for the glasses. Down and down he went into the greenish brown murk, gulls mocking from overhead. Finally he brought up a pair. They'd all cheered and hugged one another, even people on the beach had cheered, until Jeanette noticed the glasses weren't hers.

"Good Lord, Dewey," Beauregard said, glancing over. "You must have been crushed."

"No, hoss. Here's the thing. They weren't her glasses, but the prescription was so close she was able to drive back."

"Dewey," Beauregard said skeptically. He thought about it for another half mile. "Really?"

"A five-hour drive back to Birmingham, and she didn't even

have a headache," Dewey said. "That's the kind of luck I had back then."

Beauregard pressed on in the Electra, passing tractor-trailer trucks going uphill, getting passed by them going down. Dewey pressed on, too, elaborating on the years after he got laid off by U.S. Steel, the debts he couldn't pay, the foreclosed house, boat, car, and truck, the fights with Jeanette, her leaving him, Sonya's estrangement, his struggle with the bottle. Finally, outside of Anniston, he spit his wad of tobacco, tipped his hat all the way over his eyes, and dropped off to sleep. Beauregard was relieved. His reservoir of sympathy, of "uh-huhs" and nods, was all tapped out. They drove on through eastern Alabama, passing a Last Chance Fireworks! stand, then another, then swept across the border into Georgia.

Georgia, the Peach State. Beauregard's father had a whole catalog of prejudices, including predictable ones against Ralph Nader and the United Nations, less predictable ones against the Red Cross and the "prevent" defense in football; but he reserved some of his greatest disdain for the state of Georgia. He still did business over there, and he and Beauregard reenacted yearly at the Battle of Jonesboro, south of Atlanta; but Mr. Forrest railed against what he called "Georgia condescension" toward their own home state. He particularly disliked Georgians saying "thank God for Alabama," an old reference to Alabama's even lower health and education statistics. A lot of Alabamians thanked God for Mississippi, but not Mr. Forrest. He tried to be consistent in his prejudice. Beauregard shared a little of that prejudice, having had to spend time around his Atlanta cousins. They couldn't stop talking about Atlanta, its major league teams, triple-deck shopping malls, seventy-story hotels, international airport, rapid transit system, status as regional hub for so many national and even international corporations, for Delta and Coca-Cola. These cousins, two spoiled teenage girls and a younger, even more spoiled brother, made pointed fun of Vulcan, the huge cast-iron statue that loomed over Birmingham, its right arm holding a torch that burned green most days, red during the twenty-four hours after a local traffic death. Whenever these cousins visited New Arlington, they'd go around with their right arms up, Vulcan-like, and profess that the statue was the tackiest single thing they'd ever seen. Beauregard sometimes caught himself wishing that Vulcan would burn bright red for his cousins for twenty-four hours. He felt bad about wishing this, but not too bad.

145

Dewey stirred as they reached the vast industrial area just west of the city. He confessed he'd never been to Atlanta. They had some time, as McArthur had predicted, so when they hit downtown they toured for a while, driving first a stretch of Peachtree, then down North Avenue to Georgia Tech, then back over Ponce de Leon to the Emory area, then up Piedmont to Piedmont Park, then back around to North Avenue for lunch at the Varsity, the world's biggest drive-in restaurant. After polishing off two chili dogs and a tall frosted orange each, they still had a little time, so Beauregard asked Dewey if there was anything else he cared to see.

"Let's go see that Pig," he said.

"Aw, Dewey."

"I mean it, hoss. I want to. I can't get the damn thing off my mind."

So they went to Rich's and saw the Pig, and it didn't matter to Dewey that it was roped off for repairs, and that they, as adults in houndstooths, wouldn't have been allowed on it anyway; to him it was a thing of wonder. He wished he'd brought Sonya and Jeanette over here, when he had money. A ride on the Pig might have made the difference.

By now it was midafternoon, time to proceed to their intersection, Piedmont and Peachtree. They got in the Electra and headed that way. Beauregard knew that Piedmont and Peachtree formed one of the city's busiest intersections. It was a wealthy area, too. The cars would be expensive, the drivers impatient.

"I'm wondering exactly how do we do this," Beauregard asked as they idled a dozen cars from the stoplight.

"Your guess is as good as mine," Dewey said. "This is one kind of work I've never done."

"I suppose we should try to get where we can do the most damage," Beauregard said.

"Not in the middle of the intersection, hoss. That's too damn dangerous. And we'll get towed from there for sure."

"How about right up there, then?"

"That looks good."

Beauregard gestured and pleaded his way over to the middle lane, feeling bad that those drivers kind enough to let him over would be blocked by him momentarily. When he got two spaces from the light, which had turned red, he cut the engine.

"Okay, Dewey. I guess we better go to work."

"I guess you're right."

146

They got out and went around the long amber hood, opened it to its fullest extension, and leaned in for the pretend inspection. Dewey proved a good actor. He knew cars and looked quite natural reaching over to check various belts, meters, and gauges. Beauregard, who didn't know cars, felt phony and obvious leaning in beside him. Dying on a reenactment battlefield was easier. There he could curl up, close his eyes. Here he had to stand in the sun and fumes and pretend to check things he didn't understand. He was sweating big time already. The nose clips of his sunglasses were digging in. As Dewey continued to pretend tinkering, Beauregard stepped away to gauge the reaction of the drivers and passengers in the cars creeping around them, cars they'd delayed.

Sympathy was one reaction. Beauregard noticed a homely there-but-for-the-grace-of-God-go-I look on a number of faces. A more common reaction, though, was irritation. Some people were just plain angry. Beauregard wondered guiltily if they might be keeping someone from something important: a child from a ballgame, say; a mother from a delivery room. Not that they had it easy out here. He was wringing wet now, as was Dewey. He could taste the fumes. Fumes, as it happened, weren't all that different from those Varsity chili dogs. Still, Beauregard had rarely been so physically miserable.

After a half hour, with Dewey's enthusiastic endorsement, he dodged the traffic and bought a big dollar cup of Coca-Cola at a nearby convenience store. As he started back, he noticed a VW Bug in the store lot. It had an AP decal on the front windshield. He went over. A thin, balding guy in a khaki shirt and jeans was leaned against the fender, loading film into a thirty-five-millimeter camera.

"Are you the photographer?" Beauregard asked.

The man, no older than Price, thirties maybe, looked blankly at Beauregard, then down at the camera, then at himself, then back at Beauregard. "Hey, I guess I am," he said in mock wonderment.

Beauregard, in the interest of his story, ignored the sarcasm. "I'm Beauregard Forrest," he said, removing his sunglasses. "I'm with the *Standard-Dispatch*. Price's friend."

"Great. Really. That's just about the greatest damn thing I ever heard in my whole life."

"What's your name?"

"Me? I'm Alfred Eisenstadt."

Beauregard stuck out a hand. "Real good to meet you, Alfred."

"Hey, kid," the photographer said, refusing the handshake. "I'm not Alfred Eisenstadt. He was a famous photographer. You ought to know that." He stared at Beauregard, then sighed at length. "Look, I'm sorry, man," he said. "I'm having a real bad day. How 'bout letting me have a swig of that Coke? It's hotter than hell out here."

Beauregard did, and watched with chagrin as the swig became a gulp, then a second gulp. The photographer gave the much lighter cup back to him.

"I really, really don't want to be here," he said. "My German shepherd died last week. My condo roof leaks. I've got company coming, and the new bureau chief is an utter asshole. When I say 'utter' I mean utter. No hype. Then Price asks me to shoot this damn thing on my day off."

"It shouldn't take long," Beauregard said. He was used to photographers: a crusty lot, essentially good-hearted. "Hey, I'm sorry about your dog."

"I'll bet you are." The photographer looked out at the Electra. "I guess that's the 'stalled' car." Dewey was still leaned in, checking everything for the fortieth or fiftieth time.

"Yeah, that's it," Beauregard said. "You want to follow me out there?"

"I think I can get it from here with the zoom. Are you supposed to be in the picture?"

"Uh-uh. No."

"Then stay here for a few minutes."

Beauregard waited as the photographer adjusted the lens and clicked off a couple of rounds of Dewey. The older man withdrew from the hood and peered at Beauregard, then waved at him, urging him to come forward with the Coke. All Beauregard could do was put on a helpless expression, which didn't satisfy Dewey, who had his hands all the way out now, as if everything in his life had gone wrong.

"Actually, this is pretty good stuff, photographically," the photographer said, continuing to shoot. "The hat and everything. All the cars in front."

"Yeah, make sure you get the cars," Beauregard said.

"What's all this about, really? Price didn't say much."

So, as the photographer continued to click off exposures, Beauregard gave him a synopsis. "Price," the photographer muttered from behind the camera. "Birmingham." When he finished shooting, Beauregard saw him to the VW, wrote Dewey's name for him on a photo-assignment sheet, then dodged the slow traffic back to the Electra.

"Sorry it took so long," he said when he reached the museum guard. He handed over the lukewarm cup. "It was important that I stay out of the pictures."

Dewey took a long drink, wiping his mouth with his coat sleeve. "Getting rough out here," he said. "A young guy, some kid on a motorcycle, shot me a bird."

Beauregard looked at his watch. "We've got another hour to go."

"I'm beat, hoss. I'm going to stretch out for a few minutes in the back. Call me if you need me."

So Beauregard had the engine to himself for a while. Mostly he pretended to fool with it, but once he stepped back and counted the cars behind them. It was an impressive train, thirty cars easily, but getting an exact number was impossible because of a tall truck blocking the way. He leaned back over the engine. The hood afforded some shade, but that didn't matter. The declining sun had made of Beauregard's back one last target. He could feel the bulls-eye circle of sweat.

Dewey, up from his nap, rejoined him under the hood. Soon afterward they had two visitors. The first was a police officer on a motorcycle. When Dewey told him they had a wrecker coming, he nodded and left, apparently just as glad not to have to deal further with a grandfather and grandson in houndstooth hats.

The other visitor was a clean-cut young man who suddenly appeared and stood by the engine with them. He had neatly trimmed blond hair and wore a brown sports shirt that adhered to his muscular torso like skin. Around his neck hung a chain with a gold cross—not an ostentatious one, not one of the huge wooden swinging jobs Beauregard sometimes saw around Birmingham, but a cross nonetheless. He had a red metal tool box in his hand, and he smiled at the engine as if it were an old buddy. He wedged in between Beauregard and Dewey.

"Stall out on you?"

"Sort of," Beauregard said.

"What's the trouble?"

"Boy, I don't know."

"Let *me* take a look."

When the stranger set the tool box down and began to test

149

various belts and hoses, tugging here and there, seriously, Dewey grabbed his arm. "Just what the hell do you think you're doing?" he said.

"Dewey," Beauregard reproached.

But the stranger, unflustered, turned his head and smiled again at the museum guard. "Sir, it's part of my ministry to help motorists in trouble," he said. "It's just a thing I do, a Good Samaritan thing. I'll see if I can figure out the problem. If it's not major, I should have you on your way in a few minutes."

He punctuated his claim with another smile, then resumed testing belts and hoses.

"Whoa, wait a minute," Dewey said, tapping him on the shoulder. "We don't need no Good Samaritan. We got a wrecker coming."

"Just let me take a look. Might save you a few dollars." He opened the tool box, pulling out a screwdriver. He leaned well over the engine and began to tighten or loosen a part Beauregard couldn't identify.

Now Dewey grabbed him roughly by the arm and pulled him out. "Go on, now," he said, pushing him toward the creeping traffic. "Git."

"Hey, take it easy, old timer."

"I will once you walk back to your car."

"All right, then. Okay."

The Good Samaritan picked up his tool box, shaking his head as he dropped in the screwdriver. He stood looking at Beauregard and Dewey, forgiving them. Finally he smiled again and said, "God bless you, gentlemen—you *and* your wrecker. I hope it gets here. And I hope you have forty-five dollars when it does."

Loudly, for effect, he latched his tool box. As he turned and walked off toward his car, parked somewhere in the long column behind, Beauregard asked Dewey why he had chased him away.

"He 'bout messed us up, hoss," the museum guard said. "He was fooling with the starter. Starters are delicate. I *had* to stop him. If I don't, we're all broke down here in the middle of Atlanta."

They stayed another half hour, then as traffic thinned and dark fell they got back in the Electra and drove over to the store where Beauregard had bought the Coca-Cola. He called Price from a pay phone. To Beauregard's surprise, Price had him wait while Shealy got on the line, too.

"All right, B-Four," Shealy said, not bothering with "hello" or any other greeting. "Price told me about your little scam. Very clever. I should fire you—both of you—but it sounds like you got a good story. How'd it go at your intersection?"

"Pretty well," Beauregard said. "It happened, which was the main thing. And I was here to see it. Did the photographer call?"

"He called a while ago, B-Four," Price said. "He got some pretty good stuff. He couldn't get over your hat. He said he'd never seen a reporter in a hat like that."

"Listen, B-Four," Shealy said. "Did you see any other reporters out there?"

"No, sir. Nobody."

"In that case, we're not going to run this story tomorrow. We'll save it for day after tomorrow, when we can give it really good play. You can have the morning to make some more phone calls. You can write the story tomorrow afternoon. You might want to stop by tonight, though, just for a few minutes. Type your notes into the computer. While they're still fresh."

"All right, Bubba." He didn't have any notes, having spent most of his time driving around and leaning over the engine. But he had lots of impressions. He'd type those in.

When Shealy hung up, Price stayed on the line.

"Front page, B-Four," he whispered.

"You really think so?"

"B-Four, it's practically done. Shealy's going to have the desk make up some sample fronts before they go home tonight. He wants to give this story a good ride."

"Did Lorena call?"

"A couple of times," Price said. "That was a hell of a move sending her flowers. You're on a roll, B-Four."

At Dewey's insistence, they stopped back by the Varsity for dinner. Then he wanted to see Atlanta at night. It was almost eight-thirty when they pulled out of the gas station and hit the interstate for Birmingham. Even with the time change, they'd be late returning.

Dewey quickly dropped off to sleep, so Beauregard, hat and sunglasses off again, sipped black coffee and let himself contemplate the inevitable for just a while. Front page. And, as front-page stories went, this was a good one. One people would talk about. The morning disc jockeys might pick up on it, or the talk show hosts. It might be a "brite" on the wires. Hell, it might even win

151

an award. Not a Pulitzer, of course, but maybe something from the Alabama Press Association. They gave lots of awards.

Near Anniston, he could still feel the houndstooth hat, though it had been off his head for the last hour and a half. He was used to wearing hats, what with golf and military school and reenacting, and he knew well the feeling of having a hat on his head long after he'd actually removed it. "After Hat" he and Jackson called it, and tonight's case was fierce. It would take another couple of hours, maybe a shampoo, to get his head back. That was all right. After Hat was a small price to pay for a front-page story that would eliminate or make ironic his nickname, thus advancing his cause with Lorena.

Dewey barely stirred during the trip back. Even the twinkling city lights across the wide valley of Birmingham failed to open his eyes. Beauregard had to shake him when they pulled into a parallel space by the entrance to Tidwell Buick.

"It's probably better for you to return the car," Beauregard told the museum guard. "McArthur didn't notice me in the crowd this morning. He couldn't help but notice me tonight."

"All right," Dewey said sleepily. "I can handle that. I don't need a license to drive fifty feet."

"I appreciate your help," Beauregard said. "You told me everything. You posed for the pictures. Hey, it was nice of you just to let me go with you."

"I'd go anywhere with you, hoss. You're good people."

Beauregard was glad it was dark in the Electra, because his eyes were moist. They'd been through a lot together, he and Dewey. Maybe he'd keep in touch with him, as Price did his valued sources. Maybe they'd meet periodically at IHOP or Waffle House or Dunkin' Donuts. Anywhere would be all right, as long as it wasn't that little trailer with the Bear Bryant carvings. And no more softball.

He climbed out and watched as Dewey pulled the Electra into the driveway of Tidwell Buick. Then, very tired, he turned and started walking the ten blocks to the Birmingham Boosters building. When he got there, he drove back to the newspaper to type in his impressions. It was late now, almost eleven-thirty. They'd be putting the last edition to bed.

He could tell something was wrong as soon as he hit the linoleum corridor leading to the newsroom. There were too many people around for this time of night, and they were too busy. Then he saw Shealy, sleeves rolled up, pimento-cheese-stained tie loosened almost to the solar plexus, arguing with the front-page layout man. Shealy was never here this late.

Beauregard walked on into the newsroom. One copy editor noticed him, then another, then they all did and the place was silent. There seemed an odd, collective sympathy in their staring. Beauregard's first thought was that his father must have died, and they were deciding where to run the obit. Shealy walked over and draped an arm around him, started guiding him to the relative privacy of Style. Now Beauregard knew his father was dead.

"Bad news, B-Four," Shealy said.

"What is it?"

"The AP guy, Price's alleged buddy, went back to the bureau to develop the photographs of your Bear Bryant character. The Atlanta bureau chief got a look at them and wanted to know what was up, so the photographer told him. The bureau chief, by all accounts a real asshole, assigned two of his reporters to check it out. They managed to get traffic reports and a confirmation from McArthur, so they moved a five-hundred-word story. The AP national desk liked it and put it on the A wire. Now it's moving to newspapers all over the country. With pictures. In other words, B-Four, we got royally scooped."

There was a swivel chair a foot from where they stood, and though it was full of *Glamour* magazines, Beauregard plopped down. He felt warm, dizzy. Felt ruptured.

"The photographer's sorry," Shealy went on, "if that matters. And Price is devastated. He's waiting for you at Taco Bob's, with a cold pitcher of Budweiser. When I get through here I might join you. What the hell."

Beauregard looked up at Shealy. "Couldn't we at least use my story?" he said. "I could write real fast."

"Too late, B-Four. We've already laid the AP story into a hole on the front. Even if you finished your story in a half hour, we'd miss the press run."

Beauregard nodded wearily, with closed eyes. He knew the deadlines.

"You going to Taco Bob's?" Shealy asked.

"I don't know, Bubba. Right now I'm going to take a leak. I've been drinking coffee all night."

"Good idea, B-Four. You'll feel better after that leak."

He walked to the men's bathroom, stopped by the urinal, continued on to the window. It was always, even in winter, open for ventilation. He looked out over the modest Birmingham skyline, Vulcan in the distance, Sloss Furnace nearer in. Maybe everybody was right, maybe Birmingham *was* a loser city. Maybe he was a loser, too. Beauregard, Birmingham—both started with *B,* both had ten letters. He'd noticed that long ago but had never told anyone, not even Jackson. Jackson. He would never have gotten into this mess if he hadn't gone to see Jackson that morning. That was when he met McArthur. Now, though, he understood McArthur. He was like him. He had his own Pink Pig: the front page. It was hopeless, a lost cause, like the Confederacy. Recently he'd resisted the old feeling that he should have been born in another era, in the Confederacy, resisted it because that's what so many reenactors said of themselves, and he didn't want to be like them. But the feeling washed over him now. These days no one respected a lost cause. Back then they did. Lee emerged from the War Between the States a defeated hero. No one nicknamed him "Gettysburg" or "Appomattox." After the war, when he took what he meant to be a private vacation tour of the Deep South, thousands turned out at every train stop to cheer his brief, weary wave.

Beauregard walked back to his desk, the eyes of the copy desk still on him. A pink stack of phone messages rested to one side of his terminal. Lorena's name was on every one.

Quickly, without allowing himself to think how late it was, how unmannerly, he dialed her home number.

"Hello?"

"Lorena?"

"Beauregard?"

"Yes. Yes, it's me. I was wondering if I could come over. Tonight. Now."

"Now? It's late, Beauregard. I'm studying."

"I won't stay long. I won't even come in, if you don't want me to. I just need to see you. It would do me a world of good."

"Are you all right?"

"I honestly don't know."

"Should I put coffee on?"

"Yes."

"Black, right?"

But Beauregard had hung up on her. He was halfway down the hall already. The party van ran sluggishly, but he vowed he'd be in Southside, at Lorena's, before the coffee brewed.

Chapter Fourteen

He'd forgotten all about Booger. When he saw the hyperactive little dog, sockless now and running around the room for no clear reason, Beauregard thought that if he *had* remembered, he might not even have called Lorena, might instead have chosen some easier consolation, draining a pitcher of beer at Taco Bob's with Price and Shealy, or betting on the death count of "The Rifleman" with Jackson at his Devonshire Oaks condo, or just going back to his own apartment, stretching out in the shag carpeting and staring at the ceiling tile stains that more and more looked to him like Stonewall's perilous position near Dunker Church at Antietam. Faulty memory had served Beauregard well. He was awfully glad he'd come to Lorena's, Booger or no Booger.

For one thing, he liked her apartment. He decided after a few sweeping glances that he would have an apartment like this eventually. The main room's waxed wooden floor caught pools of light from the two shaded lamps, one by the coffee table and one in a far corner. The plants—two of them, ferns he believed, in clay pots—looked flourishingly leafy and green. He saw shelved around the room a goodly number of paperback novels and poetry volumes. She had the good sense to frame her posters, not rush them into position with careless jags of masking tape, as he had with van Gogh and Jimi Hendrix.

She'd greeted him at the front door in a blue terry cloth bathrobe that covered all but the wide collars of darker blue pajamas. Her skin, scrubbed free of the little bit of makeup she usually wore, was shiningly flush, and her hoopskirt of reddish blond hair was fully extended. She hugged him briefly, the terry cloth soothing to his touch, then pulled him by the blazer to the couch. She ducked into the kitchen, returning momentarily with coffee in steaming ceramic mugs. He remembered now that she didn't like plastic foam cups—bad for the environment. Maybe he'd get a work mug, although Price, the traditionalist, wouldn't like it.

"Tell me everything that happened," she demanded, sitting and turning toward him on the couch.

"You're sure you want to hear all my troubles?"

"Of course. Somebody hurt you and I'm mad about it. Mad as hell. So tell me."

"All right, then."

"Just let me put the sock on Booger."

"Still on the sock, huh?"

"Off and on. It's no panacea."

After she gathered and socked the dog, taking him into her lap for a restful petting, Beauregard began his story. Although he felt better being near her, he had no trouble recounting the details of his recent injury. He took her from Birmingham to Atlanta and back again. He got McArthur's Pig speech in there, and Dewey's chewing tobacco, and the heat and the fumes, and the Good Samaritan. He lingered on what it was like to walk into the newsroom thinking he had a front-page story, only to learn he'd been treacherously scooped.

Lorena proved a first-rate listener, nodding and sighing and shaking her head at precisely the right times. Even her blinks and sniffles (she had a slight head cold) seemed paced to suggest supportive outrage. When he finished, she summarized and passed judgment. She fingered the AP photographer and bureau chief as principal villains, cited Price and Shealy as negligent for not recognizing the danger of getting scooped, and declared Beauregard entirely the victim.

"It's too bad you can't sue all these people, Beauregard," she said. "You'd win a verdict, a big one. Hand me a Kleenex."

He handed her a pink scented one billowing up from a box at his end of the coffee table. "You really think so?"

"I do. Megabucks." She used her free hand, the one not stroking Booger, to blow her nose lightly. "Trust me."

The experience of someone listening to him so carefully was rare and restorative for Beauregard, as was the experience of someone so unequivocally taking his side. Price took his side, but with a measure of detachment and irony. Jackson usually lost interest before it was time to take a side. Not Lorena. Maybe he was misreading; maybe she was just being nice. He didn't think so. He'd know for sure when he pressed her for a good-night kiss, longer and better than the one after the avant-garde party.

"I think I'll untie Booger," she said. "He's asleep now anyway."

"Do," Beauregard said. "Excuse me. I'll be right back."

Once inside her bathroom, he noticed everything, the crocheted toilet seat cover, the feminine soaps and lotions, the tampon box, the disposable razor; then he took his leak. Afterward he quickly unbuttoned his blazer and shirt and sponged himself down. Using the flushing toilet as a cover, he gargled with her Listerine to take the edge off his daylong coffee-and-chili-dog breath. He spit the wash as the last of the blue toilet water sucked noisily into the old groaning pipes. He would be ready for that longer, better good-night kiss.

When he stepped out, she was standing by the couch, holding the bouquet of roses in front of her.

"You shouldn't have done this," she said seriously.

"I wanted to."

She shook her head. "Roses cost money, big money, Beauregard. For what these cost you could have joined the Sierra Club for a year. I'm talking full membership, too, not the student discount."

"Newspapers don't like reporters joining organizations like that. They want you to appear objective."

"That's stupid," she said. "Come smell them."

He walked over, gave the obligatory approving sniff, then briefly stood shaking his head as if he couldn't get over the miracle of roses. He noticed Lorena looking straight down into the bouquet. Despite what she'd said, her face was flusher than ever with pleasure. All her attention went to the roses. It was as if she were soaking up something beneficial from them: nectar for humans, or something. His eyes drifted down to her neck, a shade paler than her face, then to her voice box, exposed by the unbuttoned top button of her pajamas. The deep and soft-looking cave, not exactly cleavage, but in the neighborhood, aroused him slightly. He had begun to worry about this—aroused by a voice box?—when she spoke again.

"All right, I like them," she said. "*Love* 'em, God. But why, Beauregard? What occasion?"

He shrugged. "I called your office this morning. The receptionist said you were in the basement, filing. I don't know why, but I had this vision of it being really awful down there. So, to make you feel a little better, roses."

She was looking down at them again. Now she was smelling them.

"Is it awful down there?" he asked. "In the basement, filing?"

"As a matter of fact, it is." She set the roses in a water-filled vase on the coffee table, then joined him on the sofa, legs up under her, hands spreading flat the bouncy terry cloth folds. "The basement's cheerful enough, as basements go, but the people I work with, Chester and LuAnne, insist on gossiping all day. Today, for example, Chester went on and on speculating about who's gay at the school board. I hate that kind of thing."

"Me, too," Beauregard said, searching his memory for the names and mug shots of possibly gay school board staffers.

They took long sips of coffee. Beauregard was ready to move toward the front door and begin the good-night kiss. First, though, he had to tell her something. It was one reason he'd come. Once she heard this, she might not want to kiss him, but he couldn't go on without leveling with her.

She was petting Booger again. She'd gathered the dog into her lap and was stroking his head in an elaborate pattern, under the jaw, over the skull, across the narrow, loose-skinned forehead, down the indentation between his eyes. It looked like something she did often, probably nightly, a tactile lullaby. The dog's ecstasy contrasted with Beauregard's discomfort.

"Remember how you asked me one time about my nickname," he began.

"I remember very well," Lorena said. "You told me it was a newspaper nickname, an inside thing. You told me I wouldn't understand, which bugged me, to be perfectly honest. I'm not dumb, Beauregard."

"I know. I'm sorry. I didn't want you to know anything about that nickname. I was nervous about what you might think."

"You *seemed* nervous."

"Well I was."

He was standing now, looming over her and the dog, blazered arms outstretched as if a gesture might help get the words out.

"People at work call me 'B-Four' because my stories don't seem to get any closer to the front page than Section B, page four," he said in an embarrassed rush. "One time I made the B section front, but Price gave me that story, a favor. Usually I'm way, way in the back. Lorena, I honestly thought I'd make front page with this Atlanta story. Once I made the front, I figured the nickname would go away. I wouldn't have to explain it to you, the way I'm doing now."

He plopped back down.

"That's what you wanted to tell me?" Lorena asked.

"That's it," he said. "The whole damn thing."

With the hand she'd used to stroke Booger, she reached over for the right cuff of Beauregard's blazer. She didn't grab the wrist inside it, just the cuff. She jerked once, hard, a silent gavel-banging.

"Look," she said, "some of the very best stories are in the back. Even if they weren't, you just started at the paper. You'll be on the front page plenty before it's over. You'd have been on there tomorrow if it hadn't been for that AP bureau chief."

"You really think so?"

"I *know* so. What he did was criminal. Here, you probably want your wrist back."

The Stockton Pye version of "Lorena" began to play in Beauregard's mind. *The years creep slowly by, Lorena, the snow is on the grass again.* It occurred to Beauregard that of all the people in the world, four billion plus according to the *World Almanac* in the *Standard-Dispatch* morgue, he might well be the only one who had the old War Between the States ballad in mind. No telling in how many people's minds a Beatles tune was playing, or an Elvis. Probably thousands in the central time zone alone. No matter. He would be the lonely standard-bearer of "Lorena." He loved that tune, and he was feeling increasingly fond of the Lorena sitting next to him. He couldn't wait until the next opportunity to send her more roses or a good book or a classy poster with a sturdy frame.

"I feel a hundred percent better now," he said, reaching over and touching the hand that had squeezed his blazer. "You sure know how to bring a guy back."

"I'm just glad you feel better. Really."

"Did I tell you how much I like your place?"

"I think so. I can't remember."

"Well, then," he said, stretching and forcing a yawn, "I really should go. I feel bad about keeping you up so late."

159

"I'll be up awhile longer," she said. "I've got a paper due tomorrow."

"I've kept you from it."

"Not really. It's done. I've just got to proofread it. The thing is, I hate proofreading. I'm lousy at it. I'd much rather write a poem than check the spelling on a paper."

"I could help," Beauregard said, reasonably sure his offer would be turned down and they would advance to the front door for the good-night kiss. "I'm pretty good at spelling and grammar. You have to be, in newspaper work."

"You're tired, Beauregard. You've had a long day."

"I'm not that tired."

"You're sure?"

"Absolutely."

"Sit there, then," she said, abruptly dumping Booger and standing. "This is great. I'll make more coffee."

Within minutes he had doffed his blazer and moved over to a cane-back chair at the rectangular oak table across the room. He had a fresh cup of coffee at his side, and her hardback *American Heritage Dictionary,* and an AP Stylebook fetched from his briefcase in the party van. He used a slightly chewed number two pencil to mark her paper. Lorena was stretched out on the couch, underlining her psychology text with a squeaky yellow marker. Their kiss would have to wait.

Beauregard read her paper through once for content. She'd written on her stint last summer as a volunteer counselor at Crisis Intervention. Interesting subject, but Beauregard was a little unnerved to find that the interpersonal skills she had used for soothing battered people and potential suicides were more-or-less those she'd just used on him. Was he social work to her, another case? He decided to set this concern aside, to concentrate instead on making her paper bone clean of spelling and grammar errors. He inspected every word, every letter, as if the burden were on them to prove they'd been used correctly. On the first page alone he caught an *effect* that should have been an *affect,* an *accommodate* with just one *m,* and a sentence that started in the first person, shifted to the second, then slid like Rickey Henderson into third. He liked the sentence but felt compelled to note its unorthodoxy. In fact, he filled the paper with notes, most of them encouraging. "Good phrasing" . . . "Nice transition" . . . "Interesting section, but may need a 'nut graph.' See me."

He looked over once: Lorena was rubbing her eyes. He looked over a second time, twenty minutes later, and she was asleep, the psychology text rising and falling on her terry-cloth-covered chest. Beauregard had never had such a good chance to look at her when she wasn't looking at him. The relaxed scrutiny prompted even more affection in him. More lust, too. He longed to be that psychology text, rising and falling. It was an unworthy wish, un-Lee-like, so as penance he looked around the desk for anything else to proofread. He found another paper, this one for her history of Birmingham class. It was about a black minister named Fred Shuttlesworth who had kept the civil rights movement alive in Birmingham in the decade before Martin Luther King, Jr., came to lead his famous campaign of 1963, the one where police brought out dogs and fire hoses. Shuttlesworth, often acting alone, had been beaten and stabbed and had his house blown up for his outspoken opposition to segregation. He was a tough old cuss, so much so that he thought King had sold blacks out in the negotiations that ended the demonstrations.

Beauregard forgot to proofread, the paper was so interesting. He had a working knowledge of the major civil rights incidents, the King-led marches, the Sixteenth Street Church bombing; but he hadn't known much at all about Shuttlesworth. Interesting man. When he had time, he'd go down to the public library and read the books and magazine articles and scholarly papers listed in Lorena's bibliography.

Concentration and the late hour made Beauregard's eyes puffy, his shoulders tight. He turned in hopes of finding Lorena stretching, refreshed, eager to inspect his handiwork and perhaps massage his shoulders in gratitude, as Shealy did Price's after a good story. But she was still sleeping. A thin tributary of drool—visible; not unattractive—trickled from an open corner of her mouth to the little chartreuse pillow beneath her head. He looked at his watch. Two-thirty. He was tempted to wake her, to get the good-night kiss for which he'd longed and gargled; but she needed her sleep. She'd have to be at work in five or six hours. She might get docked if she didn't show up on time. Chester and LuAnne would surely gossip.

He shuffled the paper into a neat stack, set the pencil down over it, then picked up his blazer from the chair back. He did these small tasks noisily, hoping Lorena would wake. She didn't. Nor did watchdog Booger. Beauregard looked at Lorena one last time, his puffy eyes no impediment to appreciation, then walked heavily to the front door.

She'd dead-bolted it. He turned the upper knob right, the wrong way, then hard back to the left. The metal cylinder slid into place with a loud clack. He reached to turn the lower knob and let himself out.

"Beauregard?" Lorena called out in sleepy complaint.

"Yes."

"What are you doing?"

"Leaving. It's late. I finished proofreading your paper on crisis counseling, though."

"You did?"

"On the table."

"Oh, Beauregard. Thank you."

"It's good work," he said. "*A plus,* in my opinion."

"There's a lot of crisis in Birmingham."

"You make that point in the paper."

Beauregard didn't know what else to say. He remained in the foyer, hoping she'd hop up and join him for the kiss.

"Come here, Beauregard."

He tingled a bit at Lorena's husky imperative, then walked back into the main room. She was patting the space next to her on the sofa. She'd rolled over and made room for him to stretch out. For once, he was glad he was thin. They fit together easily, chest to chest, both bodies securely on the couch, though Beauregard's wing tips dangled in the distance. Her large brown eyes fluttered twice, a good sign, then shut down abruptly. Her breathing became quietly regular. So much for husky imperatives.

It disappointed Beauregard, this nodding off, but he understood that most romances were evolutionary. To be mashed into a sofa with a young woman in a terry cloth robe was progress. He would content himself with being Lorena's sentinel. If he had to be still, to keep from waking her, he could and would. He had plenty of experience on reenactment battlefields. He'd died on pinecones, anthills, cow patties. A sofa, even this old one with porcupine springs, was no big deal.

Ten minutes passed. Booger, still snoozing on the throw rug, rolled over. From somewhere beyond Beauregard's vision a clock chimed three times. He tensed his legs slightly, to keep the blood flowing. He knew from reenacting that if he didn't do this, his legs might fall asleep. That was the last thing he needed, to be lurching around, grabbing for furniture, when the time did come to rise with her and go to the front door.

Tensing his legs woke Lorena. She opened her eyes, then closed them again and leaned forward. They kissed. It was a lingering kiss, closed-mouthed yet exploratory, his lips finding out what they could about hers. They broke, then started again, this time, on her initiative, French kissing. Beauregard put his hands up under her hoopskirt of reddish blond hair. He had the fleeting thought, I have done just enough good things in my life for this to be happening. Soon he had an index finger inside her robe, then inside her pajamas. She stopped him, but only to suggest they move the coffee table, toss the cushions and turn the sofa into a sleeper.

Beauregard took care of it, quickly. He assigned himself the additional task of switching off all but a romantically moody wattage of light. They sat on the thin, sleeper-sofa mattress. Beauregard kicked off his wing tips; Lorena her slippers. They undressed in a mutual shiver, he taking some of her things off, she taking off some of his, both turning and finishing on their own.

He held up a black sock in the semidarkness.

"I thought I'd put this on Booger, to be sure."

"Good idea," she said. "And put him in the kitchen, and close the door."

"Will do."

"Make sure he's got water."

"Does it matter, with the sock?"

"He can drink with a sock on if it's not too tight. In fact, a sock makes him thirsty."

"That's amazing."

"*Hurry,* Beauregard."

The actual lovemaking started out self-consciously. It was Beauregard's self, Beauregard's consciousness; Lorena seemed more at ease. Beauregard was under the influence of letters he'd read in the *Penthouse Forum,* of what he knew of *The Joy of Sex* and especially of *I Can Suit Ya!,* which was out in the van. Jackson's manual was full of advice about how to please women. Beauregard, eager to please Lorena and to disguise his own inexperience, made the judgment call to go right into the Catfish. He tried to lift her into position, but she balked. It was hard to tell, because of the moody wattage, but she didn't look too happy that the idea of the Catfish had even come up. Beauregard abandoned it and lowered his head to her breasts. This went over better. After a few seconds, she dug her fingers encouragingly into his tapered scalp.

Jackson's book was specific about breasts. "Women's breasts are sensitive and should not be dealt with roughly," Beauregard recalled an early chapter saying. "Take one in your mouth as if it were a grape. Kiss and even suck it, but not so hard that you break the skin of the 'grape.' "

Beauregard had never liked grapes. He wasn't sure he'd ever rolled one around in his mouth, avoiding breaking the skin. He erred on the side of caution, taking a breast into his mouth but not doing much with it, just letting it sit there like a toothpick or thermometer. Hourlike seconds went by. Lorena's fingers pulled out of his scalp.

That did it. Beauregard mentally tossed aside Jackson's book, and *Penthouse,* and *The Joy of Sex.* He would make his own way now. He knew he was not an ungraceful or incompetent person. Through limberness and superior technique, he was longer off the golf tee than Jackson, despite Jackson's forty-five-pound weight advantage and thrice-weekly visits to Nautilus. The memory of this advantage rallied Beauregard's confidence, allowed him to relax. He began to think of Lorena's breasts as breasts. He sucked on them accordingly, calling on some dim babyhood memory of either the real thing or a first-rate pacifier. Her fingers dug back in. . . .

When it was over, a sweaty but on-the-whole glorious fifteen minutes later, there was plenty of room on the sleeper-sofa to spread out and wonder what it all meant. They got under a sheet and stayed close.

"Those moves," Lorena whispered. She was running a hand in a pattern around his head, the way she'd done Booger's. "Where'd you learn all those moves?"

"What moves?"

" 'What moves' he says." Now she was playfully walking her fingers across the broad plateaus of his rib cage. "At one point you tried to get me up on all fours."

"The Catfish," he admitted, then told her about Jackson's sex manual. He was a little ashamed of it now.

"The Catfish," she mused. "Your brother . . . Your brother played football for Alabama, right?"

"Right."

" 'Roll Tide' and all that."

"Yeah."

"Such bullshit."

"Lorena."

"I know, I know. Utter blasphemy to say such a thing in Birmingham. But that's pretty much what I think. Can you handle that?"

"I can," Beauregard said. "I've thought it was bullshit myself, from time to time."

He got closer and made a tendril of her hair. "Going to work tomorrow? Today, I mean?"

"Oh, sure. I can't let Chester and LuAnne down."

"Do they ever gossip about anything serious?"

"Sometimes. Chester insists there's a portable classroom missing."

"A trailer?"

"Yeah. He says some of the maintenance guys use it for a deer hunting lodge."

"No, uh-uh."

"That's what he says. It's the most disgusting thing I've ever heard, but of course Chester says he wants one. He says it'd be just the thing to roll down to his parent's lake lot for parties."

They dozed. Or, rather, Lorena dozed while Beauregard reflected on the various miracles of the early morning: the miracle of skin, of body fluids, of nature fighting its way through the sex books. When at last she stirred, he whispered that it was time for him to go. As he dressed, she slipped on her robe and freed Booger. The three of them went to the door. There, as morning's first light filtered between the foyer window ledge and curtains, Beauregard finally got his good-night kiss.

"Love you," he risked.

"Love *you,* Beauregard."

Traffic was light as he drove back to his apartment. The *Standard-Dispatch* circulation folks were out, though, hurling Tuesday papers, fat with advertising inserts and the AP account of the Atlanta campaign, onto the dewy lawns of Southside. Beauregard absorbed the sight without anger. He was going home to crash. He wouldn't think about work again for another two or three hours.

Chapter Fifteen

So much could go wrong with a newspaper story. The subscribing public, Beauregard thought, had no idea. Of necessity reporters worked fast and relied on secondary sources for information. They took what they could get, much of it over the phone, much of it on faith.

They could only hope the chatty but scatterbrained rural county clerk had pulled the right file when she identified a suspect as having a criminal record "as long as Uncle Dolph's arm, *my* Uncle Dolph, and, hon', that's a long one"; only hope the new, winningly articulate Southside psychologist quoted in Style's "Men and Stress" series hadn't had pre-Birmingham problems of his own, hadn't faked his Ph.D, say, or been barred from practicing in the Northeast for seducing entire therapy groups. All those surveys and government statistics that came across the wires—who really knew whether they were right? And what reporter, pinned by deadline, hadn't called around in search of an eyewitness account of a neighborhood fire? Maybe the eyewitness hadn't seen much of the fire, had instead been inside ironing or watching TV, but didn't want to blow a chance to make the paper and so exaggerated or even invented details: children in pajamas leaping from second-story windows onto Sears trampolines.

Even if every fact in the story was correct—and Beauregard wished someone would invent a verifying wand, like those metal detectors at the airport—so much could go wrong between the hitting of the computer terminal's SEND button and actual publication. Some copy editor might misread the story and write an inaccurate or even libelous headline. Someone in the composing room might paste on the *wrong* headline. That had happened already to Beauregard. For a Metro Brief he'd crafted on the Red Cross's quarterly blood drive, the headline had been NEPAL VOTERS JAM POLLS. The next day it was Beauregard, not the composing room foreman, who had to call the Red Cross spokeswoman for a blood drive update and absorb her "Well, it's going just fine, but no thanks to you, *Beauregard*" barb.

Beauregard would decide later that the anxiety reporters felt over all that could go wrong in their work accounted for the tide of sympathy that washed over him when he arrived in the newsroom on the morning after the Atlanta debacle. Other reporters looked at him as if he'd returned from the battlefront minus an arm and a leg. They seemed to feel sorry for him, and very glad they hadn't had to go in his place.

Midwesterners sent Beauregard computer messages.

Rochelle here, B-Four. Just heard about Atlanta. Damn. It wasn't your fault, and somebody (name of Shealy) ought to kick AP's ass.

If it's any comfort, that was a great idea for a story, B-Four. The AP was flattering you, in its own pinched, Marine Corps of journalism way—but I know you still feel awful. Hang in there. You'll get 'em yet. Bowzer.

This is Crenshaw, B-Four. What a pisser! Hey, on a related subject, some of us plan to go slumming in Atlanta this weekend. Peggy, our beloved library assistant, says you checked out the Atlanta map. Drop it on my desk when you get a chance. No hurry.

Those who didn't send messages stopped by Beauregard's desk to commiserate. Two of them actually brought him cups of black coffee. He'd gotten himself a cup on the way in, and so had three going, but he didn't mind. The rare feeling of camaraderie was worth caffeine jitters and extra trips to the bathroom.

The awkward thing, really, was that Beauregard felt wonderful. Though tired, he glowed internally from the night with Lorena.

He longed to tell someone how good it had been. He wouldn't give intimate details, of course. That would be sleazy. But he wanted to make a few select ambiguous remarks to someone, so someone would know his dawdling relationship with Lorena had recently surged.

It wasn't the sort of thing he could tell Jackson. Jackson would pepper him with specific, hardball questions. No, Price would be the one to tell. Though a first-rate reporter, Price would respect the ambiguity of Beauregard's remarks, lay off the questions, just give him a high five and wish him well, or perhaps engage with him in half-serious banter about their lives as hard-drinkin', hard-lovin' newspapermen.

Unfortunately, Price wasn't around. Beauregard figured he had either not come in yet or had gone out on assignment, though he'd left his beeper on his desk, charging. Unusual. Price started work early and usually carried his beeper. Beauregard thought perhaps he should have stopped by Taco Bob's last night, or at least called Price there. He knew Price felt bad about Atlanta. Maybe he'd stayed up all night, drinking. There was a melancholy, thirsty streak in Price that would account for such behavior.

The morning passed quickly. Beauregard went through his little bit of mail, made a few obit calls, met his quota of Metro Briefs. Just before noon he tried and failed to reach Lorena. She was back in the basement, filing. The receptionist perked up when Beauregard identified himself. She went on and on about the roses, how lovely they were, how sweet he had been to get them, how long it had been since Clarence, her shiftless husband, had bought her even a single longstem. So: Lorena had been talking, a good sign. Beauregard reflected on this, then on their night together, a highlights film of the action projecting onto his closed eyelids. He snapped out of it with the approach of breathing noises and a shaking aspirin bottle.

"Mornin', B-Four."

"Hey there, Bubba."

"Need a favor."

"No problem."

Shealy sat heavily in Price's swivel chair. He pulled closer, hoisting his elbows onto Price's desk. "A while back I promised Hanks Elementary I'd send a reporter out to talk about newspapers," he said. "Well, the day has come and everybody but you has an assignment. I know you had a tough day yesterday, B-Four, but I was wondering if you could go out to Hanks for me."

He'd never before asked Beauregard to do something—just told him. "Sure, Bubba," Beauregard said.

"Good man."

The city editor pulled a rumpled sheet of copy paper from his shirt pocket. "Let's see," he said, squinting. "It's Mrs. Tuck's class, fourth grade. You need to be there in half an hour, so you'd better head on out. Stop by the press room and grab some papers. Every child gets a paper."

"What do I talk about?"

Shealy shrugged. "Oh, hell, I don't know," he said. "You could talk about hot type versus cold type, I guess. Computers in the newsroom." He failed to suppress a grin. "Maybe, in your case, a good topic would be 'How I Landed That Big Story.'"

"Thanks a lot, Bubba," Beauregard said.

"Sorry, B-Four. That was cold. Listen, whatever you want to talk about is fine with me. And keep track of the gas. I'll make sure you get mileage."

Mrs. Tuck's class was performing a vigorous and disciplined multiplication drill when Beauregard slipped through the back door and squeezed into one of the downsized school desks. A few small heads turned, but most kept their focus on Mrs. Tuck, a formidable-looking woman wearing bifocals on a chain and a netted, mortar-shaped bun of gray hair.

"Eight times aught is what?"

"Aught!"

"Nine times aught is what?"

"Aught!"

Not the new math, certainly, but give her credit: They had *aught* down cold. Beauregard looked around. It was a basic classroom. Globe, projector screen, bookshelf. The *Niña, Pinta,* and *Santa María* sailed across a blue, paper-covered bulletin board. He could smell chalk in the air, and a revivingly strong brand of cleaning fluid.

"Twelve times aught is what?"

"Aught!"

When Mrs. Tuck motioned for Beauregard, he came forward with his stack of newspapers. They met on the other side of the desk, backs turned to the class. Looking hard at him over her bifocals, speaking in a low but still authoritative voice, she questioned him.

"What's your name, young man?"

"Beauregard Forrest."

"How long at the paper?"

"A few months."

"Reporter, right?"

"Yes, ma'am."

"Beat?"

"General assignment."

"You sound like you're from Birmingham."

"I am."

She closed the interview with a nod, then stepped around the desk and introduced him.

"Class, this is Mr. Forrest of the *Standard-Dispatch*. . . . A news reporter, general assignment. . . . Grew up right here in Birmingham. . . . You will, I know, give him your undivided attention."

With that, she almost sprinted to the door, calling over her shoulder that she would be in the teacher's lounge for the next forty-five minutes, should Beauregard need her.

"Thanks for that introduction, Mrs. Tuck," he said, though she had already cleared the room and could be heard high-heeling it down the hall.

Beauregard took a breath and sized up his audience. There were about thirty of them. Most were white, though there were a few black children, and one Asian girl. Probably a typical public school classroom for this neighborhood, but Beauregard found it interesting. At Birmingham Military there hadn't been any girls and damn few blacks. Still weren't any girls, though reportedly the board of trustees was about to change that. Beauregard hoped so. Maybe, with girls around, the soft BM era would be advanced. Maybe Crampton the biology teacher would quit draping his boa constrictor on unsuspecting cadets' necks during the middle of midterm exams.

"Well, boys and girls," Beauregard began, "as Mrs. Tuck was saying, I *am* Beauregard Forrest, and I *am* a reporter. And I guess I'd just like to begin this little presentation by saying good morning to all of you."

"Afternoon," corrected a small black boy sitting on the front row. He wore thick, wire-rimmed glasses and a blue-and-white striped dress shirt with button-down collars. He was tapping his digital watch.

"Right," Beauregard said. "Of course. 'Afternoon.' Good afternoon, boys and girls."

He handed out the newspapers, a little rattled. At Birmingham Military, tapping a watch at a guest speaker would have brought a visit to the commandant and ten demerits minimum.

"All right, class," Beauregard resumed, holding up a newspaper. "This, of course, is the *Standard-Dispatch*. And this is what we call a 'section' of the newspaper. This happens to be the front or A section of the *Standard-Dispatch*. There's also the B section, and C section, and sometimes even a D section."

Using the sections, he explained the difference between news and features, editorials and sports, long stories and Metro Briefs. He pointed out various typefaces used for headlines. He noted that photographs often were reduced, enlarged, or cropped to fit a space. He tried to define *cropped*.

"Not really anything to do with farming," he said. "It's just a term that means, well . . . Let me try an example. Say the newspaper agreed to print your class picture, but for space reasons the children on the end of the rows didn't make it in, or only part of them did, a shoulder and half of the head, say. They'd be cropped out. Got that? . . . Good. Let's move on."

He touched on circulation, then on the newspaper's history, describing how the *Birmingham Standard* and *Birmingham Dispatch* had merged after World War II. Then he discussed computers. They had a big one at the *Standard-Dispatch,* he said. There was a mainframe, and each reporter had a terminal connected to the mainframe, and the screens on each terminal split so notes could go on one side and the story on the other.

Beauregard felt he was losing them. He knew he'd lost two; their heads were on their desks. He decided to forgo his explanation of classified ads and move on to comics. The class perked up a little. He stepped forward, lowered his voice conspiratorially, and said that if they got jobs at the paper and knew where in the composing room to look, as he did, they could read the comics two to three weeks in advance.

Response to this confidence disappointed Beauregard. He saw a few nods of the head; many more stares. He looked over them to the clock on the back wall. Twenty-five minutes to go.

"Questions so far?"

"What kind of shoes are those?"

It was the little black boy, the watch-tapper. Through the early part of Beauregard's talk, he had held the newspaper in front of him as if he were a prosperous businessman ignoring the wife at breakfast. Now, though, he had spotted Beauregard's wing tips.

"What's your name, young man?"

"Hector."

"All right, Hector." Beauregard walked to one side of Mrs. Tuck's desk and lifted his right foot onto it, so everyone could see. The children raised up in their seats. Those on the front row, including Hector, walked up to study the shoe. Then everyone did. It was shoes they cared about, not newspapers. Hector took the lead, fingering the waxy laces, the perforations on the toe. Others followed. It felt strange to Beauregard, having his shoe poked by all these little fingers. But it was taking up time.

"This kind of shoe is worn by many, many professional men," Beauregard explained. "They make a boy's size, too. In fact, I grew up wearing this kind of shoe. It's called a wing tip."

Hector tilted his head in mock confusion. "Did you say 'wang tit'?"

Giggles got drowned out by shrieks of laughter. Only fourth grade, but they knew what tits were, and they seemed delighted that Hector had managed to sneak the word into classroom discourse.

"No, Hector, *wing tip,*" Beauregard said, pronouncing carefully. He lowered his foot, scattering the children back to their seats. "Other questions?"

"Have you ever been on TV?" asked a small, braided girl.

"Once," Beauregard said. "Channel Five, panning, caught me at a traffic accident I was sent to cover. A Ford truck had wrapped itself around a telephone pole. The driver came out all right, but only because he wore his seat belt. Always wear your seat belt."

"Do you have a computer at home?" a boy asked.

"No."

"What kind of car do you drive?"

"I drive a van, Hector." What was it with this kid? "You can see it from here. It's the dirty white one, the one with the writing on the panel."

Hector and half a dozen other boys sprang from their seats and made for the window as if that rare and most compelling of South-

172

ern educational interruptions, snow, had suddenly begun to fall. Beauregard walked over to shepherd them back.

Eighteen minutes. He could think of little more to say. He tried to go into the difference between hot type and cold type, got halfway, realized he was over their heads and his own, and pulled back. He was struggling. Fatigue, no real problem when he was sipping coffee with the newly sympathetic Midwesterners, undermined him now.

Hector again. Beauregard had noticed him conferring with the boy behind. They had whispered briefly, then looked at Beauregard—hard, measuring looks. Now Hector had his hand up. He had it straight up, too, not crooked shyly or uncertainly. He probably wanted to know Beauregard's nickname at work.

"What is it?"

"Could I have your autograph?"

Beauregard looked at him, then at the class, to verify that this was some kind of orchestrated joke. Apparently not. The class seemed genuinely interested in the fate of Hector's request.

"My autograph?"

Hector nodded.

"Well, I don't know," Beauregard said, coughing a little, shifting his weight. He looked at the clock. "We *do* have time."

He pulled out his ballpoint, leaned over Hector's desk, and, with summoned nonchalance, scrawled *Beauregard Forrest* across the top of Local/State.

"Now me," said the little boy behind Hector.

By the time Beauregard had finished the second autograph, he was surrounded. Everybody wanted one. Most thrust forward newspaper sections, but he also signed a couple of Blue Horse tablets, a Flintstones lunch box and the only available spot on a little boy's leg cast—just above the toes, which badly needed washing. Beauregard was shy at first, and his small, cramped writing reflected it; but before long his *Beauregard Forrest* was a large, looping thing. He no longer felt tired. The autograph session, his first little B-12 shot of celebrity, had brought him back. He wished Lorena could be here. He'd tell her about it, of course, but in telling he'd have to be modest. It would be much better if she could see for herself how they crowded around him, heads upturned.

"What's all this?"

It was Mrs. Tuck, standing in the door. Beauregard, down to his last two admirers, looked up and said, "Oh, hello there."

"Autographs?"

"They insisted."

"Good for you," she said, approaching. "Usually it's money they want."

At her suggestion, the class showed its appreciation for Beauregard. They applauded loudly and got louder—became staccato, even, under Hector's drum-major influence. Mrs. Tuck waved them off, then escorted Beauregard out. He expected her to peel away at the hall, then at the front door; but she saw him all the way to the van. She was in no hurry to get back to post-aught multiplication.

As they strolled, they talked about Hanks Elementary, how old it was, the demographics, the teacher-pupil ratio. Beauregard spotted a line of portable classrooms in a field by the main building. He remembered what Lorena had said about the rumor of a missing one.

"Have you ever taught in a portable, Mrs. Tuck?"

"One year," she said. "Really it wasn't so bad. They're bigger than they look. You have your own bathroom, you can control the thermostat, and you don't have the noise from adjoining classes. Yes, I'd say I liked it, all in all."

"Hanks has a lot of them."

"We could use more. It's not easy to get them, you know. We've got one first grade class meeting on the stage of the lunch room, because there aren't enough portables. Now that's tough. When the other children come in for lunch, it's nearly impossible to hear on that stage."

Beauregard gave a concerned little shake of the head. Privately he calculated. If, as Chester suggested, school board officials used a portable as a deer hunting lodge while children had to study on a noisy lunchroom stage, there was newsworthy scandal in Beauregard's midst. He and Mrs. Tuck shook hands, then he climbed back into the van and began the drive back to the newspaper.

Beauregard had grown used to the way reporters referred to unfortunate and even tragic events as good stories. A murder-suicide was a good story. A tornado was a great story, if bad enough. In public, reporters and editors described good stories as "strong" stories; but that was PR. Back in the newsroom they'd be smiling and raising their fists whenever they gained some key piece of information: the caliber of the murder weapon, say, or the precise swath of the tornado. All this was to the journalistic good.

174

At a stoplight, Beauregard dared to think again about making front page. The reverie carried him to the newspaper's parking lot and even inside the building. He stood at the coffee station, filling a plastic foam cup, when one of the Midwesterners approached from behind.

"Did you hear, B-Four?"

"What's that?" Beauregard said, setting the half-filled pot back on the burner.

"Hey, pour me some."

And he did, though he went over the rim, badly, because the Midwesterner told him Price was quitting reporting. He'd taken a job as Shealy's assistant city editor. Price was going on the city desk. Price, of all people, management scum.

Chapter Sixteen

The high tide of sympathy that washed over Beauregard on the morning after the Atlanta debacle had moved out to sea by early afternoon. Price was a better story. Reporters gathered in funereal twos and threes around the newsroom, shaking their heads, wrinkling their brows, sipping coffee thoughtfully, enjoying saying what a shame it was, Price quitting reporting after all these years. They worked the Price story as diligently for conversation as they would have a Birmingham mayor's resignation for print. More diligently. Suddenly they were all great reporters, and as such pressed one another for the telling details that would make this in-house story sing.

What time exactly did he tell Shealy he'd take the job? . . . What was he wearing? . . . Not Shealy, Price! . . . You say a tie, but was his collar loose? . . . And his armpits—stained?

They wondered aloud who if anybody would get Price's coveted "senior reporter" title, who would take over his several beats, whether he would bequeath the executive-size swivel chair he had talked his way into years ago or just swivel it over to the city desk.

For Beauregard, listening from the periphery, the popular analogy of reporters to birds of prey suddenly made sense. Price hadn't even gone over to the desk yet, probably wouldn't for another two weeks, and the other reporters already had his title and swivel chair in probate.

They deserved a stiff upbraiding, his colleagues, but Beauregard wouldn't be delivering it. He felt defensive. Emerging from the loose talk about Price was a theory that the Atlanta debacle might have been a factor in his decision, might even have precipitated it, been the one straw too many.

You know what a perfectionist Price is. To be associated with a bomb like that, well . . . Glad it wasn't my story that got to him. . . . You know whose it was, don't you? . . . Yeah? Well, figures.

As the afternoon wore on, an afternoon that he had fully expected to spend savoring two recent firsts in his life, making love and signing autographs, Beauregard felt not just a withdrawal of sympathy but also an actual chill from Midwesterners buying into the Atlanta debacle theory. Tankersley, who had never failed to yell Beauregard's nickname when they passed in the hall, who in fact seemed to regard "B-Four" as a *Eureka!*-like word, incomplete without exclamation, passed him and said, "Hey," only—said it weakly, too, with averted eyes. Other real or imagined slights occurred as Beauregard made brief, necessary trips around the building. The editorial writer ahead of him at the copy machine left it jammed with paper and needing ink. Later a bathroom door closed in his face—highly uncommon in Birmingham.

To hell with them, Beauregard thought as he headed downstairs for more coffee. Who cares what turkey vultures think? But as he strolled the corridor leading from the newsroom, past the photographs of plane crashes, sinkholes, and Coach Bryant, bravado wore off and he realized he did care. Shouldn't but did. He'd liked it this morning when they talked to him and sent sympathetic messages and brought coffee. Now some of them were blaming him, without trial, for Price's going on the desk, and though they were nothing but encircling Midwestern turkey vultures, it bothered him.

The afternoon turned again, though, when Shealy stopped by Beauregard's desk.

"How was it at Hanks?"

"It went okay, Bubba. Real nice kids."

"Glad to hear it." He sat heavily on Price's desk and turned again toward Beauregard. "Listen, B-Four. I'm promoting you off of Pet of the Week. You've made progress. You deserve a break from some of the scut work."

"Thanks, Bubba."

"I didn't realize how many consecutive weeks you'd done Pet of the Week."

"Quite a few."

"Price pointed that out."

Beauregard swiveled forward. "What's the deal with Price, Bubba? He's really going on the desk?"

"Yeah."

"Why's he quitting reporting, though?"

"You'll have to ask him that, B-Four. He should be in tomorrow. Maybe tonight. He had some things he needed to do."

Afternoon became early evening. Still at his desk, still swigging coffee and finishing marking up the next day's press releases, Beauregard could see the sky fading from saffron to deep blue, then to blue black. Occasionally a car or pickup truck with its horn rigged to play the first five notes of the Alabama fight song would drive by and honk, but otherwise the streets were quiet. Most reporters had left for a Southside bar where they planned a happy hour "Price Wake," though Price, still missing, was not actually expected to attend. Beauregard stayed at work. Buoyed by his promotion from Pet of the Week, he began to make notes on how to do the missing-portable story. He stopped long enough to phone Lorena at her apartment.

"Tired?" he asked after they had exchanged greetings.

"Very," she said. "And I can't talk long. I've got a class in a little while. I'm turning in my psychology paper. I made nearly all the corrections you suggested. Thanks again for doing that, Beauregard."

"There weren't many corrections," he said. "Just little things. It's a very good paper. Clear, persuasive. When can I see you?"

"Class tonight, as I said. So that's out. And tomorrow night I've got Sierra Club."

"Thursday night, then."

"The thing is, I'm supposed to go to a poetry reading Thursday night. I'm supposed to read some of *my* poetry, which I've never done in public. I'm afraid it's going to be like a little piano recital or something. You won't want to come."

"Of course I want to come," Beauregard said. "I love your poetry."

"Stop being so nice, Bernstein."

"Bernstein." Not a bad nickname. "You know about Woodward and Bernstein?"

"Yes, the great reporters. But don't be saying you love my poetry. You've never read a single poem of mine."

True, of course. He scrambled for a response, deciding against saying that last night was a poem, or that it was a poem to be near her. He'd save those good lines for later. "What I mean is," he said, "I've loved hearing you talk about your poems. And I know from your paper how well you write."

She paused. "I may read the one about you."

"The one about me?"

"Would that bother you? I started it at lunch. I'm pretty sure it's finished. Sometimes they just come like that."

Beauregard didn't know what to say. He'd never expected to be the subject of someone's poem. He couldn't be sure, of course, not having read it, but it was a good bet the poem was a love poem. He felt flattered but nervous. A certain responsibility went with being a poet's inspiration. It was necessary to be vivid, to say and do vivid things. Maybe he should unload with that good line about her whole life being a poem. No, he'd save it.

"This poem's not called 'Bernstein' is it?"

"No," she said. "Listen, I've got to go."

"All right. But I'm coming Thursday."

"I'll be a nervous wreck."

"Let me drive you, then. I'll pick you up at seven."

"Seven-thirty."

"Okay."

Beauregard worked without interruption for another half hour. He thought about leaving, decided to give it one more cup of coffee, got that cup, then went to check the files on portable classrooms. Before he left his desk, he sent a computer message.

> Price: I'm in the morgue. Stop by. Beauregard. p.s.—You can't go on the desk. I won't let you go on the desk.

The filing situation was grim. There was no convenient "portable classrooms" file, only "education," which filled two whole drawers. It wouldn't be like searching the Bear Bryant file, but it would be a long hard job nonetheless. At this hour, all he could hope to do was start. As he went slowly through the first clippings, copying down names and stray bits of information, he realized this could be a complicated story, one he might not finish before winter term and Washington and Lee. He still hadn't told Lorena about

Washington and Lee. He kept meaning to, but the timing never seemed right. The problem was, certain other remarks he'd made suggested he would be in Birmingham indefinitely and might even enroll in night classes at UAB. That was an increasingly attractive future, now that Lorena was writing poems about him and making room on the sleeper-sofa. But it wasn't the future his father had in mind. Mr. Forrest had grudgingly let Beauregard move away from New Arlington, but he would make his stand if Beauregard tried to back out of going to Washington and Lee. Mr. Forrest was convinced Jackson would have become the gentleman banker he had intended him to become, had he made him go to W&L instead of letting him play football at Alabama. He wasn't taking any chances with Beauregard. If Beauregard defied him, it would be rebellion of a high order, far beyond taking the Southside apartment, and Beauregard wasn't up to it. Jackson had a gift for rebellion. Beauregard didn't. He might know everything about the Confederacy, but when it came time to contemplate secession from his father, Beauregard knew himself to be conveniently Unionist.

His ballpoint pen gave out as he was copying quotes from an early story about parents' reactions to portable classrooms. When he walked back to his desk for a replacement, he noticed the MESSAGE PENDING light on his computer. He reached over to hit the two keys that called up messages.

B-Four: Let's talk. What say we meet at IHOP, around nine? You'll probably get there before I do. Try to find a booth that's not too sticky. I realize that may be impossible. Price.

It was like Price to swoop in and out, and count on Beauregard finding his message and abiding by its instructions. He would, too. IHOP, with its "breakfast anytime" policy and copper-insulated coffee pot on every table, was perfect for emergency conversation. He and Price would be drinking coffee and sharing confidences while the Midwesterners held their Price Wake over on Southside. Excellent.

He logged off his computer, slipped on his blazer, and headed out.

Beauregard had forgotten that the Greater Birmingham War Between the States Roundtable, over which Mr. Forrest presided, met Tuesday nights at IHOP. He arrived at the break. From where he stood just inside the front door, he could see his father and the thirty or so other members chatting in twos and threes around the crude circle of rectangular tables that Rico or someone else at IHOP had arranged in the roped-off section. An overhead projector glowed in the circle's center. Against the far wall a projector screen showed an image, blurry with the lights up, that Beauregard guessed to be that of Confederate general William Hardee.

Beauregard knew most roundtable members by face and many by name. Some reenacted with Mr. Forrest's unit, and the others had been to New Arlington for the big Confederate Memorial Day picnic. The membership included professionals, of course—physicians, dentists, lawyers, architects, and bankers, as well as a Catholic priest, Father Terence, who had his own metal detector and the roundtable's best minié ball collection. But for every professional there was a workingman, a plumber or truck driver, ice house foreman or boat mechanic, who hadn't majored in history, hadn't even been to college, who probably drove a pickup graced with some irreverent bumper sticker (INSURED BY SMITH & WESSON), yet knew everything about the war. Beauregard had been to the houses of some of them, inspected their bookcases. Shelf after shelf would be lined with war books, the best stuff, too, regimental histories and generals' memoirs, Wiley's lives of Johnny Reb and Billy Yank, the great three-volume narrative history by Foote, and Freeman's indispensable biographies of Lee and Lee's lieutenants.

Mr. Forrest, in one of the groups of twos and threes, noticed Beauregard, excused himself, and walked over. He'd either been home to New Arlington or brought extra clothes to the bank. He wore a tan suede jacket, an open-collared white dress shirt, dark brown stretch pants, and a brown leather belt with a brass *F* in the buckle. Dressed like this, and with his hair combed his own way, he didn't look so much like Robert E. Lee. Beauregard knew the war would be much on his mind, though, this being meeting night. He knew what to ask, too, once they'd shaken hands.

"So is Hardee your topic tonight, Dad?"

"Yes," Mr. Forrest said. "Fred Whatley's reading a little paper he wrote on Hardee's *Rifle and Light Infantry Tactics*."

"Ah," Beauregard said, remembering easily, "the respected training manual."

"Used by which side?" Mr. Forrest demanded.

"Both sides, sir," Beauregard said. "That's how respected it was."

"Year of publication?"

Tougher. "Eighteen fifty- . . . six."

A tiny smile raised Mr. Forrest's narrow upper lip and the accompanying gray wave of mustache. "Good," he said. "Very good. I only hope you do as well on the SAT."

Beauregard didn't say anything, which was his way of signaling to his father a desire to change the subject. He'd given the signal often over the years, but his father usually missed it. "Do you need any more vocabulary books?" Mr. Forrest asked. "I saw a new one at the bookstore downtown."

"I'm still working through the first book, Dad."

"Why are you here?"

"I'm meeting Price, from the paper."

"You two could join us," Mr. Forrest said, brightening. "You couldn't sit at the roundtable—that's for members—but you could sit nearby. I'll have Rico bring some chairs over."

"That's okay, Dad. Some other time. Price and I need to talk."

They shook hands, then his father turned and walked purposefully back toward the roped-off section. Beauregard went the other way, searching for and finding a back booth.

Beauregard knew he and his father could have gone on all night with that question-and-answer game. If Beauregard knew nothing else, he knew the war—the outline of it, the minutiae. It hadn't been an unhelpful thing to know. All through school the knowledge had been available to him for reverie, and he'd passed entire class periods, whole grades, as best he could remember, lost in fantasies of performing heroically in specific battle situations— dying in Pickett's Charge, for example, or living and thriving with Mosby's Rangers. Sometimes he'd debate with himself compelling issues of the war, such as whether Braxton Bragg's migraines had affected his generalship of the Army of Tennessee, or whether a better ambassador than Slidell might have persuaded the French to fight with the Confederacy, thus tipping the balance.

He was trying to get away from war reverie now. The knowledge was there if he needed it, if he got stuck in line at a fast food restaurant or waiting at the courthouse for a press release; but that was about all it was good for. The SAT didn't have any questions about the war. Lorena was more interested in recent Birmingham history. The knowledge valued at the *Standard-Dispatch* was Price's: how to file a Freedom of Information request, how to check tax and property records, how to turn bailiffs and dispatchers and court clerks into reliable sources.

Where *was* Price? Sitting here waiting for him, alone, was a little like one of those fast food or press release situations. He had better things to think about now. There was the missing-portable story, and the autograph session, and the poem Lorena had written about him. There were his nicknames, "B-Four" and "Bernstein." He'd gone eighteen years without a nickname, and now he had two.

"Roll Tide."

Beauregard looked up. "Price!" he said. "You snuck in on me."

Price slipped into the booth's other side. "Sorry I'm late, B-Four. Been waiting long?"

"Not too long."

"I see your Dad is here with his Civil War–nut friends."

"Yeah. They meet here every Tuesday night. We could go to Waffle House—"

Price shook his head. "They won't bother us. They look typically hypnotized." Price rolled his neck around, popping it like a knuckle. "Man," he said. "I am one tired hombre."

Beauregard had never seen Price look so tired. The trappings were the same: loosened collar, rolled-up sleeves, stained armpits, Vitalis-thickened strands of hair. But he looked especially sleep-deprived. His face was more pallid; his eyelids, behind the bandaged glasses, drooped more.

"Coffee?" Beauregard asked.

"Thanks, B-Four."

Beauregard used their table's copper-insulated pot to fill Price's cup, then set the pot down. With Price he knew better than to ask about cream or sugar.

"Is it true you're going on the desk, Price?"

"Yeah, B-Four."

"Why?"

"It's hard to give any one reason. Pass that ashtray."

Beauregard, doing so, said, "Was it Atlanta?"

"Lord, no. Of course not." Price tapped out a Camel. "I mean, I was sorry that turned out the way it did. And you better believe I called the AP and blistered that new bureau chief. But that didn't have anything to do with me going on the city desk."

"That's what the Midwesterners are saying," Beauregard said. "Some of them, anyway."

"I'll clear that up tomorrow. I couldn't face those Heartlanders today."

"Hey, I understand."

Price brought out two menus from behind the wooden tray of syrup pitchers. He gave Beauregard one, then opened the other and placed it flat on the table. Cigarette dangling, he began to scan the descriptions of nations and their pancakes. Abruptly, though, he looked up.

"You just get tired after a while, B-Four," he said. "I've been a reporter for fifteen years. Let's say I've averaged a story a day, which I have, easy, and the average story ran five hundred words, and that's low, probably *way* low, and say I worked, on average, two hundred and forty days a year, which is low, too, because I've always worked weekends. That's a hell of a lot of words. I wonder how many words that is?"

Beauregard pulled out a ballpoint pen and did the arithmetic on an IHOP paper napkin. "One million eight hundred thousand," he said. "Roll Tide."

"Oh, no. More than that," Price said, setting his burning cigarette in an ashtray. "Let me see that napkin." Beauregard handed it over. Price, pausing once for a drag, did his own arithmetic. Finally he crumpled the napkin and shrugged. "Anyway," he said, "it gets to me when I think of all those yellow clippings of mine in the morgue or up in my attic. Let me tell you, B-Four, there's nothing sadder than a yellow clipping, especially from the old days, when we were still using *Negro*. See, I go back that far."

"I thought you liked the old days."

"Well, I did." Price lifted his bandaged glasses and rubbed the red, indented skin on his upper nose. He let the glasses drop back down. "What kind of pancakes are you having?" he asked.

"Silver Dollar," Beauregard said.

"They're so small."

"They give you a bunch of them."

"Fistfuls?"

"Yeah."

"All right, then," Price said, "as long as it's fistfuls." Suddenly he was mugging for Beauregard, his face a mask of tragedy. "Do you think we'll ever get served?"

"Here comes Rico."

While they were waiting for their food, and even after its arrival, Price talked about his new job. There were disadvantages. For one

184

thing, the city desk was in the nonsmoking section of the news-room. For another, he'd have to give up on reporting projects he'd looked forward to, such as "People Who Have Jobs at the Court House but Don't Really Do Anything." Worst of all, of course, he'd be management scum. He could already feel his thinking skills and integrity beginning to disintegrate.

Beauregard dislodged a pitcher of blueberry syrup from the sticky wooden tray. As he poured, he said, "Sounds like you're just burned out on news reporting, Price. Why not take six months and work on the copy desk, or write for Style? They could use a good, tight writer like you."

"You know what I think of Style," he said flatly. "That would never work."

Beauregard remembered now that Price called Style "Pathetic Subcultures." Price had no patience for its rambling accounts of railroad buffs and competitive bird-watchers.

"I guess not," Beauregard said.

Price, pouring more coffee for both of them, said, "Hey, how's it going with that new girlfriend of yours? With Lorena?" He pronounced her name with Spanish inflection.

"Better," Beauregard said. "Much better."

"But no date tonight?"

"We've got one Thursday night. We're going to a poetry reading at UAB."

"Poetry!" Price said, bug-eyed behind his glasses. "Shit!"

Beauregard smiled. This was vintage Price. Anything smacking of pretension he ridiculed. The thing was, he probably read poetry on the sly. He might even have written a verse or two. He wrote fiction, or did. As assistant city editor in charge of so many Mid-westerners, he might not be able to finish *That's Close Enough*, the computer system detective novel their slack reporting had inspired.

"So, what was the mood in the newsroom today?" Price asked.

"Everybody was really sorry you're leaving reporting," Beaure-gard said. "Then they started talking about who'd be the next senior reporter, and what you were going to do with your swivel chair."

"What about my beeper? Did anybody claim that?"

"That didn't come up. I guess they've all got beepers."

"You're getting my beeper, B-Four."

"Price, no," Beauregard said, already feeling it holstered on his belt, hoping Price would insist. "It's brand new, state of the art."

"I won't need one on the city desk."

"I couldn't."

"You will. I won't take no."

A little later, smoking, they talked about the benefits package for management employees. It was better, as was the pay. Editors didn't get overtime, but reporters never seemed to get overtime either, so Price didn't feel he was losing on that score. He'd be way ahead overall. He could make a down payment on the house he'd been renting, send his Mom a few bucks. Money was the real reason he was becoming assistant city editor.

"In fact," Price said, "I'm buying the pancakes tonight."

"No, Price. My treat."

"Give me that check, B-Four."

"Price."

"I mean it. I'm scum now. You have to do what I say."

So Beauregard, after wiping the syrup off, gave him the check. They walked to the cash register. As Price paid Rico, Beauregard rolled a toothpick from the dispenser and turned around to see how the roundtable was progressing. The question period had begun. Hands waved for Mr. Forrest's attention, he being moderator of this program, as well as roundtable president.

Beauregard had drunk coffee all day and much of the night, but he slept seven hours and awoke refreshed and ready to work. Driving home from IHOP, he'd decided he would definitely do the missing-portable story, do it for Price. He wouldn't ask his advice or even tell him ahead of time. He'd just do it. He had a head start on sources, what with Lorena and her gossipy friends at the school board, Chester and LuAnne. He knew Mrs. Tuck and the Hanks Elementary situation. He could do it.

Wednesday, when he had time, he continued going through the "education" file cabinets. Thursday, too. By late Thursday afternoon he had a notebook full of leads to follow and ideas on how best to proceed.

He wanted to talk to Lorena about it, make sure she would feel comfortable helping him. But that could wait. First they had to get through the poetry reading.

Beauregard had never been to the kind of poetry reading held in an auditorium, with a reading lamp on the dais and wine and cheese at intermission. He'd had poetry read to him, though. Mr. Forrest liked poetry, of a kind, and on Sunday nights he would take little Beauregard on his knee and read to him from a hardback anthology with portal-shaped drawings of the included poets, many of whom, Beauregard remembered, scowled behind long gray beards. Mr. Forrest, wetting a finger to turn the pages, usually began with "The Frost Is on the Pumpkin," "Wynken, Blinken and Nod," or something similarly light and appealing to children. Soon, though, he would turn to the poems he liked, darker, more complicated selections like "Casey at the Bat" and "The Cremation of Sam McGee." Often he would read "Little Boy Blue," by the newspaperman Eugene Field. The little boy in "Little Boy Blue" was dead, and his toys, gathering dust on the shelf in his room, mourned him. It was occasionally the evening's last poem, after which Mr. Forrest would switch on the television, shake Beauregard's hand, and encourage him to run upstairs to bed. Beauregard would lie awake for hours, wondering if his mourning toys would be allowed to remain in the room or just get hauled off with his clothes to Salvation Army.

Beauregard had never told Lorena that. Nor had he told her he'd had only middling success in understanding the contemporary poems assigned to him in English class at military school. He was willing to give poetry a second chance, for her sake. He just hoped he understood the one she'd written about him.

The poetry reading was in a UAB auditorium. It was a basic, windowless, fluorescent-lit lecture hall, a hundred or so seats with half desks sloping toward a wooden lectern and black chalkboard. On a table by the lectern were a half dozen empty glass tumblers and a tall pitcher of iced water.

They arrived a few minutes early and took seats on the left-hand side of the auditorium, Lorena insisting on the aisle seat so she could get down front easily when the time came. She was a wreck, as she had predicted. While Beauregard waited, she'd bolted frantically around her apartment, searching for her black ballet slippers, running a brush through her hair, attaching some dangling silver earrings, getting her folder of poems together, stubbing a toe ("*Shit!* Sorry.") as she rounded the refrigerator to make sure Booger had food and water. They hadn't been running late. She was just nervous.

Beauregard had made a number of encouraging remarks on the drive over, but to no apparent effect. He wanted to reach over now and give one of her hands a reassuring squeeze, but she was sitting on them, rocking back and forth. He turned his attention to the crowd, estimating it at thirty-five to forty. At least a half dozen were poets, judging from the number of empty glass tumblers. Most of the rest were friends, no doubt, though a few looked like doting parents. It *was* a little like a piano recital, come to think of it, but he didn't tell Lorena.

The lights went down. A heavy bald man in a brown suit, whisperingly identified by Lorena as the English professor who led the undergraduate poetry writing workshops, stepped to the dais and made welcoming remarks. He was heartened that so many would venture out on a Thursday night to hear young poets read. He would appreciate donations to help pay for the wine and cheese. Finally he introduced the first poet, Drew Jenkins.

Jenkins was a tall, slender young man with shoulder-length hair and a confident bearing. He wore jeans, a work shirt, and an army surplus backpack. He removed his folder of poems from the backpack, set the folder on the dais, then took his time pouring a glass of water. He drank most of a glass—drank it conspicuously, too, the first-rate microphone amplifying the sound of his contracting throat muscles, the resolving "aah."

"This guy's good," Lorena whispered.

"He hasn't even started," Beauregard said, bothered at her compliment of this potential rival.

"I've read his stuff."

Before each of his three poems, Jenkins explained the source of the poem, the circumstances under which he'd written it, the number of drafts, the number of titles he'd rejected, what they were. He explained key insider references, such as, in the second poem, "times, kings, lings." That was what his older brother would say to reserve the easy chair in the TV room before going to the kitchen to make a ham and mayonnaise sandwich.

Even with the explanations, Beauregard couldn't understand Jenkins's poems. The only way he knew they were over was that Jenkins would back away from the microphone, flip his long hair dramatically, smile, then pour more water. With that, applause would begin.

"Good, huh?" Beauregard challenged during light applause between the second and third poems.

"Pretty good," Lorena said.

After Jenkins finished, the professor came forward again.

"Our next reader, Lorena Miles, is a freshman majoring in urban affairs. Lorena?"

Lorena took a deep breath, then pulled her hands out from under her legs and grabbed her folder. When she turned his way, Beauregard gave her a you-can-do-it smile and nod. Lorena gave him a weaker smile, no nod, but got up and walked to the dais.

Like Jenkins, Lorena filled and drank from a glass of water, but safely away from the microphone. The overhead light caught her silver earrings, and the reading lamp's glow accentuated the blond of her reddish blond hair, making it golden. She leaned against the dais, a posture that Beauregard thought cropped to advantage her pink blouse and black vest.

She read two poems. A nervous, but not unattractive, waver invaded her already drawling soprano. Beauregard thought that must be why she gave no introduction, just read the titles and poems. The first was the one about him.

A Leaf Blows through My Window

A leaf blows through my window.
Parched, its veins visible and thirsting,
It blows over the sofa bed,
Blows past the dog, asleep on the throw rug,
Blows into my hand.

I have caught other leaves.
Now, not looking, I have caught this one.

Leaves can be crushed, ground into particles,
scattered away on the indiscriminating wind,
But can a leaf, planted, grow?

Suddenly my hand is soil.

She stepped back from the microphone. Applause began. Beauregard, applauding hard, fighting the urge to stick two fingers in his mouth and whistle, looked around. The crowd liked this poem. Why not? It was a hell of a poem, clear and vivid. He was proud to be in it. True, he'd expected to hear his name, and he hadn't expected the Booger reference, and he wondered who those other leaves were; but those were quibbles. On balance it was fine, front-page stuff. When the applause threatened to die out, he kindled a new round, and when that was going nicely he shook a fist encouragingly, familiarly at Lorena, as if she'd knocked a home run in the bottom of the ninth inning, just for him. It was hard to see her behind the water glass. She had it up high, almost like a blind. She appeared to be blushing. As usual, it was hard to tell, given the natural rouge of her complexion.

Because he was so taken with the first poem, Beauregard had trouble concentrating on the second. It was a long, Jenkins-like poem about childhood, dense with mud pie references that no doubt symbolized something. Lorena stopped once during the reading. He thought she might be making an early move for water, but that wasn't it. After squinting at her folder for a few seconds, she went on, but the waver in her voice was more pronounced, approaching a warble. She didn't go for water when she finished, just grabbed the folder, nodded vaguely, then walked back to her seat beside Beauregard. Applause—generous, though not as strong as for "Leaf"—lasted until she had settled.

"Hey, good job," Beauregard said.

"Oh, God, no," she whispered back.

"What?"

"I got the pages mixed up on the last one. I read page three before page two. By the time I realized it, it was too late to go back. How could I be so stupid?"

The professor was calling the next poet to the dais.

"Lorena, listen." Beauregard had her by the wrist now, squeezing urgently, determined to help her through this crisis as she had helped him get over Atlanta. "*Nobody could tell.* They loved both your poems. You heard the applause. Don't get down on yourself."

He expected some acknowledgment of his effort to rally her—a reciprocal squeeze, a remark, something—but Lorena stared blankly ahead. At the break, he had to talk her into going to the lobby for wine and cheese. She knew some other poet would make a cutting remark.

As it happened, she was surrounded by fellow poets and audience members who complimented her on her reading. They cited specific lines they liked, including lines from the rearranged poem. Beauregard fetched wine and cheese, then elbowed Jenkins out of the way and stood by Lorena's shoulder. He didn't want any confusion about who the current leaf was.

By the end of intermission Lorena was buoyant. She was still buoyant when the reading ended and they went back to her apartment. To extend the spirit of the evening, she prepared another tray of wine and cheese. They finished it off quickly in the front room. After that, they tied up Booger, then unfolded the sleeper-sofa. They spread out, still clothed, and Lorena read aloud from old hardback volumes of her two favorite poets, Millay and Dickinson. Eventually they disrobed and made love, and it was good, though at one point Beauregard's elbow slipped on a poetry book. Afterward, Lorena picked up the books and found more poems to read. They made love again. The lovemaking got even better; Beauregard's comprehension of the poetry stayed more or less the same.

They lay entwined under a blue sheet.

" 'Beauregard,' " Lorena said, not calling him, but pronouncing his name for the sound. "I hadn't noticed how poetic 'Beauregard' is. All those vowels."

"It was hard to learn to spell."

" 'Beauregard Forrest,' " she continued. "Hey, I was wondering, are you related to Nathan Bedford Forrest?"

"Lorena. You've been reading."

"A little."

Beauregard shook his head. "Forrest was a great general, a cavalry genius. But no. We're not related. My dad paid a genealogist a lot of money, but the guy turned up nothing on us and Nathan Bedford."

"Was your father disappointed?"

"Some. He went through a 'Forrest was overrated' phase, but it didn't last long."

"Didn't Forrest start the KKK?"

"Helped start it. He didn't mean for it to become what it did, though. Or so his biographers say."

"Still, I'm glad you're not related to him."

"I guess I am, too."

Soon, recognizing the late hour, Beauregard rose to dress. Lorena got up, too, pulling on her terry cloth robe. They walked arm in arm to the foyer, then leaned against the front door. He told her he was going to do a story on the missing portable and could use her help.

"I'll try," she said. "All I know is what Chester tells me. He's usually right, though."

"Maybe I could talk to Chester."

"I don't see why not. He loves to talk."

"We'll set something up next week," Beauregard said professionally.

They kissed good night.

He was out the door and walking away from her apartment when he realized he hadn't mentioned Washington and Lee or his upcoming SAT test. He turned to go back, then saw that she'd shut the door and turned off the porch light.

Just as well. No need to tamper with a splendid evening. He'd tell her later. Or maybe he wouldn't tell her—just take the test and see how things played out. Robert E. Lee, of course, would have leveled with her early on, before joining her on the sleeper-sofa; but was Lee really the best authority on how to conduct a meaningful fling? Wasn't Beauregard doing pretty well on his own?

As he walked down the lamp-lit sidewalk to the party van, hands in pockets, thinking about all these things, Beauregard stepped carefully, superstitiously, avoiding cracks in the sidewalk and the occasional leaf blowing his way.

Chapter Seventeen

Late Saturday morning, all quiet in the newsroom, except for the steady buzz of the fluorescent lights and the intermittent crackle of the police radio on the city desk. Beauregard leaned over *Bartlett's Familiar Quotations,* scanning the five-page Mark Twain section, confident the epigram he needed would catch his eye. If Twain didn't come through, he'd score with Oscar Wilde or Marcus Aurelius, or maybe Shakespeare. People would be drifting in later to put out the Sunday paper. For now, Beauregard had *Bartlett's* all to himself.

The book occupied a place of honor in the newsroom, a wrought-iron stand between the news reporters' area and the copy desk, next to an identical stand for *Webster's Third.* Many reporters considered *Bartlett's* more valuable than the unabridged dictionary. Somebody in the newsroom always knew how to spell a troublesome word, but finding help with a lede paragraph was harder. Thus the affection—reverence, really—for *Bartlett's.* There was nothing like it to jump start a faltering news story. Reporters would tow themselves over to the huge volume, hook up to it for a few minutes, then come away recharged and ready to push on with their stories. Sometimes it took awhile. It wasn't always easy to make a subject like asbestos removal connect with, say, Ovid. But it could be done. Even Price, in his reporting days, would use *Bartlett's.* A pool player, he called it a cheater's stick and took pride in using it only when absolutely necessary; but he *had* used it, and he'd told Beauregard it was an invaluable tool for a cub reporter.

Beauregard needed *Bartlett's* now for his story on the first grade class that was meeting on the lunchroom stage at Hanks Elementary. In a Price-like tactical move, he'd decided to do a short, tightly focused piece on the class's situation, thus educating himself on the human cost of the missing portable and possibly prompting some guilt-ridden school board official to call him with the portable's location. The short article, probably destined for Local/State, would handsomely serve the longer, front-page article on the deer lodge scandal.

The short article had taken longer than Beauregard expected. Although freed from Pet of the Week, he still had Metro Briefs and obits, and Shealy had begun to give him somewhat more ambitious daily stories: car wrecks *with* injuries. Beauregard had needed two full weeks to squeeze in interviews with the Hanks principal, the teacher of the class, a few of the first-graders, several parents, and the spokeswoman for the school board.

They had been good weeks. He and Lorena had spent time together, going out to eat, taking in a couple of movies, taking walks, advancing their dating relationship to catch up with their physical relationship. The pleasure of those dating hours helped compensate Beauregard for seeing Price move to the desk. He looked more or less the same as assistant city editor, but he was preoccupied with supervising his reporters, six of them, all Midwesterners. One was Bowzer, who had taken over Price's old desk, next to Beauregard. A nice enough guy, but irritating of voice, and a fanatic about ice hockey. It was bad enough that he left neat stacks of *Hockey News* on his desk, where Price had left leaked documents. He also used the WATS line to call home to Michigan. Instead of hearing Price say and do funny things, like calculating the number of consecutive days he'd not chuckled at Today's Chuckle, or drawing Shealy's face on a plastic foam cup, Beauregard now heard Bowzer telling Yankee friends about Birmingham's brief experience with minor league hockey, how no one had understood the game, how it had been enjoyed exclusively for violence, and how the organist had played "Sweet Home Alabama," the new "Dixie," whenever the home team scored. Beauregard knew he'd got all this from Price; still, it bugged him. After a quick "mornin'," he ignored Bowzer and worked on Hanks.

Now, finally, he had his reporting done. Time to write. Time to hook up to *Bartlett's*.

He ran a finger up and down the Twain pages. Twain, as always, amused, but his quotes didn't strike Beauregard as right for Hanks. He turned to Oscar Wilde, then to Marcus Aurelius. They too failed to yield a lede. He turned to Shakespeare.

The problem with Shakespeare was that his section went on so long. A reporter could spend ten minutes just going through major plays and sonnets. Spending so much time with *Bartlett's* wasn't considered bad form for a reporter, as was reading *Time* magazine in the morgue, but on deadline every moment counted, and occasionally other reporters would crowd around the *Bartlett's* stand, coughing and shuffling, eager to charge up and push on with their stories.

Alone in the newsroom, Beauregard felt no pressure. He started with *King Lear* and moved backwards, eventually copying into his notebook the *Hamlet* line, "When sorrows come, they come not single spies, but in battalions." Then he scratched it out. Decent line, but not specific enough. A little melodramatic, too. The Hanks situation wasn't that bad.

He went through *Julius Caesar, Twelfth Night,* and *As You Like It,* but by the time he got to *As You Like It* his concentration was shot. Quotations passed under his finger like so many railroad ties. He'd moved on to *The Merchant of Venice* when he thought he remembered seeing the word *stage*. He backtracked to *As You Like It,* found *stage,* read and jotted down the quotation, then happily snapped the huge book shut. He jogged over to his terminal and typed what now seemed the inevitable beginning of his story, "All the world's a stage."

Good old *Bartlett's,* Beauregard thought, hitting the SAVE button and leaning back in his swivel chair. You couldn't beat it.

Beauregard knew he would have to expand on the quote, make it connect with the Hanks situation, but that would be easy enough. He'd do that after lunch. He grabbed his *Standard-Dispatch* windbreaker, comfortable on these increasingly brisk fall weekends, and headed down the corridor.

Jackson had invited him over for steak and shredded lettuce. They were eating early because Jackson was going to the Alabama game. The Crimson Tide played some home games in Tuscaloosa, some in Birmingham. Today home was Birmingham, which was why it took Beauregard a few minutes to cross the narrow street between the newspaper building and the employee parking lot. Traffic was heavy, though the game was still a couple of hours away. It wasn't a Southeastern Conference game, wasn't even a good nonconference game, was instead a fish-in-a-barrel schedule filler with the University of Akron; but from all over the state, vehicles poured into Birmingham. Beauregard didn't have to look to know what the occupants were wearing. The men wore crimson sweaters. So did the women. If they had babies, the babies wore crimson jumpsuits and possibly crimson diapers. They were on sale at quite a few places around town.

Jackson had the steaks in the skillet when Beauregard arrived. The older brother wore sweat pants only, his Nautilus-toned triceps surfacing like submarines as he pressed a metal spatula against the sizzling pink steaks.

"Game day," he said by way of greeting. "Roll Tide."

"Roll Tide."

Beauregard had noticed that Jackson's use of *Roll Tide,* never infrequent, picked up on game day. Today's lowly opponent wouldn't command as many RTs as Auburn or Tennessee, but there would be a marked increase over everyday conversation.

Beauregard draped his windbreaker over a chair. Jackson, turning from the skillet, bypassed their usual handshake and handed Beauregard the greasy spatula.

"I need a quick shower," he said. "How 'bout taking over?"

"No problem."

"Medium well!" he yelled over his shoulder as he jogged toward the bathroom.

"No problem."

Within seconds Beauregard could hear a directed rush of water pouring through the one hundred needle-fine apertures of Jackson's Euro-massage shower head. The shower made for a distant stereo effect with the cooking steaks. Beauregard flipped them. It felt odd to be flipping steaks at Jackson's after so much time with Lorena. Lorena was a vegetarian. Beauregard hadn't become one, not yet, but he was going whole meals without meat, and when he did eat meat the portions were smaller and the meats less emphatically meaty—turkey sandwiches on whole wheat rather than T-bones and barbecue. He was eating more and more vegetables. He'd even caught himself using the word *veggies.* To be at Jackson's, a steak house, felt like a much-needed vacation.

He planted a forest of steak sauce and salad dressing bottles on the table, then opened the refrigerator for lettuce. He washed the head, found two bowls and began to shred over them. He knew Lorena would be slicing carrots and cucumbers, possibly a tomato and some Gouda cheese, turning the lettuce into a first-rate salad. Give her credit: She made the most of vegetarianism.

Lorena was into so many things. She worked full time, went to school, wrote poetry. Besides occasionally volunteering at the Crisis Center, she belonged to the Sierra Club and Amnesty International. She was Big Sister to an underprivileged girl, and though the girl had stolen her hair dryer, Lorena still took her camping. Lorena didn't stop at giving money to worthy causes. She got involved. That—with meat—was another clear difference between her and Jackson. Get Down! Inc. gave its fair share to United Way, but Jackson refused to throw benefit parties. Because he was so well known, everybody from the Shriners to public television wanted Jackson running their fund-raisers. His policy, arrived at early and adhered to without exception, was "no pay, no play." A form letter explained his position more diplomatically.

Jackson, wearing slacks and a T-shirt, emerged with wet hair just as Beauregard had the spread ready.

"Looks good," he said, throwing a leg over his chair. "Roll Tide."

Beauregard, studying the table to make sure he hadn't forgotten anything, answered vaguely, reflexively, "Roll Tide."

"How you been, Beauregard?"

"Fine, Jackson." Satisfied, he took his seat. "How *you* been?"

"Busy. Busy, busy." He peppered his steak lightly. "Hey, I ran into Billy McArthur the other day. He's feeling the heat from the Boosters board. They didn't like the publicity on that Atlanta mess. They want publicity, of course, but not that kind. They got calls from Yankee newspapers. Funny calls. Yankees thought it was funny, him invading Atlanta."

Beauregard, cutting his steak, asked, "He's not going to lose his job, is he?"

"No, uh-uh. Billy's survived worse than this. This is nothing compared to the roast."

"What roast?"

"Pass me a roll."

Beauregard gave him the basket. Jackson looked into it, selected a roll from the bottom, then began to butter it on top.

"Couple of years ago," he continued, "the Boosters had a roast at the country club for old man Glover, who'd been on the board from the beginning. It started out like any other roast. Lots of jokes about how fat he is, how bald he is, his golf game. Then it's Billy's turn. He starts in on how many colleges Glover's son has flunked out of. He's naming them one by one, saying how many semesters the poor kid lasted. Glover's wife is there. She's not laughing at all. Doesn't faze Billy. He's been drinking all night. He goes on to joke about how promiscuous the Glovers' daughters are."

"Misty and Dawn?"

"Yeah. And Misty *is,* Roll Tide. But that's not something you roast a guy on."

Beauregard forked some lettuce from the plastic bowl. "How does he keep from getting fired?"

Jackson shrugged. "Billy's good at some things," he said. "Frankly, it'd be hard to replace him. Promoting Birmingham is not a job a lot of people want. It's like coaching football at Tulane or Vanderbilt."

"Tough to win, given the circumstances."

"Roll Tide."

They talked for the rest of the meal about the upcoming game. Jackson had Tuscaloosa sources who kept him informed on the physical and mental condition of the team, far beyond what made the newspaper. The paper might hint at a player's attitude problem; Jackson knew it to be homesickness. He got scouting reports on opposing teams, too. Getting information on Akron hadn't been easy, but he'd managed. They had good outside linebackers, a decent secondary. The offensive line was lousy. The quarterback could run—had to, because of the offensive line—but when hit hard he fumbled.

Beauregard nodded along. After what seemed a reasonable interval, given that this was Akron, not Auburn or Tennessee, he prepared to shift the conversation. He wanted Jackson's advice on what he should tell Lorena about taking the SAT.

He hadn't told her anything yet. Once again, he'd started to, but then she'd showed him a poem she'd written. There was no misunderstanding this poem, a long unrhyming one called "Against Standardized Testing." She wouldn't think well of him for taking the SAT again, especially if it was a prelude to winter term at Washington and Lee, which he hadn't told her about either. His consistent failure to speak about going off to college implied that he had no such plans. He hadn't lied, but he hadn't leveled with her, and he knew he should have. Now it seemed almost too late to be leveling. Once you'd veered off Robert E. Lee Road, it was hard to get back on. Beauregard thought he might not tell Lorena at all, just quietly take the SAT, score badly, and buy an additional six months to spend with her and make front page. By then she might well have tired of him, and he might well be ready to go off to school. His father would be disappointed by the low score and the failure to gain admission to W&L winter term, but Beauregard could handle that. What he couldn't handle, and what he might well face if he refused to take the SAT, was his father's fury. It was hard to say what his father might do. Beauregard could see him taking away the newspaper job he had arranged for so easily. He might say that if Beauregard wasn't going to take the SAT, there was no need for the job. A call or two, and it would be eliminated. So much for making front page. But would his father *really* react that way? Jackson would know, or would at least have an educated opinion. Beauregard was eager to sound him out.

But before Beauregard could change the subject, Jackson crossed the room and switched on the radio.

"Pregame show," he said, raising his eyebrows twice to italicize the information. "Roll Tide."

"Yeah, Roll Tide," Beauregard muttered. He'd forgotten this part of Jackson's ritual. He'd have to wait for a commercial to talk to him, or walk him to his BMW.

"You look tired," Jackson said.

"I'm all right."

"Coffee? I got a new pot."

Beauregard followed him to the far end of the kitchen counter. The pot itself was clear glass, like any other, but the surrounding coffee station was tall, cylindrical and gleamingly white. Germans had made it. It had a special vent to allow the brewing coffee aroma to permeate the room. Jackson showed him where to pour the water and insert the filter. He had the special gold filter, available by mail from the manufacturers in Germany.

"Nice," Beauregard said.

"What brand do you drink?" Jackson asked.

"Coffee?"

"Yeah."

When Beauregard mentioned his discount brand, Jackson briefly feigned choking, then brightened. "Lately I've been going to Cedric's Tea and Coffee, in the mall," he said. "I've got an account there. I've been learning all about how the beans are roasted, about how to tell if your coffee's full-bodied or not, about toxicity. Cedric's been teaching me, Roll Tide."

Beauregard gave his slightest nod.

"Want some?" Jackson reached into the refrigerator for a small white Cedric's bag illustrated by a map of Central America with Costa Rica, source of these beans, lightly shaded. "Won't take but a minute to grind and brew." He shook the bag invitingly.

"No, thanks," Beauregard said.

"I thought you liked coffee."

"I do, but I've had two cups already this morning."

Beauregard wanted another cup, but declined in silent protest of Jackson's attitude. What a contrast to Price. Price scorned fine coffee, just as he scorned decaf and the mint teas popular in Style. To Price, coffee wasn't something you drank for taste. You drank it for newsroom atmosphere and energy to do the job better. He'd be laughing at Jackson's gold filter.

Beauregard, Price in mind, decided to make one more effort at directing the conversation. He walked over and turned down the radio.

"What are you doing?" Jackson demanded. "That's the pregame show."

"The game's not for another hour and a half."

"I might miss a good interview."

"I want to talk about something else."

Jackson checked his watch. Beauregard could tell he was calculating the time needed to drive to the stadium, park his BMW, and get to his lower-level, forty-five-yard-line seats. Apparently satisfied, he sat down again at the kitchen table.

"All right, what is it?"

Beauregard sat, too. He set his plate and silverware aside, to buy a few seconds. If he wasn't careful, Jackson would take control, start asking the questions. He'd want to know how Lorena figured in all of this. He'd want specifics on their physical relationship. Having listened to Jackson give specifics about his own physical relationships with women, Beauregard knew Jackson would expect return information.

To avoid discussion of Lorena, Beauregard decided to couch things in career terms. What would Jackson do if he were within months, possibly weeks, of making front page, and their father wanted to rush him off to college? Yes, that was the way to get into this conversation.

"Consider this, Jackson."

"All right. But hurry."

"Say you've been working at the *Standard-Dispatch* for a few months. You've got an idea for a good story. With a little luck, and a lot of hard work, you find yourself in a position to make front page."

"Just a minute."

The phone was ringing. Jackson took the call in the den.

"Game day, Roll Tide," he said, voice carrying into the kitchen. "Hey, Bobby. . . . Yeah. . . . Yeah. . . . No, Dexter's hamstring is fine. It's Collins's strained knee we need to worry about. If he can't play, it's Porter, and Porter's going to get you two to three illegal procedures minimum. Dumbest guy on the team. . . . Yeah. . . . Yeah."

Beauregard crumpled a paper napkin and threw it against the refrigerator. By the time Jackson got off the phone, it would be too close to kickoff to talk at length. He began to clean off the table, but then, hearing Jackson drone on, got madder still and decided to leave the table as it was. In fact, he'd leave the condo, leave right now, while Jackson was still on the phone. Jackson deserved the confusion he would feel at walking into the kitchen to find the dishes dirty, Beauregard gone. If it disrupted his pregame routine, fine. To hell with it. Go Akron. He grabbed his windbreaker and went out.

But as he walked to the visitors parking lot, Beauregard remembered that he would be driving away in a van Jackson let him use free of charge. Jackson had helped him get his apartment, too, and had furnished it for him, albeit sparely and out of storage. Jackson was generous in his own way. True, there was an imperialistic quality to his generosity, but Beauregard had never complained about that while eating his steaks. He'd eaten a lot of Jackson's steaks. The memory of them, of all Jackson had done for him, took the edge off his righteousness. He withdrew the thought "Go Akron," wishing instead for a narrow, unimpressive Tide victory. He also left a note under the wiper of Jackson's BMW, saying he'd had to run on.

As he drove toward Southside from Devonshire Oaks, Beauregard passed a city golf course. He felt the urge to play. He'd worked hard all week. He needed to walk the steak off. Nine holes would do that—would rid his mind of the Jackson encounter, too. This clear, crisp afternoon was perfect for golf. The courses would be virtually empty, because of the Alabama game. He would swing by his apartment, pick up his clubs, and head out to Flickerwood.

Before he'd gotten a block, though, he thought about Lorena again, and how helpful she'd been in his reporting on the missing portable. She hadn't stopped with putting him in touch with gossipy Chester. She'd found other school board sources as well. He hadn't yet located the missing portable, but thanks to Lorena he had lots of background. Lorena had become quite passionate about the story. It was another cause for her, like the Sierra Club. She wanted Beauregard to make front page, of course, but she also worried about the first-graders struggling to learn to read on that noisy stage. "And the poor deer, Bernstein," she'd said. "What about them?" Every time she thought about it, she got angrier and made a new list of people at the school board to talk to, to sound out.

Beauregard turned back toward the paper. If he was going to eat steak, he'd work it off at the computer terminal, not on the links. He owed it to Lorena to put in a few more hours.

When Beauregard got to the newsroom, Bubba Shealy was sitting on the desk of Crenshaw, one of the Midwesterners, listening intently as the young man made a telephone call. Shealy didn't often work Saturdays. His outfit, knit pants and a green bowling shirt, suggested that he hadn't meant to work this one. Beauregard used his own terminal as a blind behind which to watch the scene. Crenshaw, gesturing frantically with his free hand, appeared to be trying to talk somebody into something. After a minute, his posture slackened, he nodded grimly into the phone, then he hung up. He turned in hangdog defeat toward Shealy. Shealy hit the desk with an open fist. He got up, glanced accusingly at Crenshaw, then walked over to the water fountain and kicked it. He glared again at the Midwesterner before storming into the men's room.

Beauregard, logging on, knew something very bad had gone wrong with Crenshaw's story. He'd seen anger in the newsroom, but he'd never seen anyone kick the water fountain. Shealy had kicked it hard, too. If he was wearing bowling shoes, he was hurting.

Crenshaw snapped shut his briefcase and fled the newsroom. Shealy emerged from the toilet. He stopped just outside the door, his eyes catching Beauregard's. Beauregard lowered his head and pretended to work. Peripherally, though, he could see Shealy walking toward him. No doubt Shealy needed a story to replace Crenshaw's. He'd want to know what Beauregard was working on. Beauregard had planned to take a few more days with this Hanks Elementary story, mainly to work on the writing; but there was something to be said for getting it in the paper right away. He'd be that much closer to finding the missing portable.

Shealy was looming now, breathing heavier than usual. "You been in the bathroom today, B-Four?" he asked.

"No, sir."

"Somebody dropped gum in every urinal."

Shealy had recently sent a memo demanding an end to the dropping of gum in *Standard-Dispatch* urinals. He'd confided to the copy desk chief that the sight of pink, shrimp-shaped gum all soaked with urine had bothered him awfully, surfacing in his dreams. The copy desk chief had told the assistant copy desk chief, who had told everyone else. What had been an occasional janitorial problem now was chronic.

"I didn't do it, Bubba," Beauregard said. "I don't chew gum."

"What are you working on?"

"The Hanks Elementary story."

"Remind me. I'm shook up."

Beauregard recapped the story, noting that the reporting was done and that he'd started a lede paragraph. Earlier in the week he'd even taken a roll of photographs, and one of them, a black-and-white shot of a little boy plugging his ears against the lunchroom noise, had been praised by the photo editor. If Shealy needed a story, Beauregard had one for him—one that was factually sound and strong in emotion. It was there for the asking.

Shealy remained quiet for a second, letting Beauregard's offer settle. Then he said, "I sure miss Price's reporting."

Beauregard started to make the polite, accurate response, "Me, too, Bubba," but before he could, Shealy went on to say how valuable Price was in a situation like this, how he always had some story he could scramble up, and it would be good, too, often much better than the collapsed story. Midway through Shealy's tribute Beauregard lost the desire to join in or even nod. It was deflating to hear Shealy talk of another reporter's virtues immediately after you'd offered to deliver, on your day off, when you could be playing golf, a much-needed story. Shealy was always saying something deflating. No wonder people dropped gum in urinals he'd be leaning over.

"B-Four . . . ?"

"Sir?"

"You all right, son? You zoned out on me."

"I'm fine."

"Okay, good," Shealy said. "I'll give your story a try. If it's not what I want, I can always go with AP's weekend death toll. So just relax, do your best, don't worry about it. You've got about an hour. I'd give you more time, but we need to close this section as soon as possible. When you finish, come get me."

Beauregard was still nodding when Shealy walked away. The chance to displace AP was extra motivation. AP had ambushed him on the Atlanta story. Now he'd wipe out their death toll, or at least move it backward in the paper. First, though, he hustled downstairs for a deadline-size cup of black coffee.

Beauregard rather liked writing on deadline. A reporter on deadline was like a lawyer in court, a doctor in surgery, Jackson at a party on Friday night. On deadline, you felt as if what you did mattered to somebody—to the copy desk, anyway. They couldn't leave until you finished. People in the newsroom steered clear when they knew you were on deadline. A different etiquette applied. It was all right for a reporter on deadline to yell "damn it!" or "shit!" It was all right to throw things, a thesaurus or stapler, as long as they didn't hit another reporter on deadline.

When Beauregard got back to his desk, he started right to work on his lede. He knew he had "All the world's a stage" to work with, and he knew he wanted to answer quickly at least one or two of the basic reportorial questions (who? what? when? where? how? why?); but he didn't want to clutter the paragraph. It would be a balancing act. He tried an opening, deleted it in disgust, tried another, deleted that, then risked a full lede.

"All the world's a stage," wrote William Shakespeare, and though they are a little on the young side to be familiar with his many plays and sonnets, no doubt the 25 first-graders who have yet to receive their portable classroom and are forced to meet on the noisy, crowded lunchroom stage of Hanks Elementary, 2356 Porter Street, would find themselves in perfect sympathy with that statement by Stratford, England's immortal bard.

$$\star \qquad \star \qquad \star$$

He read back through silently for content, then aloud, softly, for sound and rhythm. Not bad. He could live with it. If he had all day, he might do better, but on deadline this would work. That was another great thing about deadline: lower standards. Interesting, though, how many reporters actually wrote better on deadline. Price was one. Price would consider Beauregard's lede too long, too "windy." They'd argued sometimes about what was and wasn't good newspaper writing, usually taking specific examples from the *Standard-Dispatch*. Recently they'd disagreed about a sportswriter's feature on midget league football, Price contending that it was too much to say of a pair of under-eighty-five-pound cornerbacks, "They hit like paid assassins." Beauregard insisted that the line made the piece sing.

Having settled on a lede, he flipped through his notebook for a good quote. He'd realized some time ago that though the story had plenty of emotion—little children struggling on a noisy stage—the quotes he'd elicited didn't show it. With more time, he could reinterview some people, ask the kind of leading questions that yielded good quotes. No time for that now. He'd have to go with the best quote he had. He found it and typed.

"The stage is real noisy," said Jason Garr, 6. "I don't like the stage."

All right, time for a nut graph. What was the story about? It was about children on a stage when they should be in a portable classroom. But hadn't he said that already, in the lede? Well, yes, but that didn't matter. Shealy liked a set structure: lede, quote, nut graph.

He tried a nut graph.

Concerned parents, as well as the school's principal and the class's teacher, worry that the noise is more than just an inconvenience, is in fact a serious impediment to learning.

Boring. But Beauregard, glancing at his watch, knew he must push on. He threw in a quote from the teacher, one from the principal, another from an irate parent, then wrote a long, quoteless passage explaining why the school was so crowded and why the school board claimed it was hard to get portables. He closed with the kind of punch he knew city editors liked.

> For now, Jason and the other first-graders would like a little quiet time to work on reading, writing and two plus two. They'd like to leave the stage to Mr. Shakespeare.

Which wasn't exactly true, since none of them had mentioned Mr. Shakespeare, not even the teacher or principal; but reporters were paid to be clever, to turn the ordinary stuff of life into, if not paid assassins, something memorable. "Punch it up, punch it up" was a Shealy refrain. So Beauregard had.

He hit SAVE, then went to get Shealy. Soon they were at the city desk, Shealy in his swivel chair, Beauregard leaning just over his shoulder, as he'd seen Price do on deadline so many times.

"Back off a little, B-Four," Shealy said.

After Beauregard retreated a step, Shealy called up the story. The lede filled the screen. Shealy read it, sighed extravagantly, then swiveled around toward Beauregard.

"This makes me want to go with AP's death toll," he said.

"Why, Bubba?"

"Too slow and too long."

"It flows, though."

"Yeah, it flows. The Cahaba River flows—all night, but I don't want to read it."

"We could trim, I guess," Beauregard said.

"That's what I'm going to do."

Shealy swiveled back toward the screen and poised an index finger over the DELETE button. First he eliminated the "William" before Shakespeare, then the street address of the school, then "Stratford, England's immortal bard." He started back at the top, making more cuts and rewriting. When he backed away again the lede read:

> All the world's a stage, said Shakespeare, and nobody knows better than those first-graders at Hanks Elementary forced to meet on a noisy lunchroom stage while waiting for a portable classroom.

"How 'bout that?" Shealy said.

"Shorter," Beauregard conceded.

"Yeah. Now let's look at your quote." He did, then swiveled around again. He shook his head. "Weak quote, B-Four."

"It's what he said."

Shealy grimaced before returning to the keyboard. He paused in thought, breathing loudly, then attacked the keys. He withdrew once more, and they looked at the screen together.

Six-year-old Jason Garr, fingers plugged into his ears, summed up the stage experience. "Noisy," he said, adding that he didn't like this makeshift classroom one bit.

"Better," Beauregard said.

"I put an exclamation mark after 'noisy,' " Shealy said. "Did he exclaim, by any chance?"

"Might have. It was hard to hear on that stage."

Shealy nodded, then said, "I was just guessing that Jason is the one with his fingers in his ears, the one in your picture. Is he, B-Four? Tell me he is."

"As a matter of fact, Bubba, yes."

"Hot damn! We're rolling now!"

The rest of the editing was surprisingly light. Shealy actually liked the nut graph. When Beauregard admitted he found it boring, Shealy said nut graphs were supposed to be boring. He tightened sentences here and there, cut a dead quote, moved two others around, then hit the SAVE button.

"Henry!" he called to the copy desk chief. "We're in!"

With that he was up and on his way to the photo lab. Beauregard watched him for a few seconds, then drifted over to his own desk. He sat in his swivel chair and leaned back.

It would have been nice to have had Shealy say "good job" or give him a back rub, as he used to do Price, but Shealy was busy getting the story into the paper. Beauregard sipped idly from his plastic foam cup, the coffee cold now. He felt satisfied but also spent. Having had both experiences, he could honestly say that the moments after deadline were a little like the moments after sex. No wonder Price, recovering, used to smoke a Camel and stare at the ceiling.

Chapter Eighteen

Go ahead, Betty from Irondale."

"Am I on?"

"You're on the air, Miss Betty. Go right ahead."

"All right. Woodrow?"

"Yes, ma'am."

"The polyester scraps are gone. Ed from Center Point called to say he'd pick 'em up tomorrow night after work. He's bringing *me* a sack of bib lettuce."

"Good enough. Woodrow's marking the polyester scraps off his Swap Shop list."

"Thank you so much, Woodrow. Listen, I got to go, but know I love you. We all do. We love our Woody."

"You mighty sweet to say it. Bye-bye now."

"Bye-bye."

"All right, neighbors, we're making our way through the early part of Monday morning. 'Bout ten past eight now. What say we take a little ride in the traffic heely-copter. Frank, tell Woodrow what mischief you see from up there, boy. . . ."

Beauregard, stopped in downtown traffic, could hear the helicopter buzzing and see its bulbous shadow darkening the busy interstate. Ordinarily, he wouldn't have been listening to Woodrow on the way to work, would have taken precautions not to listen to him, hurrying through his frequency or simply avoiding

AM altogether. But Woodrow was the only talk show host popular enough to have a morning drive time spot. If Birmingham was talking about Beauregard's story on Hanks Elementary, Woodrow's show would be the megaphone.

Woodrow had been on Birmingham radio for as long as Beauregard could remember. Disc jockeys came and went, but Woodrow endured, as much a part of the landscape as Vulcan atop Red Mountain. Nobody delivered the over-forty-five crowd like Woodrow. Arbitron Ratings, reported in the *Standard-Dispatch*, confirmed it. Beauregard had read a Style profile of Woodrow, which attributed his success to an absolute refusal to be slick. It wasn't slick, for instance, to acknowledge locals' birthdays and golden anniversaries, or to call strangers "neighbors," but Woodrow did. He used courtesy titles for women, conducted periodic on-air Swap Shops and recited the Pledge of Allegiance at least once every day between 7:00 A.M. and 1:00 P.M., when his show ended. He spoke in his own drawl-intact Birmingham voice, only his was even warmer than most, was a kind of heating pad that comforted middle-aged and older people all over the city. Beauregard knew that young Birminghamians' reponse to the Woodrow phenomenon was different, more critical. Lorena had told him her avant-garde friends used *Woodrow* as an all-purpose adjective for things insufficiently hip. They spoke of their parents' Woodrow dinner parties, of Woodrow all-you-can-eat restaurants, of Woodrow haircuts, though Beauregard knew from the picture accompanying the Style story that Woodrow himself was shiny bald. The Midwesterners at the *Standard-Dispatch* all did Woodrow imitations, speaking in the third person ("Talk to Woodrow! Tell him!") and conducting parody Swap Shops in which neighbors offered hard drugs for banana pudding. Price did an eerily good Woodrow, and he had told Beauregard something that wasn't in the Style section profile, that Woodrow made big money doing live, on-the-air testimonial advertisements for groceries and auto dealers and hardware stores. Price said that whenever you heard Woodrow say, "Take it from Woodrow!" you could be sure Woodrow was taking it from somebody else. But Price had also told Beauregard never to underestimate the talk show host. He insisted that the best measure of a newspaper story's appeal was Woodrow. If Woodrow was talking about a story, the story had found its mark.

So driving to work Monday, Beauregard had tuned to Woodrow instead of the progressive rock station Lorena favored and he himself was acquiring a taste for. He'd taken the long route, to give Woodrow time, but he could see the newspaper building now and had heard nothing about his story. It was all polyester scraps and heely-copter reports. At the next red light, he worked the dial to see if some other station might be mentioning the story. Birmingham radio stations, with their lean reporting staffs, often rewrote or simply read the *Standard-Dispatch* for newscasts. But Beauregard detected no theft of his story. Disappointed, he returned to Woodrow.

"Makes me sick, Woody," a twangy-voiced man was saying, "all those children squeezed in like that."

"Makes Woodrow sick."

Beauregard gripped the steering wheel with isometric force. His Hanks story? Had to be. . . .

"I've got a trailer they could use," the man went on. " 'Course, it'd have to be hosed out good."

"What size trailer, Bobby? They need a big one."

"And mine ain't big, Wood. And it's at my little sister's house, and right now we ain't friendly. But, well, you know, for education and everything, a better chance in life, I'd be willing to go over there and get it. Try to. Can't nobody push Wanda Dopson around."

"Mighty nice of you to offer, Bobby. Hold off for now. Let's see if anybody else read that story in yesterday's paper by Beauregard Forrest. Talk to Woodrow! Tell him! Tell him if you think it's right for little first-graders to have to study on a lunchroom stage!"

Beauregard let out a rare whoop and slapped his left palm against the steering wheel. It was meant as a gesture of triumph, but he hit the horn. The driver in the Chevy ahead of the party van, apparently feeling unjustly accused of dawdling, answered with a longer, more forceful honk, and soon drivers all over the four lanes were honking. Beauregard turned up the radio. He didn't want to miss anything. Woodrow had another caller on, a Miss Eloise from Gardendale, and she, too, thought the Hanks situation deplorable, though she had no trailer to lend.

When Beauregard finally got to the turn for the *Standard-Dispatch,* he kept going, and he drove around downtown until 9:00 A.M., when he had to be at work. Woodrow was still fielding calls on the Hanks situation. Beauregard counted twelve in all. Some callers didn't want to talk about just Hanks, wanted to bring in other subjects—bingo corruption, home remedies—but Woodrow kept them focused. Everyone agreed that the newspaper was right to nail the school board for failing to get those little children off that crowded stage. Beauregard, guiding the party van into a space in the *Standard-Dispatch* parking lot, whooped again.

More affirmation greeted him as he made his way to the newsroom. Beginning with Haney, the lobby guard, employees from various noneditorial departments paid tribute. Some had read his story. Some had just heard his name on Woodrow. Either way, they toasted him with raised plastic foam cups.

It got even better in the newsroom. His computer was full of congratulatory messages from other reporters, and those who hadn't sent messages stopped by his desk. The teacher of the first grade class had called, as had Hanks parents. In fact, Beauregard had an unprecedentedly thick stack of pink phone messages, a Price-size stack. The only person he expected to hear from, but hadn't, was Lorena. He'd call her later. The thing to do now was return the calls of those people he didn't know. One of them might be a new source for the missing portable.

He had the stack of messages in one hand, the phone in the other, when Price walked up with a cup of coffee.

"Mornin', B-Four."

"Mornin', Price."

"Where's Bowzer?"

"Out on assignment, I guess."

The new assistant city editor took a seat on top of his old desk. He fingered with disapproval Bowzer's neat stack of *Hockey News,* then tapped out and lit a Camel.

Exhaling, he said, "Real good story this morning, B-Four."

"Thanks, Price."

"On a slow day, that's front page. Maybe even rack card."

If a story was done far enough in advance and considered journalistically strong enough, editors could ask the circulation department to print up rack cards: construction paper cards that promoted the story and fit into wire slots in newspaper racks all over town. Price had written many rack card stories over the years. His living room was decorated with framed rack cards: Price on zoning board corruption, Price on fire department response time, Price on lobbyists' gift-giving.

Beauregard liked hearing Price's compliment, but he knew it

was inflated. "The Hanks story isn't front page or rack card," he said, "but it did make Woodrow. That's a first for me."

"Woodrow's kind of a rack card."

"I guess. I never thought of him that way."

Price flicked ash into the wastebasket, then looked up and said, "Shealy's liking you better and better."

"You think so?"

"Yeah. In fact, don't be surprised if he gives you a staff beeper today."

"I've got yours, Price."

"I know, but put it away for now and take the staff beeper from Bubba. It'll make him feel like a good guy. We don't want to discourage that."

"Okay, Price."

And, presently, Shealy showed up at Beauregard's desk. First he gave Beauregard a back rub. Watching Price get them, Beauregard had always imagined Shealy's back rubs to be relaxing, not ham-handed and mildly painful, as this one was. Still, to endure a Shealy back rub was a career milestone, so Beauregard rolled his neck and closed his eyes and "aah"-ed with summoned conviction.

"Like that, B-Four?" Shealy asked.

"Hmmn, boy."

Shealy ended with a friendly slap, then took a seat in Bowzer's swivel chair. He whistled once, a sharp, purposeful middle-management *thweet,* and by obvious arrangement a few reporters gathered around. Rochelle was there, and Crenshaw, and Tankersley. Other Midwesterners drifted over, as did Price. They made a shadowy, smiling huddle around Beauregard.

"I've got a little presentation to make," Shealy said, projecting. "As most of you know, we got caught short Saturday. Nobody's fault, really. One of those things. B-Four here happened to be in the newsroom. At my request, he knocked out a pretty good story on a tight deadline. We were actually able to lead with it on Local/State. We give B-Four a hard time, call him 'B-Four' and everything, but he's come a long way. In recognition of his effort on Saturday, I've got something to give him. Where's that sack, Price?"

Price pushed through the crowd and handed Beauregard a white, crinkled Taco Bob sack. Beauregard, standing as he took it, noticed barbecue sauce across the tilted bell of the trademark

212

sombrero; but he smelled no food. He assumed the sack was a newsroom substitute for wrapping paper.

As Beauregard reached inside, Shealy said aloud, to everyone else, "It's a beeper. His first beeper."

"All right!" a Midwesterner said.

"Hey! Hey!"

"Roll Tide!"

Beauregard, grinning dutifully, brought out the staff beeper and held it up like a golf trophy. It was a genuinely proud moment, undercut only a little by Shealy saying "his first beeper" as if it were a first bicycle or train set.

"Over here," someone said.

Beauregard pivoted. More people had gathered—some from Style and Business—and now someone was applauding, and now everyone was. Beauregard knew the whole thing was out of proportion, but what the hell. It sounded good, felt good. He shuffled a bit, blinked gratefully.

"Speech!"

Beauregard waved the suggestion away.

"Talk to Woodrow! Tell him!"

Eventually the circle re-formed into a short line of individual congratulators, Beauregard pumping hands and absorbing back slaps. Rochelle gave him a quick, embarrassed hug. Finally Shealy took Beauregard aside.

"Your Hanks story was damn good, B-Four," he said.

"Thanks, Bubba."

"We've been getting all kind of calls on the desk. The Hanks principal phoned just before you came in. He said somebody from the school board had already been over to see where to put the new portable. They should have it by the end of the week. The principal, of course, thinks you're God's gift to journalism. He wants to change the name from Hanks Elementary to Beauregard Forrest Elementary."

"Now, Bubba," Beauregard said in modest reproach, "you know he didn't say that."

But Beauregard could see the workmen changing the block-letter sign on top of the school building.

"Words to that effect."

"Mr. Mackey's a good principal," Beauregard said. "Hard-working. Bright. Nice guy, too."

The workmen were lowering the dingy *H* now, lifting the shiny new *B* into place.

"I didn't tell him we call you 'B-Four,' " Shealy said.

Beauregard, who knew the embarrassment of ambush from his years in reenacting, waited for the taunting bayonette of Shealy's wheezy laughter. It didn't come. Shealy, expressionless, was looking into his own shirt pocket, sticking a hand in there for something. Maybe this wasn't an ambush. Maybe the flattering conversation with the principal really had occurred and Shealy had withheld the nickname out of loyalty and new respect. Though the matter was open to interpretation, Beauregard felt better than he had all day.

Shealy handed him a slip of paper. "Call this guy."

Beauregard glanced at the name and number.

"He claims to be a Vietnam veteran on a hunger strike for better benefits or something," Shealy continued. "He called me last Thursday, but he'd only been fasting for two days, so I told him to call back if he held out much longer. He called again this morning. Go see him. If there's a story, come back and write for tomorrow's paper. I'll put somebody else on Metro Briefs and obits."

"You don't want a follow-up to the Hanks story?"

This had just occurred to Beauregard. He'd been so dizzy from praise that he hadn't thought about a follow-up. If Hanks was getting a portable, that was a first-rate follow-up. He'd rather do that, and sneak in a few calls to possible sources on the missing portable, than spend all day on a fasting veteran.

"Later in the week, if the portable comes through, we'll do a follow-up," Shealy said. "Today I need a story I can count on for Local/State. So call this guy."

"All right, Bubba."

Beauregard, as befitted his new status, took his time carrying out Shealy's assignment. He sipped coffee and again enjoyed looking through the thick stack of phone messages. He checked his mail. He chatted briefly with an editorial writer who was already at work on a short, punchy piece berating the school board for its treatment of Hanks. Finally he returned to his desk and phoned the fasting veteran. The man said "Yo!" with more force than Beauregard would have expected from someone who hadn't eaten in a week, but he was probably just excited about meeting a reporter. Beauregard got directions and told the veteran he'd come right on out. When he put the phone down, he caught Rochelle looking at him from across the room: a first. Maybe she was evaluating him as a romantic prospect. Maybe she had a thing for reporters who'd been mentioned on Woodrow.

As Beauregard descended the stairs to the lobby, the morning's many good events welled up in him, cascaded. Things were working out. As soon as he finished the fasting-veteran story, he'd jump back on the missing portable. He'd see Lorena tonight, press against her with the new beeper, then lead her to the sleeper-sofa. He felt ready to try the Catfish again—that's how confident he was. Why shouldn't he be confident? Shealy himself had remarked on how far he'd come.

He'd pulled open the stairwell door and begun to cross the lobby when Haney grabbed him by the arm.

"I just called upstairs, B-Four," he said. "There's somebody here to see you." He pointed across the lobby. Lorena was there, sitting in the chair she'd sat in on Booger day, the day they'd met. She was looking the other way, at the people in line to place classified ads.

"Thanks, Mr. Haney," Beauregard said, collegially slapping the jittery security guard on the back, another first. "I'll take care of it."

So that's why she hadn't called. She'd seen his story and had come to congratulate him in person. Crossing the polished floor, looking at her, noticing the blue-and-chartreuse print dress he'd never seen before, the way her hoopskirt of reddish blond hair was tied behind her head, her work coiffure, no doubt, he felt himself smiling far more broadly than usual, almost ear to ear. Then their eyes met. Something was wrong. She kept looking at him, but she didn't return his smile. Her face had reddened from normal flush to angry crimson. He continued forward, wary now, dropping his smile. She stood before he arrived.

"SAT, huh?"

"What?"

"You're taking the SAT in three weeks," she said. "Chester found out. You didn't have the decency to tell me."

The test was in two weeks, but this was no time to correct her. "Lorena, listen," he said, hands up, palms out, aggressively pushing back the idea of himself as heel. "Okay. *Yes.* I did sign up for the test."

"Where are you sending your scores?"

"What?"

"*Where are you sending your scores?* Someplace far off I'll bet."

215

He lowered his hands and his eyes, then exhaled conspicuously. Humility and candor were his new, desperate tacts for regaining favor. "Washington and Lee," he said quietly.

"Where's that?" she snapped. "Virginia?"

"Yes."

"You bastard."

"Lorena, please. I'm sorry."

"No, Beauregard. I won't accept that. You lied to me."

"Lied?" He knew what she meant but asked the question to buy time for God knows what. He could try to tell her that he planned to bomb the SAT, but that would sound desperately implausible now. Anyway, she wouldn't respect such a plan. She was Lee-like, in her own way.

"Not saying is the same as lying," she said. "You carefully, painstakingly omitted the truth from all our intimate conversations. I can't believe I ever thought you were trustworthy."

"Lorena, please. Let's take a walk. People are noticing us here."

Stalling again, but he knew at once that he'd picked a bad time to sound as if he cared what others might think.

Her eyes narrowed now; her mouth set hard to one side. "Bastard," she whispered in cruel privacy. She started to walk away, then pivoted and slapped him hard against the right cheek. The motion and clap caused a definite rustle in classifieds. Haney bounced up from behind his guard's station. Lorena stood there for a second, amazed at what she'd done, then turned and rushed out the door.

Beauregard was still rubbing his cheek when three sportswriters came downstairs from the newsroom and brushed by on their way to lunch.

"Good story this morning, B-Four." . . . "*Damn* good." . . . "My kid goes to Hanks. Son, I want to thank you."

Beauregard, numb, nodded just enough to keep them from asking what if anything was wrong. When they left, he tried to pull himself together. Like it or not, he was still on deadline with a story scheduled for Local/State. Finding Lorena, pleading his case, would have to wait. He stumbled out the door and across the street to the employee parking lot.

When he cranked the van, Woodrow and his crowd were still talking. They were off the Hanks story, on to pit bulldogs.

"Talk to Woodrow!" Woodrow said. "Tell him!"

Beauregard switched the radio off and drove on to the fasting veteran's.

216

Chapter Nineteen

His name was Earl Bottoms. He was a thin enough red-haired man dressed in fatigues, dog tags, and combat boots. He lay back now in a green chaise longue in the living room of his dusty, sparsely furnished east Birmingham duplex. When he wasn't talking, he spooned ice chips from a pink Tupperware bowl on his lap.

Beauregard, seated precariously in the trough of a black plastic beanbag chair, pretended to look down at his notebook. Really he had shut his eyes. He was trying to gather himself. He was supposed to be working now, but he wondered if he could, feeling as he did, gutted. Of course he would work. He *had* to. He'd work fast, too, in the interest of a quicker reconciliation with Lorena. If the story was shit, too bad. Everyone would have to understand. He opened his eyes and saw the fasting veteran spooning another ice chip. Beauregard felt a little sorry for the old guy—one chance in the limelight; all dressed up in his fatigues and dog tags; starving to death—but he had to hurry this story. He turned to a clean page and began to lash him through the early phase of the interview.

"Age?"

"Forty-four."

"Branch of service?"

"Army."

"Rank?"

"Private in the infantry. What they call a 'grunt.' "

"How many days fasting?"

"It'll be a full week tomorrow."

"Weight loss?"

"What?"

Beauregard looked up from his notebook. "How much weight have you lost?"

"I don't know."

"What do you mean you don't know?"

Beauregard was more exasperated than angry. It was just his luck to draw a fasting veteran who didn't know how much weight he'd lost. The guy was defensive about it, too. The guy was *weird*. Beauregard hadn't really pressured him that much, but he was shifting his butt in the chaise longue, fingering his dog tags chain. "This weight thing, Mr. Forrest," he said, looking away, totally defeated by the question. "I just don't know. I didn't think to keep track. I guess I should have."

"Do you have any scales around here?" Beauregard said. "We could check."

The fasting veteran shook his head. "Tina took the scales. The judge gave her the furniture, and Tina said scales was furniture. I didn't question it."

"Can you *guess* how much weight you've lost? It's an important detail. My editor will definitely want to know."

"I'd guess ten pounds. At least ten. You can put that down. Say, Mr. Forrest, do you do all your interviews this quick?"

"No, not all," Beauregard said. "How long are you going to be fasting?"

"As long as it takes, I guess. . . . I'd appreciate it if you'd hand me those cigarettes."

Beauregard tossed him the Marlboros and book of matches from a nearby folding table. He watched impatiently as the fasting veteran lit a cigarette and took a drag. Smoking on a fast was a violation, no doubt, but Beauregard wasn't going to make an issue of it. He was in a hurry.

"What's the purpose of this fast?" he asked. "Just briefly, Mr. Bottoms."

The question seemed to rally the fasting veteran. He pulled up in the chaise longue, and as he spoke he gestured with the burning cigarette. "I want better job training and medical benefits for the local Vietnam veteran," he said. "And I want to meet with top local officials."

"Specifically who?"

The fasting veteran angled his head, surprised. "You don't want names, do you?"

"Yes, I do," Beauregard said. "Of course I do."

The fasting veteran collapsed back into the chaise longue. "I can't give you names. . . . Pass that ashtray."

Beauregard did. "Why not, Mr. Bottoms?"

"I, uh—I just can't think in those terms right now."

"Why not?"

Suddenly the fasting veteran was up, standing over Beauregard, breathing hard. "Because I'm *hungry*, Mr. Forrest!" he said. "Can't you understand that, man! I'm just real, real hungry right now!"

"All right, okay. Easy."

"You never fought in Vietnam."

"I know I didn't."

"What the hell do you know about it?"

"Easy." Beauregard held up his reporter's notebook, the white pages fluttering like a truce flag. "Let's just forget that last question. Let's just calm down now and move on."

It went back and forth like that for a while, the fasting veteran handling certain questions easily, others not at all. Beauregard decided that he was as crazy as he was hungry. The opinion was confirmed by the crude, handwritten press release the fasting veteran gave him. Half a word was in cursive, the other half in print. Some letters leaned east, some west. Tiny consonants jammed up against large, rounded vowels. And, of course, like quite a few of the press releases Beauregard handled, it made little sense.

"Mama, she don't understand about this fast," the fasting veteran was saying now. "She keeps bringing over baked beans, my favorite, which makes it that much harder."

He was looking at the old lady's framed picture on the dusty fireplace mantel. He began to sniffle. Then, abruptly, the sniffles became great shoulder-heaving sobs, rattling the flimsy chaise longue. Beauregard climbed out of the beanbag chair and went into the kitchen. Scanning the room for a paper-towel roll, he looked past a fruit bowl and a loaf of white bread and various open sacks and containers. He ripped off a couple of towels and walked back into the living room. The fasting veteran accepted the towels gratefully and honked into them a couple of times. Beauregard patted him on the shoulder. Still patting him, he looked away at his watch. "Mr. Bottoms, I really need to go."

219

The fasting veteran blew again, then looked up and asked quaveringly, "When's this going to be in the paper?"

"Maybe tomorrow. Maybe. I never promise."

"You need a picture of me? I've got some snapshots."

"We'll probably send a photographer out."

"You think your story will get me on TV?"

"I don't know."

"On Woodrow?"

"Maybe."

The afternoon traffic rush had begun. At one intersection, Beauregard had to wait five long minutes to pull into traffic. Every time it was all right one way, it was all wrong the other. It was as if the motorists had synchronized their trips to mess up Beauregard's. Finally, gunning it, he made his turn and headed on to the paper.

As he drove, he thought about the fasting veteran. The medical benefit he needed was psychotherapy. He was more than a little crazy. He'd seemed astonished when Beauregard suggested that fasting privately, in one's duplex, might not attract as much publicity as setting up in the courthouse park, or in front of the VA Hospital. In ways small and large, the guy had his fast all wrong. There ought to be a license for fasting, Beauregard thought. Ought to be standards.

When he got to the newsroom, deadline frenzy had set in. People were yelling, "Damn it!" and, "Shit!" and standing in line at *Bartlett's Familiar Quotations*. Even Bowzer was hard at work on something.

Beauregard thought fleetingly about telling Shealy how crazy the fasting veteran was, in case he might want to kill the story. But did it really matter if the fasting veteran was crazy? Lots of people in the news were crazy. A fast was a fast, however crazed or incompetent. Besides, if Beauregard backed off the story, Shealy would have a hole to fill, and he'd be pissed. Beauregard might even get a Bowzer-like reputation with Shealy. Shealy had sent Bowzer to cover a fire once, and he'd returned saying, "Nothing to it," though his *Standard-Dispatch* windbreaker reeked of the blaze. He'd been in Shealy's doghouse for days. That's where Beauregard would be if he didn't fill the hole in Local/State.

So after doffing his blazer and fetching a cup of coffee, Beauregard sat at his terminal and rode the newsroom energy like a large, cresting wave. First he made a photo assignment through the computer system, then he called the VA office, getting the "no comment" he expected. Now he was clear to write. He flipped through his notebook, took a sip of coffee, banged out the top graphs.

A Birmingham man hasn't eaten for a week in protest of what he claims is a lack of job training and medical benefits for himself and other local Vietnam veterans.

Earl Bottoms, 44, of 9857 Bass Street in east Birmingham, vowed to continue his fast until he meets with unspecified "top local officials" to discuss the situation.

He said his fast has been hard.

"Mama, she don't understand about this fast," he said, reclining in a chaise longue and spooning ice chips from a Tupperware bowl. "She brings over baked beans, my favorite, which makes it that much harder."

Bottoms said the lot of Vietnam veterans has improved in other cities but not in Birmingham. He's not sure why. Local Veterans Administration officials refused comment.

Beauregard read back through what he'd written. Boring, he decided, but he could live with it. He would withhold style and a rich vocabulary in the interest of finishing quickly and finding Lorena. He took another sip of coffee before banging out the remaining paragraphs. He hit the SAVE button and sent Shealy a computer message saying the story was ready to be edited. He looked across the newsroom and saw Shealy and Bowzer together by the city desk, no doubt editing whatever Bowzer had written.

Price walked up with his own steaming plastic foam cup. "How's that staff beeper working?"

"Okay, I guess," Beauregard said. "No one's beeped me, yet."

"You all right, B-Four? You don't look too good."

"I'm okay. Tired."

"How'd your fasting-veteran story turn out? The guy still standing?"

"Yeah. It's a weird story, Price. I gave it a shot. That's all I can say. . . . Listen, Price, any chance *you* could edit my story? I need to get out of here."

"Sorry, B-Four, but Shealy's got me all backed up. He should be free in a minute. You're after Bowzer."

"What's Bowzer working on?"

"I don't know. You want me to find out?"

"No, Price. That's okay."

Beauregard watched Price walk away, then went back downstairs for a coffee refill. He finally had time to be miserable about Lorena. He realized how happy he'd been the past few weeks, how far past a meaningful fling they'd gone. At last he'd had someone to talk to, to touch, to think about in random moments, rather than the War Between the States. He knew he should have leveled with her about the SAT and Washington and Lee. There were people you leveled with, like Lorena, and people you didn't, like his father, and he hadn't known the difference. He knew now, and from now on he'd level with her. But first he had to make up with her. He hoped, when he found her, he would know what to say.

Back in the newsroom, he noticed that Bowzer was no longer with Shealy on the city desk. Shealy sat alone at his terminal, still editing something. Beauregard sent him another computer message, reminding him the fasting-veteran story was ready, then picked up the "Missing Portable" file to distract himself. It was no distraction. It was, in fact, proof of the serious professional consequences if he didn't make up with Lorena. She was his key to this story. Over the weekend her friend Chester had come up with a serial number for the trailer and the names of three suspects from the school board maintenance department. Two young guys and an old guy, and they had access to the trailer, and they hunted together most weekends. The old guy was named Rufus Tate, and he was legendary around the school board for his wiles and in-house ruthlessness. Chester believed a disgruntled underling would eventually leak him the trailer's location. If so, and if they could find it, Beauregard had his front-page story. But everything was in jeopardy with Lorena angry at him. Chester was Lorena's friend, not his.

Beauregard looked up from the file and saw MESSAGE PENDING on his computer screen. He called up the message.

B-Four: I went ahead and edited your story. I made a few changes, nothing big. Good job. Good *writing* job. If the art's okay, we'll put this on the Local/State front—probably above the fold. Thanks again. Bubba.

Beauregard glanced over at the city desk. Shealy was holding up a layout sheet, talking to a copy editor who stood beside him. Amazing. He'd actually pleased Shealy with this slapdash deadline story. It was something he hadn't counted on, like throwing in a basketball from half court. A little encouraged, he slipped on his blazer and hurried out.

It was the barely illuminated half hour after sunset, a winsome transitional time known in some quarters of Birmingham as "dusky dark." Beauregard flicked on his headlights, then guided the van into sparse, post-rush-hour traffic. When he had a free hand, he buttoned his blazer. He felt chilly even inside the cab.

Knowing it was Monday night, school night for Lorena, he drove to UAB. He had no idea where on the sprawling campus her history of Birmingham class might be meeting, but that didn't stop him. He parked and began to walk the campus, questioning people. Someone suggested that he go to the student center for a course schedule. He did, though it meant a long, chilly hike. When he got there, he asked at various desks until he found the thick newsprint document. He identified the building and classroom number, got directions, and began another cold trek.

By the time he found the lecture hall, it was almost 8:30 P.M., an hour into the two-hour class. The lecture hall was in a building where all the classrooms opened outside, onto concrete breezeways. This particular breezeway was like a wind tunnel, chilling and accelerating the air. Beauregard huddled against a bulletin board that offered snow skiing trips and discount magazines. He would wait for her here. When she came out, he would be impressively red-faced with cold. She'd appreciate what he'd endured for reconciliation.

Standing there, getting colder and colder, teeth actually chattering, which was good, because it would help make his case, he noticed the odd looks given to him by students passing by. He couldn't really blame them. He was, after all, a shivering, rather formally dressed young man without books or backpack, without even the sense to pocket his increasingly red hands. Beauregard shrugged off the odd looks. Nothing mattered now but reconciliation, and it would begin as soon as she walked out that door and saw him frozen.

When the bell finally rang, he took his place to one side, in a shadow, where he could chatteringly call her name and step into view. But she didn't walk out alone as he'd imagined she would. She was with a group of students, four young men, and they were talking and laughing, obviously full of some witty note on which the class had ended. They turned down the corridor without even noticing Beauregard. He waited a second, heart sinking, then ordered himself out of the shadow. "Lorena!" he called.

She stopped, obviously recognizing his voice. The others stopped with her, a couple of them looking back, annoyed and ready to be hostile. Lorena did not look back. "Let's go," she said after a second. And the entourage proceeded on, talking and laughing as if nothing had happened.

This was worse than the lobby slap. Beauregard fell back against the bulletin board, feeling through his blazer the blunt end of staples and tiny plastic handles of pushpins. He was punished further by another round of laughter, then by slamming doors and cranking engines. He looked down the corridor in time to see her green Vega in a short, collegial line of departing traffic.

She would expect him to give up now. *No way.* He sprinted across campus to the van, then drove as fast as he could to her apartment, taking every Southside shortcut. She wasn't an especially fast driver. He knew he had a shot of being on her porch when she pulled up.

When he got there her car was nowhere around. He cut the engine and waited, hands still gripping the steering wheel. Maybe she'd stopped off for a drink with her friends. Maybe, God, she'd gone home with one of them.

A chilly and insecure half hour passed. He got out and waited on the brightly lit porch. Then he got back into the van to wait. He was back on the porch again, hands in pockets, when she pulled up.

He walked to the very center of the porch, facing her and the Vega, his shadow cast forward over the front steps. She studied him from behind the windshield. Then, deliberately, as if nothing special were going on, she got out of the car with her backpack and came forward.

"Go home, Beauregard," she said quietly as she brushed by. "I'm not impressed."

He turned to face her. "Lorena, please. I'm not trying to impress you. It's really cold out here. Let me just come in for a minute."

"I'm sure the dorms will be toasty warm at Washington and Lee."

"Lorena . . ."

"No, Beauregard." She'd been turned toward the door, inserting the key, but now she looked back at him. "*No.* You weren't

224

honest with me. I thought you, of all guys, would be. But I was wrong."

"I'm sorry, Lorena."

"Go home, Beauregard. I mean it. I think you better just run along home now."

Before he could think of anything else to say, she'd let herself inside and shut the door.

A half hour later he sat in Taco Bob's office, sipping black coffee after having polished off a pork plate and fried apple pie. Still officially devastated, he'd at least warmed up and filled his belly. Taco Bob had fetched the food and sat with him. Now the smaller man returned from the very back of his office with a painted canvas.

"What is it, Bob?"

"Architect drawing."

"Your bed 'n' barbecue?"

"Ro' Tide."

Architectural drawings were, by definition, romantic; but if this building came anywhere close to the artist's conception, Taco Bob would have a first-class establishment. It would be a two-story redbrick building, columns and shutters, with a swimming pool on one side and a Flickerwood-like gazebo on the other. The grounds would be beautifully landscaped and out front would be a small, dignified hand-painted sign, not a big green Coca-Cola job like the one atop Taco Bob's.

"Nice, Bob," Beauregard said politely. "Real nice."

Taco Bob pulled a brochure from his apron and handed it to Beauregard.

"Let me guess," Beauregard said. "This is the slick for your bed 'n' barbecue."

Taco Bob nodded. "You read for grammar," he said.

So Beauregard proofread the four-color brochure. The guest rooms, he learned, would include furniture and crafts from different Southern states, the main barbecue states. There would be a North Carolina Room, a Georgia Room, a Tennessee Room, and so on. The gift shop would sell crafts, recipe books, and sauces. Besides the pool, there would be tennis courts and an exercise room. Free shuttle service to and from the airport, of course. And a conveniently late checkout time, since the main meal would be a barbecue brunch.

225

"Looks clean to me, Bob."

"My daughter wrote."

"She did a first-rate job. Really. I wouldn't change a thing."

As he watched Taco Bob take the slick back and return the canvas to its place against the wall, Beauregard felt humbled, as he always did, by the slender immigrant's achievements. Oh, well. At least he could pull together an acceptable newspaper story from dubious material. And do it on deadline.

They were clearing away Beauregard's paper plates and plastic-ware when one of Taco Bob's younger children stopped by with a rolled-up *Standard-Dispatch*.

"You're just getting today's paper?" Beauregard asked.

"Tomorrow's paper," Taco Bob corrected proudly. "Taco Bob's first on route."

"Let me see, Bob. I've got a story running."

They leaned together over Local/State. The fasting-veteran story was right there on the front, anchoring the section, with a good shot of Bottoms smiling and spooning ice chips in his chaise longue. Beauregard read the story. Shealy, true to his word, had made only small changes. The story jumped inside, though, so Beauregard wanted to check the jump. He started to turn the page, but Taco Bob stopped him. He had a finger on the fasting veteran.

"I know that guy," he said. "That guy eat here."

Beauregard's mouth went dry, but he managed to chuckle non-chalantly. Then, because he had to, he asked, "Recently?"

Taco Bob nodded.

"*This* guy?"

Taco Bob looked again at the newspaper. "Eat here yesterday. Eat here today. Eat here *every* day, Beau'gard. Come in first thing, order bake bean. Some day two order bake bean. Gas out dining room."

Beauregard listened with increasing depression as Taco Bob explained how Bottoms was always talking ignorantly about Vietnam, always misplacing rivers, deltas, mountain ranges, even the big cities, Hanoi and Saigon. Taco Bob was sure he'd never stepped foot in the country. He bet he'd never even been in the service, that he'd got those fatigues and dog tags at the army/navy store on Sixth Avenue.

"Bob, I need to use your office," Beauregard said quietly. "I need to call somebody."

As Taco Bob closed the door behind him, Beauregard reached

226

for the white pages. He wished he could call Price, but it would have to be Shealy. He'd have to call him at home, too, and right away, so Shealy could phone the paper and have the story pulled for the later editions.

He was listening to the dial tone, waiting with dread for Shealy's voice and breathing noises, when he pulled out the A section and saw Bowzer's story on Hanks Elementary's new portable classroom. It was obvious what had happened. The portable had arrived early, and Shealy had given the story to Bowzer. The front-page story.

"Hello."

"Bubba."

"B-Four?"

"Yes, Bubba. Listen, Bubba. We've got a serious problem."

Shealy's treachery was a hammer blow, to go with all the others, but Beauregard would ignore it and tell him about the fasting veteran. Telling the son of a bitch was the Lee-like thing to do.

227

Chapter Twenty

Press run on the first edition was only a few thousand copies, so the fasting-veteran story didn't get widely circulated, but Shealy insisted on a correction for the next day's paper. "Due to a reporter's error," the indictment began, "an article on a so-called 'fasting veteran,' the entire premise of which proved erroneous, appeared in the early edition of Tuesday's *Standard-Dispatch*. We deeply regret the article's publication." It did not escape Beauregard's attention that this correction, run in a little box on page A-Three below Today's Chuckle, was closer to the front page than anything he'd written.

"You know, B-Four," Shealy said later in his office, all eyes having followed Beauregard there as he crossed the newsroom to answer Shealy's yelled summons, "Price gave me hell for assigning Bowzer the follow-up story on Hanks Elementary. He called me 'management scum,' the way he used to, and told me I was thwarting your career. My position, of course, was that you were out on assignment already. I didn't want to pull you off one story for another one, especially when I had Bowzer sitting around. Still, I felt pretty bad about it. I was at home, drinking a beer, feeling pretty bad, when I got your phone call. After that I didn't feel bad at all."

"I guess not."

"See, B-Four, I don't have to thwart your career. You perform that task just fine all by yourself."

Beauregard didn't respond, just looked down and away at Shealy's leaning stack of AP Stylebooks. He could hear Shealy rocking back and forth reproachfully in his swivel chair. "Bottom line?" the city editor said.

Lord God, Beauregard thought. Not this. Not the bottom line. Shealy had recently been in a phase of asking "Bottom line?" then answering himself, after a pause. When Beauregard first got to the *Standard-Dispatch,* Shealy was in a phase of encouraging reporters to use "Upshot: . . ." in their stories. He'd want a reporter to round off a complicated explanatory passage on, say, homestead exemption, by writing, "Upshot: lower taxes." Even when the story was inconclusive, when there was no upshot, not yet anyway, he would want one, asking aloud, "Can't we get an 'Upshot: . . .' in here?"— only he'd pronounce the word *colon,* too. The phrase *upshot colon* gained currency in the newsroom, became a thing to say behind Shealy's back. Price introduced Upshot J. Colon as a peripheral character, a "helpful but flatulent bailiff," in his computer system novel *That's Close Enough.* Price even did a health story on roughage deficiency just so he could get "Upshot: colon problems" into the paper.

Now Shealy was in a "Bottom line?" phase.

"Bottom line is," he answered himself importantly, "you let us down. I'll have to take some disciplinary action. Don't want to, but have to. I'm not sure yet what it will be. I'll be sending messages."

By the end of the long day, Shealy had put Beauregard back on Pet of the Week and taken away his staff beeper. He'd huffed by late in the afternoon, just after deadline, when reporters were staring at the ceiling, unable to leave or do more work. Without breaking stride he'd snatched the little black instrument from Beauregard's desk. Later Beauregard would decide it was just an impulse on Shealy's part, but at the time the act seemed as deliberate, conspicuous, and painful as the ripping off of stripes in a court-martial.

Although a couple of reporters bestirred themselves enough to send Beauregard consoling messages, Price was the only one to counsel him at length. They retreated to a Waffle House after work.

"Cigarette?" Price asked, reaching for his Camel pack as soon as they settled into their corner booth.

"That's okay, Price. I've pretty much quit. Bowzer doesn't like it around the desk. Anyway, I was never that crazy about smoking."

Price shrugged. "Bowzer," he repeated, shaking his head in regional and professional disapproval. "What the hell, though, maybe I'll quit smoking, too. I'm not allowed to smoke on the city desk. It's too much trouble to walk across the room or go outside."

"Quit, Price. It'd be good for you."

"I'm seriously thinking about it."

"Don't think about it. Just do it."

"Next week."

Price lit his Camel, took a long drag, then reached across for a menu. Before long they had ordered, received, and begun to eat their waffle stacks. They sipped black coffee from brown ceramic mugs.

As the meal proceeded, they talked about the fasting-veteran story. It was a Price pep talk, mostly. First Price told Beauregard he admired him for phoning Shealy right away. "Not all reporters would have done that," he said. "A lot of reporters would have kept quiet, ridden it out, hoped for the best." When Beauregard didn't say anything, just shrugged and kept eating waffles, Price added that all reporters make mistakes. He himself had had two corrections in his last year as a reporter. Early in his career, he'd had one every couple of months. He recalled a city council story in which he'd used *trash* and *garbage* interchangeably.

"They're not the same?" Beauregard asked. With anyone else, he would have laughed knowingly, then later looked up the terms in his handy AP Stylebook.

"Not in that jurisdiction, B-Four," Price said, pouring syrup. "In that jurisdiction, and quite a few others, trash is technically twigs and leaves and other kinds of yard crap. Garbage is food and other stuff from the house. Pork chops and coffee grinds. Old burned-out light bulbs."

"Yeah."

"Anyway, I didn't know any better and used *trash* for *garbage,* *garbage* for *trash.* I think I even threw *refuse* in there. It was Synonym City for the last half hour of deadline. The correction took two paragraphs." Price waited a second, then asked, "Feel better?"

"I guess so."

"Good. You *should* feel better. That Hanks story you did was first-rate. The Atlanta story would have been, if I hadn't screwed you up by calling the AP photographer."

"No, Price. It wasn't your fault."

"Yes it was, B-Four. People get in your way, but you do good work. I mean it. Hanging around you almost makes me want to be a reporter again."

It took awhile, but Beauregard did feel better for having talked to Price. The next day he clipped on Price's old beeper. Doing so, he couldn't help but think of the reenacting term *farbing,* which meant fighting in nonauthentic clothes. Beauregard considered himself farbing, sort of, by wearing the beeper, because no one would beep him as long as he was only doing Metro Briefs, obits, and Pet of the Week. Still, he would wear the beeper, for Price's sake and in mild defiance of Shealy. For those same reasons he resumed using spare time to work on the missing-portable story. He could tell that Bowzer, back on the WATS line with his hockey buddies, wasn't going to pick up on it.

As he had feared, though, the sources he had developed with Lorena's help had all dried up. Even when Beauregard could reach them by phone, which was rare, they no longer had anything to say. Chester was the only one who proved helpful. They talked on the phone one night. A precise, nasal-voiced young man, he provided insight not on the missing portable, but on why Lorena had turned against Beauregard so strongly.

"In her mind you turned out like the other guy," he said.

"What other guy?"

" 'Spencer' something. I can't remember his last name. Anyway, this Spencer cretin never said anything about going off to college either. He and Lorena had dated for two years. They were talking about moving in together. Then one Thursday night he announces he's leaving for Auburn. Leaving the next day."

"God a'mighty, Chester."

"I know. That's why she got so upset when I told her about you and the SAT. Then when you told her about Washington and Lee—bad move, Beauregard—she *really* lost it."

Later Beauregard pondered the new, salient information. He'd thought she'd overreacted, but now, knowing the history, he had to reevaluate. Lorena saw him as another Spencer. That was unfair, but he could see how she would. "Spencer," Beauregard said aloud. What the hell kind of name is *Spencer?* Beauregard wondered what this Spencer looked like, what kind of personality he had, and whether Auburn was his school of choice or just the best he could do.

Beauregard renewed efforts to reach Lorena, but she continued to avoid him, ignoring letters and hanging up the phone. Days passed. Rejections accumulated. He kept writing and calling. She bought an answering machine to screen her calls.

"We can't come to the phone right now," her message began. Beauregard hoped the "we" referred to her and Booger. "Leave your name and number at the beep, and we'll get back."

But she didn't get back when Beauregard called.

Eventually, because nothing else had worked, he wrote a sarcastic letter. He told her he wanted to nominate her for an international pouting award and needed her lip measurements in millimeters. It was something he remembered Jackson writing to a girlfriend one time, with some success. Three days later Beauregard got a letter back. Actually, there was no real letter, just an envelope full of crushed oak leaves and little strips of paper containing one typed word each. Beauregard, pulling them out one by one in a private corner of the newsroom, realized with a chill that he was looking at a shredded version of "A Leaf Blows through My Window," Lorena's poem about him.

Later that day Chester called.

"Check your mail?" he asked.

"Yeah. Wait—she told you she did that?"

"It was my idea."

Beauregard paused, breathing hard. "Congratulations, Chester," he said finally. "Congratulations to you and Lorena both for making me feel like total shit."

"Hey, we had to do something, after your lip letter."

"What doesn't she tell you, Chester?"

"She doesn't always tell me, Beauregard. I like to poke around, like to *find* things."

"Chester, do I have a chance with her?"

"Maybe. A slight chance, perhaps. The lip letter didn't help."

After two more miserable days, Beauregard sent a last letter encouraging Lorena to pass along any information about the missing portable to Price or Bowzer. "This story is bigger than either one of us," he wrote. "It needs to be written. I don't care who gets the byline."

He felt sure she'd respond one way or another to this bald-faced lie. When she didn't, he gradually withdrew on both the romantic and journalistic fronts. He decided, in the absence of any better plan, to do the expected: take the SAT, go to Washington and Lee, forget all about this abnormal interlude in which it actually seemed possible that he, an underachieving younger son, small-boned, without the family nostrils, subdued by manners and tradition, could actually be a kick-ass, front-page reporter with an unconventionally beautiful girlfriend who wrote poetry, volunteered at the Crisis Center, and engaged him in vigorous, guilt-free sex, if not the Catfish. In short, Beauregard gave up. He started coming to work on time rather than early. He quit making extra calls on Metro Briefs, obits, and the missing portable. With Pet of the Week, he didn't go down to the Humane Society, just read the press release, looked at the photograph, and described mixed-breed "Pete" as "frisky," nothing more.

One cool, rainy afternoon he arrived home from work and found the front door wide open. Burglars had made off with his black-and-white TV and a few other things. He drank a beer, to calm himself, then called the police. Two officers arrived within the hour and walked around the little apartment, inspecting and making notes. Just before leaving, one of them, a black guy with a mustache, took Beauregard by the arm.

"Sorry about your place being ransacked," he said. "I know it's a strange feeling to see home sweet home looking like this."

"Thanks, officer. I appreciate it."

"Get a dead bolt, man."

"I will, sir. First thing tomorrow. Thanks for coming out."

But Beauregard's place had not been ransacked. In these post-Lorena days he had become lethargic about housekeeping, just as he'd become lethargic about journalism. If anything, his place was neater now, the burglars having made off with a percentage of the clutter.

Beauregard didn't tell anybody about the incident, not even Price or Jackson. He'd resumed eating T-bone steaks at Jackson's on a fairly regular schedule, but he didn't confide in him about the burglary. Silently, against the physical evidence, Beauregard clung to the notion that he'd been ransacked. The place hadn't been, but he'd been. It was some small comfort to think so, anyway.

Chapter Twenty-one

Beauregard was first to arrive at Dryson High on the morning of the SAT. It was a brisk morning, the breeze rattling the flagpole chain. When he found the front doors locked, Beauregard walked across the street to a convenience store, bought a large plastic foam cup of black coffee, and walked back. He drank his coffee in the van. He didn't read the newspaper or listen to the radio, just sat there, face forward, hands encircling the steaming cup.

Eventually a crowd of young people began to form outside the locked doors. They lined up, sort of, not wanting to appear too eager, also not wanting to miss any advantage in being early.

Beauregard continued to sit in the van.

He'd risen before sunrise and slipped on the nearest pants, a work pair draped on a folding chair by the bed. He grabbed a heavy shirt, a windbreaker, and tennis shoes from the closet. He dressed in semidarkness, and when he finally flicked the light switch he realized that the shirt was really the gray wool vest to his Confederate uniform. He didn't change. No one at the SAT would care; and, anyway, he would have the windbreaker covering most of it.

His search for a sharpened pencil led first to a kitchen drawer, then, successfully, to a paper box of miscellaneous items on the hall closet floor. He locked up his apartment, flicking the new dead bolt, then drove the party van to New Arlington. There, the sun pinkening a low bank of clouds in the eastern sky, but providing, in Beauregard's view, damn little warmth, he loaded a reluctant Snuffy/Traveller into the horse trailer for his father.

After he latched the door, Beauregard turned and saw Mr. Forrest in the bright fluorescent square of the kitchen window. He sat at the table, uniform on, hair combed the other way, Lee's way. He was sipping coffee and leaning over the *Standard-Dispatch*.

Beauregard, knowing that his father would disapprove of casual wearing of any part of the Confederate uniform, zipped up his windbreaker. Then he went inside.

"Hello, Beauregard," Mr. Forrest said, rising.

"Dad."

They shook hands.

"Ready for the SAT?"

"I think so."

"Have you got pencils? I had some sharpened for you at the bank."

Beauregard smiled. "I've got a fine pencil, Dad," he said, patting his windbreaker pocket. "Thanks anyway."

Beauregard poured himself a mug of coffee, then joined his father at the kitchen table. Mr. Forrest started in on the upcoming reenactment practice. It would be at the old Calhoun site, between Birmingham and Huntsville. The next few weekends would consist of highly structured practices for the important February reenactment at Olustee, Florida, but today's would be unscripted, a free-for-all to boost troop morale. The Chattanooga boys were coming with artillery. The Montgomery crowd might show up, too. As usual, postbattle festivities in the modern camp would include deli sandwiches and a cold keg of Budweiser.

Throughout the briefing, Beauregard sat across from his father, alternately nodding and saying, "Yes, sir." At Price's suggestion, Beauregard had tried to cut back on saying "sir." While acknowledging that there were occasions when it was advantageous, Price maintained that *sir* usually introduced an unfortunate hierarchy into reportorial conversation—the subject on one level, the reporter way down below. Beauregard had cut back some, but in addressing his father it was impossible. He might as well try to quit blinking. Nearly everyone younger said "sir" to his father, even Jackson. Beauregard had, over the years, loosened to the point of omitting the word every so often, to show anger or disagreement; but this was not an occasion for that. It was too early in the morning. And, actually, it felt comfortable and even reassuring to be here in the kitchen with him, nodding and "sir"-ing again. After all that personal growth in the newspaper business, it was nice to contract a little, to again be a mere aide-de-camp.

"Why don't you come join us after the SAT?" Mr. Forrest was saying now. "We always need a good infantryman."

"Thanks, Dad. But I imagine I'll be pretty whupped."

"If not, you know where we'll be."

"I do, sir. I'll keep it in mind. . . . Have you heard anything lately from Washington and Lee?"

Mr. Forrest tensed. Then, as quickly, he lightened. "You let me worry about Washington and Lee," he said. "You just concentrate on the SAT."

"Yes, sir."

Mr. Forrest reached across the table and squeezed Beauregard's forearm. "I know you'll do well, son. This stretch as a cub reporter was all you needed."

"Maybe, sir. I sure hope so. We'll just have to see."

Now, unzipping his windbreaker, Beauregard filed in with the rest of the test-takers. They moved as a column down a linoleum corridor, then left, through a double door, into a lunchroom. It was a huge, brightly lit space with long tables and alternating silver and black plastic chairs, perhaps the school colors. Beauregard took a black chair. He set his pencil down, and his coffee cup. It was probably against the rules to have coffee here, but he didn't care. For better or worse, he was a reporter, not some rules-bound high school student. He sipped from his coffee cup.

Though the others tried hard to look nonchalant, or even vaguely pissed at being up so early on Saturday, Beauregard saw through them. They chewed their fingernails even as they slumped in their seats. Most had brought more than one pencil; some, several. Many had already placed their watches on the table. The SAT preparation books, Beauregard knew, suggested this. Looking away at one's wrist took time and increased the chance of losing one's place in the test booklet or, disaster of disasters, getting off line on the answer sheet. Bright futures had been postponed because of a misaligned answer sheet, young Farnsworth knowing the answer to Question 31 was *b,* but marking the *b* space for Question 32, thus throwing everything off and not immediately getting into Princeton.

Beauregard knew that his own problems with the SAT were more fundamental. He was one of those unfortunates who, as the solemn pronouncement went in military school, "doesn't test well." That last semester at the Bowel Movement, when he'd failed for the third time to crack 520 on verbal, he felt as if he must have a D.T.W. badge on his uniform, so often did he hear the phrase spoken of him by counselors, teachers, cadets, Mr. Forrest, and even Jackson. He'd scored well enough on math, but needed another fifty points on verbal to get into Washington and Lee. Goddamn verbal. Was that what college was about, rushing to choose the "most nearly opposite" antonyms and analyzing short, numbing, nutgraphless passages on tapestry weaving? They were never about the War Between the States, always something like tapestry weaving. When the SAT asked of such a passage, "The author's primary purpose is to . . . ," Beauregard felt like writing, "lower my SAT score."

Would this test be different? Did he care? Well, yes, some. To fail to get into Washington and Lee would be a family embarrassment. He didn't want to go there, but if he couldn't make front page and retain Lorena's affections, worse fates existed. His father might send him to The Citadel. There was always, lurking like death, the possibility of a four-year sentence to V.M.I. Actually, Beauregard had begun to have one pleasant fantasy about Washington and Lee. He'd show up winter term, settle into his dorm room, drop down to the campus newspaper, find the editors in a panic to get out the first post-Christmas edition, volunteer, and end up writing two or three front-page stories on deadline. They'd be thin, collegiate versions of front-page stories, and Beauregard would know the difference; but the grateful editors would slap him on the back, buy him a beer at a local pub, maybe even offer him his own weekly column.

The proctor and his assistants passed out the thin, one-page answer sheets and thicker, more formidable-looking test booklets. Beauregard printed his name, address, Social Security number, citizenship, sex, race, and age in the cells at the top of the answer sheet. When the proctor, a lanky, shiny-bald man in rolled-up sleeves, said with practiced calm, "You may begin," Beauregard could hear the seals of test booklets popping all over the lunchroom. The collective turning of the first pages made a brief, brisk wind.

The test started with a verbal section—antonyms, his old buddies, fifteen of them trailing down the page like stations of a marine obstacle course. The first was easy enough. The most nearly opposite word for *undermine,* given the options, was *support.* He darkened *c* on the sheet. The second *(purify/pollute)* was as easy, and though the third *(spirited/unanimated)* was harder, Beauregard felt pretty sure he had it right. He pushed on. Sometimes he knew the answer instantly, sometimes he used process of elimination, sometimes he went with what looked right. Of the fifteen, he felt confident of twelve and liked his guesses in two of the other three.

Next came a section in which he had to choose the word or pair of words that best completed a sentence. Just five of these, and Beauregard, the circles on his answer sheet growing fuller and darker, felt sure he had them all. Then came a reading section. Amazingly, he liked this little tale of "the 100 small regions of isolated volcanic activity known to geologists as 'hot spots.' " He easily determined the passage's main purpose and that the hot spot theory may eventually prove useful in interpreting "e) major changes in continental shape."

Suddenly he felt his momentum. Maybe he'd lucked into the one version of the SAT he could ace. Maybe, though, his father's crazy notion had proved right. Maybe six months at the newspaper really had improved his verbal skills. He'd learned quite a few words (many of them newspaper words—lede, pica, double-truck, sig, dink, nut—but not all), and he'd had a thorough grounding in usage and grammar. He certainly didn't seem as awed by the test, or even by the people taking it with him. Before, he had granted superior intelligence and poise to those sitting around him. Now they just looked young to him—immature gum chewers whereas he sipped black coffee.

As he moved to the next passage, he heard a slight, high-pitched noise nearby but resolved not to let it distract him. A noise might bother the others, the kids, but Beauregard was used to concentrating in a noisy newsroom, phones ringing, police radio crackling, people on deadline yelling, "Damn it!" and "Shit!" He bore in on the next reading passage, a tougher one, on the history of the mandolin. He heard the noise again. Louder now, but he could still shake it off. He was into the second paragraph, the mandolin invented but not refined, when an object bounced off his forehead and onto the table by his answer sheet.

Confused, then angry, he picked up the projectile. It was an eraser: one of those pink, ski-slope-shaped kind that stuck on to a pencil. Beauregard couldn't say where it had been thrown from, but he made a guess and scowled that way. He saw not one likely hurler but several. Beauregard was the one with the grievance, the grainy, still-stinging spot on his forehead, but they scowled him down, faces contorted in anger, a hanging jury. A flush young man in wire-rimmed glasses said aloud, "It's your beeper, asshole," touching off a chorus of "shut *up!*"s from around the room, but chilling Beauregard, because it was true. The sound he'd tuned out hammered him now, and it was getting louder. He must have slipped his work pants on without remembering to remove Price's beeper. He felt for his belt, fingers edging around the leather as if it were a guide rope. Near the back loop he found the instrument, but not its *off* button. The beep continued, prompting more angry exhalations of breath, deliberately dropped pencils, and frustrated rearranging of bodies in plastic seats. The area of disturbance was spreading. Beauregard could see the bald proctor coming toward him, pointing at the exit and mouthing "Out! Out!" Beauregard nodded, stood, and stumbled down the aisle, trying and failing to find OFF as he went, finally cupping the whole instrument with a hand in a futile effort to muffle the beep. He pushed the side door open and slipped through. The door wheezed back, then rattled closed. Someone's applause at his departure met with still more groans and "shut *up!*"s.

Beauregard crumpled against the concrete block wall, his heart competing with the beeper. He straightened and ripped the instrument off his belt, holding it up like a specimen bottle until he had found and flicked the OFF button. He leaned back against the wall, savoring the quiet. Dressing, he must have hooked the beeper backward, so the button was beltside, hidden. Oh, well. It was over now. But who the hell had beeped him? Probably no one. Probably one of Price's old sources, wanting Price. He started not to check, then decided he would, to buy just a moment more outside the lunchroom. The mood would be ugly when he went back in. He'd have to look deeply concerned, as if some unfolding family medical emergency merited beeper updates.

He held the beeper up again and hit "play." Emerging from the rude crackle was a voice, tinny and unsure, but also unmistakable.

"Beauregard? . . ."

Lorena!

"Beauregard, call me. As soon as you get a chance, Beauregard, just give me a quick call."

Her voice alone worked on him like a tonic, and all those "Beauregards" made it double strength. He congratulated himself on having included the beeper number in all his letters to her.

Now: Was there a REPLAY function on this beeper? Better yet, why not call her right away? He checked his watch. Only three or four minutes had elapsed. If he hustled, he could call her quickly, arrange for a longer conversation or rendezvous, then get back to the lunchroom in time for the test's next section.

But where to call? He crossed the linoleum and tested the door to the reception area of the principal's office. Open, but the lights were out. He stepped inside and slipped behind a desk. Straining to see the buttons, he dialed her number.

"Hello?"

"Lorena?"

"Oh, Beauregard. Where are you? I've been calling your apartment all morning."

Beauregard hadn't counted on her asking where he was. To answer honestly would remind her of the SAT, sorest of subjects, the reason she broke up with him. To answer disingenuously—well, hadn't his previous disingenuousness, his refusal to level, been the reason for the breakup?

He stammered for time.

"Oh, it doesn't matter," she said. "Finding you was the important thing. Thank God for beepers, right?"

"Right," he said, meaning it even as he rubbed the spot where the eraser had bounced off his forehead. "That's exactly right."

"Beauregard, I've been up all night. I didn't know what to do."

"Are we making up now?"

"We can talk about that later." The way she said it held out the possibility but guaranteed nothing. She sounded anxious. "I've got something to tell you. Listen, Beauregard. Brace yourself."

He didn't, just closed his eyes and waited to hear that she was pregnant or transferring to Auburn.

"Beauregard, I think I know where that missing portable is."

Chapter Twenty-two

Speeding north on the familiar two-lane highway, passing landmarks he hadn't seen in months, here a white-frame church with steeple, there a hubcap-and-boiled-peanuts stand, Beauregard kept his left hand on the wheel and used his right to reach through the unzipped gap of his windbreaker into the side pocket of his gray vest. He rummaged, then brought out a piece of hardtack.

How long had it been since he'd eaten the saltless biscuit relied on in lean times by both Northern and Southern troops? Much too long. He'd acquired a taste for hardtack while camping authentically. Men in the authentic camps went to great lengths to re-create the exact dietary experience of Johnny Reb and Billy Yank, eating the same foods they ate, having the same difficult bowel movements. Hardtack being the authentic snack of choice, Beauregard had eaten his share, usually late at night around the campfire, some private in the flickering shadows playing flickering period tunes on a period mouth harp. Now Beauregard bit into his hardtack, which was the size of a motel soap bar, though much harder. In fact, as hardtack went, this was a rock, testing the roots of Beauregard's healthy, though increasingly coffee-stained, teeth. He enjoyed the hardtack. He was hungry. He bit again. It didn't bother him that pebble-hard crumbs bounced off his chin, onto his rumpled gray breast. Hardtack crumbs on Confederate uniforms were a good thing, a kind of medal or merit badge. Some reenactment soldiers, even authentics, couldn't choke down hardtack.

Beauregard pressed the accelerator. The party van, against the odds, against its own sluggish history, responded like the real Traveller or some other magnificent steed. They bolted down the highway, passing cars and trucks. Beauregard felt good behind the wheel and good in his gray vest, which was wool, the right fabric for such brisk weather. It felt good too to be traveling away from his half-completed verbal section of the SAT and toward a newspaper story, a damn good one, maybe front page. Mr. Forrest would be furious, but Beauregard would deal with him later. He took another bite of hardtack. He was one with the road. He pressed harder on the accelerator and sped on into north Alabama.

At long last, an acquaintance of Chester's in maintenance had come through with the portable's location. There had been a party scheduled for the deer hunting lodge, and this employee hadn't been invited, so he got the location from an invited colleague and gave it to Chester. Chester had let Lorena decide whether to leak the information to Beauregard. After a sleepless night, she had, in part because the source believed the portable might soon be moved for security reasons, having been exposed to so many people at the party.

"The portable's near Sibley," she told Beauregard. "There's a little road, just off the county highway. It's supposed to be at the end of that little road. Chester says look for a big painted rock on the left-hand side of the highway, going north, a mile or two after Sibley."

"God a'mighty."

"What?"

"Nothing." Beauregard was writing everything down on Dryson High hall passes in the darkened reception area of the principal's office.

"It must be something, Beauregard. You've never used that word with me before."

"Sorry."

"Don't apologize, Bernstein." Bernstein? He took heart. "Just tell me why you said 'God a'mighty.' "

"Lorena, I know that area. I *think* I've seen that rock."

Sibley was the one-caution-light town near the old Calhoun property where Mr. Forrest's unit had reenactment drill most Saturdays, including this one. There might be lots of dirt roads marked by painted rocks, but Beauregard thought he could find

242

this one. If he left now, he'd have a better chance—perhaps his only chance—of confronting the thieves. Of course, if he left now and encountered his father, as he would eventually around Birmingham if not Sibley, he'd have to explain why he hadn't finished the SAT. His father had gone to great lengths to get him into Washington and Lee next term, and everything depended on a higher verbal score.

What would Lee have done? It wasn't always easy to apply the Lee test to contemporary situations. This one was perhaps more complicated than most, given that Mr. Forrest *was* Lee, in a way, that he had invented the Lee test, and that the university in question carried Lee's name. Still, it seemed to Beauregard that Lee would have gone right after the missing portable. Lee was always bold. For all his vaunted dignity and integrity, boldness was his salient trait. He'd been bold taking over for the wounded Joe Johnston during the Seven Days' Campaign at Richmond, bold again at Second Manassas, at Sharpsburg, Fredericksburg, Chancellorsville, Gettysburg. He might have been too bold at times— Gettysburg, Lord—but the Southern rebellion lasted as long as it did because of Lee's boldness. It was time for Beauregard's rebellion, time to do what he felt he should do, not what was expected. The way to rebel was boldly. Like Lee, he was reluctant; once in, though, he too would be bold. He would go after the missing portable. He would go right now, even though he was wearing half of a Confederate uniform.

"I'll see what I can find out," he told Lorena.

"Beauregard, be careful," she said. "It's still deer hunting season. Those men have guns."

"I'll be careful."

"Wear an orange hat."

"I'll wear something."

His only stop before leaving Birmingham was at Jackson's, to borrow a camera. It was game day for Alabama. Jackson, half dressed already, his pleated trousers on but not yet his white dress shirt and red sweater, walked into the den as Beauregard loaded the Minolta. Jackson was toweling dry his William-cut hair.

"Roll Tide," he greeted Beauregard. "What's happening?"

"I need this camera," Beauregard said as he threaded film to the spool. "I'm on to a good story. Some school board employees are using a portable classroom as a deer hunting lodge in north Alabama. I've got directions. I'm on my way."

"Roll Tide."

Beauregard first assumed Jackson was encouraging him to pursue the story. Then he remembered it was game day, and Jackson would be saying "Roll Tide" at every opportunity. Perhaps he was Roll Tide-ing for both purposes: encouragement and superstition. Jackson was that complicated, but there was no time to interpret him now.

"Got to go," Beauregard said, snapping shut the camera's back and slipping an arm through its leather strap. "I'll return this in a day or two."

Jackson hooked his other arm, stopping him. "Weren't you supposed to take the SAT this morning?"

"Yeah," Beauregard said. "My beeper went off during the verbal section. It was a call on this story. I had to leave right away."

Jackson clucked. "Marse Bob's going to be pissed, Roll Tide."

"I know."

"A beeper call, though," Jackson mused seriously. "That's good, Beauregard. Impressive."

Beauregard shrugged himself free of his older brother's grasp. "That's what beepers are for, Jackson," he said impatiently. "I've *got* to go now. I'll talk to you later."

It was a cool, windy day, white clouds hurrying across the sky as if to get to some place warmer. Beauregard sped on into reenactment territory. Hunched over the wheel, he looked to his right and saw large black birds circling in the distance. Turkey vultures. It had long been a fantasy of Beauregard's to die so convincingly on a reenactment battlefield that turkey vultures would begin to circle overhead and even light near his prostrate body. It had never happened. There was so much noise on a reenactment battlefield. Even now, a full two miles from the site where he always parked his father's Cadillac and the trailer carrying Snuffy/Traveller, he could hear musketry and occasional blasts from the twelve-pound howitzers brought down by the Chattanooga crowd.

As he got closer, the sounds began to rattle the half-open passenger window and shake Beauregard's nerve. He knew Mr. Forrest would explode like those howitzers upon learning that he had walked out on the SAT. He might well have made a sizeable monetary contribution to Washington and Lee, to grease the wheels of early admission. It was wasted grease now. Beauregard flinched at another, louder round of howitzer fire, then rolled up

244

his window and turned on the radio full blast, to drown out the battle. He would be disciplined in this crucial hour. He would worry about the story first, then his father.

A couple of miles past the reenactment site, Beauregard came to Sibley. It wasn't much of a town, just a caution light and a white-frame country store with gas pumps and a phone booth. A mile farther he spotted the painted rock on the left-hand side of the highway, about where Lorena had said it would be, about where he remembered it from the time he and his father had taken home a Huntsville reenactor. Beauregard slowed and turned down a dirt-and-gravel road bordered by tall deciduous trees. It was cooler, darker, and noisier now in the van. There was enough gravel under tire to drown out the radio, but not enough to keep orange dirt from swirling up behind. An occasional branch slapped the side of the van, as if in some fraternity initiation rite. Was this really the right road? A trailer could squeeze through here, but not without a fight.

Continuing on, the rumble having replaced gunfire as an un-nerving noise, Beauregard began to realize that if he confronted these thieves, they would hate him. It was a sobering thought to have here, the swirling orange cloud obscuring his path of retreat. He had never really had anyone hate him for a story. Billy McAr-thur might have hated him, although probably not; McArthur seemed defiant, even proud, after the AP story about his Atlanta traffic campaign. These portable-classroom thieves would be dif-ferent. They had a lot to lose. They would hate him.

Price, Beauregard knew, had had many people hate him. He seemed to revel in others' hatred, to draw strength from it. Beaure-gard had seen taped to Price's file cabinet a three-by-five-inch card with a typed quotation from his hero, the great and much-hated investigative reporter Seymour Hersh. The Hersh quote said, "I like to write stories that make people jump up and down." So did Price. People all over town had jumped up and down at the best of Price's stories, the rack card stories, and though most of the jumpers were readers, upset about the scandal in question, some were people Price had written about, the bad guys, and they hated Price. "That guy hates my guts," Price had said to Beauregard of any number of rogue businessmen and politicians around Birming-ham. "I think I'll give him a call." Beauregard had no such experi-ence to draw on. He was nervous now, rumbling down the dirt-and-gravel road.

245

Ahead, through gaps in the trees, he detected a flash of some-thing inorganically white. The road wound twice more, offering tantalizing glimpses, then straightened. It was the portable class-room all right, still on tires, in the midst of an acre-wide clearing beside the road. No other vehicle was around.

Beauregard, palms moist against the steering wheel, pulled the van into an area where cars or trucks had recently been, judging from numerous tire tracks and mashed down grass. He grabbed his notebook and got out and walked toward the portable. Because there were no other vehicles around, he didn't expect anyone to come to the door when he knocked, and no one did. Good. He had some time. He stepped over a generator and crawled under the back left wheel, where he knew from his sources that he could find a small metal plate with the serial number. Yes, he saw it: 94476B. That matched the number Chester had come up with. He crawled back out and made a note.

Quietly, feeling more than a little self-conscious, he stood on tiptoe and peeped into one small window after another. The gray screens and lack of interior light kept him from seeing anything clearly. He *thought* he saw antlers, a terrific detail, but no good until confirmed. He decided to write it down anyway, on speculation. He turned another page of his notebook.

It was then that he remembered he'd only knocked on the door, not tried to open it. Price would try. Hell, he'd jimmie it if he had to. Beauregard went back to the door. Looking around, making sure he was alone, he felt the metal knob. Unlocked. Standing there, hand still on the knob, wondering whether he really should enter, he heard the faint far-reachings of reenactment artillery. He thought again of Mr. Forrest, no doubt up on Snuffy/Traveller now, riding around giving orders. Beauregard decided he better do this story, do it all the way, Price's way, to have something to show for the unfinished SAT. He stepped inside cautiously.

He could smell last night's party. It was a stale-beer-and-cigar-smoke smell, familiar to him from tagging along with Jackson a few times in recent years. If it smelled like this now, it must have been overwhelming around midnight. Imagine: a first grade classroom filled with stale beer and cigar smoke. He felt for a wall switch, then flicked on the overhead lights.

Beauregard had smelled party sites, and seen them; but he'd never seen anything quite like this. An eight-point buck's head hung over a bulletin board filled with construction-paper letters of the alphabet. A pyramid of beer cans tottered beside shoved-to-gether school desks. There was a cigar butt ground into a hole of the pencil sharpener, and the classroom globe, all shot up around Australia, was completely out of its stand, rolled into a corner like a basketball. Someone had hooked a VCR up to the educational TV. A glance at the stack of videocassettes confirmed Beauregard's suspicion. They were blue films, XXX-rated, every one.

Readers would find this detail particularly disgusting, Beauregard knew. They'd jump up and down when they read it. Broadly speaking, but especially in details like blue films on an elementary school TV set, this was a wonderful newspaper story. It had the ironic juxtapositions, the "color," Bubba Shealy loved.

What it didn't have was a photograph. Beauregard jogged to the van and got Jackson's Minolta. He took a few shots of the portable as framed by the north Alabama woods, then popped the flash and crawled underneath for a shot of the serial number. He stepped back inside for some degradation close-ups (he particularly liked the cigar in the pencil sharpener), then stepped back outside and locked the camera in the van.

Still no hunters. It occurred to Beauregard that he could leave right now. He could return to the newsroom and write an eyewitness account buttressed by the photographs. He wouldn't have to name the thieves, just make clear that someone was using a portable classroom for a deer lodge. It would still be a strong story—probably page one. The school board would be forced to respond with an investigation that would eventually, possibly even quickly, result in arrest of the thieving employees.

But that would be chicken-shit. Price wouldn't do that. He would stick around as long as possible, in the interest of positively identifying the thieves and making the strong story even stronger. It was a good bet that the thieves would be back here before long, having hunted through the morning and early afternoon. Beauregard resolved to stick around—maybe not as long as Price would have, but a respectable interval—in hopes that he could get a quick interview or even a terse "no comment," and be on his way.

He went back inside to look for more details. He noticed a bag of potato chips, rolled up and sealed with a rubber band. Beauregard opened the bag and reached inside. There was a journalistic purpose to this, he told himself—the chips in his story would be accurately "fresh" or "stale." This first one was fresh enough. He verified with a second chip.

He was walking around the portable, stepping over mattresses, eating more chips, when he noticed a familiar receiptlike sheet taped to a cabinet door across the room. He squinted but couldn't read it. He stepped closer. He was within three or four paces when he recognized the logo across the sheet. He stopped and closed his eyes hard, as if to blot out what he'd seen. It was Jackson's logo. Get Down! Inc. had thrown last night's party. Not wanting to, knowing he must, he stepped forward for the confirmation. It was all there, the list of services provided, the fees, the Visa card voucher. Taped behind it was one of Jackson's slick brochures—a new one, with the words "As Seen on 'PM Magazine'!" printed across the top.

Beauregard turned around and leaned with his back against the front door, chip bag dangling from his right hand. He needed to calm himself, think clearly about what this meant. Jackson knew he was trying to break this story. They'd talked about it less than two hours ago at his condo, and Jackson hadn't said the first word about throwing this party. Probably, though, Jackson hadn't been listening carefully. He'd been in his usual pregame stupor. In any event, he or someone at his firm had thrown a party last night in a stolen first grade classroom. Maybe they hadn't known in advance that it was stolen, but once on site, setting up amid the school desks and chalkboard, it should have been obvious. Beauregard had always cut Jackson some slack, but not this time. This was so clearly wrong, so clearly a thing Robert E. Lee would never have done or even contemplated. It also made Beauregard's job harder. Now, in addition to reporting and writing this rather complicated story, he would have to cover his brother's butt. He shook his head and reached for another chip.

He was crossing the room again, in search of more details, when he remembered that he hadn't looked at the signature on the voucher. He went back and saw that the name was different from the names of the three maintenance men Chester had identified as the likely thieves. Either Chester was wrong or last night's party had been paid for by someone else. That might make sense. Maintenance men—even three of them—would have a hard time affording one of Jackson's parties.

After looking around the trailer a few more minutes, Beauregard, of necessity, started to step into the bathroom. The sight and smell stopped him. Someone had hugged the toilet seat last night, but imprecisely, fouling the bowl and even the linoleum floor. Beauregard decided he'd rather piss in the woods.

He shut the front door behind him and made the short jog from the trailer. It was cooler here, and the wind in the trees overrode the sound of his pissing. He was comfortable with pissing in the woods. He had done it many times. Usually he was in full Confederate uniform, which meant he buttoned up instead of zipped up. When had the zipper come into common use? His father would know. He himself used to know. Things slipped away. . . . He had finished zipping and begun to step back out of the woods when he heard an automotive rumble coming down the narrow road. He froze for an instant, then knelt behind an oak tree.

A red pickup with a gutted deer on its hood rode into view. The truck stopped about ten yards short of the portable, and three men climbed out, leaving their rifles in the rack behind them. The heavyset, flush-faced, orange-vested man with a butte of gray hair was Rufus Tate, a supervisor in Parts and Maintenance and reputed leader of the three. The driver, a young blond man with the biggest Adam's apple Beauregard had ever seen, fit the description of Mike Dunston. He wore an Alabama jersey, number 16. That left Terry Finwick as the man with wavy black hair, a bad complexion, and a mustache that looked like an upside-down horseshoe print.

Rufus held up a hand, as if he'd heard something. Beauregard hunkered behind his tree blind. Then, as the other men stood silent, Rufus started a long loud fart which he and the others drowned out with laughter. Rufus turned to the slain deer. "That Bud was for you," he said, and they all laughed again.

Men alone, Beauregard thought critically. He'd heard that "Bud" line many times after farts in the modern camp. He'd never heard it delivered to a dead deer, though. These guys were especially crude, or drunk, or both.

Soon Rufus walked over to the party van, the other men trailing him like hound dogs.

"Hell, I thought they got everything last night," Rufus said.

"Me, too," Mike said.

Terry, looking in the van window, added, "They must be in the portable. Ain't nobody in here."

Beauregard continued to kneel behind the oak. His fear of going forward, of confronting the crude and possibly dangerous thieves, competed with his need not to be cowardly. At first it was a standoff, but as the seconds passed he felt more and more ashamed of his cowardice. He imagined important people in his life—Price, Lorena, Jackson, Mr. Forrest, Lee—above him in spirit forms watching and making various observations, the stinging essence of which was, "Why doesn't he *do* something?" Reluctantly, Beauregard hugged the tree trunk, pulled himself up, and stumbled out of the woods.

The thieves, who had been shuffling toward the portable, turned at the sound of crunching leaves. "Hello, there!" Beauregard called, trying to gain the initiative.

The thieves said nothing. Beauregard, sweating, stopped a few feet short of them. Finally Rufus came forward. He walked right up to Beauregard, then around him as if he were a mannequin wearing a marked-down suit. He reached out and fingered Beauregard's vest, exposed through the unzipped windbreaker. He even slipped a fat thumb in the pocket where the hardtack had been. Beauregard's notebook was wedged in there now.

"Where'd *you* come from?" Rufus demanded, tugging the vest. "You get loose from all that crazy shit across the way?"

"Sir?"

"Son, I see your uniform. I know you're one of those Civil War nuts who fight near here every Saturday, scaring hell out of our deer. Now you're lost and you need a ride back over there. Dandy fine. We'll give you a ride, all right, only not right now. Right now we've got to see somebody inside the trailer. Sit your butt down here and wait for us. While you're waiting, you can forage or clean your gun or something. Hell, you can clean *our* guns."

He grinned at Mike and Terry, who grinned back on cue. They all turned to walk toward the portable.

Beauregard suddenly realized he held a card of unknown value: the Jackson card. Looking at the backs of the hunters, riled by Rufus's tone and his gratuitous slap at reenactors and his confusing of a gray vest with a complete uniform, he decided not only to play the card but thump it down, in the interest of more details or an admission. It was deceptive, in a way, invoking Jackson's name. But Lee had been quick to deceive in the interest of vanquishing the much larger Northern army. Rufus and his hound dogs had Beauregard outnumbered three to one. If anyone deserved deception, they did.

"I'm not here with the reenactors," Beauregard called out, voice steadying with each syllable. "I'm Beauregard Forrest. Jackson's brother."

Rufus turned first, then the others did, like magnets. "I'll be damned," Rufus said. He walked back over to Beauregard. "You at the party last night?"

"No, sir."

Rufus began to laugh, then behind him Mike and Terry did. "Kind of hard to remember who all *was* there," Rufus said. "Let me tell you something, Beauregard. Your brother's company puts on one hell of a party. Those hostesses, my God! I'd seen them before, of course, but last night they were wearing little antlers on their heads and skimpy little deerskin outfits. They had me dancing and running around that trailer like a young man. Shit, I had to take a second nitroglycerin tablet."

Beauregard grinned with Mike and Terry to help keep things going. Then, gesturing at the portable, he observed purposefully, "Nice place to have a party."

"Oh, it's all right," Rufus said, sniffing and looking away.

"Buy it in Birmingham?"

Rufus nodded, but quickly, as if it were an obvious question not worth spending more time on. He pulled a cigar from his orange vest pocket and flicked a lighter at it. He took a puff, then blew the smoke out horizontally, just missing Beauregard. "You here to pick up the rest of the stuff?" he said. "I see that van. . . ."

Beauregard chose his words carefully. "I could do that."

Rufus turned and looked back at the portable. "Hell, there ain't much," he said. "I *thought* they got everything last night. All those dirty movies are mine." He turned again to Beauregard. "Hey, son, how much does your brother pay you? Or does he just give you one night a week alone with those hostesses?"

They were all laughing now, dirty, back-of-the-throat laughter which had as its subtext that Beauregard couldn't find female companionship on his own, but had to depend on Jackson. Beauregard started to laugh along but stopped. What the hell was he doing? He *had* them. He didn't have to take their mocking crap. They should be laughing at *his* bad jokes. God a'mighty.

He waited for the laughter to subside, then said as evenly as he could, "Actually, I'm not on Jackson's staff."

"No?" Rufus said. He started to relight his cigar, which had gone out during the laughter.

"I'm a reporter."

Rufus stood there, lighter flame extended but missing the cigar. With narrowed eyes he was looking at Beauregard, beginning to hate him. Behind Rufus, Mike and Terry muffled nervous, phlegmless coughs.

"I thought you were Jackson's brother," Rufus said finally.

"I am," Beauregard said, "but I work for the *Birmingham Standard-Dispatch*. I'm doing a story on a missing portable classroom. On *this* missing portable classroom, 94476B. I checked the serial number before you drove up."

The ensuing silence was interrupted by distant reenactment explosions. Mike and Terry continued to look stricken, Rufus merely flushed and angry. He recovered first, smiling weakly and saying, "Okay, young man. Mawn inside. Let's talk."

During the short walk to the trailer, Beauregard decided he'd start soft with his questions, then gradually harden them, the way Price did. He might even start off sympathetic, to get them talking. He'd say he knew it wasn't easy maintaining so many schools and portables. Maintenance people, here and elsewhere, were notoriously overworked and underpaid. They needed something, if not a deer hunting lodge, to work off tension.

Once inside, Rufus said to Beauregard, "You stay here, son. We need to step outside and discuss this situation among ourselves."

"Wait, now. That's not fair," Beauregard said, but they didn't wait. Terry, the last one out, slammed the door and locked it behind him. Beauregard went to a window and watched them huddle in the field. He could see Rufus leading the urgent discussion.

That they'd locked him in was troubling, but Beauregard still felt he had the upper hand. He made notes on what had just happened. Then he looked around the portable again. On a folding table, near a back windowsill, he noticed snapshots from the party. The most incriminating was of four smiling, obviously drunken men seated on the couch, a deerskin-clad and antler-topped hostess sprawled across their laps on her stomach. She was smiling at the camera, too, though differently, professionally. Beauregard didn't recognize the men. Probably hunters from the area. Still, he dropped the snapshot into his pocket, to show Price. He looked around some more. For the first time, he noticed writing in one corner of the chalkboard. R, M and T had been written on it, and next to each letter was a series of slash marks, five for Rufus, four for Mike, only one for Terry. Probably slashes equaled deer kills. If so, and if he could confirm it, Beauregard had another terrific detail. He would press the point during the tougher phase of his questioning.

"Yoo-hoo!"

Rufus, smiling, had stuck his broad gray head in the door. He came in, as did Mike. Beauregard accepted Rufus's gestured offer to join him on the couch.

They settled in, Rufus turning heavily toward Beauregard, Mike standing in the background. "Now, here's what we're going to do," Rufus explained matter-of-factly. "Terry's getting the truck. He'll hook it up to the portable. In a minute, Mike and I'll start getting things ready here on the inside. You're welcome to sit here and watch us. In fact, we insist you do. When everything's ready, we'll drive the portable back to Birmingham. It'll be available for use next week, which is what you want. We'll be out of this little situation, which is what we want. It's win-win. So, son, just make yourself at home here, and we'll go ahead and get started."

He started to rise, but Beauregard grabbed him by the arm. "Wait, sir," he said. "You said 'win-win.' Are you crazy? What do I win?"

"I just told you," Rufus said. "We take the portable back to Birmingham."

"But I need a story."

"I can't help you there, Beauregard. I wish I could. I'm truly sorry."

"I'll do a story anyway."

"You've got no witnesses. No proof. It'd be your word versus ours. We'll have the portable back at the school board long before you can get a story in the paper. I'm in charge of inventory, so any questions you raise with the superintendent come right back to me."

"I'm a witness," Beauregard said. "I've got notes."

"We thought of that. In fact, we're going to take care of that right now. Go ahead, young Mike." Mike walked over and snatched Beauregard's notebook from the vest pocket. He retreated to a corner where he tore the pages into little strips that fluttered down into a plastic garbage bag. No one spoke until he finished.

"There now," Rufus said, as if Beauregard were a small boy whose shoes he'd tied. "We're going to get started. Feel free to pop a dirty movie in the VCR, if the urge hits."

For the next half hour, Beauregard sat on the couch as the men bustled about preparing the trailer for departure. They picked up garbage, swept the floor, cleaned the bathroom, removed mattresses, removed the cigar from the pencil sharpener, erased the blackboard, carried out the incriminating deer head with antlers, and tied down anything that might shift in transit. Their mood improved as the cleaning progressed, as Beauregard's darkened. Rufus actually began to whistle. Beauregard, interrupting him, asked when he could leave. Rufus said they wanted him to stay until they were absolutely on their way. "We want to look in that rearview mirror and see you waving," he said. "It'll mean a lot to us." And then he laughed that dirty, back-of-the-throat laughter of his again. It was a terrible sound to Beauregard, worse than the whistling, and he was glad when Terry returned and drowned it out by flicking on the vacuum cleaner.

It was an old model vacuum cleaner, so loud that Beauregard felt separated from the others, felt alone. He brooded behind the wall of sound, thinking, So this is how it ends, without even a Metro Brief to print, just a journalistic fish story, the huge front-pager that got away, bigger even than Atlanta. What had made him think he could pull this story off? He wasn't Price; never would be. Price would have prepared better. He wouldn't have just rushed in, expecting the thieves to give him an exclusive interview. He would have devised backup verification, a hidden observer, something more than the photographs, which by themselves were flimsy evidence. The serial number photograph was separate from the others of the portable, and a lawyer, if not a city editor, would ask for proof that they were related. Without that, the portable in the woods could belong to any school board or no school board—might be one an individual had bought *from* a school board, secondhand. Beauregard had gambled by leaving the SAT, and now he didn't have the SAT or a front-page story, and he wouldn't have Lorena, once she found out how royally he'd screwed up. She'd see him for the loser, the cub reporter, the B-Four, the city of Birmingham, he really was. What if Rufus, no dummy, traced the leaked information back to her? He might have her job.

Lord God.

He had to make a run for it. With all the noise from the vacuum cleaner, he thought he might be able to slip out the front door and sprint for the van. It was the longest of long shots, escaping first, then quickly finding someone around Sibley who would return with him to verify that the portable had been in these woods. Still, he would try.

He waited until their backs were turned, then strode quickly to the door, taking care not to knock over anything. He could hear the vacuum cleaner still running, so he figured he might be escaping. He turned the knob, opening the door just enough for him to squeeze through, thus minimizing the entering shaft of light. He had cleared the door and begun to pull the knob shut when it hit something. He looked back: a boot. He released the knob and started to run, but first he had to leap off the two small portable stairs. He stumbled. Terry fell on him like a linebacker over a fumbled football. Then Mike, too, was over him, holding down his arms.

"Bring him back in here," Rufus called wearily from the door. "God knows I didn't want to do this."

They brought him back in and tied him with rope to a folding chair. They tied his legs to the chair legs, and his arms behind the chair back. Then, for good measure, they gagged him with a kitchen towel. Beauregard didn't know why they gagged him. He hadn't been talking. Even if he had been, they couldn't have heard him over the vacuum cleaner. There he sat, though, bound and gagged. At first his thoughts were defiant. These thieves might not know it, but he had been in rigid positions on reenactment battlefields for hours at a time. Soon, though, he began to feel sorry for himself. It wouldn't be so bad if someone important in his life could see him like this. But no one would, because Rufus was smart. He'd have Mike and Terry untie him just before they left. The bit about being bound and gagged would just be another wrinkle, another pound, to the whopper fish story.

The thieves kept working. Gagged, Beauregard had no choice but to smell the Lysol that Mike was spraying all over. It was a distraction, along with the screaming vacuum cleaner, but soon Beauregard was punishing himself again. His thoughts bounced around like a pinball, from the SAT to Lorena to the thieves to Lorena to his father to the thieves to how everything was all messed up. He was probably the only reporter in *Standard-Dispatch* history to be bound and gagged, and no one at the paper would ever know. He himself wouldn't tell. It was too pitiful to talk about.

He was thinking on these things, spirits sinking accordingly, when with his keen peripheral vision he noticed a blue flash in the curve through the far trees. A police light? Probably not. Could be anything, he told himself. He wouldn't hope. He would find some War Between the States reverie to calm himself and pass the time. John Singleton Mosby capturing a Yankee general in bed, pulling

back the covers and spanking him on the behind. . . . Another flash.
. . . Had Lorena called someone? She'd sounded worried. It
wouldn't be past her to have called the sheriff's department, giving
them information and directions. Lorena, I love you, Beauregard
thought. Please have made this call. He checked to see if Rufus and
the others were looking at him, then twisted in his chair to get a
good look out the window. Far down the dirt-and-gravel road
came a sheriff's deputy car, blue lights flashing. Maybe it had its
siren on, too, but no one could hear because of the deafening
vacuum cleaner.

"Mmmnnn," sounded Beauregard. It was the start of a rebel
yell, involuntary and loud despite the gag. "Mmmmmnnnnn."
They still couldn't hear him, but when he twisted back toward
them he tipped over and crashed to the floor. Rufus, noticing,
screamed at Terry, "Cut it! The boy's gone nuts!" As the vacuum
cleaner whined down, the police siren took its place. Even to
Beauregard, who knew what was up and had his right cheek
mashed into the floor, it was a chilling segue. He heard the thieves
rush to the window. As the siren shut off, car doors opened and
slammed.

"Rufus?" Mike asked tremblingly.

"I know. I see them," Rufus snapped. "Why do I always have
to be the one who decides what we're going to do?"

But in a second he'd rallied, ordering Mike and Terry to untie
and ungag Beauregard, a task they finished just before the deputies
came through the door.

Chapter Twenty-three

Other squad cars came and went while Beauregard, armed with a fresh notebook from the van, conducted interviews. In fact, the cleared area around the portable became something of a scene. Officers from other jurisdictions drove over, as did the county coroner and some local paramedics. Everyone in public service wanted to see the stolen portable and shake their heads at the Birmingham thieves. Beauregard was preoccupied with reconstructing his notes and talking to everyone he could, but at some point he noticed that the deer was gone from the hood. He hoped it had been taken away for evidence, not some venison blowout at the local police lodge. Either way, he couldn't worry about it. One scandal at a time.

The first deputy he interviewed happened to be the young man who had come to the reenactment field during the territorial dispute with the Society for Creative Anachronism. Only a few months had passed, but Beauregard could tell he was more confident in his work now, which was nice to see.

Beauregard got most of his information from the sheriff. He was an older man, compact, neatly groomed—a dead ringer for Grady Fee, a *Standard-Dispatch* editorial writer who had in recent years become a Christian fundamentalist. Price claimed Fee wrote in tongues, and he *was* the most confusing of the three editorial writers; but Beauregard liked him. He liked this sheriff, too. He was polite and, more important, quotable. Gesturing at the thieves, now locked up in the back of a squad car, he lamented in colorful, complete sentences the very existence of human beings so low as to commandeer a first grade classroom for a deer hunting lodge. Country people, he went on, had enough problems without having to worry about criminals from the big city. He saw the Birmingham menace every day—drugs, burglary, car and truck theft. Now this deer hunting lodge thing.

Beauregard, writing all that down, asked, "Who called you about the portable classroom? Was it a young woman from Birmingham?"

"Yes, sir," the sheriff said. "Only she didn't call. She came by headquarters."

Beauregard looked up. "She drove here?"

"Yes, sir."

"Where is she?"

"Waiting for you at the store at Sibley. She told me to tell you that. I would have, but you kept asking me questions."

Beauregard, rumbling as fast as possible down the dirt-and-gravel road, sent up a little prayer that Lorena hadn't given up and gone home to Birmingham. How could that dipshit sheriff have waited so long to relay her message? Country people—they took all day.

He was through the Sibley caution light and pulling into the parking lot of the store when he spotted Lorena leaning against the door of her green Vega. She wore blue jeans and a red sweater jacket with a hood, and she had her hoopskirt hair tied in a ponytail. She was studying a textbook, yellow marker in hand. He hadn't seen her in weeks, not since that cold night at UAB, and looking at her now caused him to break yet another emotional sweat—the day's third or fourth. He drove the van across the lot. She saw him finally, lowering her book and marker, looking at him hard through the windshield. He didn't know what to make of that look. She wasn't smiling. He stopped the van and hopped out.

Early on, Price had told Beauregard: If you're going to be a reporter, act like a reporter. Beauregard told himself to act like a boyfriend here. He no longer knew whether he was one, but he would act like one. He walked around the van and strode toward Lorena, taking her in his arms, pulling her close. She hesitated, then hugged him back, albeit conservatively. They stood like that for a few seconds. It was hard to say in what spirit she was hugging him.

Beauregard noticed Booger bouncing around in the Vega, not barking. Having been gagged himself recently, he felt new sympathy for the little mongrel. If things worked out, he would spend more time with him, take him to the park again.

For now, though, all attention belonged to Lorena.

"I'm so glad to see you," he said.

She pulled away, enough to study his face. "You look all right," she said. "Are you?"

"I'm fine."

"I was worried about you. The more I thought about it, the more sure I was they would hurt you. That's why I decided to come find the sheriff."

"You did right."

"I hope so. When I was following the sheriff to Sibley, I heard all this gunfire. More like explosions, really. It was terrifying. I just knew you were dead."

"I was okay. But you did right to come. . . . Hey, Lorena, we got 'em."

"What?"

"The men who stole the portable—they're in custody."

"Beauregard!"

Another, longer hug, which became a parking-lot waltz, Lorena leading. When they stopped he gave her a bare-bones account of the episode, promising a full account later. He had to phone the newsroom right away. It was getting late, and this was a strange, complicated story. No one at the paper even knew what he was up to.

"What can I do?" Lorena asked.

Beauregard thought for a second. "I've got film in the van," he said. "What I really need you to do is take it back to the paper for developing. You might as well take this photograph, too."

He pulled from his vest pocket the party snapshot he'd found in the portable. Lorena took it and studied it, then looked up wide-eyed. "Beauregard, all these men work at the school board."

"They do?"

She nodded gravely. "They're pretty high up, too. The guy on the right's an assistant superintendent."

"What's his name?" Beauregard asked.

"Dennis McNulty."

"That's the guy who signed the Visa voucher for the party they had last night. . . . Can you identify the rest of them?"

"Every one," she said. "God, that deerskin outfit is disgusting."

"Would you? On the back of the photograph?"

"Gladly."

"Great. I'll get that film now. When I call the newsroom, I'll tell them you're coming."

"When will I see you?" Her tone was different now, more cautious. "We *do* need to talk, Beauregard. We need to talk about us."

"We haven't made up yet, have we?"

"No. Afraid not."

"I was hoping we'd found a shortcut. Gotten there already."

"Sorry, Bernstein. Nice try."

Beauregard nodded. "We'll talk tonight, Lorena. Are you going to be at home?"

"I can be."

"Please. I'll get there as soon as I can."

Beauregard, in the country store's phone booth now, dialed the *Standard-Dispatch* newsroom. Price answered. Beauregard, excited over all that had happened, excited Price had picked up, rather than Bubba Shealy, began a flustered recitation of the day's events.

"Calm down, B-Four," Price said. "Give me what you've got, slow. *Tell* it to me."

So Beauregard did, chronologically, beginning with the SAT and carrying through to the arrests. He told Price that Lorena was bringing photographs, including a particularly incriminating snapshot. He himself was ready to dictate, if anybody there could take it down.

Now Price was excited.

"This is a hell of a story, B-Four."

"You think so?"

"I *know* so. . . . They really tied you up?"

"Yeah, Price, but I don't want that in the story. This story isn't about me."

"I see your point." Price paused, breathing into the line, then said, "As good as the story is, it needs working from this end. Somebody should call the school board members for reaction."

"I'm way up here."

"I know, and I'm short on reporters." He paused again. "Tell you what, B-Four. Bubba's off today, but I'll have him come in and work the desk. I'll make the calls myself."

"Okay, Price."

"You're right about dictating. If we waited until you drove back here, we'd miss at least one edition, maybe two. We don't want to miss any editions with a story this strong. This is front page, above the fold. I'll go ahead and take the dictation. Give me a second to get the computer fired up. . . . All right, I'm ready. Roll Tide."

Beauregard, flipping back and forth in his notebook, leaning against the smudged glass of the spidery phone booth, began to dictate. He tried to think in complete sentences, to come up with a lede, a good initial quote, a nut graph and color, but he was both tired and excited, so he had trouble keeping things in order. He dictated his nut graph before his lede, his color before his good initial quote. He had background in the foreground. It was as if he'd dumped puzzle pieces into Price's lap and challenged him to put them together, on deadline. Price wasn't complaining, though. Beauregard finished the dictation, then risked raising a lingering concern. He figured he could tell Price, who was management but not yet scum.

"One more thing," he said. "My brother's company threw the party. I don't think Jackson was there or anything, but Get Down! Inc. handled it."

Beauregard could hear Price taking a sip of coffee, then another. Finally Price said, "You don't want that in the paper, do you, B-Four?"

"Not really."

Price paused, no doubt weighing the consequences of omission, then said, "I'll keep it out, but don't tell Bubba. You know how he hates your brother. The old Alabama-Auburn thing . . ."

"I won't say a word."

"Tell you what, B-Four. Ride back out to the scene and see if the cops have finished up. If they've taken Rufus and the rest of them to the jail, call to make sure they've been booked. And find out what the bail is. I'll be busy for a while, making my own calls and getting this story in shape. Call me again in an hour."

Beauregard finished his work in a quarter of that time. The crime scene was nearly deserted now, so he returned to the store and called the sheriff's department and jail. Deputies at both places confirmed that the charge was grand theft and that the three men were being held on $100,000 bond each. As it was Saturday, and deer-hunting season, bail bondsmen were scarce in Turpin County. The men would be spending at least one night in jail.

261

All this was important information, but Beauregard had a forty-five minute wait before he could phone Price. He bought a cup of black coffee and drank from it, leaning against the cab of the van. He was going over his notes, making sure he hadn't left out anything, when he heard a distant twelve-pound howitzer. The reenactors were still at it. He thought for a second, then downed the last of the coffee and swung back into the van. He would go level with his father. There was just enough time.

Chapter Twenty-four

F*arbing* was the term for a reenactor dressed inauthentically, and Beauregard, as he parked the van and jogged down a path toward the authentic and modern camps, knew he was farbing big time now. He'd left his windbreaker in the van so the Confederate vest would show; but he'd had no time to remove and replace all the other offending items—the tennis shoes, work slacks, wristwatch, beeper, and Archdale T-shirt. He would have to fight this battle as he was. He *wanted* to fight. He missed reenacting, he realized. Civilians didn't realize how therapeutic it was to step out of one's time and get the "period rush" of reenactment. You could feel your own little contemporary problems diminishing as you assumed those of a mid-nineteenth-century soldier. Reenactments were sensual, too. The best of them were, if not a "riot of the senses," as the Style writers might put it, at least a good rumble. Beauregard was still in the woods separating the car field from the reenactment field, but he could already smell the powder: a sweet, sulfurous smell. The guns were blasting. His friends at Birmingham Military had talked about how loud rock concerts were, but Beauregard, the one time he went with them, had been disappointed. He had a reenactor's idea of noise. Those electric guitars and tree-tall amplifiers didn't measure up. Nor was there, at a rock concert, a sight as stirring as a bullet-perforated battle flag, U.S. or Confederate, still erect and waving against the odds.

When he reached the field, he could tell how far this unscripted reenactment had progressed. Dead soldiers everywhere. Beauregard paused just long enough to assess more carefully the individual quality of their deaths. Some were quite fine; others, well . . . At least no one in his father's unit was truly awful at dying. He'd seen reenactors from other units die in impossible positions, on their sides, even, so they could watch the rest of the battle. At the reenactment in Jonesboro, Georgia, south of Atlanta, he'd marched past two dead men playing cards. He'd been shot and killed himself before he could decide whether to report them.

He'd be reported for farbing today, for sure, but no matter. He had to get across the field. Powder smoke made distance vision difficult, but he knew that his father would be at the field's far end, by the headquarters tent, probably poring over some of his antique maps, Snuffy/Traveller tied to a post or nearby tree.

This was the Yankee side, so Beauregard, following protocol, found the paper box with blue-mesh "Yankee" jerseys and slipped one on. He advanced to the nearest dead man, Cecil Henry, and reached down to touch the nearby barrel of his .557 caliber long Enfield rifle musket. Cold. Henry had been dead awhile. Beauregard quickly stripped him of his rifle and forage cap, then reached into his haversack for some spare cartridges and powder.

"What the hell?" Henry said, eyes still closed. Some men didn't take kindly to being stripped, although it was authentic.

"Sorry, Mr. Henry." Beauregard was adjusting the cap to his own head. "I need these things. I'll get them back to you."

"Beauregard?"

"Yes, sir."

"I'll be damned! Welcome back!"

"Thank you, sir," he said. "It's good to be back. I'll see you later."

Beauregard ran forward to where a dozen Yankees were pinned behind an island stand of sweet gum trees near the center of the reenactment field. All pounded him on the back in welcome. Given that he had a cap on and a rifle in hand, and that the situation was distractingly tense, no one seemed to notice the degree to which he was farbing. Fred Costello, the Hueytown grocer who always brought beer and deli sandwiches for the postreenactment gathering in the modern camp, gave Beauregard a shouted briefing. The situation was grim. A superior force of Confederates had amassed across the way. If he knew Tom Ballard, their commanding officer, they would charge with twenty or so men, then flank with most of the rest.

Beauregard, his own agenda in mind, proposed a counterattack. They would ignore the flanking threat, instead rising together and firing a concentrated volley at the charging Confederates. If the Yankees were lucky, the majority of the Confederates would be flanking, too far away to offer support, and the relatively few charging Confederates would be surprised by the counteroffensive. The Yankees could either defeat or slip by them, moving on to capture the makeshift breastworks the Confederates had left behind. Beauregard could almost guarantee that Ballard, easily the most scatterbrained of Mr. Forrest's field commanders, would leave only two or three men to protect home base.

Beauregard had always thought he would be a good reenactment tactician, if given the chance; but even he was surprised at how well his plan worked. Ballard had his numbers all mixed up, flanking too many, charging too few and leaving only one green private as guard. The Yankees wiped out the charging Confederates and moved on without harassment to the breastworks, where they captured the lone private and made him put on a blue-mesh jersey. "Galvanizing," it was called—common in the real war and in reenactments.

The Yankees all pounded Beauregard on his back again. Once they'd ended the congratulations, though, they could see that this new position was even less safe than the old one. They'd moved deeper into Confederate territory, and straight ahead they faced a larger and more intelligently led force than Ballard's. Beauregard proposed another charge. This one, he knew, had little chance of success, but the men, drunk on the previous advance, followed him and Costello blindly.

Again, surprise and audacity served them well, the front line of Confederates falling as the Yankees fired, reloaded, moved forward, and fired again. As they died their B-grade movie deaths, the Confederates' faces dissolved from imagined agony to genuine surprise—surprise that young Beauregard, who usually got himself killed early in any reenactment, had been the agent of their deaths.

But a second line of Confederates stepped up and blasted away. Yankees fell on Beauregard's right, on his left. Costello went down ahead of him. Soon Beauregard alone was standing. The whole second line of Confederates, thirty men at least, was shooting at him, but Beauregard refused to fall. He ignored the first rule of reenacting. He wouldn't die. It was too important not to. He rushed on, acknowledging only an arm wound, at last breaking through the bewildered Confederate line like a Heisman Trophy halfback. He ran another twenty yards to where his father had been standing on a folding chair by the headquarters tent.

"Beauregard?"

"Yes, sir."

"Have you lost your mind?"

"No, sir."

An aide-to-camp, plus some of the Confederates whose line Beauregard had penetrated, looked on to see what punishment the general's son would get for dressing this way and refusing to take a hit. Mr. Forrest stepped down from the chair.

"Come with me," he ordered conspicuously. Beauregard followed him into the tent.

"Close the flap."

Beauregard did, then turned around. The tent was close quarters—stuffy and dark. He could think of better places to have this confrontation. He bought a couple of seconds by stripping off and pocketing his blue-mesh jersey, then setting the rifle in a corner. He looked up to meet his father's stare.

"Son, you've really put me on the spot by behaving like this."

"I know, Dad."

"You're not even half-dressed."

"I'm sorry."

"Is that a beeper on your belt? Your *L.L. Bean* belt."

"It is, sir. Yes."

"My God."

Mr. Forrest paused at length, severely, then surprised Beauregard by smiling a little behind the Lee's beard. "Good move on Ballard, though," he said.

"Thank you, sir."

"Unfortunately, you panicked a little once you got past him. What you should have done, given the situation, was . . ."

"I didn't panic, Dad," Beauregard cut in coolly.

"You most certainly did."

"No." He'd upped the ante by leaving off "sir."

"Son, I saw you."

"*I didn't panic, Dad,*" Beauregard repeated. "I knew exactly what I was doing. My objective was to cross the field and talk to you. I knew if I didn't fight my way across I'd just have to stop and explain to everybody what I was doing, so I fought my way across. True, I lost a few men, and I didn't fall when I was supposed to at the end, but I got here. Here I am talking to you. Mission accomplished. So don't be saying I panicked."

Mr. Forrest didn't say anything. He just looked at Beauregard, eyes wider than Lee's ever were, at least as revealed by the surviving photographs and oil paintings. Across the way a howitzer went off, shaking the support pole of the little tent.

Beauregard waited for the noise to fade, then said, "You're probably wondering what happened with me and the SAT."

"Something happened?"

"I walked out, Dad. I had a beeper call. I had to go to work."

Mr. Forrest continued to stare at Beauregard, eyes narrower now, face flush. Then, in a transition familiar to Beauregard, he lowered his head, closed his eyes, and began rubbing his eye sockets with a thumb and forefinger. He shook his head slowly and let a prolonged stream of air blow noisily, disappointedly through his impressive nostrils. The closed eyes were the main thing. As bad as it was to get one of Mr. Forrest's saber-sharp stares, Beauregard thought it worse to have him refuse to make eye contact.

"Listen, Dad," he blundered on. "I can't go to Washington and Lee next term. I'm just not ready. There's a girl I like here, and I'm beginning to get the hang of things at the paper, and I just don't think now is the time for me to go. It might be good for me, at some point, but not now. Dad, I had to make a decision this morning. I was actually taking the SAT, taking the verbal section, no less, and doing pretty well, when this beeper went off. I had to decide whether to go after the story, which was what I thought I should do, or stay and finish the test, which is what I knew you wanted me to do. Dad, I went with what *I* thought I should do. It wasn't easy. *This*—talking to you like this—isn't easy. I could very easily have died crossing that reenactment field back there. I was tempted to. It's something I enjoy and do well. But I had to level with you about Washington and Lee. I can't go. Dad, I just cannot go to Washington and Lee next term."

"Stop repeating yourself."

"I want to be clear."

"I know you're not going to Washington and Lee—at least not next term."

"Sir?"

Mr. Forrest continued to avoid eye contact, but for a different

267

reason. He'd turned shy, embarrassed. He had his hands in his double-breasted frock coat pockets. "Their admissions man called last week," he conceded softly. "There's no way you can get in early. They have a rule that all freshmen start in the fall, and they wouldn't bend on it. I pushed them hard—believe me—but they wouldn't bend. I, uh—I suppose I should have told you all this."

"You sure should have."

Mr. Forrest looked up. "I didn't want to distract you, Beauregard. You'll need that higher SAT score at some point."

"I suppose."

It was Beauregard's turn to sulk, and he did, but only briefly. He didn't have time to sulk at length. Besides, he could tell his father was mortified at having to admit his lack of influence with Washington and Lee. Beauregard was a little mortified for him. He remembered now having read in the W&L catalog that all freshmen started fall term, but he'd assumed his father could get around that. His father had considerable influence around Birmingham— all of it, in Beauregard's view, earned. He'd led the bank through an unprecedented era of growth and profitability, and he'd taken on his share of civic responsibilities, always discharging them faithfully. He was practically the father of reenacting in Alabama. It was Mr. Forrest who lent money at low interest to units and individuals wanting to get into the hobby. He had been the one willing to run interference with state and federal parks officials so that reenactments could be held on or near historic sites. He had negotiated with the historical-movie people for the reenactors' work as extras, making sure they got fair pay, access to the commissary, and proper credit in the titles. He'd practically invented reenactors' insurance. As a result, reenactors would do anything for him, as would many other people around Birmingham. The thought that he couldn't bring his will to bear against W&L was a little unnerving. The school was right, of course, in a narrow, Lee-like way. And the result suited Beauregard's purposes. But he didn't like to see his father hurting.

"I'm sure if they would have made an exception for anybody, they would have made one for you, Dad," Beauregard said.

Mr. Forrest, eyes still downcast, waved the sympathetic thought away. It took hold nonetheless. In a few seconds he was sniffing again, looking up. "What's this about a girl?"

"We started dating a few weeks ago," Beauregard said.

"What's her name?"

"Lorena, interestingly enough."

"I like that. Tell me more." Mr. Forrest was like Jackson in this way. "Tell me everything."

"Not now, Dad. I've got to get back to work."

"Good story?"

"I think so."

"Excellent. I'll look for it in Local/State."

This wasn't meanness, Beauregard knew, just habit. He smiled forebearingly and thrust out a hand. When they finished the handshake, he grabbed the rifle, left the tent, and started back across the field.

This time Shealy answered. A lightness, almost a gaiety, marked his breathing noises.

"Great story, B-Four," he said. "I mean it. As pissed off as I was at first, I'm glad now that Price called me in."

Beauregard was back in the country store's phone booth, running a hand through his hair to soothe the itchy effects of After Hat. "That's good to hear, Bubba," he said.

"All right, here's where we stand," the city editor went on. "Price got everything we need from the school board. The superintendent confirmed the arrests and promised an internal investigation. The school board members—the three Price reached, anyway—expressed outrage. They're thanking us for bringing the matter to their attention."

"Good."

"As far as I'm concerned, the story's ready to go. I'll read it to you. Here we go."

Beauregard listened as Shealy, starting with "By Beauregard Forrest, Staff Writer," read him the whole story. Because of a truck whining by, he had to ask him to repeat the lede, but he heard everything else the first time. Price had done first-rate work. He'd taken Beauregard's material and arranged it to best advantage, adding transitions and the pertinent quotes from school board members, nimbly avoiding the Jackson issue. Still, it was Beauregard's story. Price had kept the language of Beauregard's dictation whenever possible, and he'd put his own stuff, the school board stuff, near the bottom.

"Any problem with that, B-Four?" Shealy asked finally.

"One thing, Bubba."

"What's that?"

"I want a double byline. I want Price's name on there."

The city editor paused, then began to squeak disapprovingly in his swivel chair. "No, B-Four," he decided. "I don't think so. Price is an editor now."

"I don't care."

Another pause, Shealy's breathing noises turning heavier, darker. "We've never given a reporter and an editor a double byline, B-Four," he continued. "It might set a bad precedent or something. Tell you what, though. Let's take him out for a drink later. Price likes to drink. It'll be on us—on me. What the hell."

"No, Bubba."

"Come on, B-Four."

"If his name's not on there, I don't want mine on there."

Beauregard knew he had Shealy. The *Standard-Dispatch* couldn't very well run a story about finding the missing portable without a byline reference to the reporter who'd found it. The *Standard-Dispatch* was tight with pay and benefits, liberal with bylines. A front-page story without one would look naked.

"All right, B-Four," Shealy said after a respectable holdout. "Price's name goes on there, too."

"Thanks, Bubba."

"You know, B-Four," Shealy said, softening, "we had a reporter one time who wanted to get on with the Atlanta paper. He actually whited out Price's name on stories they'd done together, stories he sent to Atlanta with a résumé. He got the job, too. He's at the *Washington Post* now, making more money than all three of us put together. More power to him, I guess, but I know you'd never do anything like that. You're the kind who insists on a double byline, even when you could have it all to yourself. I admire you for that, B-Four. I really do."

"Bubba?"

"What, B-Four?"

"My name first on that byline, right?"

"Right," Shealy said. "Of course."

"I just wanted to get that straight."

"A story like this—hey, I don't blame you."

He drove straight from Sibley to Lorena's, not bothering to change from his farbed outfit, arriving well past dark. She wore the same red sweater-jersey, but it was loose now at the collar. She'd undone her hair, too, and brushed it out. She smelled of jasmine and wore no shoes.

"What's that on your face?" she asked.

"Probably a powder burn," he said. "I'll have to explain."

He had a lot of explaining to do—they both did. To help things along she'd made black coffee and a vegetable soup. Coffee and soup, a hot combination, but Beauregard wanted seconds on both. Early on, he excused himself and took a sponge bath in the bathroom, the flushing toilet covering his quick, efficient splashings. He offered to make another pot of coffee, but she did it herself, adding cinnamon, a corruption by Price's standards, but this was no time to get into all of that.

"I'm sorry I wasn't straight with you about the SAT or the chance I'd go off to college," he said.

"You should be," she said. But there wasn't much sting in her voice.

"Well I am."

"Good."

They were sitting in the living room, on either side of the folded-up sleeper-sofa. Abruptly, though, Lorena stood and loomed over him, thumbs hooked nervously in the pockets of her sweater-jersey. "Now I'm sorry for something, too," she said.

"What?"

"For beeping you during the SAT." She sat back down and took his hand. "God, Beauregard, I hate the thing, but I wouldn't have beeped you out of it. I thought it was next Saturday. I didn't know until I called Chester a little while ago."

Beauregard shrugged. "I'm glad you beeped me. It forced things. I'm not ready to go off to school. I want to hang out with you and work at the paper."

"Then forgive me for being such a shit the past two weeks. I had cause, sure. But I took it too far."

"No, you didn't. Chester told me about Spencer running off to Auburn. I understand completely."

The setting couldn't have been better—soft lights in the corners; piano jazz on the FM radio; Booger locked up in the kitchen—but tension lingered from the last exchange. Beauregard decided Lorena actually wanted to apologize, and he, in his politeness, was thwarting her.

"It sure was a long two weeks, though," he threw in.

"I know. I'm sorry."

"All those notes I sent. The unreturned phone calls. I was a hurtin' puppy."

"I know it, Bernstein. I'm so sorry. Believe me, I was hurting, too."

They caught up on other things. They talked easily, pleasurably, almost greedily. Each waited to be the one talking, like children in line for a diving board. She told him about everything that had been happening at UAB and the school board. She couldn't wait to get there Monday. The whole place—not just the basement—would be abuzz.

He told her about the fasting-veteran debacle, about the burglary of his apartment, about playing golf again. He gave her a full account of the day just past. He explained how he got the powder burn crossing the reenactment field, and how the thieves had briefly had him bound and gagged. He was a little nervous when she sympathetically suggested they check his wrists and ankles for rope burns. Fortunately, they found some promising discolorations, which she insisted on rubbing with some kind of white lotion from the bathroom. Though it burned, he "aahed."

At eleven P.M., they got into the van and drove down to the newspaper. While Lorena waited, Beauregard slipped into the production building and walked over to a large cylindrical trash barrel by the presses. He pulled out an inky, rejected first edition. As casually as possible, he rattled it up in front of his face. There was his story, on page one, under the forty-eight-point headline, CLASSROOM WAS HUNT LODGE. In smaller letters, the subheadline read: "3 Arrested Near Sibley; Investigation Continues." Underneath that was his byline, with Price's, as Shealy had promised.

The story, with photographs of the lodge and the snapshot of the partying school-board officials, took up most of the front page. The only items above it were the *Standard-Dispatch* masthead and the scores of the Alabama and Auburn games. Beauregard folded the paper and closed his eyes hard, as if to seal into memory this first sighting of his accomplishment. Killer tornadoes yielding golf-ball-sized hail might strike suddenly and bump the story inside for future editions, but in this first one, rolling off the presses right now, he had made front page.

"Hey, hey, what do you say, B-Four?"

"What? . . . Oh. Hey there, Bobby. Caught me off guard."

A pressman walking by.

"Good story."

"Thanks, Bobby."

"Man, I've hunted around Sibley hundreds of times. Thousands."

"Is that right?"

"All my life . . ."

When the pressman finally walked on, Beauregard reached back into the barrel and brought out another dozen copies.

Lorena proved to be, if anything, more excited than Beauregard. She kept the van's inside light on all the way back to Southside so she could read. Back in her apartment, they took the papers to the sleeper-sofa, which they folded out and climbed onto. She insisted on reading the story aloud. Beauregard was embarrassed when she started, but the further she got, the better he felt. It *was* a good story. If he had come across the story in an out-of-town paper, he might actually have clipped and saved it. At the least he would have toasted the reporter with a raised plastic foam cup.

When she finished reading his story, Lorena followed with a few of her poems. They were new—the latest written just this afternoon, after she talked to Chester. "Blazer on the Chair" was all about Beauregard, and very flattering. All right, maybe the rhymes—new for her—seemed forced; but he wasn't going to tell her. He was no poet. Besides, you could take the candor thing too far.

They undressed and made love with the lights still on. Two weeks had passed, but it wasn't a desperate, groping, deadline reunion—more a slow, grateful, savoring one. Beauregard took a little nap afterward and had a rare good dream. In it he led a successful reenactment infantry charge, harassed only by Jackson with a strange, muzzle-loading vacuum cleaner. He woke to find Lorena sitting up, naked, rereading the newspaper story. She had it right up in her face, and her brow above it was knitted in concentration, as if she were finishing a good mystery novel. Obviously she hadn't slept. Too keyed up. The experience of helping to find the portable classroom and expose the school board thieves had proved a kind of stimulant for her, or so it seemed to Beauregard. He thought she would make a terrific reporter.

He tugged the top sheet. "Hey, there," he called softly.

"Bernstein! You're awake!"

She dropped the paper and straddled him, bending down to whisper in his left ear, reddish blond hair spilling all over him. "How do you feel?" she asked.

"Fine. Refreshed."

"Let's do it, then."

"What? Make love again?"

"The Catfish."

"Lorena . . . you're kidding."

"I am not, Beauregard. I want to. I've never felt quite this way."

He pushed her back enough to look at her, expecting a chink of smile. Nothing. Not a trace. She was looking him right in the eyes.

Chapter Twenty-five

Attendance was excellent for the surprise party Jackson threw for Beauregard the following Thursday night. Beauregard, thinking he had arrived to cover a political speech, opened the door of the Hotel Jefferson's Evergreen Room only to find most of the *Standard-Dispatch* staff standing on either side of a blown-up version of his front-page story.

They were looking at him, smiling, punch glasses held high.

"All right, everybody!" yelled Bubba Shealy, who used his empty glass as a baton. "Here . . . we . . . go!"

And then, in a tuneless confluence of Southern and Midwestern voices, they gargled an a cappella chorus of "For He's a Jolly Good Fellow!"

Beauregard stood there taking it, smiling and blushing and waving and shaking his head, but he was less surprised at the gathering than at the sight of Jackson in the background, giving instructions to a few of his hosts and hostesses. That Jackson would throw a free party was big news, up there with the stolen portable. It had to be free. The *Standard-Dispatch* would never have paid for anything like this, and it was outside the means of newsroom staffers.

More surprises followed. Jackson had hired Taco Bob to cater and the food was Vietnamese, not barbecue. There were as many hosts as hostesses assigned and they were all dressed conservatively. The band was not the young, bawdy rhythm-and-blues party band

Jackson usually used for important affairs but rather a jazz band of dignified older black musicians who had grown up in Birmingham and retired there. There were no blue films. It was, in a sense, a tasteful party, progressive, even (by Jackson's standards) feminist.

Still, the party worked in the way Jackson's parties usually did, to near perfection. People forgot themselves at Jackson's parties. A Jackson party was like a little Mardi Gras, only better, because there was always a clean bathroom nearby. Jackson never failed to observe his principles of party science, especially the first one: Involve the uninvolved. If necessary, he himself would drag a person out onto the dance floor. Many of his dances were group dances, in this case line dances and a limbo that had everyone clapping and waiting his or her turn. Jackson's parties unfolded suspensefully. There was always a new course of food, always a new, even more interesting bowl of punch. There were always party favors. Beauregard couldn't help but notice the effect party favors had on this crowd. There they were, many of them with master's degrees in journalism, but they couldn't quit blowing their little party horns. If Jackson had asked, Beauregard would have predicted no interest among his colleagues in party favors; but Jackson didn't have to ask. He knew these things. It was his business, his art.

That Jackson was a master party planner was obvious from the comments Beauregard heard from Midwesterners. Normally so hard on Birmingham, they suspended criticism for this one evening. They hadn't had so much fun since their respective years in Columbia, Bloomington, Madison, and Iowa City. Even Bubba Shealy, an Auburn alumnus, was won over by Jackson. Shealy became a sweaty fixture on the dance floor. Price controlled the limbo bar, and whenever Shealy came through, he dropped it to management-scum depths; but Shealy, to the mock then admiring cheers of his reporters, managed to get under and through.

"Going pretty well, huh?" Jackson said, sidling up to Beauregard in the crowd of limbo watchers.

"It's going fine, Jackson."

"Dad couldn't make it, but he insisted on covering half my expenses for the party."

Beauregard turned to his older brother. "Dad's helping pay for one of your parties?"

"He sent a check over this morning."

"Amazing."

"I know. This whole thing has brought the family closer together." Jackson put an arm around Beauregard. "Thank's for keeping Get Down! Inc., out of your story. You saved my butt, little buddy."

Beauregard shrugged. "You should thank Price, the assistant city editor. He made the call."

"Which one's Price?"

"That guy with bandaged glasses. The one holding the limbo bar."

"I'll speak to him."

There was plenty of time between dances for aftermath stories—stories of how AP had picked up Beauregard's account of the missing portable for the "A" wire; of how the *New York Times* and *Washington Post* had sent correspondents to Birmingham for follow-ups; of how Woodrow had been on the story all week.

At first everyone at the party called Beauregard "Beauregard." Shealy, it seemed, had sent out a pre-party memo to that effect. But as the evening wore on, and as more and more of Jackson's punch was sipped and guzzled, "Beauregard" was forgotten and "B-Four" again became Beauregard's name. He didn't mind. It was odd, even a little disconcerting, hearing the newsroom staffers struggle with "Beauregard." Except for Price and one or two others, they had the accent and vowel sounds slightly wrong. They spoke it conspicuously, too, like "Good morning!" in a foreign language. "B-Four" was easier and better, especially now that it was solidly ironic. Any colleague who called him "B-Four" in front of a stranger would be obligated to tell the full story, how he had persevered and made front page.

Lorena showed up late, having come from class. She behaved warily at first, because Beauregard had told her of Jackson's involvement with the deer hunters. She didn't approve of that or of his party business or of this obvious attempt at penance. She was won over in part, though, by Taco Bob's good spring rolls and by the jazz band. They played a medley of standards, including "Tuxedo Junction," which she'd learned about in her history of Birmingham class.

Beauregard noticed her foot tapping. "We've never danced," he said.

"I know."

"I can dance a little."

"Me, too."

"This sure is nice music."

"Sure is. . . . Let's dance, Bernstein."

"Good idea."

The party was still going strong at midnight when they slipped out, Beauregard carrying the blown-up front page under his arm. Lorena had to be at work early the next morning. Beauregard didn't but would be. He'd been congratulated throughout the party, but the nicest thing he'd heard was that there was going to be a staff reshuffling, and that from now on he would be working under Price. Price had confirmed the rumor and told him they would proceed at once with the long-delayed series, "People Who Have Jobs at the Courthouse but Don't Really Do Anything."

Tomorrow was Friday, the best day to document idleness at the courthouse. Beauregard wanted to be there bright and early.